Originally from Tarragona, Spain, Elena Moya has written three fiction novels (*The Olive Groves of Belchite, The Spanish Maestra* and *La Candidata*), which have been published in English, Spanish, Catalan, Italian and Portuguese. In Italy, *The Spanish Maestra* was short-listed for the Puglia school system literary award.

Elena holds a BA in Journalism from the Universidad de Navarra, Spain, an MA in Arts from the University of Nevada (Reno, NV, US), financed by a Fulbright scholarship and a Diploma in Creative Writing by Birkbeck College, University of London. Elena currently works as an investment writer, following a fifteen-year career in financial journalism, working for Bloomberg, Reuters and *The Guardian* newspaper. She has also been Chairwoman of Catalans UK. An ardent traveller and footballer, she lives in London.

Acknowledgements

Atsede Aemro-Selassie photography.

Peter Gold transaltion.

The Spanish Maestra

Elena Moya

The Spanish Maestra

Pegasus

PEGASUS PAPERBACK

© Copyright 2016
Elena Moya

Translation into English by **Peter Gold 2015** ©

A CIP catalogue record for this title is
available from the British Library

ISBN- 978 1910903 01 8

Pegasus is an imprint of
Pegasus Elliot MacKenzie Publishers Ltd.
www.pegasuspublishers.com

Published in Spanish: September 2013, Suma de Letras (Santillana)

First Published in 2016

Pegasus
Sheraton House Castle Park
Cambridge CB3 0AX England

Printed & Bound in Great Britain

To María

1

The first time she looked into his eyes, she guessed who he was. Although that first encounter happened almost a year ago, and much had happened since, Vallivana Querol was trembling before the meeting they had arranged. Maybe he was waiting for her behind the centenary gates, or observing her through one of the gothic windows of that majestic building. Maybe he was as nervous or felt as unsure as she did about their meeting.

Sitting on a stone bench and with the patience she had learned over eighty-nine years, the old lady sighed as she contemplated the two symmetrical brick towers, now growing darker and more imposing in the cold and gloom of the gathering dusk. She had been there for quite some time, apparently calm, still feeling the warmth of a cup of tea in her big, strong hands, which reflected a full and committed life. They were hands that had worked and suffered, that had fought and defended, and that were alive. Her face, however, was delicate, pale, wrinkled and looked extremely tired. It was totally dominated by her huge, bright dark eyes.

Valli, as she was known, was still wondering whether to enter the building or not. She thought that going through those old, wooden doors into Eton College would betray a lifetime dedicated to fighting for certain ideals. But now, after the latest events, she no longer knew whether that battle had even been worth it, or if it had all been a mistake. Her whole life could have been a complete mistake.

The old lady sat still, wrapped in a long, tweed coat, with a thick woollen hat on her head that almost covered her eyes. She did not want to see much, anyway. She preferred to close her eyes and think about the long road that had now brought her to the gates of that college, going back to when she was born a lifetime earlier in Valencia to a family of farmers who could barely read and write. Eight decades later, there she was, invited by Charles Wrigglesworth, head of the foreign language department of this prestigious institution, which had educated prime ministers, writers, artists, lawyers and bankers of many countries for more than five hundred years. The schoolmaster had invited her to share her vast experience with his students and Valli had accepted in principle, but not because she wanted to get to know Eton as such.

Valli only wanted to find the peace that had evaded her all her life, despite spending many long years trying to find it. Now, at last, with decades of experience behind her, she sat down to think, trying to link together the events of a lifetime. She had arrived in London two days before the meeting so that she could wander through the streets of a city that could have changed her destiny more than fifty years earlier. During those two days, Valli had reminded herself of the months she spent in a small bed & breakfast in Bloomsbury in 1953 – the same one she had chosen to stay in this time.

Charles had insisted that she should stay in Eton itself, just an hour outside London, in a small, charming hotel close to the college. But Valli had never liked posh neighbourhoods and Eton certainly was one of those: it was full of tea-rooms for middle-aged ladies of leisure, Aston Martin dealers for their banker husbands, or boutiques for those who were into upper-class fashion: tweed jackets, top hats, bow ties and ties or waistcoats with heraldic crests. The old *maestra*, who had spent her life fighting for those in need, felt that such an environment was, frankly, nauseating.

But unlike years ago, she now accepted it. And the years when she travelled around Spain teaching hundreds of poor children and adults to read and write now seemed buried in time. Everything had changed. Even her adored Bloomsbury, home of the British and European intelligentsia, had now been taken over by clothing and food chain stores, full of students who seemed more interested in consumption than in changing the world, let alone improving it. She had been taken aback by the deafening music in the shops: an incentive – it seemed to her - for people to walk in, do their shopping and leave as quickly as possible. The cafés didn't have any comfortable chairs to sit in for a quiet conversation, or just to stop and rest for a few minutes. London was no longer the creative society that she once knew; it had turned into a retail metropolis with hardly any book shops, Valli thought to herself as she walked down the streets of Bloomsbury and Fitzrovia, thinking of her much admired Virginia Woolf. In 1953 she had spent weeks sitting on university floors or even in pubs discussing the state of the world, talking to anyone and everyone – it didn't matter to her, for she thought that everybody was equal. But now, just two days into her trip, she had hardly spoken to anybody. Everybody was in their own little world, moving at a dizzying pace.

The train journey that morning from Waterloo to Eton had reminded her once more that the strong young woman who had once rejected a comfortable and stable life in England to fight for Spain had turned into a small, vulnerable old lady, overwhelmed by a fast-paced world of consumption that nothing or nobody – not even her – could change. What's more, the disparities against which she had fought so hard seemed even greater: the tall, grey tower blocks just outside London, home to families that would probably never improve their social status, were not far from vast golf courses and pristine red-brick houses, which she saw as the train progressed towards Eton. The council football pitches, full of muddy puddles and holes, near Waterloo station were immediately followed by the immaculate rugby fields of the public schools along the Thames that Valli observed as the train moved westwards. Valli knew that in England, rugby was a sport practised by gentlemen, whereas football was the top sport amongst the working classes.

England and its classes: just like Spain, but a bit more refined, she thought as the train travelled on.

At least the English elites were better educated and there was no doubt about the excellence of British public schools. In contrast, in Spain, a sudden building boom was taking even the best students out of the classroom and into the construction business, where they seemed to earn much more and do so much more quickly than by becoming a doctor, a lawyer or an engineer. Valli could not believe the thousands of apartments and houses that were springing up around Spain. Two years earlier, in 2006, she was astonished to see dozens of cranes building detached houses in Alcañiz, a small, poor provincial town in the middle of nowhere, not far from her own village. Valli wondered who on earth could afford a detached house with a swimming pool and a garden in wretched Alcañiz, if the farming town barely had any industry or services. She had been saying for some time that it would all end badly. She kept telling everybody that the only three factors that determine the wealth of a nation are: education, education and education. Everybody laughed, as the Spanish press, politicians, and even her own friends and acquaintances only seemed to acknowledge one single industry: construction. It seemed extraordinary to her that, all of a sudden, everybody had homes and cars out of all proportion to their income. Having been brought up on a farm, Valli knew very well that you can't spend what you haven't got, and she had already read somewhere that some foreign banks were starting to struggle. But Spain was fine. Spain was always fine. Spain never had any problems – that was what everybody said.

Watching all the while as she continued to sit on the stone bench right in front of the famous college, Valli saw two students leaving the main building through the huge old wooden doors. The two boys were wearing the usual black tails and waistcoat, pinstripe trousers and well-ironed white shirt with the famous stiff collar. They walked fast, heads up, looking straight ahead. Their confident air, rosy cheeks, white skin and unruly hair that was slightly longer at the front marked them out as members of their class.

They didn't look at Valli as they walked past her, despite the fact that she was the only person on the street. Their parents paid more than thirty thousand pounds a year for them to learn who they should mix with and who not. They had learned well.

Valli looked down. She had lost that battle a long time earlier. The world belonged to the elites, who seek out and find each other in order to keep their privileges. Her heart filled with sadness as she had dedicated a lifetime fighting against this unfair but very real fact. With half a smile she recalled the time when she drove a cart pulled by a donkey across Spain, with her friend and well-known Spanish playwright Alejandro Casona, then Director of the "Educational Missions" established by Spain's Second Republic. Together they toured the Maestrazgo region, between Catalunya, Aragón and Valencia, teaching children and adults how to read and write. They were following the example set by the old *maestro* Menéndez Pidal, who years earlier had travelled across the plains of Castile collecting stories and folklore that farmers had passed on to each other, generation after generation, down the centuries. It was a magic culture. Alejandro and Valli told some of those ancient stories to the children they visited. They also organised plays and taught them how to stage them in the open air, under those nights of a million stars only seen in remote villages. More often than not, parents and grandparents also joined the reading classes, some more embarrassed than others, but all with the hope for change that the newly-established democracy had inspired in 1931.Valli remembered how grateful those people were, as they had never received anything from anybody; sometimes they gave them chickens or quails, on other occasions they just received a heartfelt hug, always accompanied by a genuine smile. Valli, however, always felt that the best reward was the sparkle she could see in their eyes as they learned. Until the light was extinguished.

Still lost in her thoughts, Valli heard the two students laugh disdainfully as they reached what they must have thought was a safe distance. They were not looking at her; they continued straight ahead, with their hands in their pockets, their heads well up, always looking forward. Always confident, always self-assured, they walked off with their fast, superior stride. Those boys knew where they were heading, now and in life, Valli thought. They were going where they have been told to – whilst she could barely thread together the events of an aimless existence, at best, or simply, a life with a misguided destiny.

Valli looked at the strong, wooden door, now closed. Closed to those who could not afford the privilege, to those who had not been taught how to pass the entrance exams and above all, closed to women. What will those boys think of women, who are denied a place in the world's top schools just because they are not men? Naturally, if those students became country or world leaders they would not treat women on an equal basis, give them opportunities or promote them, because, simply, they were just not part of their system, their world. And this is how habits were perpetuated.

Valli looked at the sky, now almost completely dark, and felt the cold in her bones. After a sad and solitary Christmas, the former *maestra* had purposefully started the year with a mission. She had not come all the way to London to win the equality battle - she lost that one a long time earlier. Now, she was here to win the battle against herself.

2

He was looking at her from the gothic windows of Durnford House, the college building that he shared with a select group of fifty students. He knew that she would not turn to look towards his window as, like thousands of tourists, she thought that Eton College mostly occupied the wide area and stone buildings around the imposing chapel. In fact the college was made up of more than fifty buildings that were spread throughout the small village of Eton but were all close to each other. Eton College, he thought, was not like schools in Spain, where students sit in the same classroom eight hours a day to absorb a string of facts, most of them of dubious relevance. Instead, life in Eton was a constant back and forth, with students changing classrooms and buildings almost every hour, non-stop from eight in the morning to sometimes well past eleven at night, when the after-dinner club meetings or cultural events ended.

From his elegant wood-panelled room, Charles had been observing Valli during the full hour that she had been sitting on the street bench. She had arrived well ahead of time, as their meeting was not scheduled until two-thirty in the afternoon. At that hour, right after lunch, the masters had a short break while the students played sports, making good use of the last hour of natural light.

It was almost fifteen minutes before the old wall clock – one of the few objects from his father that Charles had kept – chimed the agreed hour. Charles, in his immaculate tailcoat, black waistcoat and white shirt and bow-tie, reached for his long black cape, which distinguished masters from students. Eton was all about symbols. The colours of the waistcoats, trousers, hats or scarves indicated which house or club one belonged to – and that in itself could also be a sign of one's academic level or achievements amongst the school's one thousand plus boarders. Everybody knew their place, as in life.

Tall and handsome, Charles had never questioned his place. At fifty-four, he was head of department, with two dozen teachers under his leadership. The house he was in charge of, Durnford, was one of the most popular and students competed to be members of it or to become its captain. Each boy had a single room, simple but warm, and always located on the lower floors, below the much bigger attic flat occupied by the house master. In other houses, the house master – always a man – shared his home with his spouse, but Charles was not married, rather happily so, so travelling was his only hobby outside college life. He either worked or travelled: there was nothing in between.

Since graduating from Oxford in the sixties, Charles had visited one hundred of the nearly two hundred countries in the world. After university, and without parents to take care of, Charles spent three years travelling in Asia, mostly in India. He had been invited by old friends from Eton – which he had also attended as a student - who were descendants of British colonial civil servants in the country and who had developed strong ties with the Raj. Charles spent months studying Hindi and Indian culture, staying in a sumptuous room in one of the towers of a Jaipur fort, courtesy of one of its owners – a friend of a friend, of course. After another year exploring Africa in similar circumstances, Charles eventually returned to England to do what everybody expected of him: a friend's uncle offered him a very well-paid job at a merchant bank in the City, where he started making money surprisingly easily. All he had to do was to take one of the owners' businessmen friends to lunch. After that, and back in the office, he had to assess the value of their business, applying a well-known easy formula. By mid-afternoon, he would call people on the contact list that his boss had given him and sell them bonds or shares in that business in exchange for a hefty commission. By six o'clock, with the job done, he would have two glasses of sherry at his favourite Mayfair club.

Money flowed fast in the City in those days. Margaret Thatcher, after only one year in office, was breaking down barriers, emasculating the unions, deregulating industries and selling public assets. Opportunities came thick and fast, and so did the champagne and the parties. On one of those nights, an indifferent Charles easily won the heart of the sister of Robin, an old Oxford friend. Meredith, aged nineteen, was shy, respectful and also very beautiful. She was like a little porcelain doll, slim and fragile, with big blue eyes dominating her pale face and beautiful curly, long, blond hair. They married a few months later, moving into the Chelsea home that her parents had given them as a wedding present – despite the fact that Charles could also call on the small fortune that his own father had left him.

Happiness at the large, white stucco home that they planned to fill with children did not last long and Charles, less than one year later, left the large house, wife and City job to return to Eton as a master. Living with a woman who had been brought up to sew and keep quiet held no interest for him, and he soon realised that he could not face what lay ahead: he was exasperated by his friends' homes full of screaming children, no matter how many nannies they employed. Charles preferred the silence of castles and libraries, the quietness of the remote lakes and mountains that he escaped to in his free time. He came to the conclusion that family life was banal and lacking in stimulation. It made him long for the intellectual challenges of the Eton and Oxford life that he was used to. He found marriage and domesticity supremely dull.

Eton, of course, welcomed him with open arms, giving him as much support as it had in his second year as a boarder, when he was fourteen and his father suddenly died of cancer.

Charles had always admired his father, even though he had barely known him. At seven he had already been sent to a boarding school near Cambridge, where Professor Wrigglesworth was an eminent Hispanist at the University. His father had always addressed him in Spanish, while the nanny they employed for years and with whom Charles spent most of his time as a child, spoke to him in English. His father's insistence that he should speak perfect Spanish was such that the first boarding school he went to had to hire a special teacher so that Charles would not forget the Spanish he had learned at home. Charles did indeed keep the language, but lost his father, whom he barely saw afterwards. Years later, when he died, Charles had already been at boarding school for almost seven years, half of his life. During that time, he saw his father only about once a month, when he visited him in Eton and they went for lunch at a nearby restaurant. Those meals were rather cold and distant, as the two exchanged few thoughts other than the latest theory about Cervantes' works or the like. Just once, when his father must have already known about his illness, he advised him to go through life using the English language in his head and Spanish in his heart.

Charles never quite understood the meaning of such a statement, just as he never really understood his father, although he suspected the two of them were more similar than not: solitary and eccentric gentlemen who enjoyed life in silence and in their own way. Men made for the gothic quadrangles of Eton, Oxford and Cambridge, well-adjusted and polished, who went through life in a refined and discreet manner, never needing to roll up their sleeves or take too much risk. They were happy – in their own way.

Like Valli, Charles noticed the two students leaving the college through the main wooden doors. They were in his Spanish class, which had been studying in the small town of Morella in the Valencia region - where everything had started.

With a sigh Charles looked at an old photo of George Orwell, an Eton old boy, on the wall. Orwell was looking at something with inquisitorial eyes whilst his classmates seemed to be listening to something else, rather passively. Even as a youth, Eric Blair – his real name - had revolution written in his eyes. Some of his works, like *Animal Farm* or *1984* had excited Charles from a very young age, partly thanks to the insistence of his own father, who had been a friend of the famous writer since they met in the Spanish Civil War. After the conflict ended in 1939 both Orwell and Wrigglesworth returned to their privileged lives in England – the one as an already successful writer and the other to a lectureship at Cambridge. The two kept up a more or less regular correspondence until Orwell died in 1950. Charles' father, who died years later, had left his son some of the letters, as well as hundreds of books, the wall clock and the silver cuff links that he always wore. He also left him a substantial sum of money and the family house in Cambridge, which Charles sold after his divorce, having realised that he would never want to create a home in which to bring up children. In fact, what he remembered most of that large property just outside Cambridge were the long, lonely hours in the library or playing in the garden with one of his nannies. The term *family home* was an oxymoron to Charles – at best.

He thought that trying to be happy with a small group of people – who you can´t even chose – was just a waste of time. Besides, he had always felt that families, as they were conceived in Roman times, were no more than a civic device for the transfer of wealth, never a place for emotional support. He also had enough resources so that in case of need he would be able to afford as much assistance as he required, without having to ask for any favours. On special days, such as Christmas, the best thing was to travel and rest, which was much more satisfying and intellectually healthy than doing exactly the same year after year: stuffing yourself, always in front of the same people, with whom you don´t have anything to say that is actually worth saying. Charles loathed staged happiness, which to him was what Christmas had come to be all about. He was in South Africa the previous year and the year before that he went to Singapore to visit some friends. In the 1990s, he used to spend Christmas in New York, the world´s financial and cultural centre that always fascinated him. Sadly, he now had to follow his friends to different places as they were more likely to have settled in Shanghai, Qatar or Abu Dhabi than in North America. But he did not mind. Singapore and Cape Town had been fabulous – precisely because nothing had been about Christmas at all. For him, the trees with the flashing lights, the nativities and Santas were, to be honest, beyond bad taste.

Charles' ordered and peaceful life had, however, been disrupted almost a year earlier, in February 2007, when he started looking for a place in Spain to host a Spanish language and culture centre for his students. He knew the country well and, like most Britons, preferred the sunnier and cheaper South, where he boasted of having visited most of the villages. Charles did not like big cities; he much preferred the silence and quietness of rural life. Searching in Google, he found an advertisement from the local council of Morella, a lovely medieval town in the province of Castellón, completely surrounded by dry, bare mountains. The property was a large, rather grand old school that the council wanted to sell, following the construction of more modern premises for its students. The old building was therefore available to be refurbished for new activities.

Charles had looked at the online photos with much interest and became very excited about spending a week with the boys in Morella. The town seemed ideal: small, with narrow cobblestone streets, almost in the middle of nowhere, but only two hours from Valencia airport. The web also said that a new airport would open soon near the coastal town of Castellón, only fifty minutes away.

Charles was more than used to the fact that not every Spaniard answers emails promptly and so he called the council offices directly. Unfortunately, he was told, the building was not for rent, but only for sale. With a sense of disappointment, Charles put the matter to one side, although he never stopped taking an interest in Morella.

One month later, and driven by his innate curiosity, he decided to use his Easter holiday to get to know the place. So off he went.

3

Seated by the large, stone fireplace, the Mayor of Morella, Vicent Fernández, was waiting for his guests while having his usual breakfast of sausage and toast.

'Where's the brandy,' he asked his wife, Amparo, as he lounged in his favourite leather armchair. 'The sausage is getting cold and I haven't been able to have a nip yet, and I need to be on top form today!'

Vicent looked towards his wife of more than forty years, as she rushed to the kitchen to satisfy his needs, something she had done all her married life. He crossed his short, stout legs and smiled with pride. Seconds later, Amparo, short and like her husband not particularly slim, delicately placed a glass of brandy on the side-table next to Vicent's armchair, just as he liked. He looked her in the eyes, perhaps for the first time in months. They were both sixty-seven, although she looked much older, her skin more wrinkled, her face tired, her eyes with barely any spark. Her rounded belly was hidden behind the white apron that she wore every day except Sundays, when she wore a black dress to go to church. Vicent took her hand and looked down at the floor, expecting her to squat down. Of course, she did.

'Today, my little Amparo,' he said solemnly, 'our fortune is going to change. We have waited for an opportunity like this for years and finally the moment has arrived. We need to be attentive and kind to everybody, without losing sight of our objective for a second. I will briefly introduce the project, just before lunch. Please don't serve anything while I'm speaking, or if President Roig also says a few words. And above all, don't say anything to anybody – just ask our guests if they like the food or if they need anything. Make sure everybody knows where to leave their coats, where the toilets are and all the domestic details. Don't say anything about the school or the apartments. Just leave this to me, as I'm the one who knows all about it.'

Amparo nodded, her eyes fixed on the floor. Despite her age, the daughter of the local chocolate-maker still had a baby face, with a small, round nose and a large head, well-covered by thick, black, curly hair. As a young woman Amparo was never short of suitors, perhaps because she was the daughter of the wealthy owner of Chocolates El Gorrión – who in the end died penniless. The family business went to Amparo's younger brother despite her being the older sibling, but in those days it was unthinkable for a woman to run a business. They say in the town that there would still be a factory if she had inherited the business, as she was much smarter and more aware by far than her brother, who ended up ruined only a few years later. From an early age, Amparo had always worked hard and faced whatever challenges came her way without complaining. She had always known her place.

'What about the children, are they aware of everything?' she asked her husband, picking up and folding the newspaper that Vicent had just dropped on the floor.

'Ah, the children.' Vicent sighed. 'No, I haven't given them the latest instructions. But Manolo will be here soon and I don't know what Isabel is up to. I imagine she's wandering around doing nothing useful, as usual.'

His wife gave him a quick, disapproving look, although without losing the note of kindness that she had managed to sustain over all those years.

'Oh, Vicent, leave the girl alone. She already has enough to worry about, with the job situation and such like. I don´t think things are going as well as she says.'

'Like everybody else,' her husband answered quickly before taking his first swig of the brandy. 'I feel like a bull!' he said, placing his big hands on his chest, before burping.

Amparo returned to the kitchen, where she had been since five in the morning preparing *tortillas* and canapés. The catering service of a nearby luxury hotel, right in the middle of the Torre Miró mountain pass, would be delivering some *hors d'oeuvres*, salads, wine and spirits, but Vicent had been adamant that it should be Amparo who cooked the meat and the *tortillas*. His wife had also spent the previous day in the kitchen, preparing the *chorizos* and the lamb that she would cook on the barbecue.

The Fernández's were expecting about fifty people, from Catalunya, Aragón and Valencia, as Morella sat right in between those three regions. Such a location had always given the town a business advantage, as the locals were able to get along and trade with everybody, unlike other parts of Spain which were stuck in a paralysing, old-fashioned provincialism. However, Morella had also felt the cold shoulder from people or politicians who did not appreciate such an independent stance. The town had often been left to its own fate, without much outside help. Now, however, after substantial investment in the roads, this small medieval town was much more accessible and Vicent, who had only been in office for a year, was determined to revive the community. Morella had already converted its former agricultural economy into one based on services, but its own limitations, like the medieval wall around the town, prevented further growth. Now the town needed to create capital, and turning the school into a new, highly successful venture would be a quick and efficient way to do so. Vicent was very keen on the project. After all those years in the shadows, today he would become king.

The Mayor stretched his legs, placing them near the corner of the stone hearth, which was now burning strongly to keep the house warm on that cold February morning. He looked proudly around the house. The living room was spacious and well lit, full of the charm he had been able to retain of the old sixteenth century farmhouse that he had bought two years earlier. The wooden beams across the high ceiling had seen centuries of life; they were slightly twisted in places, but they remained firm and strong and bursting with personality. The white stucco, the old stone walls, the terracotta floor tiles and a thick, cream carpet gave the room a great sense of well-being. Next to his favourite armchair there was another chair, albeit a bit less presumptuous, and a big four-seater sofa, also in front of the fireplace, creating a satisfying sense of well-designed, luxurious cosiness. The son of a member of the Civil Guard, Vicent had always lived in houses or apartments without any charm or personality, making him envy his school friends' farmhouses that were secluded, silent and full of history and where families happily gathered around a blazing hearth. Now he had his own, although, in truth, he could hardly remember seeing his wife and children sitting smiling by the fire. Maybe at Christmas, and probably out of a sense of obligation.

Vicent gently stroked back the few remaining hairs on his head and, somewhat uneasily, propped his head on his hand as he stared at the fireplace. He brought his other hand to his chin, gently moving it back and forth to check the smoothness of his shave. His eyebrows, for once, had been trimmed, giving him a more refined appearance than usual.

He looked impatiently at his watch. It was just after ten. Vicent stood up to open one of the large windows in order to check the track that led to the farmhouse from the nearest road. All he could hear was some birds singing and the whistling of the wind, which gave some slight movement to the tops of the trees – olive, chestnut and oak – that surrounded the house. The beautiful landscape, right in the middle of the mountain pass, was also home to ravens, eagles and falcons, as well as dozens of different types of birds that cheered the mornings with their song. Vicent looked at the sun, which by this time was already high, and smiled.

As soon as he heard the sound of the first car – his son, Manolo's old, white van – the Mayor walked towards the main door.

'You're late,' he said as soon as he saw him, pointing at his watch and then buttoning up the leather jacket that he had decided to wear.

'The printers made me wait longer than I was expecting to, but all the brochures are ready,' his son replied, barely looking at Vicent as he took some boxes of drinks out of the van. As he carried them towards the house, Manolo tripped on a stone and almost lost his balance, although he managed not to.

'Careful! Don't drop my Moët & Chandon!' his father shouted in annoyance.

Arguing that he was too old to load and unload, Vicent watched his son, fortyish and scruffily dressed, bring one box after another into the house. Vicent had actually been surprised about Manolo's apparently genuine interest in organising the day.

Maybe he just wants to feel important, he thought. He would be delighted if his son ran the little hotel the family owned in Morella with the same industriousness, he told himself, as Manolo continued to bring in the boxes. But since he had passed the business on to him, the hotel had only gone downhill. Vicent had left it in a sound, profitable state with an established clientele – symbol of a prosperous, *nouveau riche* Spain that was just discovering the weekend-away culture and a liking for the comfortable life, away from the stoic, Catholic respectability that had cast a dark shadow over the country for centuries. Young women did not have to act like nuns any more, so young or student couples used the weekends to escape from the parental home, where they were still likely to have to stay until they got married.

But Manolo hadn't been able to hold on to the clientele or foster any new interest. As it happened, two boutique hotels had opened in the town since Vicent left the business, taking some clients away and making their hotel look relatively old-fashioned and cramped. From what he could see, Manolo didn't really have any plans to refurbish the place or give it a new lease of life. It was his son's lack of ambition, rather than the decline of the hotel itself, that upset Vicent the most. He hadn't loved the job either, which he had held since the age of fifteen, when his father died and he had to take care of the business to support his mother and himself. That's all they had. The pension they received was not enough, so the business had to work no matter what. Fortunately, and after long years of hard work, Morella started to attract more than a few palaeontologists in search of fossils, plus some enterprising individuals keen to make some money by finding and selling black truffles that had recently been found in the area. This kept the hotel going until the weekend-away became the fashion, filling the coffers and providing him with the opportunity to start saving. Vicent remembered quite clearly how it all started, in the 1960s, when Morella was an isolated town only visited by French tourists looking for a rainy-day alternative to their cheap hotels on the coast. Only one hour from the seaside at Castellón, those same tourists that scandalised Spaniards by filling the beaches with their bikinis and skimpy clothing, were astonished to see the price of local lamb cutlets. They practically threw them around when they found that a full plate for at least ten people was only forty pesetas, which for them was peanuts. Amparo had always been an excellent cook and that is really what kept the business afloat. The following years were a bit easier and Vicent could afford to send his two children to university in Valencia, although only the daughter graduated – in Philology or Philosophy, he couldn't quite remember. The son, though, who was sent off to do Business Studies, was never up to it and a year and a half later he was back in the village, doing some construction work and helping out at the hotel. He finally handed the business over after he decided to go into local politics as an independent in the year 2000, when he was sixty. He was elected Mayor six years later, a job which he was now fully enjoying, especially on days such as this one.

Vicent heard a second car and quickly realised it was the old, clapped-out Renault Clio belonging to his daughter Isabel, a secretary at a tile factory in Villarreal, near Castellón. At forty-three, Isabel was still single, something that surprised her mother, but didn't surprise him. His daughter, despite her mother's unconditional love and support, had not been blessed by nature – rather to the contrary. The poor thing had always had most things stacked against her: she was short, somewhat ample in size and had to wear thick, bottle-bottom glasses that almost concealed her eyes. What was to be done? Vicent wondered; there had to be someone out there for her. Shaking his head, he watched his daughter step out of the car carrying several bags and boxes, and as she walked towards him she stepped on exactly the same stone as her brother. But unlike him, she fell flat on her face. The crystal glasses that she was carrying in one of the boxes fell to the ground and shattered to pieces.

'What on earth is happening with you both today? Why do I have the clumsiest children in the world?' Vicent complained, rushing up to check how many champagne flutes were still intact.

Amparo came out immediately to help her daughter, who had already started to pick up the pieces.

'Oh, my love, did you hurt yourself? This wretched stone, I always trip on it as well. Please, Vicent,' said Amparo, turning to her husband, 'can you remove the damn thing? What if our guests, or even the President, fall over like that?'

Alarmed by such a possibility, Vicent quickly removed the stone while mother and daughter headed towards the kitchen, having removed all the bits of glass from the ground. What a disaster it would be if Eliseo Roig, President of the Region of Valencia, broke a leg in his home, thought Vicent. It had taken him a year to get him to come, as well as the more than fifty potential investors that he was also expecting. Nothing must go wrong.

Vicent adjusted his woollen tie, which was both elegant and informal, and walked through the garden towards the show-jumping arena to make sure everything was ready. Along the way he checked the swimming pool, which was immaculately clean and surrounded by a perfectly cut lawn. The show-jumping arena, the size of two football pitches, was indeed ready, with the fences all set up around the circuit and the horses quietly waiting in the adjacent stables. Vicent wasn't a good rider but had always loved horses, ever since he played with them as a child at the farmhouses of his school friends.

As he did every morning, Vicent went towards Pablo, his favourite horse, big and handsome, although rather short-legged and not very tall. Pablo was calm by nature, but always looked ahead and acquitted himself well. Nobody would have called him fast, but by putting extra effort into his long strides he was capable of proving people wrong. Maybe it is true that love is ultimately narcissistic and people tend to love those they see as a reflection of themselves, thought Vicent. As with his horse, few people would have bet on him – the son of a middle-ranking member of the Civil Guard with few qualifications. But look where he had got to, he said to himself as he looked at the stables. Slowly, he started stroking Pablo´s mane, something that the horse only let Vicent do. All the stable lads were seen off with kicks and neighs, but the understanding with Vicent was almost perfect. They had been together for more than ten years, after the Mayor bought him cheaply from a farmer friend who was getting too old to take proper care of the – then - young pony. Pablo stayed with the old man three more years, until Vicent bought himself the farmhouse, a place where he could finally give Petit – as he renamed him – the space he had always dreamt of. As soon as he had bought the magnificent building, Vicent arranged for the construction of an arena and the stables, happy to be able to give some freedom to his horse and dreaming of days such as the one he now had ahead of him.

Vicent looked around and everything seemed ready. The cushions were in place on the chairs around the outside tables, the horses had been fed and the circuit tracks were neatly laid out and marked. Vicent puffed out his chest and breathed in the fresh, dry mountain air that he loved so much. To him, rivers, green valleys and lush forests were for the movies. The real mountains were hard and dry. They smelled of rosemary, small trees flourished, they were home to animals who knew how to protect themselves from the cold and the wind. His was an open and direct landscape, a panorama with no place to hide. The real mountain was macho, like him, he said to himself with pride.

Three waitresses, wearing smart black dresses with white aprons and caps, opened the doors of the small wooden pavilion by the arena and prepared the outside bar, table and sofas. On the wooden terrace, overlooking the oval arena, they lit two brick barbecues and laid the tables with starched white linen tablecloths and shiny silverware – the only valuable items that Vicent had inherited from his mother. A few moments later the waitresses brought out two giant ice-buckets full of bottles of Moët & Chandon and two large pans full of hot soup that would give the guests a warm welcome.

The President of the Valencia region arrived driving his own Porsche, followed by an escort car. His tall, blond and surgery-enhanced wife stepped out of the car first, and it soon became apparent that she was unable to walk around the estate in the tall, stiletto heels she was wearing. Vicent rushed to help her, although of course there was little he could do. Slowly, and with the assistance of Amparo, who had also run to help, the two women went into the house.

'That's some little mansion you've got, big man!' said Eliseo Roig, President of the Valencia region, giving Vicent a bear-hug, which was more like a collision. Eliseo was tall and stocky, with a direct gaze and a polished political presence – nice eyes, in his case green, white teeth, broad shoulders, smart clothes and, most important, a good-little-boy smile that concealed a monster-like politician. 'My goodness me!' he said, shaking his head as he surveyed the vast estate, which had spectacular views over the mountains for miles and miles without another building in sight.

That privileged location, of course, came at a price. In the first place the Fernández's had to build a five-kilometre dirt track to connect the old farmhouse to the nearest country road. Then they had to bring the water and electricity supply, which came to over two hundred thousand euros as more than a dozen workers spent almost three months digging and burying pipes and power cables. The four-storey, ten-bedroom house had not been inhabited since the last century, when some landowning family must have been self-sufficient, while trading their goods at nearby local markets. Morella had always been a wealthy area, surrounded by large estates, which survived through the breeding of highly regarded livestock, such as lamb, wild boar and, of course, the world-famous acorn-fed local pigs.

President Roig came back from his brief, self-guided tour of the garden nearest the house, admiring the bright, delicately carved wood of the windows and balconies. Tall and graceful like the cypresses around it, the building conveyed power and control over the vast lands that surrounded it.

'And you seemed such an innocent little bird, keeping ever so quiet... but sometimes silence speaks louder than words!' said Roig, patting Vicent on the back but without being able to take his eyes off the landscape, which had clearly impressed him.

'Well, one does what one can. I have worked very hard over many years,' Vicent replied looking down. A bit of false modesty would reassure Roig that he was the main protagonist that day and not himself, Vicent thought. The Mayor had always known that envy in Spain was rife and today he needed Roig more than ever. He had to please him at all costs.

'Come on in, please, go right ahead, you're the first to arrive.'

The two men went into the house and sat by the fireplace, where Amparo, who had been chatting with Adela, Roig's wife, served them a brandy.

'Ah, this is the life,' said Eliseo looking Amparo up and down, without being able to conceal his slight disappointment.

Vicent gave Adela a quick look and then turned to Eliseo, whose eyes seemed to say: "You have the house, you bastard, but I've got the job and the girl – oh, yes! – she's twenty years younger than me. Screw you."

The two men had met before, always at meetings about the new airport in Castellón, when Vicent had always supported the President. That once brought him into conflict with the Mayor of Castellón, who thought the city could not afford such an investment. But given the President's persistence and that of his associates like Vicent, the plan was going ahead – at least for now. The need for support for his airport was probably the reason why Roig had accepted Vicent's invitation that day.

The Mayor, who wasn't that bothered what Roig thought of his wife – as he already had what he wanted and when he wanted it – pressed on with his plan as he had no time to lose. He cleared his throat and picked up one of the brochures that his son had neatly arranged by the fireplace, exactly where Vicent had told him to.

'I'm delighted to welcome you to my home and I'm sure we'll have a splendid day,' he said, leaning forward. 'The horses are ready and the lamb will taste like heaven. You'll see...'

'Now you're talking!' Eliseo interjected. 'Well, I don't really care much about horses. I'm here to see you, and for the lamb, and of course to discuss business.' Before going on, he leaned towards Vicent, using a more confidential tone. 'Tell me, Vicent, I'm so very curious: what are you really after with this school? Because I need to warn you: things are going well, but there aren't any fireworks. We've done lots in a short space of time and we've already achieved our objectives.'

Vicent smiled, acknowledging the warning, but confident that he would be able to deal with any challenge. As far as he knew, Roig only wanted one thing now and that was to win the next election.

'Don't worry, Mr President, everything is under control,' said Vicent, feeling sure of himself as he leant backwards and crossed his legs. 'As I said in my email, we have an old school in Morella, a huge building that has been abandoned for years. It's right next to the church, an ideal location that offers great possibilities.'

'I am listening,' said Eliseo, crossing his legs and joining his hands on his knees with presidential deference.

'It's a unique investment opportunity for anybody willing to turn the building into an apartment block, and there is also room for a cinema or a supermarket. As a matter of fact, we really need a big store as this town is dominated by small shops that charge the customers what they like. Having said that' – Vicent stopped for a second to add power to his words – 'the real coup would be to bring in a casino, Las Vegas style, which could lure thousands and thousands of tourists. With the airport in Castellón fully up and running, the foreigners would flock like sheep. It would be one of those projects that fill the coffers, keep the locals happy and employed and, most importantly, win votes,' said Vicent, looking Roig straight in the eye.

Eliseo raised an eyebrow, indicating both surprise and interest.

'Look at this small-town mayor, how clever he's turned out to be,' he said with a cynical smile. 'Go on,' he added, serving himself another glass of brandy, which Amparo had left on the side-table right next to him. Her husband had been insisting all week that the President had to have everything immediately available at all times.

'This is a great opportunity that I will unveil to the select group of investors that I've gathered here today.' Vicent stopped again to serve himself another brandy. He had to be loyal to Roig, but he also had to win his respect by having a conversation between equals.

Eliseo took a large swig from his glass. With his age and experience, he had learned not to waste any time.

'What do you need from me, exactly, and what are you offering in exchange?' he asked.

Vicent coughed nervously, although he had been preparing himself all week to deal with any questions.

'I am only a small-town mayor, as you say, an independent, without any sponsors or backers,' he humbly replied.

'To the point, Vicent, please, we are all grown-up here,' said Eliseo, cutting him short.

Vicent adjusted his tie and now spoke more assertively.

'I need your support to sell this project to potential investors and I need a financial cushion as well. The school is in a dreadful state and refurbishing will cost about ten million euros, a sum which of course would be difficult for any investor to write off. Any help from the Valencia regional government to finance the refurbishment would really help the sale process. Of course, once it was sold we could direct some funds towards the Castellón airport. I understand that you've invested a good deal of your financial and political capital in that project.'

Eliseo took a deep breath and pulled out a cigar from the inside pocket of his expensive-looking leather jacket. Swiftly Vicent passed him an ashtray, but Eliseo rejected it dismissively and threw the first ashes into the fireplace. It was clear who was boss.

'I see, I see...,' said Eliseo, slowly puffing on his cigar. 'The airport situation is a bit delicate; I'm saying this in confidence, Vicent. It's not going as we all hoped. Unfortunately, there have been some delays, but nothing that can't be sorted. Things will improve, I have no doubt.' The President was silent for a few seconds, whilst he gently rolled the cigar in his big, fat hands. Powerful hands. Eventually, he said: 'So how much do you think you could put into the airport?'

'If we sell the building for five million euros and you put, say, another five into the refurbishment, we could invest two into the airport.'

'Well,' the President quickly responded, 'why should I spend five million to get two?'

Vicent, who wasn't afraid of putting the knife in when necessary, immediately replied:

'Because I think that the political capital invested in the airport project has all but evaporated. Also, allocating five million to Morella is easily justifiable because the town hasn't received a penny from the regional government other than for roads, whereas more money in the airport would be difficult to justify after the millions that have already been poured in – so far, with no visible results.'

Eliseo looked intently at Vicent.

'There's one more thing,' Vicent went on, aware of the importance of the moment, 'and then I'll finish. Everything would be much easier if we combined efforts to lobby Madrid to build the damn Parador in Morella, which they've been talking about for ages. There's a small hotel in the town that could be turned into a Parador, giving Morella a lot more prestige and attracting thousands of national and international tourists.'

'I like your thinking, Vicent,' said the President, his eyes fixed on his cigar, when just then they heard what sounded like a van outside.

Vicent thought it would be the group from Zaragoza, who had arranged to travel together. So he had to bring the conversation to an end, although he'd managed to get across the most important points, he thought, with a sense of satisfaction.

'I don't need an answer today, President, no, not at all. You can think about it and call me when it suits you. I am entirely at your disposal. Needless to say,' he added quietly, 'a successful deal could be the beginning of a long and fruitful collaboration.'

Vicent was convinced that a Parador plus well-filled council coffers that would enable him to finance major projects would make him one of the most popular mayors in the entire Valencia region. This would at last offer him access to Roig's party, the good old-fashioned right-wing party of Valencia. Vicent had tried to get into such a club for a long time but the big landowners of Morella had always prevented him from doing so. Despite his increasing wealth and the hotel he owned, Vicent had always felt an outsider amongst the Morella elite – all of them descendants of the land-owning families that looked on him with a superior air because, at the end of the day, he was an incomer and a working person. Those big landowners were also rather worried that Vicent, bourgeois that he was, could try to change the law and split those big estates around Morella into smaller farms, diminishing the power they had held for more than three centuries. During that period, the land map around Morella had not changed an inch.

The two men stood up as soon as they heard voices outside. Roig gave Vicent a frosty smile, but shook the hand that the Mayor offered him. Wearing their leather jackets, they both went out to receive the guests.

*

At twelve noon precisely a loud gunshot started the first flat-race, in which ten horses and jockeys headed by the Marquis of Villafranca competed against each other for over five minutes. His beloved Petit, lent to Roig as a special concession, was soon left behind, although fortunately he didn't finish last. Vicent knew that his horse only responded to his commands rather than the random signals from the hefty President.

The Mayor, together with the riders' wives and the other guests, watched the race from the pavilion terrace, although more of them spent their time admiring the mountains and surrounding landscape than looking at the race itself. Vicent, who didn't really want to ride as he felt his time was better spent acting as host, uncorked the first bottle of Moët & Chandon and started serving the champagne in the fine crystal glasses that the waitresses had already handed to each guest. The businessmen and their wives were not slow in showing their liking for the bubbly and the bottles were emptied so fast that Vicent had to send one of the lads to fetch further supplies from Morella. Unlike his guests, Vicent wasn't bothered about champagne or expensive wine: as long as there was good food and a buxom woman like his – or any other – you could keep the rest, he thought. But he knew that the Moët was important today, so he went around pouring it, talking and joking with everyone as he did so. Politics had taught him to find as many allies as possible and never to create enemies.

'I'd love a top up! Oh, you're such a darling!' said the Marquis' wife, explaining as she tossed back her long, blond hair that she was very thirsty after such a long trip from Zaragoza.

'Of course,' said Vicent, pouring more champagne into her glass. 'But I'll have you know that my father *walked* between Morella and Zaragoza at least once a week after the war. Can you imagine what he would have given for a glass of Moët along the way, eh?' Vicent joked, giving a loud and rather forced guffaw. Still, the Marquis' wife and her friends laughed at his joke even more and gave a toast to Vicent before carrying on drinking.

'Goodness, what extraordinary times they were,' the Marquis' wife said after a pause. She had clearly spent thousands of euros on surgery, Vicent thought. She hadn't yet gone near any of the horses, but she was wearing tall riding boots, a well-padded green jacket and a silk headscarf around her thin and visibly ageing neck. 'What did your father do?' she asked with more deference than real interest. 'I've heard stories about fortunes being made around here after the war from selling olive oil at highly inflated prices when it was so difficult to come by…'

'My father was an honest man,' Vicent quickly responded. 'He was only a Civil Guard who came to this area in 1946 after some years in Jaca, where I was born. He had to deal with a lot of thieves and crooks around here. In these remote towns and villages everyone was quick off the mark. It's truly unbelievable how creative people can be when they need to.'

'Now, now, Vicent, let's not cut off our nose to spite our face – we're very honest here and we've earned everything we have,' said Ceferino, or Cefe as he was known in the town, breaking into the conversation. Tall and thin, Cefe spoke with a cigarette in his mouth from a corner table he was sharing with Eva, the young secretary at the Town Hall in Morella and also a local. Cefe, who was about fifty, had spent half his life running the Morella branch of a well-known Valencian bank. The two of them stood out in such a refined group, as they wore large, home-made woollen jumpers and well-worn mountain boots, in great contrast to the immaculate riding boots worn by most of the guests and which seemed to have come straight off the shelves of the shop.

'Of course,' said Vicent, cutting Cefe short. He didn't want to allow too much attention to be given to Cefe, who he only got on with out of necessity. The banker, as a matter of fact, had very few friends – only an irreverent old lady who had spent half her life in exile and who now wanted to become the town's saviour. But Vicent didn't want to concern himself with such trifles on a day like today. 'Of course we've earned everything we've got… and what's about to come, as I shall explain to you all soon…,' he said, in a slightly teasing tone.

'We can't wait!' said Paco Barnús, one of the investors behind the brand new glass skyscraper in Cullera, until recently a small fishing village on the Valencia coast. 'I already have some experience in turning towns and villages into real centres of progress, so I'm all ears,' said Barnús, leaning back in his chair and doing up the golden buttons of his blue jacket. The investor then raised his hand and clicked his fingers for more champagne, but without looking at any of the waitresses at all.

The young girls, unaccustomed to being treated in that way, didn't notice the gesture and Vicent had to alert them by looking at them intently and giving a slight cough. Finally, one of them rushed towards Barnús and asked in a friendly way but in Catalan:

'Would you like a bit more?'

The businessman was surprised at being spoken to in Catalan, the local language, at such a gathering and glanced at the waitress disparagingly and with some exasperation. Turning away from her, he replied in Spanish:

'Yes, please.'

Her hands shaking, the young waitress filled his glass and withdrew as quickly as she could. Just as she got back to her place by the wall, Ernesto Mitjavila, one of the main investors in the Valencia bank where Cefe worked, decided he, too, wanted more champagne. No-one broke the tense silence as the same waitress, bottle in hand, crossed the terrace again and nervously served the gentleman, with the eyes of everyone present upon her. Ernesto watched the Moët fill his glass and waited in expectant silence until the waitress had returned to her position in order to pick up the conversation. Before doing so, he gave a sigh that indicated he was getting to the end of his patience.

'In Valencia,' Mitjavila finally said, looking at all the guests, 'we have become an example for the rest of Spain, at least according to what I heard the other day in Madrid. Who would have guessed, only a few years ago, when we only had a few acres of oranges and lemons?' he asked, laughing and drinking more champagne. 'Now look at Valencia, it's a centre of international tourism and has also hosted Formula One Grand Prix races. As a matter of fact, I was having lunch with Bernie Ecclestone the other day,' he said, smoothing back the few white hairs that he had left and adjusting the silk scarf around his thick neck.

'We're also making progress in Zaragoza,' pointed out Federico Muñoz, who was standing by one of the burning braziers. 'We've even developed a plan for the Monegros region: it won't be a desert any more. We're going to build a nature theme park right there that will create thousands of jobs and, most importantly, bring in capital that'll stay in the region.'

Eyebrows were raised in admiration and some of the guests looked at each other with a sparkle in their eyes. They all felt as though they were at the forefront of a new Spain.

Vicent was enthralled by the scene, as it was exactly what he had dreamt of. Spain had at last turned into a country capable of generating capital, a giant step for a place that was used to supplying cheap labour for centuries. Many people he knew were doing well out of that change, and now it was his turn.

Standing by the barbecue where the lamb was already cooking, and after the races had finished, Vicent thanked the riders for their efforts and gave a medal to each one of them. After a round of applause, he turned once more to his guests, this time looking more serious.

'Dear friends,' he said. 'Thank you very much for coming all the way here. It's an honour for me to welcome such a select group of people' – Vicent paused briefly to look at Eliseo. 'I would especially like to thank Eliseo Roig, the President of our region.'

Without further introduction, the President stood up to speak, accustomed as he was to being the centre of everything, thought Vicent.

'My dear friends and Mayor Fernández,' said Roig in a loud, clear voice, his back as stiff as a ramrod. 'This wonderful smell of roast lamb is killing me, so I will be straight and direct: a style that has brought so much success to the Valencia region, the fastest-growing area in Spain.' The President paused to look up at the mountains. After a few seconds silence, Roig took a deep breath before continuing, a well-known trick in politics to give the message a bit more resonance.

'The possibilities for our towns and villages,' he went on, 'some of which are still anchored in the past, are now better than ever; but this also means that there's still plenty to do. We already have examples of marvellous developments, such as in Cullera, where entire communities have leapt almost a century in a couple of years with just a bit of investment. That's why our Government is proud of initiatives such as Mayor Fernández's – about which we're anxious to know more details.'

Roig looked at Vicent with a broad smile. The President, visibly proud of himself, looked at each guest and turned back towards the Mayor, patting him a few times on the shoulder. Vicent, his chest all puffed out and his head up, took the floor again.

'Thank you very much, Mr President,' he said in a firm and confident voice. 'Gentlemen, I have invited you here to spend a fantastic day and to unveil an amazing project: the redevelopment of Morella's old school. In the Town Hall we want to make Morella as rich and as prosperous as other medieval towns in Europe, such as San Gimignano in Italy, Germany's Rotenburg or Carcassonne in France.' Some guests exchanged looks of surprise and curiosity, as if they had never heard the names of those places before. Vicent continued his short speech. 'These towns have made capital out of their history and beauty, while in Morella we only have a few shops and hardly any medium-sized businesses. We want more.' The Mayor paused to take a deep breath, something he had been practising all week. The words were coming out well, although he hoped nobody would ask him about the towns he mentioned as he had never set foot in any of them. He went on: 'As I shall show you after lunch, the old school building is the biggest and grandest in town. More than one thousand square metres ready to be transformed into a hotel, a cinema, apartments or even better: a casino like the ones in Las Vegas, which would attract thousands of both Spanish and foreign tourists.'

Vicent noticed the smiles on a few people's faces. Everything was turning out just as he had wanted.

'Refurbishing the building, however, will be costly, something close to five million euros, which we expect to share with other local and regional governments. I've already been told in Madrid that the rest of the investment must come from private sources – for them this is a great opportunity as new apartments in such a location would sell very easily. And if we decide to build a casino, success will be guaranteed as it'll be the first one like it in Spain.' Vicent paused to observe his guests' reaction.

'A casino, what an original idea,' whispered Barnús to the Marquis of Villafranca sitting next to him. They nodded in agreement. 'This could be very, very interesting,' Barnús now said out loud, raising an eyebrow and gently stroking his chin with his forefinger and thumb.

'I won't say any more,' Vicent added. 'We've left some information on the table,' he said, pointing to the brochures next to the ice buckets, now replenished with more bottles of champagne. 'Please let me know if you have any questions. A bus will take us to the school in about an hour, after lunch; the ladies can come as well, of course,' he said, smiling towards a small concentration of blond heads on one side of the terrace. 'We'll come back here afterwards at about six to finish the day with some coffee, cakes and drinks. I hope you find the project as succulent as the lamb that is ready and waiting for us. Cheers and *bon appetit!*'

Vicent, who was enjoying every second of the party he had been preparing for months, basked in the applause and the pats on the back that he received from his guests. The champagne was flowing and the shellfish were plentiful, brought in especially from the coast for those too refined to eat meat. Everybody was laughing, joking and telling each other their self-congratulatory business success stories and their grandiose future projects. In his triumph Vicent had almost forgotten about *Lo Petit*, who he hadn't looked at for a while and who was standing not far from the main terrace, head down, looking nowhere in particular with his sad eyes. He seemed exhausted. He had never been a racehorse and had only been raised as the friend of an old farmer, who he helped as much as he could. In contrast, the other horses looked quite composed after their efforts. Four were thoroughbreds, bought by Vicent at the April Fair in Seville the previous year, and five had been hired for the occasion from a stud farm in Barcelona.

At the corner table, Eva and Cefe were sucking their fingers in appreciation of the lamb stuffed with truffles. The other guests were, of course, using a knife and fork to eat the cutlets.

'How's this all going to end?' Eva asked, looking at the group sitting some way away.

'I don't know, Eva, I just don't know,' was all Cefe replied, as he lit a cigarette.

4

As she sat in the back row of the Gothic rooms of the Town Hall, smartly dressed for the occasion and with her neat hair a brighter white than usual, Valli couldn't believe what she was hearing. The wonderful building with its half-pointed Gothic arches, polished wood floor and neat stone walls, was practically empty. That was no doubt intentional, the old *maestra* thought, because to arrange a meeting at three o'clock on a weekday afternoon was frankly inconvenient for most people. And to hold it on a Wednesday also left out the people from Morella who worked in Castellón or Vinaroz and only went into town at the weekend. However, there she was to look after everyone's interests. Only three women a little younger than her and two retired old men had heard the Mayor's presentation on the possible sale of the school. Valli noticed that despite the brevity of the statement, some had taken advantage of the comfortable chairs and the warmth of the room to have a little doze.

As no-one had any questions or comments, Vicent immediately closed the session. Valli watched the Mayor pick up his papers and look once more at the almost empty room. Their eyes met.

He quickly looked away, but Valli got up surprisingly nimbly for someone her age and moved towards him. Despite the fact that Vicent had clearly seen her do so, he finished putting his things together and headed for the door, forcing Valli to quicken her pace in order to catch him.

'Mayor!' she shouted. 'Not so fast!'

Vicent, who had almost reached the door, turned round, and with little enthusiasm responded:

'What can I do for you, Señora?'

Valli looked him straight in the eye. They knew each other sufficiently well for him to call her by her first name, but it didn't surprise her that he preferred to keep his distance. Eventually she said:

'I imagine this proposal will have to be voted on. Have you thought of organising a referendum or are you relying on the support of your Council to take it forward?'

Vicent burst out laughing.

'A referendum? For heaven's sake! What age are you living in, Señora Querol? When have we ever had a referendum in Morella?'

'Quite often during the Republic, actually,' she replied, prompting further loud laughter from the Mayor.

'Just look how much the world has changed since then,' he said crossly. 'But to answer your question, of course I'll need to get the support of the local Council, which has people on it who are well versed technically in these complex financial and socio-economic processes. So don't you worry; everything's in good hands.'

And with that said, he gave her an icy smile and walked off to his office. Valli followed him with a hard, serious stare. Things could not be left like this, she thought.

Valli hurried out in order to catch up with the others who had been there and exchange impressions, but they had already gone to take refuge from old-age boredom in their homes. It was only mid-afternoon and Valli didn't want to go home and face the solitude that still visited her every night since her partner died many years earlier. Valli was not at all religious but she went out into the countryside once a week to cast flowers along the paths around Morella in tribute to the person who accompanied her for over twenty years and who now lay in a cemetery in Paris. It was that death and the death of Franco that prompted her return to Spain in 1977 after a long exile. Now, alone, she didn't know if she had the strength to try to stop the Mayor and his outrageous plans. Apartments in the old school! It was *her* school, where she taught during the Republic and again more recently since returning to Spain and settling in Morella.

At the sound of a familiar voice her slow, sad steps came to a halt. She was always pleased to hear it.

'What are you doing here? I thought Wednesday was your day for going into the countryside,' said Cefe, going over to her and leaving his friends at the door of Casa Masoveret, where they were debating whether to go in and have a game of cards or go for a walk along the Alameda that went round the town behind the castle.

'Oh, my dear boy, how wonderful to see you, Cefe!' Valli replied, raising her arms to give her friend a kiss. 'I haven't seen you for ages. Where have you been?'

'I've been in Valencia for a few days at a bank meeting; they're putting more pressure on us every day,' he added, giving a rather nervous laugh.

Valli gave a little frown.

'I thought you only went for the Christmas dinner. Now they're getting you to go there in the middle of March? When they call extraordinary meetings it means that things are either going very well or very badly…'

Cefe looked both ways along the street and then at Valli, who was looking straight at him. The banker, now over fifty and still wearing his country style suit and tie, took her by the arm and told his friends he'd be back in a while after taking Valli home.

The old *maestra*, happy to walk across the square with her friend, asked him directly as always:

'Is something up?'

Cefe immediately shook his head.

'No, absolutely nothing, there's no need to worry. As you know, there's a lot of construction going on and it's pay up time! No, the bank just called us together to ask us to be careful because although there are a lot of interesting projects on the go, we have to take care with the typical clever clogs who think that everything will keep on going up, and we have to keep our feet on the ground. We've lent a lot of money and we've got to start calling in the loans.'

'That's what I've been saying for a long time!' said Valli, defending her view that had been subjected to a lot of comments accusing her of being an old unsophisticated conservative. 'Everyone thought that I was encouraging people to keep their money under the mattress. But that wasn't the case at all. I was only saying that you have to assess risk very carefully. We farming families certainly know that, don't we?' she said to Cefe, looking at him intently with the eyes of a long-standing and close friend.

Cefe smiled and without saying a word the two carried on walking until they reached Pla d'Estudi, the attractive square of white houses where Valli had her apartment, which was easily recognisable by the bright plants that always decorated her balcony. It was the largest square in the town, open to the mountains on one side while the rest was dominated by a pleasant assortment of old houses no more than three floors high, all with balconies of dark wood. That uniformity and the broad but small central square with just a few fairly young trees dotted around brought peace and quiet to most people as they walked across it heading for the Alameda.

Encouraged by the pleasant, almost spring-like afternoon sunshine, the old *maestra* and the banker continued on their walk. The weather was too agreeable to stay indoors, where she only had her large number of books for company, she thought to herself.

Valli met Cefe just after he was born, wrapped in a woollen blanket by the fire in his family's farmhouse, which was very near her own parents' place. Cefe's house was the last one she saw in Morella for almost twenty years, for it was there that she went to collect a blanket and some tins of food that her friend's mother had got together for her, knowing that that night she was embarking on her journey to France. She couldn't go to her parents' house, which was being carefully watched by the Civil Guard who were on her tail. Valli got to France on her own in just under a week, having gone through woods and over mountains without any help, other than what like-minded people were able to offer her. The hardest thing about that journey was knowing who you could trust rather than the cold or hunger.

Valli never had any doubts about Cefe's parents. She knew his father well, as she had had him as a pupil just before the outbreak of the war, when she was doing teaching practice with the Educational Missions in Morella. Along with another teacher they brought together children of different ages from the farms to meet in houses, barns or even stables and give them classes. Many children, like Cefe's father, who was also called Ceferino, had never been inside a school because his parents needed him in the fields. But they loved the school, because they spent the whole day learning and playing, almost always in the open air. Valli still remembered how, shortly before he died about ten years previously, Cefe's father proudly recited one of Machado's poems that she had taught him, almost certainly in the open countryside.

Cefe's father always said that if it hadn't been for Valli and the Missions, he would never have sent his son to school, and so his son would never have become a respected banker. Cefe had gained the respect of the town because although he was known for being austere and was aware of the limits to what he could do, he didn't hesitate to help and understand those in need. He had been head of the office for more than thirty years and in that time it had never had any serious problem and many people from Morella were still grateful to him for having helped them out of their difficulties at some time or another.

'What a lovely afternoon, Valli,' said Cefe as he lit up a cigarette and stopped at one of the viewing points of the Alameda that had recently been created, with designer wooden benches. From there they looked at the spectacular views of the mountains, arid, tough and distant, that seemed to stretch endlessly into the province of Teruel.

Valli felt tired and sat down on one of the benches, where she was joined by her friend. Cefe accompanied her on the Alameda walk as often as he could, especially since his father died. It was a lovely, peaceful walk; sometimes they talked and at others they simply looked at the countryside or the imposing silhouette of the castle. They breathed in the smells and absorbed the tranquillity. The Alameda had looked undeniably lovely ever since the new mayor had invested heaven knows how much money in getting rid of holes, levelling it out, putting in more play areas and period lamps that were very bright and painted black. Older people said with pride that at night it looked like New York, while the younger ones complained that what had been gained in safety had been lost in privacy. Mayor Fernández had also built a similar walk just a few metres below the main one, creating space for cars and tourist buses that came at weekends.

Cefe and Valli carried on walking and said hello to two elderly ladies who were well wrapped up in modern anoraks and walking arm-in-arm. Further on was an old man with a beret and a stick who was slowly coming towards them. It was a lovely afternoon, perhaps the first sign of the arrival of spring after a long, cold winter.

'With the weather like this why haven't you gone on your usual walk in the country?' Cefe asked out of curiosity.

'Oh, my dear boy, you can't imagine,' she said in a tired, dejected voice. 'I've come from the Town Hall, where the Mayor called a meeting for three o'clock to pull the wool over our eyes with an idea that even he shouldn't have any faith in. He's proposing to convert the old school into apartments and he even wants to set up a state tourist hotel. This Mayor will ruin us, don't you think?'

Cefe looked at her closely.

'What makes you say that?'

'Because Morella isn't America or Valencia, which is the same thing in this case,' Valli replied angrily. 'If you fill the town with new apartments, what'll happen to prices? I don't know much about economics, but I do remember from the farm that if you sell wheat to people in the capital, they always pay more and leave prices at a prohibitive level for people in the towns and villages, so they're left without any bread. My father always said that the markets are for local people, and that if you open them up to other communities, you've gone and done the wrong thing.'

'You're against globalisation, then!' said Cefe with a smile.

'What do I know about it?' Valli conceded, relaxing her shoulders. 'I don't know, I just don't know, I don't get this thing about apartments in the school. Besides, shouldn't we be dedicating the building to a more enriching social initiative, rather than apartments?'

'That's the thing, Valli, that's the thing. What is there more enriching than apartments?' said Cefe, looking down at the ground.

'Yes, it's enriching, but who for?'

Cefe didn't reply, but looked ahead at the dark, arid mountains that he knew so well.

'Besides, that school holds so many memories for me…' added Valli after a brief silence. 'It should be converted into a university summer school, or a theatre or something like that. It's probably not that bad inside, and the classrooms could be renovated, but of course, it's been such a long time…'

'The place is in a terrible state, it's completely ruined,' said Cefe. 'I was there not long ago, and of course you'd have to spend a fortune on it. It's been abandoned for nearly fifteen years.'

'Goodness, is it that long? But in any case, I'd like to see it,' Valli insisted. 'They always tell me it's locked, but I'd like to go and see what exactly this Mayor is up to. Besides, who knows, there may be some books and other things of mine there. There are at least some interesting memories. But whenever I've asked they've said no, that it's barred and bolted, because it's dangerous to go inside.'

Cefe waited a few seconds and finally looked at Valli.

'I've got some keys. If you like, I can let you in, if you'll keep it as our secret. The best time is early on a Sunday morning when there's nobody about. What do you say?'

Valli's eyes lit up.

'That's fantastic. What about next Sunday?'

'Sunday it is.'

The smell of freshly baked bread made Valli feel hungry as she walked along Virgen Street towards the church. She'd left her house good and early, about half past six, so as not to have to rush. Half-way there she stopped to look at the clock and to check that there was no-one else in the street. In fact there was no-one at all and even the birds weren't yet singing. The first rays of the sun had not yet reached the houses, which were still reflecting the gentle and calm light of dawn.

Suddenly Valli felt very hungry, as she'd hardly had anything to eat since the day before because she felt so nervous. With time still in hand she decided to go down the hill to the street with the arcades, the most commercial street in the town, to buy a roll in the bread shop. From the smell that came wafting towards her it was obvious that Paca was getting everything ready early as usual, she thought.

'Hey, Vallivana, you're up early today!' exclaimed the jovial, stocky baker, whom Valli had known all her life.

Valli gave a vague reply and Paca didn't pursue it. People had learned in the towns to protect their privacy, which in itself was quite difficult given the extent to which people had less space and socialised more. Valli thanked her and with her roll in her hand was on her way again to the school a few moments later.

The cobbled streets were clean, empty and silent. Morella had always been an attractive town, a mesh of hills and narrow streets located on a hill crowned by a medieval castle, and all encased within a wall with five majestic gates, one of which was flanked by fortified towers. The imposing whole, set in the heart of the Maestrazgo region, was remote and silent, arid and hard, like the people who lived there. They had learned to survive with very little, in a tough environment, with icy cold in winter and hardly any outside help. The imposing town had won its battle against time and neglect and had managed to retain a proportion of its young people, who no longer saw themselves having to emigrate in order to survive. In spite of the services, shops and other features of modern times that had come to the town as they had everywhere else, Morella retained the smell of the countryside and of rosemary from its surroundings, but above all it had retained the spirit of survival in its inhabitants, who remained strong and enterprising.

The early risers amongst the older people were now very patiently beginning to climb some of the hills, protected from the cold by jumpers made from local wool and a traditional black beret which, however much they were thought to be old-fashioned and countrified, were now sold in the smartest boutiques in Paris and London, according to what Valli had read somewhere.

So as not to be noticed the old *maestra* left the street with the arcades and took another that was straighter and far less commercial towards the small church square. It was some time since she had walked alone along the town's streets, she thought, as she listened to the sound of her shoes on the cobblestones. She stopped for a second to reflect, and couldn't remember a similar sensation since Franco's troops entered Morella on the fourth of April 1938 following three days of stand-off. By then the majority of Republicans in the town had fled to the coast, thinking that British and French boats would pick them up and take them off into exile. How many of them died waiting, Valli remembered with sadness. After the fall of Morella the streets were as empty as they are now, although then the silence lasted all day, as people didn't go out because they were so afraid. The Nationalist soldiers, who were encamped in Colón and Estudis Squares, patrolled the town in their green uniforms with red berets, as most of them were militiamen from Navarre. Morella quickly succumbed to their presence and the firm, rapid sound of their boots. Valli still retained in the recesses of her memory the hammer-blow sound of those confident steps that always filled her with terror.

Fortunately that had gone now, just as the twenty years of exile in Paris were now behind her, she said to herself as she set off again towards the Placet. The relatively small square was dominated by a basilica, which was not very imposing but had a more accessible and less arrogant Gothic beauty than the big cathedrals. It wasn't very high, but the main arch was flanked by two smaller ones, so that the entrance in the wide and horizontal part appeared to be inviting the townspeople to come inside. The dark colour of the stone blended perfectly with the traditional cobblestones of the square, which had not changed since it was built, stone by stone, decades earlier.

Valli sat down on a long stone bench facing the church just as the first rays of the sun began to strike the square. From her cloth bag that she carried with her everywhere she took out the still warm bun that Paca had made for her. It was delicious, she thought, as she took the first mouthful. There was no way you could do this in one of the big cities, she said to herself, enjoying her breakfast and looking around her beloved Placet, which was free from cars and tourists.

Valli was feeling nervous inside. She hadn't been in the school for a long time, at least for the fifteen years when it was closed and since they built the new buildings next to the Alameda, which were more modern and most importantly had central heating. Valli looked around her, at the acacias that had been there as long as she could remember, now bare and sad. As sad as during the war, when some Republicans set fire right there to whatever religious symbols they could find. Morella had initially been in what the Nationalists called the 'red zone', but the townspeople, calm and always practical, had spent the first few months of the conflict keeping things as normal as possible under the circumstances. Until suddenly and to everyone's surprise, a Republican column from Barcelona came and destroyed crucifixes, bibles, and images of saints of all shapes and sizes. The revolutionaries went into the church and ransacked part of the sacristy and the altar and put it all on a bonfire in the middle of the Placet and set fire to it in the night. Aged eighteen and brought up to be respectful, Valli did not understand why there was so much hatred and destruction. The fact is that a few hours later Placet was full of ashes and drunken anarchists dancing around in their smelly red shirts, while the more conservative people were seized with panic and didn't dare come out of their houses. The young Valli, who was more surprised than terrified, went straight off to find a broom to clean up the square and then carry on at school the following day.

'A very good morning to you!' said Cefe out of the blue, with his usual cigarette in his mouth.

It certainly startled Valli.

'Oh, my dear boy, you gave me such a fright!'

'But a woman like you isn't frightened by anything. What have you got to be afraid of at this time of life?' Her friend smiled, put out his cigarette on the ground and helped her up.

'Oh, get away with you,' Valli replied. 'I may not be up to much but I suspect I've still got a few battles left to fight.'

'Leave them to others, Valli, it's their turn now and it's your turn to rest,' said Cefe, in his usual affable way.

Valli gave no response and within a couple of minutes the two of them found themselves at the front of the old school, founded by the Escolapian Brothers more than a hundred and fifty years earlier. The main door on one side did not do justice to the majesty of the enormous classical building, which could only be admired in its full splendour from outside the town. It was long, built of dark stone and had large wooden-framed windows. Next to the entrance there was a triangular pediment that topped the façade of the building and could be seen from the Placet.

Having given it a good kicking to get it unstuck, Cefe opened the woodworm-riddled door with its flaking paint. With all the windows closed the entrance was dark and gloomy. The only bit of light was coming in through some darkened windows, on which an image of the Virgin had been painted beneath the word "Pietà".

Taking care not to tread on any broken glass or something that smelt like stale urine, Valli and Cefe moved towards the main courtyard, a quadrangle from where they could see the two floors of the building, covered by an almost transparent plastic roof where clearly the light did get in. In the centre stood a statue of an Escolapian Brother with two children.

Valli felt her heart miss a beat at the sight of the desolate state of her old school. She sighed, looked at Cefe and said:

'You don't know what all this was like in the days of the Republic. I can still see your father running around the vegetable garden that we had here, in this very courtyard that has been cemented over. We didn't have any statues then or symbols of power and authority, only lettuces, tomatoes, turnips and carrots, and even chickens that the pupils looked after with great care and attention.'

She took a deep breath before going on.

'I was very fond of your father. You know that we were neighbours from when we were very small, as our parents served the same master, the Marquis, who they spoke to only once or twice in their entire lives. And they were so poor, devoting all their labour to him, for nothing. The fact is that he robbed them, them and many others, deducting part of their wages if the harvest wasn't good, even if it was due to the weather or to a lack of mules for ploughing.' Valli sighed. 'The Marquis was stoned to death as soon as the Republic was declared. Nothing more was heard from that family,' Valli continued in a serious voice. 'I'm not saying that what happened was a good thing, far from it, but the fact is that it liberated my father, who was able to buy the small hotel after a few years and move the family into the town.'

Cefe looked at her very attentively, as he always did with everyone. His years in the bank had taught him to listen more than to speak. As a banker and as a person, he always preferred stability and discretion, avoiding jokes, which generally made situations worse – even more so when it came to money, as he used to say.

Valli carried on walking through her school, and now slowly went up to the Escolapian statue.

'Goodness me,' she said, turning to Cefe. 'I remember when they took away this stone Escolapian as soon as the Republic was declared, when I was just twelve and came here to the school. I had always liked reading and writing, partly because I loved the person who was my lifelong teacher – she was called Eleuteria. She was kind and patient with everyone, she never got angry and she seemed to know everything. She explained history to us with an enthusiasm and such detail that it was as if she herself had been in the midst of those battles. She encouraged me to apply for a grant, or rather she applied for one on my behalf because my parents didn't understand what was involved, and so I managed to get into the Young Ladies' Residence. I had a wonderful time in Madrid, completing my secondary studies, and in 1935 I joined the Teacher Training School. A year later, just before the war broke out, I was here doing teaching practice with the Missions, so the war kept me in Morella. It could have been worse, because at least I could be with my parents, and not on my own far away in Madrid.'

Valli looked around her, still devastated by the sad state of her old school. She went on:

'During the war, both under the Republicans and the Fascists, I always tried to keep classes going as normally as possible, because we didn't want to have an illiterate country as well as a devastated one which was ruled by Franco, making it even worse. You've no idea how many illiterate people there were then. Like our parents, the majority couldn't really read or write. It was worst on the farms, of course, because the families wanted the sons and daughters to work in the fields. That's why we went on the backs of donkeys distributing books to all the farms. It was great fun and they were so grateful.' Valli at last revealed a smile. 'After a lot of effort I was able to persuade my friend Alejandro Casona to come to Morella; it was a whole day's journey from Madrid, but he did turn up. We put on some impressive drama productions; I remember your father doing Hamlet, with a skull he provided himself, small though it was, saying that he'd found it in a field. He certainly gave me a fright with it!'

Cefe smiled, quietly remembering his father, who was loved by the whole town.

'My father always told me that if I didn't study, I would never be anything in life, like him, with so many years working for the Marquis and then working on his own land, but without ever earning a penny,' he said regretfully.

'He was a lovely man, your father… I was very fond of him. Although we were quite young, I'd looked after him when I was little and your family was in the fields. It was quite funny to have him in class when I came to Morella to do my teaching practice.'

While Valli was talking, Cefe took out of the inside pocket of his jacket a small parcel wrapped in brown paper, which he tenderly held out to his friend.

Valli immediately broke off what she was saying and with great curiosity took hold of the small package. Without asking any questions she quickly opened it to find a very old-looking edition of *Platero and I*, the almost poetical story by Juan Ramón Jiménez.

'*Platero…!*' she uttered in a quiet voice.

With eyes full of excitement and trembling hands, Valli opened the small paperback copy whose spine had been protected with sticky tape and saw that it was a 1916 edition published in Madrid. But her heart beat a lot faster when she saw the unmistakeable stamp of the "Educational Missions" on the next page.

'It's one of the books we handed out!' she exclaimed, her eyes filling with tears.

'My father read it to me at night,' Cefe explained. 'I've always cherished it, but I wanted to show it to you.'

Valli stroked the yellowing book with its smell of old paper, the print still perfect after nearly a hundred years. As she used to do back in the thirties, the old *maestra* couldn't wait to read out loud the wonderful opening to the story that describes the most famous little donkey in Spanish literature – with no offence to Sancho Panza's

Rucio – as "small, furry, gentle", and with jet-black eyes that were "as hard as two beetles made of black glass".

'Do you know that I met him – Juan Ramón?' she said full of emotion. Cefe looked surprised. 'Yes, yes, when I lived in the Young Ladies' Residence that he used to visit, one day he invited us to his house in the Salamanca district. A group of us students went and his wife, Zenobia, invited us in and offered us a wonderful afternoon tea of drinking chocolate with fritters. What I remember most is that he spent little time with us and that he had a study soundproofed with a kind of cork on all the walls, because he said that noise distracted him. He had some odd little ways.'

Valli sighed and looked towards the main staircase, now covered in broken glass and well-trodden bits of paper, that went up to the first floor. Two large murals with religious motifs had replaced a painting of La República, the beautiful semi-naked woman, with the tricolour flag in her hand, which had been drawn in 1931. Valli was a member of the group who went to get ladders, brushes and other materials from the house of the painter Alfredo, who helped them as much as he could. When the militiamen seized the town, they immediately covered it with spiritual motifs and reinstated the statue of the Escolapian brother that Señorita Eleuteria had hidden in the school's attic during the Republic.

'Just imagine,' said Valli as she went up the stairs, 'we lined up here every morning singing the Riego Hymn, with all the students shouting "Liberty, Liberty, Liberty!" Those were the days. They still hadn't put on that horrible plastic roof then, as the teachers preferred sunlight and fresh air. If it rained in the courtyard, we just got wet. No-one ever died from it. The walls were brightly coloured and the classrooms did not have platforms; music could be heard everywhere, especially in the afternoons, when the students signed up for theatre workshops, dance or playing in the school band. Everyone took part in one activity or another, and they stayed until nine o'clock at night, until it got dark or until we threw them out.'

Cefe shook his head several times.

'Well, I don't remember anything like that,' he said. 'In my years here we sang the Falange's *Face to the Sun*, and we attended classes wearing uniforms like a regiment, always feeling sad and bored, and with a priest on the platform ready to hit us on the knuckles if we made any mistakes.'

'Yes, yes, my dear boy, I know, I know.' Valli briefly took his arm as she looked at the magnificent building from the first floor. 'I didn't want to stay. I could have got a teaching licence, because at that time I was only a student, I hadn't belonged to any union or party and my family, being farmers, weren't involved in politics. But I refused. I refused to live in a way that was the opposite of how I had been taught in the Residence. I couldn't bear the idea of going against my ideals and I decided to go into exile, as the majority of my companions did. I crossed into France with Antonio

Machado and his family, all of them very tired and weak. Just think what happened to the poor man and how quickly it happened. Like Manuel Azaña, buried like a poor wretch in Montauban, or like so many others.'

Slowly they went into one of the classrooms, with some of the desks piled against a wall and the chairs, many of them broken, shoved into a corner.

'This is where we taught English,' Valli continued. 'There was a young Englishman who I met in the Students' Residence who came through Morella with the International Brigades during the war.' She stopped and looked at the floor before going on. 'His name was Tristan, he was very English, attentive and well-mannered, he couldn't have been more than twenty. He was more poet than soldier, so it was fortunate that he was never called to the front. They always put him in supplies or in some school or other, where he did a fantastic job. And how he laughed when he saw Shakespeare done Morella-style!'

'What a pity that they never taught us English,' said Cefe.

'They made your generation study French, because the practical and protestant Anglo-Saxon mentality always made Franco's National Catholicism feel uncomfortable,' replied Valli. 'Apart, of course, from the fact that England fought against Germany in the Second World War and Franco never forgave Perfidious Albion for that,' Valli added sarcastically.

'Well, look how useful English would be now for finding investors.'

Valli looked at him questioningly.

'What investors are you looking for?' she asked.

Cefe sighed and looked her in the eye.

'The Council is looking for capital to refurbish this place,' he said, looking at the ground.

Valli raised her eyebrows in surprise.

'Are you involved in this plan to turn the school into apartments?'

'No, no. I'm not part of the plan, but as we're the Council's bankers and we know some of the investors, they have involved us in the process. Plus, as the debt is with us, they can't sign anything without our agreement.'

'Well, I'm very glad to hear it and I hope you'll put a stop to such nonsense. How can they sell this building when it ought to be turned into something cultural, like a theatre, a summer school or an academy?'

'That would be fantastic,' Cefe admitted, 'but the Council needs the money and the apartments are the quickest way to get it.'

'If they need the money, they shouldn't have spent so much on the new Alameda, the new schools, so many parties and firework displays that they organise just to get votes,' said Valli, all fired up. Her cheeks were burning despite the cold in the building. 'If they want money, let them go and find it elsewhere.'

Cefe cleared his throat before adding a bit more information.

'That's not the worst,' he said. 'Another option on the table is to turn it into a casino, Las Vegas style.'

'A casino?' exclaimed Valli, taken aback. Her eyes were bright with anger; she couldn't understand it. 'Well, he didn't mention that in the meeting the other day, the rogue. Who in their sound mind wants a casino next to the Placet?'

'It would create a lot of jobs and fill the Council's coffers,' Cefe replied, without much conviction.

'It can't happen,' Valli repeated, shaking her head. 'Since when do we want to fill the town with gambling addicts?'

Cefe said nothing, before concluding:

'Maybe we have no choice.'

'What do you mean?' asked Valli impatiently, looking Cefe in the eyes as if she were about to eat him. 'This is all about money, isn't it? How much, how much does this greedy man want for this place?' Cefe said nothing. Valli went right up to him. 'Tell me, Cefe, tell me for the love of our parents and the good of our town, how much are they asking for?'

'Five million… but you didn't hear it from me.'

Valli took two steps back and opened her eyes wide.

'Good heavens, five million…' She gripped the *Platero* book tightly in her hand and said: 'Well, if it's five million they want, five million they shall have. We'll present them with an alternative plan. I'll do it, even if it's the last thing I do in this life. That fascist rat will have to walk on my grave before he puts a casino in my Republican school.'

5

Charles had no idea what to expect when he opened room number fourteen in the small hotel, the closest thing he had been able to find to a Bed &Breakfast in Morella. The other hotels had looked too modern for the break in the country that he had been hoping for - and felt he needed - that Easter. The winter in London had been long and hard, and stressful for the first time in many years. Only a few weeks earlier Charles had had to ask three students to leave Eton because their parents could no longer pay the college bills. No-one mentioned the crisis, but some bankers, like these parents, were starting to have serious problems.

The three expelled students were amongst his favourites, bright boys who would now have to move to a state school and face the taunts of their new classmates, who would no doubt make fun of their loss of privilege. Charles had supported them throughout, even after they had left, inviting them to dinner in London and writing letters full of good advice, all in his own time.

Now all he wanted was a few days' rest and relaxation in a different and distant environment. He had been captivated by Morella from the moment he saw the Council's advertisement about the school, which disappointingly wasn't available for rent, as he had hoped, but only for sale, because it needed a complete refurbishment. Always sceptical, Charles had gone over there to see it for himself. Eton was facing increased competition and the cost of new technologies was taking up more and more of the budget. The parents paid thirty-five thousand pounds a year, and as he had just confirmed, raising the fees was not an option if some parts of the financial system were already beginning to show signs of strain. These warnings came as no surprise to Charles, who had been watching the huge extravagance of the British Government for years, and also the applications to Eton, which had gone up tenfold in the past five years. He was suspicious of the fact that in such a short time such a large number of families had acquired such wealth. Something was going to end badly, he had warned his friend Robin in the City, who admitted that he was right.

Even so, his obligation was to maintain or to improve the quality of the department of foreign languages of which he was the head and which employed nearly twenty teachers. Other private colleges, such as Westminster and Harrow, had specialised in science or arts subjects, and he believed that Eton should go for languages and sport, subjects that were clearly more practical than physics or chemistry when doing business in a global market. Besides, Eton didn't want to produce scientists but bankers and lawyers. Like Robin, Charles believed that the best opportunities would arise in Latin America rather than in Asia, so that having a residential centre in Spain where his students could practice the language could offer a convincing sales pitch for parents. In fact, American universities were already making use of this model: Chicago had a campus in Barcelona and some Masters degrees involved study in four different countries.

Tired after almost a whole day travelling, Charles entered the small room he had been assigned and closed the door behind him. Without looking around, he put the key on a small desk and stared at it for a minute. He felt a little jump of joy when he realised that it wasn't a plastic card with a chip, but a piece of plated metal that was large, heavy and had the number fourteen on it in the middle. It was ages since he'd seen a real key in a hotel.

Having carefully placed his leather jacket on a chair, Charles sat down on the single bed, which responded with a noisy creaking sound. He took a deep breath, relaxed his shoulders and looked around the room. The floor was covered with traditional neat, reddish tiles that looked as though they had not seen a broom in weeks, although in general the place was neither dirty nor untidy. It was rather the case that it didn't look as though the room had been occupied for some considerable time. The sheets gave off a certain smell of mothballs and the white paint on the bare walls had been there for many years. There was no television, which he was glad about, but only a plastic telephone on a wooden night table that matched the chair and the desk.

Feeling in need of some fresh air Charles drew back the woollen curtains, coloured in strong reds and greens, which perfectly suited the place but which could never be hung in Eton unless the boys were celebrating some Peruvian carnival. He smiled and opened the window to enjoy the spring sunshine, happy not to be in one of those modern all-glass hotels where not even a drop of fresh air can get in. He took in the views, mainly the small but beautifully cobbled square that contained the public library, as he had noticed on a map. No building in Morella was more than four floors high, so that he was able to catch a glimpse of a bit of countryside in the background and slope after slope of bare hillside with scarcely any vegetation or buildings. A clear blue sky and no pollution or aeroplanes confirmed that his destination had been a good choice.

Charles began to unpack his small, well-worn suitcase, that chiefly contained books and some work reports he had to read. When he opened the plain but functional wardrobe, he was surprised to find the figurine of a flamenco dancer in the centre of a niche at the back of the second shelf.

He was slightly taken aback but a second later gave a little laugh. Who would build a sanctuary in such a place? He recalled the words of his father: "Think in English and feel in Spanish", which was also a way of reminding him that logic was not paramount in Spain.

Out of curiosity Charles stretched out to touch the small figure and saw that it wasn't made of plastic as he had expected but of good quality porcelain. It looked like a Lladró, a make that Charles knew well, since his father had a few pieces in his house… which he hadn't hesitated to leave behind when he sold the family property in Cambridge. He had always thought they were horrible.

Carefully Charles established that the statuette was not fixed to the pedestal it was standing on and brought it out of the wardrobe.

The outfit was surprisingly well stitched and made of good cloth, despite the dust that covered it. As if he were returning to the mischievous deeds of his childhood, he couldn't resist the temptation to look beneath the skirts of the flamenco dancer, whose clothes were much more cheerful than the sorrowful expression that she wore. As he investigated the underside of the figurine, Charles discovered a statue of the Virgin Mary, painted in dark tones that were more in keeping with her sad expression. In his surprise he proceeded to remove completely the flamenco dancer's clothing and studied the piece, trying to assess its value. He looked around but couldn't see any clues as to the origin of such a strange object inside a wardrobe in a small-town hotel. Suddenly there were two loud raps on the door, so he quickly put the Virgin's clothes back on and replaced it where he had found it. Just in case, he closed the wardrobe again.

'Come in!' he said in a clear voice.

'May I?' asked a soft female voice from outside.

Charles stepped towards the door and opened it. In the darkness of the hallway he saw a rather large figure of a maid wearing an apron and carrying some sheets and a mop. She looked middle-aged, with eyes that were tired and rather sad but also smiling.

'Sorry to bother you, Mr Wriggle…' The poor woman stumbled over his name and blushed.

'Wrigglesworth,' prompted Charles with a certain authority as he looked the woman up and down.

'Wigglesworse,' she repeated, clearly making an effort. She smiled and without moving from the doorway went on: 'Sorry to bother you,' she repeated, 'but we've had a problem this morning and the person looking after your room hasn't come in. So if you don't mind, I'll do it myself now, if you have no objection.'

The woman, who Charles noted wasn't that big after all, lowered her eyes towards the sheets and towels she was carrying.

Charles fully opened the door and invited her to come in.

'Of course, thank you very much,' he said. 'But if you don't mind, I'd prefer to finish unpacking before I go out.'

'That's no problem,' the woman replied, rolling up the sleeves of her ample smock. 'I'll get this done very quickly while you deal with your things. No problem.'

With a greater determination than the room-maids that Charles was used to, she came into the room and in the blink of an eye got stuck into it. She was quite a strong woman and shook the bedclothes energetically, as if she was trying to shake the very devil out of them. Then, more gently, she added the final touches, removing the slightest wrinkle with a rather maternal air. It was a long time since Charles had seen a woman plump up the pillows against her chest to make sure that they were nice and soft.

Charles was arranging his books on the desk when in the distance he heard the band striking up, indicating that the Good Friday procession had emerged from the church. Charles turned to the maid, who was now heading to the bathroom, mop in hand.

'I'm sorry you're missing the procession,' said Charles, who had spent a few Easters in Spain and knew how Good Friday was celebrated in the small towns. 'Señorita...' For the first time he looked into her deep green eyes, which he noticed with surprise.

'Isabel,' she replied.

Still looking into her eyes, Charles went on:

'Señorita Isabel, I wouldn't want you to miss the procession on account of doing my room. It's fine if you finish it tomorrow,' said Charles considerately.

Isabel, who was almost in the bathroom, turned round in surprise.

'Don't worry, Mr Wig...'

Gallantly Charles helped her out.

'Call me Charles.'

'Well, don't you worry, Mr Charles, I'm not one for processions, they're always sad and gloomy,' she said, kneeling in the bathroom, scrubbing the bath tub and the toilet and covering them in a large amount of soap and bleach. Charles carried on with his books and then arranged his clothes in the wardrobe. Isabel finished in the bathroom.

'And are you not going to the procession?' she asked, taking a handkerchief from her apron and gently mopping her brow.

Charles looked at her with interest. She seemed intelligent and strong-minded for a maid, but she had an air of distraction that he found it difficult to get to grips with.

'No, no thanks,' he replied. 'I've also seen a lot of processions and I'd prefer to sit in the sun and have a good meal than watch a Calvary. I've just arrived from London and it's been a long journey.'

'From London!' exclaimed Isabel, as if she'd never met a British person before. 'Goodness me!'

Charles saw that Isabel was about to ask him something, but out of discretion didn't dare do so. With his perfect upbringing, he filled the silence so that Isabel shouldn't feel uncomfortable.

'I'm a teacher at a college near London and I've come to look at a school that's for sale,' he explained.

'Oh!' exclaimed Isabel, leaving the mop on the floor. 'You must be the one who's arranged for my father to show you round tomorrow,' she said. 'But he didn't say anything about you being English.'

Charles asked in surprise:

'Are you the daughter of the Mayor?'

'I am,' she replied unenthusiastically, looking at the floor.

Charles tried to put two and two together.

'And the hotel belongs to the Mayor, as well?'

'Yes, it belongs to the family, although my brother runs it,' Isabel replied, shaking the mop outside the room so as to lessen the strong smell of bleach. When she returned with a dusting cloth she began to wipe the table and chair but carried on talking: 'My brother, Manolo, who you'll meet tomorrow, works in reception. I only help out at weekends and during the holidays, since I normally live in Villareal where I work for a tile company. My father doesn't come here much since he became Mayor, although he's run this business since he was fifteen.'

Charles was pleased to think that he could solve the mystery of the flamenco dancer right there. Discreetly, while Isabel was wiping the doors to the wardrobe, he went over to her.

'I'm sure you can help me with something,' he said.

Isabel turned towards him enquiringly.

'What is it?'

'I don't know if this is normal, but when I opened the wardrobe I came across a Virgin dressed as a flamenco dancer. Is that typical of Morella or is it some kind of superstition?'

Isabel burst out laughing. After a few seconds when she could speak again, she replied:

'My goodness me, it's been so long since this room was used that I'd completely forgotten about the story of room fourteen,' she said, finding it difficult to stop laughing.

Charles waited patiently without saying anything. Isabel noticed and immediately adopted a more serious tone.

'Don't worry, Mr Charles, it's not anything bad.'

'I'm pleased to hear it,' said Charles ironically.

'It's rather a long story, but I'll tell it if you like.'

'Please do.'

Isabel put her duster down on the table, adjusted the white cap she was wearing and put her strong hands on her broad hips.

'The former owner of the hotel, the original one,' she said, 'was an abusive Marquis who was beaten to death at the hands of his labourers as soon as the Republic was declared.'

Charles was slightly shocked, because he was expecting a trivial and amusing story to do with Andalusia rather than a tragic one. Nevertheless he followed the explanation with great interest.

'The fact is that the Marquis had two sisters who were very religious,' Isabel went on. 'They took over the hotel when their brother died and basically they used it to hide fascists and priests who were on the run. They also kept the most precious objects from the church and from some private houses, like a silver chalice, religious paintings, bibles and such like to save them from the great bonfire that the Reds started in the Placet.'

Charles found it hard to believe and felt more and more curious about that Virgin.

After a deep sigh, Isabel went on:

'One of the very religious sisters, who spent all her time praying, fell in love with a tradesman from Seville who was a lodger in the hotel for a while. In the town they said that he was a black marketeer, but no-one knew for sure. The fact is that they got engaged and he returned home. The sister, stuck in a town held by the Reds, remained here protecting her works of art, including the Virgin Mary, for whom she made a flamenco dancer outfit in order to hide it from the Reds and as a tribute to the city that she was about to move to. During these years under the Reds, the sisters lived practically cloistered in the hotel, for just opposite, where the library is, stood the Republican Casino, which the Reds used for spying on them. At the end of the war the sister immediately moved to Seville and nothing more was heard of her. She left in such haste that she even forgot to take the Virgin.'

Charles couldn't conceal a brief smile at the incredible story and the ease with which Isabel told it, as if it was the most natural thing in the world. Full of curiosity, he asked:

'And why don't you put it somewhere more prominent, downstairs in the entrance or in the dining room, instead of it being hidden up here?'

Isabel agreed.

'I think the same, but my father wants to keep it where it was hidden, here, in the sister's room. So this is where it has stayed, laughing its head off.'

Charles thought about it but still didn't understand the situation.

'You must be tired of explaining the same story every time someone stays in this room,' he said.

Isabel sighed audibly and added in an almost confidential tone:

'I've not told you this, but it's been some time since anyone slept in this room,' she confessed. 'We only have an average occupancy of four or five rooms and we usually give guests the ones upstairs as they have the best views, but we couldn't do it this time as an entire family of about ten people has come from Barcelona and they've taken them all.'

Isabel stretched her neck towards the half-open door, as if she was trying to check that there was no-one there. She felt that she had probably said too much already.

'But don't you worry,' she said, gathering together her cleaning things and leaving the room. 'Don't worry, the room's absolutely fine now and you won't have any problems.'

'Of course, and I'm very grateful,' said Charles, causing Isabel to look rather surprised. She's probably not used to guests being nice, he thought, before saying goodbye.

If it hadn't been for the horrible cup of tea he'd been given, it would have been a perfect morning. After home-made soup with fresh egg-yolk seasoned with thyme, two tender farm-fresh sausages and a glass of brandy, Charles leaned back on his chair feeling like a king. It was exactly eight o'clock in the morning and there was no-one else in the dining room, apart from Isabel, who did the serving as well as the cooking and cleaning.

The other guests, especially the family from Barcelona, must still be asleep, he thought. He realised that eight o'clock on a Saturday was rather early for breakfast in Spain, but it didn't even occur to him to change the habit of a lifetime. From when he first went to boarding school at the age of seven, Charles had always had breakfast at that hour, although never, of course, with quite those ingredients.

He looked out the window. It was a splendid morning and he was keen to get to know the town and its people. He always looked impeccable and was eager to create a good impression, so he had put on his elegant but rather informal two-tone shoes, brown corduroy trousers and a woollen waistcoat on top of a check shirt. His favourite silk handkerchief was knotted around his neck and his smoothly shaven face gave him an air of distinction, which is what he liked to achieve.

His meeting with the Mayor was not until nine, so he still had time to take a short walk before returning to the hotel where they had arranged to meet. Forgetting about the tea, which had unbelievably been served with the bag in the cup, Charles looked around him and noticed a number of paintings on the walls that he hadn't observed during breakfast, so absorbed was he in what he was eating. They were painted in strong, lively, eye-catching colours, something that in principle wasn't to his taste; but the straight lines used to depict the mountains and the villages made the canvases rather Picasso-like, with an almost gentle violence that was rather attractive. At least it made you look at them, he thought.

Isabel came out of the kitchen carrying a small pot of boiling water.

'More water for tea?' she asked in a friendly way, but horrifying Charles who had never seen a worse way of serving tea in his life.

He tried to hide his feelings and said nothing, although Isabel immediately noticed his cup, which was still full of tea, probably cold and with the teabag floating in it.

'Is the tea not to your liking?' she asked quietly.

Charles looked down, and being English thought that to lie was always better than to protest.

'It's just that this morning after the brandy, I didn't really feel like it,' he replied.

Isabel gave a broad smile and accepted what he said, which Charles was rather pleased about. In any case, he knew that many Spaniards couldn't decode the English language and its ability to conceal negative or harsh concepts beneath a gentle, polite or simply hypocritical language.

'Yes, I know brandy is better than tea!' Isabel exclaimed.

They both laughed.

Before she went back into the kitchen, Charles looked at the pictures again and wondered if they, too, held some sort of secret like the flamenco dancer.

'They're very interesting pictures,' he said. 'Are they by a local artist?'

From the kitchen doorway Isabel turned and looked at him in surprise for a few seconds.

'Well, yes, very local,' she said. 'You're looking at the artist right here.'

Charles lowered the glass of brandy that he was about to put to his lips and looked at Isabel with great interest.

'They're very nice,' he said in a kindly way, although he was still dealing with the fact that the person who had initially introduced herself to him as the maid also turned out to be the daughter of the Mayor, the cook and now also an artist.

'Thank you very much,' she replied, not quite sure whether to carry on with the conversation or go into the kitchen.

Charles saw her dilemma.

'Have you ever held an exhibition?' he asked. 'In my very humble opinion, I think they're good enough, don't you?'

Isabel went over to Charles' table with a broad smile, her green eyes shining brightly.

Charles said nothing, but when he looked at her more closely, he noticed that she had a bit more colour in her cheeks that morning and she even looked a bit taller.

'An exhibition? Good Lord, no,' Isabel responded, adjusting the same white cap that she wore the day before. 'I just work as a secretary in a tile factory in Villareal and that's what I live off. The painting's just a hobby; I don't do it for money. I'd be struggling if that were the case!'

'Well, you ought to,' Charles commented, as he looked closely at the paintings one by one and then again at Isabel.

'Thank you, that's very kind of you, Mr Charles,' she said with a hint of shyness.

'Just call me Charles, please,' he replied straight away.

Isabel lowered her eyes and went on:

'Well, once or twice a friend or a bar has bought one of my paintings, but only because they couldn't afford a proper one.'

Charles raised his eyebrows.

'What do you mean, "proper"? These seem to me to be intriguing and original.'

He got up to look more closely at the pictures, particularly the one that had most attracted his attention, an abstract view of Morella, which was very angular and rather dark but clearly recognisable. Obviously it wasn't a masterpiece, but it was sufficiently good to be marketable. As he went closer, he could see the brush marks as those of a firm, determined hand. However, he thought that the picture would benefit greatly if it were in a fine, dark wooden frame instead of the horrible golden baroque one that currently surrounded it.

Charles went round the dining room looking carefully at each of the five works on display: two of Morella, another two of places that looked like somewhere in the town and the last one of a naked woman, which was very aesthetic and not at all erotic. Charles was impressed by the work's sensuality, especially as it came from someone whose large, ample shape was far from attractive. Charles looked at Isabel full of curiosity.

'Do you have any more paintings?' he asked.

'Yes, I keep some in the garage downstairs, next to the entrance.'

Excited at discovering an artist but also at the possibility of finding a bargain that he could then re-sell in London, Charles wanted to see her paintings straight away. He had done enough travelling to know that you had to make the most of opportunities when they presented themselves, especially abroad, otherwise you often didn't get a second chance.

'If there's no-one else coming for breakfast and you've got a moment now, I'd love to see them; your father's not quite due for a bit,' Charles proposed, putting on his most charming smile. It was some time since he had tried to seduce a woman, but when it was a question of achieving an objective, Charles could be as irresistible as Don Juan himself.

Isabel shrugged her shoulders.

'Fine,' she said, 'if you like. You're by yourself today because the Barcelona family went out good and early with some sandwiches I made for them, as they were going out for the day.'

Charles looked surprised.

'And I thought they were all sleepyheads!'

'You foreigners always think that this is a rubbish country; well, it's not true,' said Isabel, looking serious and placing her hands once more on her ample hips with a defiant air.

'True,' Charles replied, more to himself than to Isabel.

He followed her downstairs to the garage, which was cold and as big as the dining room. It contained a farmer's type of Renault pick-up and some bags of food supplies. Next to some dusty shelves full of half-used tins of paint, boxes of tools and an old sewing machine, Isabel uncovered a pile that had been miraculously protected from the dust and humidity. The young woman – for that is how he had come to look upon her – switched on a huge lamp that threw light upon a dozen paintings leaning up against each other without anything in between them for protection.

Isabel showed them to him one by one: a bunch of flowers, an isolated farmhouse, a cat on a window ledge, a flock of sheep, a bunch of grapes… all in the same rustic-cubist style that had so impressed Charles earlier and that, now he could see the consistency, he appreciated even more. They were mundane, rural objects raised to an attractive, pleasing level of abstraction that were agreeable to look at because of what they evoked. It was an innocent vision, closer to the concept that a child might form of the object depicted than that of the eye of a great artist. That vision gave the works an endearing quality that Charles couldn't stop looking at.

'When did you start painting?' he asked, still staring at the paintings.

Isabel leant on the shelving and somewhat nervously wiped her hands on her apron.

''I've always painted,' she said. 'There's not a lot to do in the town, or at least not when I was young, so I liked to go out into the countryside with my paints and amuse myself.'

'Someone will have taught you.'

'Well, no,' she replied without pretence.

'Or they gave you some canvases, didn't they?'

'My mother did, she gave me an easel and a beautiful box of oil paints one Christmas time,' she commented, looking in surprise at Charles, for she was not used to being asked so many questions.

Isabel was just about to say something, when suddenly they heard voices.

'Where on earth is everybody?' shouted a strong, male voice from outside.

Isabel immediately covered the canvases with an old plastic tarpaulin and as she put the lights out she said:

'Let's go, quickly, it's my father and he always wants us to be at the ready up there.'

'But there's no-one there,' said Charles, following her rapid footsteps.

'It makes no difference; come on.'

'For heaven's sake, you're never where you're supposed to be!' complained Vicent to his daughter before he realised that Charles was following behind her. He then fell quiet.

Without rushing and as charming as ever, Charles stood up straight and extended his hand to the Mayor as soon as he reached him at the top of the stairs.

'Charles Wrigglesworth,' he said. 'You must be the Mayor.'

'At your service,' Vicent replied. Looking at Isabel out of the corner of his eye, he continued: 'I hope my daughter hasn't been a nuisance.'

'No, of course not,' Charles responded at once. 'You must be very proud to have such a fine artist in the house. I'm impressed,' he said, looking at Isabel, who was heading towards the kitchen.

Vicent waited until he heard the door close before continuing.

'You're very polite, Sir,' he said in a confidential tone, 'but you shouldn't flatter her too much otherwise she'll start to believe you. It's fine for her to paint for herself, and we've got some of her paintings up here because that's all they're good for, but you have to be realistic: these paintings are just rubbish and no-one's ever bought one off her.' Vicent let out a quick, false laugh. 'In any case,' the Mayor went on, 'it's always a good idea to keep women occupied, isn't it?' he added, with another, more natural laugh this time.

Charles was taken aback, finding it hard to believe what he was hearing. Finally, he said:

'Well, I think that she has talent and that she should show her pictures in a gallery.'

This time the Mayor laughed his head off.

'Get away with you, what an idea!' he said.

Charles wasn't sure what bit of that conversation he'd not grasped or why from then on Vicent began to treat him with greater familiarity.

'I see your breakfast agreed with you, old boy,' the Mayor went on. 'How many glasses of brandy did that daughter of mine give you?' he asked as he headed towards the dining room, still laughing.

Charles followed him, not quite knowing what to think.

The two men sat down at the largest table in the middle of the room.

'Isabel, bring us some bread and wine!' shouted Vicent, hardly turning his head towards the kitchen.

Before Charles could say anything, Isabel appeared with a plate of bread and tomatoes, another of ham and a bottle of red with two small glasses.

'Thank you,' said Charles, feeling very uncomfortable and, of course, with no desire to eat.

Without saying a word Isabel left the room.

During the brief presentation about the town that Vicent had prepared, the two men finished off the wine and then got ready to go out to see the school, which the Mayor had promised to show Charles. Although Charles wanted to rent and not buy, he still wanted to see the building in case it turned out to be a good opportunity. The pound sterling had been revalued and thousands of Brits were selling their small houses in London and buying magnificent villas in Spain, especially in the south and on the Valencian coast. Working class English people who had spent half their lives in the poorer districts of the capital were now lying on their sun loungers looking at the sea. There are rich countries and poor countries in the world, Charles said to himself.

As they walked through the town, Charles patiently listened to the two-hour promotion that Vicent gave him, sparing him no detail. At the end of the morning, he knew more about the new walkway and the brand-new public swimming pool than he really wanted to. Out of courtesy he couldn't turn down an invitation to the inauguration of the two sites that were planned for the following day. Charles hadn't liked the way Vicent treated his daughter, but, being a rational person, he decided to be practical. He was there to look at a building and to consider whether the town would be a suitable place for his students; he hadn't come either to buy paintings or make friends, so it was best to concentrate on the building, he told himself.

Charles wasn't able to get away from the Mayor until after six in the evening, having been shown every single street in the town, some of the new roads and finally the school. Apart from being shown some mountain paths and introduced to half the residents, he had also had to eat a large meal that hadn't entirely agreed with him. He was more accustomed to a few thin slices of roast beef than to roast goat which, in quality and quantity, could have fed Henry VIII himself, thought Charles when he could finally relax.

Seated on a solitary bench in the Alameda, Charles watched the sun going down, warm, peaceful and bright-red like sunsets in India, he recalled. Despite the eccentricities of the hotel and Vicent's odd ways, he had been impressed by the town and charmed by its silent and laboriously cobbled hills, its low houses, the smell of chimney smoke and of countryside and the attractiveness of a walled community that was proud and aware of its beauty.

In just a few minutes the sun went down behind the mountains, causing the light in the walkway gradually to fade. As it did so the old black street lamps came on, reminding Charles that he had promised to call his friend. He searched for his mobile in his jacket, the same one that he had been using for the past ten years.

'Robin?' he shouted a few seconds later. Charles only raised his voice when he used his mobile phone, which was once or twice a month. He preferred letters or emails, which were always less direct.

'Hello, my boy!' Robin replied at the other end. 'How's Spain? Have they put you on a holy cross yet and are you carrying a Calvary?' he said, giving a loud laugh.

Charles patiently closed his eyes. Ever since Oxford his friend had always been a rebel, a professional provocateur. The best thing to do was to go with the flow.

'Yes, I'm wearing my crown of thorns, but don't worry, it's not doing too much damage and the insurance will pay for my repatriation,' he replied.

After a brief silence, which always indicated that his friend was busy, Charles went straight to the point:

'Listen, great god of finance…' he began.

'At your service,' Robin quickly jumped in.

'I've visited the school I spoke to you about and sent you some photos,' he said. 'It's in a frightful state inside, and everything needs refurbishing, but outside it's a real gem. It's in a perfect location in the middle of the town, which is lovely. There are some internal courtyards with a lot of potential and very appropriate for a college or a hotel.'

'They've already taken you for a ride, my dear boy,' Robin pointed out. 'You yourself said that it's rubbish inside, but with potential. Well, of course all rubbish has potential! As soon as you do something with it, it's improved!'

'Hold on, just listen,' said Charles. 'The Mayor says that the regional government can put in five million for the refurbishment, which is very generous.'

'It's so generous that it'll finish the Spaniards off,' replied Robin, now more serious. 'There's not a week goes by without a group of Spanish politicians or businessmen in London selling me some magnificent buildings, one after another. *No, gracias.*'

Charles remained in a passive-aggressive silence.

'And may I ask how much they are wanting for this building, which in the photo you sent me looks more like the general headquarters of the Inquisition,' his friend went on.

Charles started to get exasperated.

'Robin, please, at least listen to me.'

'Okay.'

'They're asking five million…'

'Are you crazy?'

'That's the asking price, but of course we can always negotiate.'

'I wouldn't put five, or four, or two or even one million into Spain, and even less into that region, where they've put up skyscrapers in tiny fishing villages. Not even as a joke.'

'Robin, please,' Charles persisted.

'My dear friend, I'm not joking,' said the financier, whom Charles pictured in his usual brazen pose, sitting imperiously in his leather chair in his office, perhaps smoking a cigar or drinking a glass of sherry. He went on: 'You know I'd never mislead you, Charles. Believe me, I watch the markets every day. Spain is a bomb waiting to go off, especially the region that you're telling me about. The fact is that I can see it coming, there's no way that a poor country can pay for such extravagance. The only possible operation in Spain is a movement to go short, which relies on things going wrong.'

After a brief pause Charles replied:

'You're exaggerating. There's no sign of anything like that around here.'

'Charles, believe me, the markets are never wrong, the only people they surprise are fools. I can see the signs very clearly, more clearly than I would like to… because they're hurting me now as well.'

The two remained silent.

'But enjoy your holiday,' Robin concluded. 'Although since you're in Spain, you'd be better off looking at the women and the food than at buildings. It'll do you more good!'

Charles smiled and hung up.

Looking ahead of him he could barely see the outline of the now dark but imposing mountains. It concerned him that Robin, in over thirty years of friendship, had never said anything about him that wasn't accurate or that didn't actually come to pass.

6

On Palm Sunday the whole town was about to find out who Vicent Fernández really was. It had taken him more than six decades of hard struggle, but today he would finally do himself justice and Morella would recognize his true worth.

With a smile on his face, the Mayor of Morella was crossing the mountains between the town and Xiva, one of his favourite excursions, mounted on the back of *Lo Petit*. He was dressed in his most elegant riding outfit, although it was highly likely that at this hour of the day and in the middle of Easter, nobody would see him. He didn't care. On such an important day he had left the house at eight o'clock precisely, proudly wearing his tall, spotlessly clean riding boots, leather breeches, a black velvet riding helmet and a green Barbour jacket that made him look a bit like an English aristocrat. However, his figure, like that of his mount, was rather stocky; even so, the two of them, looking smart and feeling happy, went on their way along the slopes of the Maestrazgo. The smell of lavender and rosemary, the sound of his horse's hooves on the stones, and the comfortable feeling after eating a hunter's breakfast made for him by Amparo, all made Vicent see the first rays of the sun as something like a new dawn in his life. The moment had arrived to bury sixty-seven years of being a loser, as he described himself, and start playing smart.

Vicent lovingly but solemnly struck *Lo Petit*'s thigh to get him to slow down. He took him off the path they were following to go cross country over the slope until they reached an abandoned farmhouse. Without dismounting Vicent cast his eyes over the building, which he hadn't visited in nearly two years and now barely had three sides standing. Since he had become mayor he hadn't been able to get anywhere near the place, as he had been too busy completing his grand projects: becoming a famous mayor in the region, selling the school and promoting the airport at Castellón. He was convinced that everything would be wonderful after that. In two or three years' time he would be able to retire and relax in his splendid mansion of which he was so proud. At last.

Behind him was a life of fifteen-hour days, including weekends, keeping the hotel running. At the age of only fifteen he had taken over the business after the *maquis* killed his father in the very place that he was now looking at. The poor man, a middle-ranking Civil Guard who spent half his life chasing after the Reds in the mountains of Huesca and Teruel, ended up being assassinated by the La Pastora group, the guerrillas who were most successful at outwitting the Civil Guard during Franco's time. On the very night when he was killed, his father had told him and his mother that that very day he was going to deal with that transvestite about whom there was so much mystery. No-one knew if La Pastora was a man or a woman; the only certain thing was that no-one could catch him or her.

The Mayor moved his horse forward to get closer to the roofless building, whose rotten wooden beams lay on the ground or against the walls. A few metres from the ruins Vicent pulled on the reins to bring the horse – the creature he loved most in all the world – to a halt. He gently stroked his mane, which the animal acknowledged with a whinny. He thought about his father, an authoritarian man who hardly ever said anything positive to him. There were frequent beatings, sometimes of his mother, too, and always for some trivial thing he couldn't even remember. He couldn't say he loved him, because it became impossible to love someone who had beaten him, but the strict structures of family at the time obliged him to promise his mother that he would avenge his memory. However, he never had the time or the money to do so, as he needed all his energy to keep the hotel going. He didn't have much support, either, especially from the people of Morella, who had always seen him as an outsider and the son of a Civil Guard whom they had never liked. The Fernández family had arrived in the town when he was barely five years old.

Now, at last, the day for revenge had arrived. The town had only brought misfortune and the exclusion of his family, but today, he thought, they would all finally be at his feet. His father would be proud of him. He gave a deep sigh, closed his eyes and felt a huge sense of relief.

The Mayor finally moved on, confident that he would be putting his past behind him forever.

The procession came out of the basilica shortly before one o'clock. The parish priest and his sacristans, the captain of the Civil Guard flanked by three subalterns and the six deputy mayors escorted Eliseo Roig, the President of the Region, and Vicent, both of them wearing morning suits and as many medals and decorations as they could. Eliseo looked at the crowd that was building up to see him and to wave to him, while Vicent was working out how to walk with the standard of the town's coat of arms, which was very heavy to manage by himself, so somehow he had to support it on his waist. He eventually succeeded.

The Placet in front of the church was packed with townspeople on that sunny, spring-like Palm Sunday, ideal for the fiesta that Vicent had organized. The town band struck up the Morella anthem, which was bright and a bit repetitious, but good for setting the pace, Vicent told himself, clinging on to his standard. The Mayor smiled this way and that while the procession went down Mare de Déu Street at a pace that was significantly faster than that of the processions on previous days.

'You don't know how excited the whole town is to have you here,' said Vicent, looking smart and well-groomed, to Eliseo, who seemed happy to keep on smiling. 'The local radio and television stations have been talking about your visit all week. I think it's been over ten years since a President of the Region has been to visit us,' Vicent told him, attributing greater importance to himself for bringing Eliseo than to Eliseo for coming.

Eliseo did not reply, for he was concentrating on smiling and waving to the people of Morella who were lining the streets to see him go past. Vicent wasn't bothered, although he knew that he had to make the most of this opportunity to strengthen their relationship.

'Has your good lady not been able to come today?' the Mayor asked, trying to shift the standard from one hip to the other. As he did so the heavy cloth covered his face at the very moment when Eliseo turned towards him.

The President let out a little laugh, although he crossed his hands behind him and lowered his head, as if he was feeling embarrassed for him. With a sense of superiority, as if he were doing him a favour, Eliseo eventually deigned to reply to his question, but waving to the crowd all the while.

'No, Adela wasn't able to come today, she went to Mallorca to do some shopping,' he said.

'To Mallorca?' Vicent asked intrigued. 'She's off to Mallorca just for the day?'

Eliseo looked at him and replied as if he were explaining something obvious:

'She's gone in the private jet with some friends. They're there in half an hour, they go shopping, have some lunch and then off to the beach and they're back in time for dinner. It's quick and comfortable.'

Vicent tried to avoid looking at him so as not to reveal the look of surprise that was no doubt on his face. Gradually the amazement turned to envy and finally to wishful thinking. He wasn't that far from being able to do something like that. Although rather than go to Mallorca, he'd go off with *Lo Petit* to ride across the Pyrenees of Aragón, near Jaca, where he spent the first few years of his life. But before that, he had to finish the task in hand.

'Mr President,' he said as they entered the Pla d'Estudi, just before the Alameda. 'About our discussion the other day in my house concerning the school, would you be happy if I announce today in my speech that the Region has agreed to invest five million in refurbishing the old school? The people of Morella would be really impressed.'

Eliseo stopped immediately and turned to Vicent with his eyes ablaze. With furrowed brow and looking the Mayor straight in the eye, he said:

'Don't even think about it. These are delicate transactions and there needs to be due process.' The President started walking again, having brought the whole procession to a halt when he stopped. Waving to both sides, the President addressed Vicent once more but without looking at him. 'Don't even think about saying a word. If you do, there's no deal.'

Feeling more and more weary and fed up with carrying the standard, Vicent nodded several times.

'Of course, Mr President, don't you worry at all,' he replied.

'That's how I like it,' said the President, now turning towards him.

The procession crossed the gateway to the Alameda before coming to a stop in a small square just above the new school at the foot of the castle. The authorities and the rest of the crowds, about three hundred people altogether, arranged themselves around a small platform that had been placed there for the occasion while the band played the last few notes of a pasodoble. Everybody seemed happy and proud of their town.

Everybody except one person.

With her Republican flag in her hand, Valli, who had not been to the church, had spent more than thirty minutes waiting for the procession. In fact she hadn't stepped inside a church for over fifty years. Vicent saw her just as she was crossing the gateway to the Alameda, which caused him a certain amount of annoyance. That woman, he said to himself, was rather like the trees along the walk, always there, always getting herself noticed, but at the end of the day, irrelevant.

Eliseo also noticed the Republican flag.

'What the fuck is that tricolour doing there?' he asked Vicent discreetly.

'Don't worry, President, it's the town's official madwoman,' the Mayor replied.

The two men straightened their ties and stepped up on to the small platform to inaugurate the redevelopment of the Alameda and the construction of the new public swimming pool. The band eventually finished playing and the voices hushed so that the only sound was the animated cry of the birds. With his black hair brushed as straight back as it was when he came out of the church, Vicent prepared to address the crowd under a clear blue sky. He cleared his throat and waited for a few seconds in order to feel three hundred pairs of eyes upon him.

He enjoyed that sense of expectation.

'It is a great honour for me, as Mayor of this loyal, strong and wise town of Morella,' he eventually began, 'to welcome the presence of his Excellency the President of the Valencia Region, Eliseo Roig,' he said, looking at Eliseo and gently putting a hand on his shoulder as if he were welcoming a dignitary to the White House. 'In just a year and a half since I had the honour to become your Mayor, we have planned and then executed some impressive works. The covered Olympic-sized pool, for example,' he said, pointing towards the construction, 'will be key in ensuring that priority is given to sport and good health in our town.' Vicent waited for a few seconds so that those present could look at the roof of the covered swimming pool. Turning towards the walkway, he went on: 'The works on the Alameda have made our walkway more accessible, free from potholes and awkward ruts, and safer at night thanks to the wonderful street lamps,' he said, pointing to one of them. Vicent stopped once more, turning to left and right, while looking into the eyes of as many residents of Morella as he could. 'But this is only the beginning: I have a number of plans that will turn this town into the best, the most enterprising and the richest in the whole of Spain!' he exclaimed with his arms held aloft in triumph.

The crowd applauded, without a great deal of enthusiasm but enough not to embarrass the speaker. As the applause fell away, Vicent got ready to introduce Eliseo, when a voice exclaimed:

'And can we be told how we are going to pay for all of this?' Valli shouted in a surprisingly powerful voice, with her Republican flag raised aloft.

Vicent ignored her and looked at Eliseo.

'Today we have the honour...'

Valli interrupted him.

'I'm asking what funds we're going to use to pay for these plans that you've referred to, Mr Mayor!'

'Please,' he said, looking towards the sky with an air of exasperation. 'The town council's accounts are open to public scrutiny. Now is not the time, so we shall continue.' He smiled once more at the crowd and went on: 'It is an honour for me...'

'You're not going to shut me up, Mr Mayor!' Valli persisted. 'How are you going to pay for the plans for the school? It's quite clear that we can't. They shall not pass!'

Vicent and Eliseo exchanged looks and smiles of superiority, ridiculing the elderly rebel. Vicent whispered to the President:

'Don't worry, she's always like this; basically she's quite harmless.'

Valli finally kept quiet, although she didn't lower her tricolour throughout the fifteen minutes of the ceremony. Eliseo gave what was no doubt the same speech that he gave in every town every Sunday, without any reference to the locality, and the two men proceeded to cut the inaugural silk ribbon. To the sound of cheers, applause and more pasodobles, the procession, the three hundred people who had attended and anyone else who chose to do so, made their way to Colón Square, where the Council had invited the entire town to a barbecue to celebrate the occasion.

The Square was festooned as if it were the special six-yearly festival, the Sexenio. All of the balconies that looked out on to the Square were covered in the flag of Morella, courtesy of the Town Hall, and the trees were decorated with dozens of garlands made of coloured paper. In the middle of the Square huge screens showed photographs of the town, as if it were some kind of National Geographic exhibition. At the far end the largest refreshment stall had been set up to offer a free bar serving water, Coca-Cola, wine and beer for all the townspeople, who were there in their numbers and ready to eat.

Two huge ranges and a further two barbecues had been set up in the four corners of the square. On the ranges two paellas were bubbling away, one of them sponsored by the businessman Paco Barnús, who, despite wearing an elegant blue jacket with gold buttons, had donned an apron and was throwing a fistsful of salt into his creation. The businessman, who was behind the Cullera skyscraper and who had attended the horse-racing day at Vicent's house a few weeks earlier, hadn't wanted to miss the fiesta as he was convinced that Morella offered plenty of investment opportunities. This was his first appearance in the town, so to make a good impression he had thrown more than three hundred langoustines into the rice and the same number of clams; none of your chicken and bacon.

Alongside the barbecues, where more than five hundred pork chops and the same number of sausages were roasting, Charles stood by himself surveying the spectacle, as Vicent observed, with a look of astonishment on his face. Without wasting any time the Mayor headed over to the Englishman, who he assumed was in charge of a bank account loaded with pounds sterling. He had investigated as much as he could, and certainly this inoffensive, lanky man who was evidently no friend of the sun was there representing the best college in the world, the very college where the Shah of Persia, multimillionaire Orientals, oil-magnates from the Middle East or Russian Mafiosi sent their sons to study. This could be a goldmine, he told himself.

Just as Vicent reached him, Isabel appeared with two glasses of wine, which she was intending to share with Charles. Vicent quickly decided that the last thing he needed was interference from his clumsy daughter, so unceremoniously he seized one of the glasses for himself and handed the other to Charles.

'Thank you, my girl, how thoughtful of you,' he said in front of Charles, who raised his head slightly as an indication of his surprise, because he had also seen her arriving with a smile that was not directed at her father. Vicent put his hand on Charles' shoulder and clinked glasses as he proposed a toast to the best town in Spain, as he put it. Turning his back on Isabel, the Mayor downed the wine in one go and looked straight at Charles. His daughter disappeared.

'How are you, my English friend?' he blurted out.

Charles seemed annoyed. He had barely had a sip of the rough wine, which was a lot stronger than the smooth Bordeaux to which his palate was accustomed.

'Come on, drink up, it's free!' said Vicent, to which the well-mannered Charles responded with a very small sip. Vicent gave him a couple of pats on the back and turned towards the square. 'Just look at that. I bet you couldn't organise something like this in London, eh?' he said in a voice that was louder than it needed to be given how close they were to each other.

Charles was somewhat taken aback but then replied:

'It's a spectacular show, of course. Do you always organise such big fiestas?'

'Nooo,' Vicent exclaimed, raising his hands. 'Only to celebrate the good times, for this town has changed a lot since I became Mayor,' he said, and gave a great belly laugh. He turned towards Isabel, who was looking at them from just a few feet away, and shouted: 'Bring a bit of Barnús' paella, my girl, I want this chap here to have a taste of something delicious. Quickly now!'

Vicent noticed how Charles followed Isabel with his eyes as she walked in front of Valli, who was still holding her flag and sitting at the foot of the fountain next to Cefe from the bank.

'That lady with the flag,' said Charles, 'who is she?'

Vicent raised his eyes in a sign of torment and then smiled.

'That woman is a pain in the neck, a real relic of the past, more stubborn than a mule, and well past her sell-by date.'

'Well, she seemed to know what she was talking about,' Charles commented and giving Vicent a cool look.

The Mayor didn't want anyone or anything to spoil the fiesta, especially this posh Englishman who looked as though he was dressed for a carnival rather than a barbecue. Who would think of going to such a public cookout wearing an immaculate white shirt, a suede jacket and corduroy trousers, which must be making him feel the heat in any case? Vicent was wearing a morning suit because he was the Mayor, but everyone else had come dressed mindful of the fact that basically you eat barbecued food with your fingers. Looking him up and down, Vicent decided that Charles had probably never torn his clothes in his life. But he wasn't really bothered; all he wanted was his investment.

'Where's that daughter of mine got to with the paella? She's slower than a snail,' said Vicent with a laugh.

'Can you see – there's quite a long queue?' Charles replied.

'But for heaven's sake, she's not the Mayor's daughter for nothing. She can jump the queue and say it's for me!'

Charles fixed his gaze on the long queue that had formed for Barnús' paella until he saw Isabel eventually emerge with two plastic plates full of the steaming rice dish. Seconds later the two men were tucking into the succulent food while Isabel disappeared once more.

'But tell me about the old lady,' Charles persisted. 'Does she belong to a local group? Could she obstruct the sale of the school? She looks quite capable of doing so.'

Vicent laughed again.

'That woman can do absolutely nothing about it and she has no support. Look, the town is today celebrating the successes of the Town Hall. Don't worry, everything's going along fine.'

'Are you sure?' Charles asked, looking at him with one eyebrow raised.

Vicent was surprised by the Englishman's scepticism, as he wasn't used to anyone questioning him. Foreigners can be a great nuisance when they want to be, he thought to himself. In any case, if he has a problem, it's best to nip it in the bud.

'Well, if you have any doubts, check it out for yourself: come with me and I'll introduce you,' he proposed, unaware of the consequences that his action would have.

Without waiting for a reply the Mayor set off and Charles followed him, trying not to drop his enormous plate of paella as he went.

They reached the fountain where Valli was gnawing on a chop alongside Cefe.

'Hello, my dear friends,' said Vicent with a forced smile.

Neither of them responded as their mouths were full, although they gave a slight nod of the head.

'I can see, Valli, that despite your protests, you're quick to take part in the council's festivities,' said Vicent. 'I'm sure that essentially you're delighted with the way we are running things, as indicated by your presence here.'

'Look, Mayor, we're all paying for these sausages through our taxes and so I've as much right to them as anyone else, whether or not I like the way you're running things,' she replied.

Vicent gave a paternalistic smile and turned to Charles.

'My dear Charles, may I introduce you to Ceferino, manager of the local bank, and Vallivana, one of our most active citizens in local politics,' he said sarcastically.

'Pleased to meet you,' said Charles to both of them, bowing slightly to Valli.

She looked at him in surprise but also with interest.

'Where are you from?' she asked, direct as always.

'I'm Charles Wrigglesworth, head of the department of languages at Eton College, and I've come to see the school in Morella,' he explained.

'The school? What for?' Valli asked, looking at Cefe with an air of suspicion.

Vicent and Charles also exchanged glances. Vicent thought that the best thing would be not to give too many explanations, because Valli would wear Charles out in a matter of minutes and he had no time to waste. But before he could put an end to the conversation, Charles got in first.

'We're looking for a place in Spain where our students can stay for a few months, practice the language and learn about its fascinating culture,' said Charles in his usual elegant way.

'Well, bad luck,' Valli quickly replied. 'Find a hotel if you want to come, because that school is never going to be sold.'

'Take no notice of her, Charles,' Vicent promptly responded. 'The lady doesn't know what she's taking about; she has no say in the matter,' he added, looking at Charles and ignoring Valli completely.

'I know very well what I'm saying!' Valli exclaimed furiously, as she vigorously waved the chop about that she was still holding.

Cefe put a hand on her arm to calm her down.

'Steady, Valli, now's not the time,' he said.

Valli calmed down. However, she went on with her attack.

'You're from Eton, you say?' she said to Charles, looking at him with her piercing big dark eyes.

The eyes of a cobra before it bites, thought Vicent.

'Yes, Eton College, in Windsor. Do you know it?' asked Charles in surprise.

'Yes, of course I know it,' Valli replied, looking at him with an air of disdain. 'It's the most class-ridden, elitist, capitalist college in the world. It represents everything I have fought against all my life.'

Charles was taken aback, but without losing his composure he asked:

'If you don't mind my asking, I am curious to know how you know about my college.'

'And why would I not know about it?' responded Valli, who was really on form today, thought Vicent, having seen her much quieter and subdued on many occasions. Valli went on: 'Do you think because I'm a woman, I'm old and a country bumpkin that I haven't seen the world?'

Charles shook his head.

'No, of course not, I'm not saying that at all. I was just a bit intrigued, but I don't want to upset you.'

'Ah, the refined Englishman. Don't think I can't recognise a wolf in sheep's clothing,' Valli spat out, to the surprise of the three men.

Vicent was about to intervene, as the conversation was going nowhere, but Valli's poison was gaining momentum.

'If you think your little gentlemen with their tailcoats and top hats are going to prance around my town, you've got another think coming. Go back home and sort out the class structure that still corrodes your society and then, if you want, you can come and see us,' Valli said, stretching to her full height as she finished.

Vicent didn't know how to apologise, and immediately regretted having suggested that they meet.

'Please forgive her,' Vicent said to Charles, 'she's very old and doesn't know what she's saying. But come on, let's go and find some of the charming people from the town who you should meet. I'm sorry, Charles, come, follow me. Heavens, such people!'

The two men took to their heels and went back to where they had been standing earlier, evidently rather put out. Fortunately Eliseo Roig arrived shortly afterwards, clearly bored and keen to talk.

'What a successful fiesta,' he said to Vicent, patting him several times on the back.

'Morella is an excellent investment,' the Mayor replied, looking at the other two and proposing a toast to the future of the town.

Vicent took the opportunity to enable the two potential investors to get to know each other better by leaving them on their own and going over to Paco Barnús, who had been signalling to him for some time from the huge paella that he'd been managing. After a few minutes the two men were able to talk freely in a quiet place beneath the shade of a lone mulberry tree in the corner of the Square.

'At last, my boy, it's more difficult to get to talk to you than to a minister,' Paco said.

'You know today's a special day; I have to be everywhere and with Roig here I have to be on my toes,' Vicent replied in a conciliatory tone.

'Listen,' said Paco, putting a hand on his shoulder, 'about your school: in principle the project interests me – me and the Marquis of Villafranca.'

Vicent's eyes lit up.

'I knew that a financial shark like you wasn't going to miss this opportunity,' he said with his eyes growing wider.

'Okay, okay,' said Paco as he buttoned up his very elegant jacket that now stank of garlic and chops. The shark of Cullera, as he was known, went on: 'But there is one thing. As you'll appreciate, we'll need a guarantee that the region will put in that five million for the refurbishment, as you assured me the other day on the phone.'

After hesitating briefly, Vicent replied:

'Of course, but you've got the President himself here supporting Morella – what better guarantee do you want than his presence and support for the town?'

'Confirmation in writing,' the investor replied.

Vicent looked at him in surprise.

'Why the formalities?'

'You yourself called me a shark,' he replied. 'The name is not for nothing.'

Vicent pondered for a few moments, looking towards Roig, who was still talking animatedly with Charles.

'Well, don't worry, I'll sort that out right now,' he said, giving him a quick pat on the back and heading straight for Roig.

But before he reached him a voice interrupted him.

'Mr Mayor, thank you very much for such an impressive fiesta; we've never seen such generosity on the Council's part,' said Fernando, the owner of the service company in charge of the construction of the new swimming pool.

'Thanks very much,' Vicent replied, without any intention of stopping.

'A moment of your time, Mayor, if you please,' Fernando insisted, almost standing in his way.

Vicent had no choice but to listen to what he had to say.

'What can I do for you?' he asked drily.

'We're delighted with the outcome and the opportunity to have worked with you, but you'll also understand that I have to plan the coming year and deal with monthly payments. I know that things to do with public works move slowly although of course safely as well, but I would like to know if you can tell me more or less when we can expect payment,' said Fernando, quite a small, rather chubby man and a lifelong resident of Morella.

The Mayor looked him up and down in a superior way and waited a few seconds before replying. Fernando lowered his eyes and while he was waiting for an answer he began to play nervously with the beret he was holding.

'Don't you worry, Fernando, everything will work out,' Vicent answered finally. 'And now if you will excuse me I have important business to attend to.'

Settling more matters than he had been expecting to, the Mayor immediately found himself back with Roig and as politely as possible sent Charles to the bar, telling him that they were just serving some Irish coffee and that if he hurried he might get one. Charles got the indirect message and took himself off.

'Our Englishman likes the school, you've got him where you want him, you son of a bitch,' said the President with a certain amount of pride. 'You've got everything sorted with the school, then?'

'That's just what I wanted to talk to you about, President.'

'Again?' asked Roig. 'But we spoke about it before.'

'There are investors who need confirmation in writing of the public investment, the five million,' said Vicent in a fairly soft voice.

Roig looked around him and lit up a Marlboro that he pulled out of his tailcoat pocket but without offering one to Vicent. He took a first, long drag.

'No way,' he answered, exhaling the smoke.

Vicent didn't know what to say, while Roig remained impassive.

'Not unless you can relax the conditions a little for me,' the President commented.

Vicent frowned.

'I don't understand.'

'Ah, my poor man, how little experience you have at the highest level,' he said, looking straight ahead. 'Tell me, why should I go out on a limb to convince parliament about this investment, when it's all the same to them?'

'Because you can get all the credit for the project and after that, we can put two million into your masterpiece, the airport at Castellón.'

Eliseo took three short puffs, one after the other, but looking ahead all the time.

'Yes, I know all that, but what do *I* get out of it?'

Vicent raised his eyebrows. He began to understand, although he hadn't seen anything like it at that level; he'd only seen a few local *inducements*.

'I see,' he said, in a tiny voice, as if suddenly his tailcoat was rather too big, as if he couldn't feel his shirt on his skin.

When he saw Roig throw the butt end of the Marlboro against a nearby tree, Vicent nervously took out from the inside pocket of his jacket two cigars that he had brought for the occasion. They were two Havanas and cost nearly a hundred euros each. While he searched in his pockets for a lighter, Roig quickly, almost violently pushed his, already lit, nearly into his face.

Vicent sniffed the cigar several times, one after the other, which made him cough slightly. The President gave him a few pats on the back, this time quite strong and not particularly friendly ones.

'Come on, lad, are you with the big boys or not?' he asked him, looking straight ahead.

Vicent, with the cigar in his trembling hands, said almost the first thing that came into his head:

'Five percent commission?

'Fine,' replied Roig, puffing on his cigar.

'But in respect of what?' asked Vicent, unaware of any of the techniques.

'There's a cement supply company in the name of Adela in the Cayman Islands. There's only one with that name, it's very easy to find,' he said coldly.

Vicent looked at him with incredulity, although he had always suspected that there was only one way to get to Roig's level and his private jets to Mallorca: precisely that one. If those were the rules of the game, he thought, he was just one more who would observe them.

'Okay,' he said, struggling to keep calm, but without being able to prevent a few beads of cold sweat appearing on his forehead. Vicent swallowed hard and crossed his hands behind his back to throw the cigar on the ground so that Eliseo wouldn't see his slight tremble.

'Good man,' the President replied.

Vicent gave a huge, noisy sigh almost without being aware of it.

'One more thing,' Roig added, causing Vicent to straighten up all of a sudden and to look from side to side like a frightened cat.

'What?' he asked, swallowing hard again and fixing his gaze somewhere in the distance.

'I also need, and I'm telling you this man to man, not two, but three million put into the airport first thing tomorrow morning without fail.'

Vicent could no longer carry on appearing to look cool and turned to the President, who didn't bat an eyelid.

'That's impossible,' he replied, with an almost pleading look.

'Nothing's impossible if you really want it.'

'This is a small town, with few resources…'

'But big dreams, eh?' Eliseo responded, now looking at him with the eyes of a fox on the prowl. 'You have to put resources and dreams on the same level, dear boy.'

Vicent felt a cold shock run through his whole body. While the band struck up for the dancing, he remained immobile, with his hands firmly clasped behind his back. He felt as if his blood had frozen and his complexion turn pale at an alarming rate. All he could do was plead.

'I need more time. Plus, tomorrow's a holiday, it's Easter Monday…'

'No,' argued the President, interrupting him. 'In the rest of Spain it's a work day, so you won't have any problem. Do we have a deal or not?'

Vicent gulped once more and felt his eyes growing moist. He cursed the day, which he was expecting to finish on a pedestal of popularity and not plunged into such a predicament. He looked at the townspeople dancing and leaping on to the barrels of wine that was still flowing for free. Some, now drunk and with naked torsos, were clearly enjoying themselves more than he was. His wife, Amparo, who he had pictured in a private jet heading for Mallorca, was still sitting on a bench in the corner of the square, together with their children, eating and drinking very little.

After a long pause and despite the setbacks, Vicent told himself that the time had come to take a chance, as all great men had done in their time. It was time to show everyone what he was made of.

'You can count on it,' he said finally.

Turning towards the Mayor and flashing his white teeth, Roig gave Vicent a gentle embrace, a few pats on the shoulder and swiftly took his leave.

All he said was: 'It's been a pleasure.'

Vicent was unable to say anything in reply, but simply nodded his head. He looked around him. His family continued to do their own thing, as did Valli and Cefe, and the rest of the townsfolk were cheerfully enjoying themselves. They were all happy in someone's company, except him, the person who had organised it all. Vicent felt like escaping with *Lo Petit* into the countryside, but he couldn't, he was the Mayor and he had to stay until the end. His life continued to be a sacrifice.

He was still thinking that way a few hours later, his elbows on his substantial mayoral desk and holding his head in his hands. He was exhausted, but he had to show composure now that he'd heard the arrival of Eva, the administrator, who had hastily been summoned from Valencia in order to carry out the operation. He couldn't do it directly without arousing suspicions. He took out his favourite bottle of Chivas Regal and poured himself a small glass, which immediately revived him.

The young administrator, a native of Morella and someone who was always obedient – that's why he had hired her – gave him a friendly greeting.

'Goodness, how strange to be here on a Sunday night,' she said, taking off her coat and leaving her bag on the large round table that the Mayor had in his sizeable office.

The office was well-decorated in Morella-style, with woollen curtains in strong colours, well-maintained stone walls and black iron rustic lamps that gave out a gentle yellow light. The parquet flooring gave it a warm feel, as did the wide carpets that covered a good part of the room.

'It must be something important,' said Eva, sitting down opposite the Mayor.

The young woman, who was about thirty, looked visibly excited, maybe on account of doing something different from her routine work, thought Vicent. Good thing that he'd hired someone who would do as she was told, he said to himself; if not, the situation would be much more complicated. Trying to hide his nerves and his almost unbearable tiredness, Vicent stood up trying to pretend that everything was totally normal.

'Eva, my dear,' he said, 'there's nothing wrong, it's just that I forgot to send a bank transfer last week. It turns out that the Regional President himself, Roig, has reminded me today that they were waiting for it last week for reasons to do with liquidity. So we have to do it tonight so that the funds are there tomorrow without fail, that's all,' he said.

Eva responded in surprise:

'But tomorrow is Easter Monday...'

'Yes, I know, but we can do it through our bank in Madrid, because it's not a holiday there.'

Faced with Vicent's insistent stare, Eva appeared not to hesitate.

'Of course, Mayor, I'm at your service for whatever you need,' she said dutifully.

'Well, let's get to it,' said Vicent, sitting back down again.

Eva moved to a small desk in the corner, where there was a computer at which she sometimes worked. She booted up the machine, which was old and noisy, especially given the deathly silence that pervaded the room – in contrast to the daily comings and goings that had always characterised the Town Hall, which was active and enterprising by nature, whatever the political colour of those in power.

Nonchalantly, as he gathered together a few papers on his desk, Vicent finally came out with:

'It's only to do with a contribution to the Castellón airport that I agreed to with Roig.'

Out of the corner of his eye he could see Eva turn towards him.

'Oh, I thought we'd decided to wait until others had invested or until the project was more advanced before committing ourselves,' she said.

Vicent gave a slight cough.

'Yes, well, things have changed. Now that things are going extremely well, if we don't keep on the ball we could still get left out,' replied the Mayor, without looking at her.

Eva seemed to hesitate.

'Oh, I hadn't realised.'

'That's okay, it's not a problem, you can't be on top of everything,' he said, now looking at her in a fatherly way.

His position was difficult for him because Eva had always been honest and loyal. It was undoubtedly an uncomfortable situation, but he had no option.

'I'm very sorry to have asked you to come in at this hour, Eva, and I'll make sure you're well rewarded for the overtime, that's a promise,' he said, sighing and feeling an honesty that he hadn't felt for several hours.

He knew better than anyone that he wasn't perfect, but his heart was in the right place and basically he wanted to protect his own people. In any case this was another way of doing so, so he carried on.

'The thing is that it's quite a lot of money, but in time it'll seem like a bargain,' he said.

'The town will be full of foreign tourists, Mr Mayor,' Eva replied, now back in a good mood, as she opened documents on the old desk-top.

'Well, as soon as you can, please, transfer a million euros to the airport account,' he said, looking at the floor and with his back to Eva.

'A million!' she exclaimed, turning towards him once more.

Vicent had to turn back to her and face the situation.

'My dear, a million is not as much as you think these days, and just wait and see how much we'll earn. It's not very much at all compared to the total budget for the project,' he said, still shuffling his papers.

Eva remained thoughtful.

'Yes, I can imagine that an airport is very expensive,' she said, 'but the million from Morella hasn't been approved, has it?'

'It's a project agreed with the President of the Region himself, so it comes from the very top. It forms part of a major strategic plan for the whole of Valencia, in which we should feel proud to be able to participate.'

'But what about the opposition, what'll they say when they find out? They've always been against the project.'

'What do they know?' Vicent replied, feeling increasingly sure of himself. 'It's a project that has Roig's blessing and that's all that needs to be said. And besides, we have to be discreet and wait a while before publicising it. We'll talk about it when it starts to bring in profits and everything will become clearer.'

Eva looked at him incredulously.

'Are you asking me to transfer one million from the council budget and not tell anyone?'

'No, Eva, you're very young, my poor thing, and you don't understand,' he said, getting up and crossing towards her. When he was barely a few inches away and he could look at her, literally, from head to toe, he went on: 'I'm only asking you to carry on being as efficient and discreet as always and that you trust me. I'll let you know when we're ready to talk about it, but for now you have to promise me discretion. I'm not telling you to hide anything, only to trust me and wait until I can explain things. Now, please make the transfer, because it's urgent; the town will never forgive me if we miss the boat of progress.' Eva was about to ask something else, but Vicent got in first. 'Shhh,' he said, putting a finger to his lips. 'There are times when we simply have to do as we're told, even if we don't understand. It happens to me, too.'

Vicent went back to his desk, put some papers into his leather briefcase and put on the jacket of his morning suit, which now felt much heavier than it did earlier in the day.

'This will take me hours, because I'll have to redo some accounts so that the system will let me transfer the funds,' she said, looking rather scared.

Vicent went over to her once more and put his hand on her shoulder affectionately.

'I'll pay you very well for the overtime; just tell me how many hours you've spent and you'll get paid.'

When the Mayor was on the point of leaving, Eva ran after him. Looking at him directly, she said:

'I can't, Mr Mayor, I can't do it.'

He looked her straight in the eyes.

'Of course you can, Eva,' he said. 'I trust you.'

And without further ado, Vicent went out of his office, feeling proud of the way he had acted and convinced that it was the best thing for him, for his family and for the town.

7

The first time Valli ever went in, she looked so young and innocent that it was obvious it was the first time she had left her home town. She had two long carefully woven plaits, a baby face covered in freckles and lively dark eyes that darted everywhere. Eulalia Lapresta, the secretary, opened the door and invited her in with a broad, warm smile. It was 1931 and Valli was setting foot for the first time in Number eight, Miguel Ángel Street, home to the Young Ladies' Residence. It was the female version of the already famous Students' Residence, a male-only college where prominent figures such as Lorca, Dalí and Buñuel had met only a few years before. It was only a few weeks since the Second Republic had been declared and everywhere there was hope and optimism.

Valli barely knew the famous intellectuals who regularly came to the Young Ladies´ Residence. Until moving there she had concentrated on her high school exams, which she hoped to take in Madrid, before going to University. Her teacher in Morella, Eleuteria, had read in *El Defensor* an article by a Minister in the Republic, Luis de Zulueta, about the Young Ladies' Residence and straight away she had encouraged her most outstanding student to apply. After long discussions with her parents, the Querols finally agreed to allow their only child to go to study in Madrid as the grant she had won was enough to pay for everything, plus, as a woman, it was not as though she could take care of the farm. The other options available were to marry a bachelor or become a nun – choices that made Valli even keener to go. At thirteen she barely knew anything, but she had all the curiosity that her teacher had sown in her. Every night Valli would read by candlelight books by Cervantes, Dickens or Balzac that Eleuteria regularly lent her. She devoured them all.

Seventy years later, on a sunny afternoon just after Easter, Valli found herself gazing at the majestic building on Miguel Ángel Street. When she had first arrived as a teenager she had travelled up the Castellana on a tram that she had caught at Atocha – then called the Mediodía station. It had taken her an entire day to get to Madrid, having left Morella at the crack of dawn with only an old cardboard suitcase and the home-made sausage sandwiches that her mother had prepared for her. Today, it had taken just three hours to get to the capital.

The Miguel Ángel building looked exactly the same as the last time she saw it in 1936, at least from the outside. Its graceful facade and pale pink colour contrasted with the light stone around the windows, which gave the building presence and distinction in a street that was formerly quiet but now was full of cars and businessmen. Two stone columns on either side of the main door supported a rather imposing balcony on the first floor. The building was topped off by a small tower, which originally served as an observatory.

It wasn't the best moment to walk in, Valli thought, given the rather informal clothing she had worn to travel in. Who would take seriously an old lady in jeans and a home-made, loose-fitting woolly jumper? Her taxi was also waiting nearby, plus it was getting late, so she thought it might be better to wait until the following day, when she had actually arranged a meeting. The trip on the high-speed train from Zaragoza, where Cefe had driven her from Morella, had been quick and comfortable, but at her age she knew that it was better to pace herself.

Under the gentle spring sun, the taxi crossed the Castellana, now free of trams, and started to go up the steep Pinar Street until Valli asked the driver to stop. She preferred to arrive at the old male Residence on foot. This was where she learnt to struggle and to strive, so she wasn't going to arrive now in style in a taxi when she could perfectly well walk. It was at the Residence that she learned that the more natural, simple and good things were, the better. Everything else was superfluous.

With her small rucksack on her back – she didn't need much for just two days – Valli walked up the street until she reached the Residence, where she had arranged to stay.

Feeling as if she was fifteen again and attending some event or conference, Valli went through the main gate, ignoring the security guard in his little booth, and walked along the small track, now covered by asphalt, but still bordered by rosemary, thyme, rockrose and lavender. She stopped to look at the famous red-brick building with its dark green shutters where the students stayed. She held her breath as she thought she could still see Dr Marañón saying a friendly "Good Morning," or Dr Unamuno walking along deep in thought, or hear the almost hysterical laughter of Lorca and Dalí, always irreverent, often even making fun of the female students who went to the male Residence to attend some event or other. In that building, Valli had seen Marie Curie, or Keynes, the economist, presenting papers and she had participated in debates organised by Ortega, Menéndez Pidal or Gómez de la Serna. She could see those characters now, all in their suits, ties and hats, chatting away as they walked around the same gardens where she was now, almost a lifetime later.

Valli sighed and continued towards the main entrance in silence as there was hardly anybody about. She passed through the oleander garden, planted by Nobel Prize winner Juan Ramón Jiménez, who called it "the beach" as that's where they gathered in the summer, under the shade of the lime trees to escape the blazing Madrid sun. The oleander was still there, with the blossom now fully out. Its scent brought

Valli memories of the many afternoons that she spent right there, debating the state of the world with her male counterparts. She particularly enjoyed talking to the British students; they were more open to having women join their groups than the Spanish men, who were often real male chauvinists, barely paying them any attention or just completely excluding them from their activities.

It was under those lime trees, and while practising her – at the time – poor English, that Valli had met Tristan in the summer of 1936. He was there thanks to the British-Spanish Committee, a programme financed by the Duke of Alba to promote exchanges between students at the Residence and those at the Universities of Oxford and Cambridge. Tristan was a Hispanist at Cambridge who spent five years at the Residence in Madrid and later joined the International Brigades to fight against fascism. A born intellectual, but physically rather delicate, he went back to his country before the end of the war as he could help the Republic more with his writing in Britain than at the front in Spain.

Valli walked slowly towards the main door of the building and looked at the bench that still bore the name of the Duke of Alba, Jacobo Fitz-James Stuart, who also was Duke of Berwick and a keen anglophile. His money and his presence amplified the already strong British feel that the Residence always had, as it had been modelled on the British colleges where the elite had been educated for centuries. The Residence´s main aim was to turn Spain´s old-fashioned and decadent nobility into well-cultivated and modern gentlemen.

Valli walked into the main building, which was surprisingly quiet for a Monday afternoon. The last people were leaving the communal dining hall, which was being cleared and about to close. Rather than students or researchers, the guests looked like middle-aged civil servants who had just finished a two-hour lunch at taxpayers' expense. They weren´t carrying any folders or paperwork with them, or any other sign of intellectual activity.

Valli was still very excited just to be back, after so many years, in the institution that could have changed the history of Spain, but did not do so. She finally arrived at reception, where a young woman, probably underpaid, welcomed her with a forced smile, while continuing to chew gum.

Having been given nothing more than an explanation about time-tables and the Wifi password, Valli took her key, telling herself that the ignorance of a youngster who was not aware of the legacy of where she was, was not going to affect the happiness that she felt at that moment. Valli had not been at the Residence since the end-of-year party in June 1936, when she said good-bye to her class-mates, thinking that she would see them again in September. It was forty-one years before she returned to Madrid.

Without anyone helping her or knowing who she was, Valli walked along the corridors, now sad and silent, with only a high wooden skirting board for decoration. Still, she was so excited about coming back to her "*Resi*" that she went up to the third floor as quickly as she could. She was hoping the rooms would be similar to the ones she and the other female students once occupied in the Miguel Ángel building. Walking quickly and with her heart starting to pound, Valli nervously opened the door to her room. After a few long seconds, in which her expectation conflicted with what she saw, Valli felt the world falling apart as she contemplated the sad and half-empty room that could well have been in a hospital. The walls were white and totally bare; they had not even got a single picture on them. The entire contents of the room consisted of a small single bed, a functional desk, metal lamps and an old TV. The curtains, no doubt from Ikea, were closed, making the room rather dark. The bathroom was completely white and had no windows. This was nothing like the small Bauhaus-style study rooms that she stayed in for five years. In her day everyone had their walls covered in posters of conferences, exhibitions or other events, with dry flowers on a small round bedside table and a comfortable armchair to read in. They also had a lovely, wooden desk as well as a pine chair. Those rooms marked a real change for most of the girls who came to Madrid from the provinces, where all they had were small, dark alcoves that they tended to hide rather than show. At the Residence, however, the dormitories were as well-lit as drawing rooms and the beds were seen as a comfortable place to read or rest, not a sombre and intriguing symbol of a sinful life. Life at the Residence bore no secrets.

The only things from her time there that felt familiar to Valli were the big, arched windows, with the lovely green, wooden shutters, which she immediately opened. The room overlooked the main garden; the sight of it made it feel like her old "*Resi.*" She took a deep breath of fresh air. She had come all the way to Madrid with one objective and she was intending to fulfil it. If forty years of Franco's dictatorship and thirty years of nascent democracy had managed to wipe out the old ambiance of the Residence, time had taken nothing away from the zest for life that that institution had inspired in her. She had come here because she was convinced that many former residents would help her in her mission, and she was ready to give everything she'd got to achieve it.

'Well, no, we don't have one,' the receptionist said the following day when Valli asked whether she could have a list of the names and addresses of former residents. Maybe her request came too much out-of-the-blue, she thought. Perhaps it would have been better to have arranged a meeting with the current Director, as she had done at the International Institute. 'Well, most of them are dead, anyway,' said the receptionist, who was even younger than the one the day before.

Valli decided to ignore her.

'May I speak with the Director, please?'

'She's not here right now,' the girl was quick to answer. 'Do you have an appointment at all?'

Valli shook her head.

'Well, without an appointment…'

Valli cut her short.

'Look, it's not as though this place is bursting with activity, so I'm sure they can find a moment to see me in their busy schedule,' she said, almost immediately regretting it, as she knew that being confrontational wouldn't get her very far.

And she was right.

'Well, then, just call this number and ask, maybe somebody there will be able to help you,' said the girl as she handed Valli a business card and, without looking at her, turned back to her computer.

Valli was left speechless and walked down the corridor without really knowing where to go, as it was still two hours before her meeting at the International Institute. She went out into the garden and tried to enter another building that housed the old library, but it was closed. She looked through the windows and saw that it had been turned into a classroom that didn't seem to be used much. Undaunted, she went down to the old brook, now with only a small trickle of water and surrounded by walls full of graffiti. She remembered the sound of running water that could be heard back in the 1930s as the students strolled along or chatted about articles in newspapers like *El Sol* or *El Imparcial*, or about the books of poetry that they had been reading. There was nobody there now, other than herself and her memories.

Valli headed towards the large courtyard behind the main building, now home to two basketball courts that were also empty. She went past them, assuming that she was heading towards the impressive auditorium where she once heard Einstein give a talk. The site was now occupied by the Church of the Holy Spirit, built after the auditorium had been demolished. Valli knew that soon after the war Franco destroyed the site – and with it the work of a group of intellectuals who wanted to mobilise a country in which eight out of ten people couldn't read or write. It suited dictatorships, as well as many religions, to keep the people ignorant as they are easier to control.

Valli's heart sank when she walked past the church and into the site now occupied by the CSIC, Spain's leading research council, which now managed the Residence. The purpose of the CSIC, consisting of several unremarkable, grey buildings, was to foster the scientific – but never the intellectual – development of the country. However, she didn't see a single soul going in or coming out of the buildings or walking around the grassed area in the middle. It was no surprise that the organisation had barely achieved anything since Franco founded it more than fifty years earlier, while her Residence, which survived for no more than two decades, was associated with four of Spain´s seven Nobel Prize winners: two scientists – Ramón y Cajal and Severo Ochoa – and the writers Juan Ramón Jiménez and Vicente Aleixandre.

Valli sat on a stone bench, feeling small and overwhelmed by those large, rectangular, soulless buildings. She had played hockey right there, at that time the end of Serrano Street and also of the city itself. They often met the shepherds walking their sheep and dogs, as it was just an open field. Those herdsmen seemed quite relaxed about a group of young females who gathered there for their regular gymnastic exercises, usually to Mozart´s "Turkish March". The ladies sometimes even played football, a game that was looked upon at that time as suitable for men only. She had also been up on that same hill to debate, to read and study, laugh and play, smoke and drink. Where she now felt alienated and insignificant, she once had known freedom and happiness, surrounded by trees and books, more than seventy years earlier.

Finding the silence and stillness disquieting, Valli continued her walk slowly down Serrano, turning at Pinar Street down a little side road to the Castellana. She passed the Zalacaín restaurant, which she had heard of, and looked at the long queue of dark and well-appointed Audis and Mercedes, each one parked up with a chauffeur inside. This was very different from her day, when the students went bouncing up the street in happy groups, more often than not warned by their tutors to behave with more composure and decorum.

In any case, social differences hadn't changed, Valli said to herself. Now, those drivers just dozed or idly watched the comings and goings of the posh people who lived in that neighbourhood. Back in her day, workers used to sit right on that same street, eating from an old tin the *tortilla* or pork stew that their wives had made for them. Meanwhile the young ladies in the Residence were eating fillet of veal using knives and forks, as the place insisted that sport and healthy food were the key to studying. In the end, not much had changed, Valli told herself as she walked past the chauffeurs. Whilst the rich eat and play, the others work or wait, she thought. It´s always the same.

With the help of a young man who noticed her advanced age, Valli crossed the Castellana as she headed towards the International Institute, the college created by a North American missionary at the end of the nineteenth century to improve the education of Spanish women as well as to host American women who wanted to learn the local language and culture. The Institute, which was well endowed, worked closely with the Young Ladies´ Residence, and some students lodged in its headquarters on Miguel Ángel Street. There the Spanish students lived side-by-side with their American counterparts, sharing the library, the garden, the communal areas, as well as some classes and the many events that they all organised. That exchange opened Valli´s eyes to the world, as the Americans, generally tall and blond, were far more liberated and they already came with their PhDs. Valli, who was just out of a small town where they still believed in miracles and superstitions, soon wanted to emulate them: they always seemed to have a grand time, they questioned everything, practised all kinds of sport and dancing, always with the music playing very loud. One of them, Katherine Bates, had travelled around Spain with a female friend – something unheard of in those days – to write a book about it all and have it serialised in *The New York Times*. That truly was another world compared to early twentieth century Morella and Valli, like the other Spanish residents, wanted to be part of it as soon as possible.

She reached the International Institute and with her legs trembling climbed the stairs to the main entrance. She reached the glass door, still framed with the same white wood that opened into the large foyer. Once inside, strong emotions started to well up inside her as she saw the familiar cast-iron staircase with its wooden handrail, climbing floor after floor until it reached the small dome at the top of the glass ceiling. It was a wide and majestic staircase that fostered the concept of interchange and a sense of wellbeing in a building that had been conceived as open, light and free. She had spent hours on those steps, learning the most diverse facts and ideas from informal conversations with other students. Valli sighed as she noticed that the graceful, white iron columns were still there, supporting the simple, plain ceiling. Nothing had changed. As it did in her day, the building had an air of quality and simplicity. Instinctively Valli turned to the left to walk into her old classroom, now a cafeteria, but with the same windows still overlooking the garden. She looked and saw that grass and some benches had replaced the old tennis court, where they used to play in the mornings before breakfast. Valli smiled, realising that she hadn´t held a racket since then. She couldn´t see the house that belonged to the well-known artist Sorolla, now turned into a museum and hidden behind an apartment block.

Valli looked at the classroom, now bereft of the paintings that Sorolla himself had donated. However, the room still had the dark wooden floors, worn and warm, that had always made her feel so comfortable. She closed her eyes. Right there she had taken philosophy classes from the Residence´s Director, María de Maeztu, who always wore a cloche hat, a *petigris* coat and a pearl necklace. She could still see her lively, round face, her eyes always alert. On the very first day she asked them about a gold medal that King Alfonso XIII had awarded to some man from Sigüenza who had built a house deep into a rock. Maria, with an assertive tone only associated with men at the time, asked her students: "Do you think that awards should be given to troglodytes, or should we instead reward the scientists who make the world move forwards and not backwards? We have to become more European in order to get Spain out of this pit of poverty into which we have sunk." Valli soon realised where she was. After two weeks she had cut her hair short; three months later she was wearing trousers, smoking and using tangee lipstick.

Valli walked slowly towards the auditorium that was now closed. She turned to look around her: the corridors were still clean, everything gave an impression of quality, activity, neatness and simplicity – all attributes that María de Maeztu personified. Valli remembered when, just a few days after her arrival, she dropped a scrap of paper on the floor just as the Director was walking by. María looked at her intently and, without saying a word, picked up the bit of paper, threw it in a wastepaper bin and went on her way, still without saying anything. At that moment Valli wanted to die, as she would rather have had the bit of paper thrown in her face than suffered that silent humiliation. She had never dropped a piece of paper on the floor ever again.

Valli straightened the jacket and skirt that she had chosen to wear for the occasion and knocked on the Director's door. She immediately came to open it.

'Do come in, Señora Querol, and make yourself at home,' said the friendly Director, attentively helping her to a comfortable chair. 'Former residents are always extremely welcome here. It is an honour to have you with us.'

Valli sighed. Finally someone had shown a bit of interest in her, and in a place that was so special to her. She looked around the spacious office, which was full of books and some black and white photos of the Institute's founder, Alice Gordon Gulick. The place, which now offered English courses and was used as the centre in Spain for some of the top American universities, seemed full of activity.

'Thank you very much for finding the time to see me,' said Valli, always ready to go straight to the point, as she had learned to do in that very place. 'Well, I am not here to learn English, but to ask you a favour.'

The Director, a small, middle-aged, dark-skinned lady, dressed in a rather bo-bo style, smiled and leaned back in her chair.

'I am all ears,' she said in a soft voice.

Valli told the Director, whose name was Soledad and who seemed to be rather surprised by what she had to say, that she needed to contact former residents or their families in order to raise five million euros. She had to save the old school in Morella – a place the Director had never heard of – to prevent the local Town Hall from turning it into an apartment block or, even worse, into a casino.

Soledad's eyes opened wide and as she cleared her throat she looked straight at Valli.

'Señora Querol, much as we would love to help you, I don't really know how. I already have enough problems here trying to maintain this place and its history, and I don't really know where such an enormous amount of money can be found,' she said in a serious and respectful tone.

Valli dropped her shoulders, but looked straight at her.

'So there's nothing that the Institute could do to help me? Valli persisted.

Soledad raised an eyebrow and pursed her thin lips.

'Don't think for a second that I wouldn't love to help, but I am afraid I can't. The Young Ladies' Residence, as you well know, all but disappeared after the war without leaving any funds or property. The International Institute rented them some facilities, but the two organisations were always independent from each other. Now, we still have our exchange programmes, but we are a private centre and we don't receive any help from anybody. And I can assure you that, sadly, we don't have any money at all to spare. I wish I could help!' she said, sighing.

Valli quickly responded:

'Don't you work with private foundations or other organisations?

'Nobody gives us anything around here,' said Soledad, seriously. 'We survive thanks to the classes we offer, our own work and a few other things, but it's all a big effort.'

Valli dropped her shoulders again.

'I thought that there was plenty of money around these days. At least there seems to be in my town, so I thought it would be even more the case in Madrid.'

Soledad looked at her attentively.

'Yes, there's certainly plenty of money around, but I no longer know whether that's good or bad. In any case, none of it comes our way here,' she said.

'Oh, my dear,' Valli said after a brief pause. 'I don't know where all this is going to end. Everybody's spending as if there's no tomorrow; everyone seems to be a millionaire these days. They're all buying big homes and new cars. It's like America,' she said, crossing her legs and raising her head.

Soledad, who had been nodding as Valli spoke, suddenly frowned and held her head in her hands, her elbows on the table. Her black, curly hair gave her a lively, youthful air.

'Let me think,' she said. 'Well, there must be old lists of residents, but I don't really know how to find them, I could, however, help you to get in touch with some people who I know are still alive, so at least you can start somewhere.' She paused for a moment. 'But I'll be frank with you; I am not sure you'll find much money, but I'm sure that just meeting those former residents will be a rewarding experience for you, and for them.'

Valli smiled in appreciation, but continued more seriously:

'Of course,' she said, 'but what I really need is the money, as I already have good friends in my home town.'

Just as practical as Valli, Soledad went into her computer and printed out a page with two names and addresses on it, neither of which Valli recognised. Soledad then referred her to a nearby building, the Ortega Foundation, where the Young Ladies' Residence archive was kept. She suggested that maybe Valli could find more information there.

Valli gratefully took the sheet of paper with the names and addresses and walked towards the door, accompanied once more by the Director, who gave her a warm embrace.

'Here are my contact details,' said Soledad, giving her a business card. 'Please let me know how you get on and I'll do all I can to help. I'll call the Ortega Foundation right now to let them know that you'll be visiting them. Would you like me to go with you?' she kindly offered.

'Don't worry, I can manage. I'm old but I can still cope,' said Valli, cheerfully.

Under the bright midday sun, Valli walked with renewed optimism the short distance between the building on Miguel Ángel Street and the house at Number thirty, Fortuny Street, another of the Young Ladies' Residencies. Fortuny had become a quiet, residential street, but without those old milk vendors, where residents and passers-by would stop and buy a glass of fresh milk, straight from the cow kept in the back of the shop.

Maria de Maeztu had her accommodation and office in that house, but with her irrepressible energy she was forever going backwards and forwards between the different buildings that the Young Ladies' Residencies ultimately occupied, all within easy reach of each other. When Valli was fifteen, and with her baccalaureate behind her, the Director allowed her to move freely between buildings and take part in any cultural activity she liked, as she was now a university student. Valli lived in Miguel Ángel, but she loved the activities that went on in Fortuny and didn't miss any opportunity to attend the numerous lectures and talks that were organised there.

During the Spring Valli also visited that grey-coloured building that hadn't changed at all, in order to study the remarkable wisteria that in April and May crept over the wall covering the frontage in a bright, cheerful purple colour. Now, leaning on the entrance railings, Valli admired the same spectacle with identical excitement. Just as she did then, she approached the delicate plant that hung from the walls like a bunch of grapes, and with a trembling hand caressed its tiny violet flowers that had lost none of their brightness or delicateness, despite everything that had happened since the last time she saw them. The little flowers were just as young and fresh as before, unlike her hands that now looked old and worn. The wisteria, she thought, like so many things in life, doesn't change. It's only people who change.

Valli looked around her. The entrance railings were also covered in beautiful wisteria, in sharp contrast to a building with modern tiles in the street behind it, where the chirping of the birds and the silent memory of students like her, whose lives changed in that place, were quite unknown. The vitality and the energy that came from the wisteria and the radiant blue sky spurred Valli on to continue with her walk through the small garden. Crossing the well-tended lawn, Valli remembered how La

Barraca, Lorca's theatre company, rehearsed his plays in this very spot and even once put on some short plays of Cervantes for the first time, which she actually saw. She would not see such good theatre again.

Valli sighed and walked a few steps in silence until she reached the window of the old library, where she had attended lectures by Machado, Pedro Salinas, Celaya or Alberti. These talks were in no way pompous or boring, but participative and above all practical; the residents always learned something. She especially remembered a talk by Ramón Gómez de la Serna, entitled *On Humour*; another by Zulueta, *Childhood and Old Age*; or Eugeni d'Ors, who came all the way from Catalunya to talk to them on *The Art of Keeping It Simple*.

She looked around her. There was nothing left of the "little working girl's house" that María de Maeztu had let them build at the height of the Republic, in order to give classes and a snack to semi-literate seamstresses or girls from the provinces who were in service to the already decadent Madrid aristocracy. Although the prime movers behind the group were almost all from the Left, Valli did not recall any of the other residents – some of whom were future Falangists – looking down on them, since the Director insisted that harmony and an understanding of the ideas of others must always prevail. In the Residence there was no song and dance about things; people were neither restricted nor put under pressure. Everyone did things their own way and at their own pace. There was even a Jewish girl and the occasional lesbian, although at that time Valli didn't know what homosexuals were, she recalled with a smile. She didn't get to find out until a friend explained that in the male Residence Lorca was openly gay. She looked out for them after that, but the truth is that with so much foppishness imported from British colleges, the young writer was in no way out of place in such a refined atmosphere.

Overcome by emotion Valli went straight in, but a mature lady with white hair and a swift glance came out to meet her.

'Señora Querol?' she asked, with a pleasant smile.

Rather taken by surprise, Valli nodded. That's how María de Maeztu had taught her to receive visitors and she was pleased to see that the place had retained such good manners.

'I've just had a call from Soledad at the International Institute to say you were coming. Do come in and I'll show you where we keep the archive.'

Valli didn't follow her because she was so absorbed in looking at the old library, now still full of books by Ortega y Gasset, whom she had listened to several times in that very place. Slowly she moved towards the main room, previously filled with pine tables and wicker chairs – nothing lavish but comfortable and well-suited to the task. The wealth in these buildings was not represented by silver trays or rare ornaments, but the more than four thousand books on the shelves or the pianos, whose lively sounds could be heard on most nights. Valli looked at the library where the residents got together to study in the afternoons, having spent the mornings in the university. They were young, with their whole future ahead of them, and they read and they wrote down their own ideas in the notebooks that the Residence itself provided for them. They were eager to learn; they wanted to bring about change in their country.

The sound of a door closing alerted her to the fact that the lady with the white hair was patiently waiting for her next to the staircase that led to the archive. Without wishing to be a nuisance or cause anyone to waste their time, Valli sat down opposite some twenty boxes full of folders and chose those that were marked "Correspondence" so that she could at least get some addresses.

Valli sat in a small armchair in the bowels of the building and immersed herself in a world of names that she had not remembered for over half a century, but one above all caught her eye. Amongst the documents there was an old, very faded photograph of Victoria Kent, her tutor in the Residence and also the first female Member of Parliament, together with Clara Campoamor, in the history of Spain. Victoria saw her every week despite the fact that she was heavily involved in politics and had been appointed the Director General of Prisons – the first time in Spain that a woman held a national public position. Kent, who left the Residence when she finished her law studies in 1920, had stayed in touch with the institution thanks to her great friendship with María de Maeztu, although many residents always suspected that they were more than just friends.

Using the excuse that she needed to go to the ladies, Valli returned to the ground floor and this time headed towards the left wing of the building. There she found the small meeting room where the Lyceum Club met, possibly the first women's club in Spain, and where they regularly debated topical subjects. That's where Valli met María Lejárraga, who wrote *Canción de cuna*, the philosopher María Zambrano, the journalist Josefina Carabias and Margarita Nelken, Member of Parliament and single mother, who, like many residents, ended up in exile. Another regular attender was Isabel Oyarzábal, Madrid correspondent of the British paper the *Daily Herald*, who explained how she managed to sneak into a prison in Madrid in order to denounce the state it was in by passing herself off as the daughter of Alcalá Zamora, the President of the Republic. There they discussed the rebellion led by Sanjurjo in 1932, agrarian reform, the divorce law, votes for women and everything that was happening around them; they spoke openly and without rules but always with respect. The wives of major intellectuals also attended the Lyceum, such as Zenobia, who was married to Juan Ramón Jiménez, or the wives of Ortega y Gasset, Marañón, Baroja and Pérez de Ayala, which led to the group being called "The Marrieds Club" by the more reactionary and chauvinistic sectors of society.

Unperturbed, they continued with their meetings. Victoria Kent, a lawyer by profession and one-time President of the Club, explained to them on one occasion the finer points of the defence of her former tutor, Álvaro de Albornoz, who was accused of treason in a court martial just before the declaration of the Republic. The defence team managed to reduce the sentence considerably and Victoria achieved national notoriety. After she had been made Director General of Prisons, in the early years of the Republic Valli's tutor, who continued to fulfill that role, still attended the meetings of the Lyceum whenever her responsibilities allowed. Seated on the floor, because the room was always packed when she was there, they listened to her tell them about her plans for the prisons, such as giving rights to the prisoners or the possibility of allowing visits from their wives or girlfriends. She also wanted to put in libraries and even suggestion boxes. That's what she tried to do until she resigned after a couple of years, under pressure from mediocre men whom seemed to have a problem being told what to do by a woman. Victoria finally gave in, but also because it was more important to her to carry out her work in accordance with her ideals than to stay in a post keeping her head down just in order to advance her political career. Victoria was always a fine example for all of the residents.

Tall, heavily-built, full of life and self-mastery, Kent continued her professional work in her own lawyer's office which was situated very close to the Residence, where she practiced and lived with a friend and the friend's son. Valli, who often visited this rather unusual family for that day and age, remembered some of her still highly relevant comments. A glass of her favourite malt whisky in hand, her dark hair tied back, and gazing straight ahead, she said one day: "When men believe they are inspired by God, that's when disasters begin; when they accept their role as men, they are on the way to getting close to their equals, which is the way to understand them."

She had never forgotten that statement, nor the tragic premonition that it brought with it. Valli sighed as she looked at the large room, still with the same dark parquet flooring and the books all around. She saw her beloved Victoria, always so modern, smoking in the garden, discussing, arguing, always encouraging her to study more, to push herself. When Valli told her she wanted to become a teacher, Victoria urged her to become the Minister for Education. That's how she was. The old *maestra* smiled as she remembered when Victoria asked her what languages she spoke she replied Castilian and Morellan. Valli was sure that inside Victoria must have laughed her head off. But when her tutor responded she said very seriously that that was fine, but that it was essential for her to learn English and that she should go to England to visit the best schools and universities. Before she became a Minister she would need to learn about the world, she told her. Apart from Morella she'd only been to Zaragoza and Madrid in her whole life, so she put in a great effort and with the help of her friend Tristan from the Students' Residence she learned enough English to win a grant from the Council for Extension Studies Abroad. María de Maeztu supported and recommended her and in June 1936 she was all set to spend a year in Smith College in the United States starting in September. The plan never materialised.

Valli looked at the piles of folders on the desk and realised she was facing a monumental task. Who was going to leave her five million euros? Valli pursed her lips and thought that Victoria Kent would never have lost her nerve when she was pursuing an objective, however daunting it might have been. She also thought of María de Maeztu, who ignored the laughter of the young male students on the train from Bilbao to Salamanca, where she could only go to sit the exams because as a woman she couldn't attend classes. María had travelled all over the world on her own, studying educational models, giving lectures, taking an interest in the most up-to-date ideas. Such women took giant strides with barely any help or precedents.

Valli spent the next few hours with the archives, immersed in unforgettable memories of a life that changed her forever, however much fate tried to hold back the drive that the Residence inspired in her.

She worked solidly, writing down the names and addresses of as many residents as she could remember, and far from feeling that the task was impossible, she left the house on Fortuny Street when it was closing time at dusk, all set to achieve her objective happily, simply and efficiently. She had not lost one iota of the spirit that she had acquired there.

8

Charles took almost an hour to find the track that led off a small country road towards Vicent's farmhouse. He was driving a rented Seat Ibiza, and in spite of following the directions carefully he passed the end of the track several times without noticing it, not only because it wasn't paved but because the downpour the day before, Easter Monday, had left it full of puddles and covered the end of it completely. Eventually Charles left the car by the side of the road and very patiently went on foot until he finally found it.

Having manoeuvred around several major potholes and deep ruts, Charles was impressed by his first sight of the Mayor's house. The tall, elegant and ancient farmhouse was a solitary and imposing building in the midst of a spectacular landscape. The surroundings, at least from a distance, were not very well cared for, like the more manorial houses in England, but the undergrowth and the trees that surrounded the building in disorderly fashion gave it a unique natural charm. The stone of the building, which was a light clay colour, and the wooden windows gave it an instantly welcoming appearance. Charles, who was accustomed to English orderliness, to the impeccable lawns of Eton and Oxford, was fascinated by Spanish natural disorder. He found it highly exotic.

He parked the car in the first space he could find, next to a hut built of the same materials as the main house. That disorderliness was very deliberate, he said to himself. The chirping of the birds provided a happy welcome, and then he caught sight of a lad who, bucket in hand, was weeding around the apple and pear trees next to the entrance. Charles greeted him and, with his suitcase and a bunch of flowers in one hand, he knocked with the horseshoe that hung in the centre of the front door.

'Just coming!' he heard Isabel shout from inside.

Charles looked around him. The day had started cloudy, which he was basically pleased about because the overwhelming heat of the preceding days had left his skin feeling a little sore. He was accustomed to the grey skies of London, which were always more soothing than the intensity of the bright sunshine that befuddled and exhausted his rational thinking. This "better" climate had put him in an excellent mood. Moreover, this was the penultimate day of his holidays before he returned to England on Thursday and he was determined to make the most of it. Aroused by curiosity he had accepted Vicent's invitation to come to dinner and spend the night at his house, about which he had heard a rumour in the town. It certainly looked impressive, although he hadn't yet seen any sign of any of the exaggerated embellishments that were being mentioned, including a wine fountain.

Eventually Isabel opened the door.

'*Hola*!' she said with a broad smile.

Charles was surprised to see her with her loose and slightly wavy long, dark hair and her big, green almond-shaped eyes that were more noticeable on a grey day, as if the absence of the sun suited her, too. Her skin looked even darker than that of many Spaniards.

The Mayor's daughter, who was wearing an apron, welcomed him.

'Good morning, Charles, come in. Did you find us all right?'

He smiled and said honestly: 'Well, eventually, but if you persevere you get there in the end.'

He put down his suitcase and didn't quite know what to do with the flowers. Isabel looked expectantly at the bunch of yellow roses. Feeling somewhat nervous, he looked around the small, rustic entrance hall and the glass door that led into the house.

''I've brought these for you and your mother,' he said finally, looking nowhere in particular. 'I hope you like them, although I can see with your impressive garden you're not short of flowers or plants,' he added, stealing a glance at Isabel this time.

The Mayor's daughter took the flowers and put them to her face for the scent. The flowers hadn't yet started to open.

'They're lovely, thank you very much,' she said rather shyly. 'I love roses, and as you'll have noticed we don't have any, so my mother will also be delighted.' Isabel looked curiously at Charles, noticing his muddy shoes and also his small, rather old suitcase. 'But do come in,' she said, moving towards the glass door. 'Although in fact it would be a good idea if you took off your shoes and I'll bring you some slippers, as I can see you've been busy this morning…' she said to him.

Charles smiled.

Isabel continued with her chatty tone that Charles remembered from the hotel, as she took out a pair of slippers from the old chest that was in the small entrance hall.

'My parents will be back soon,' she said. 'My father has taken his horse out; I think he wanted to see the state of the paths before going out with you this afternoon, and my mother has had to go to the hotel to sort out a few things with Manolo, who will be joining us this evening for dinner.'

They exchanged comments on the rain and the droughts as they entered the main living room, which Charles looked at in amazement. The rustic style, with well-kept stonework, very comfortable furniture and the glow of a fire in the hearth, reminded him of the nicest English houses that he had seen. But it was the age of Vicent's farmhouse that on top of everything else gave it an incomparable charm. He noticed the twisted wooden beams in the ceiling, the wood-fired stove and the old farming tools hanging on the walls. He was surprised not to see any of Isabel's pictures, but before he could ask, she said:

'Come on, I'll show you your room. My father said that after lunch you'll go out for a ride and then spend the night here, because to be honest driving on these God-forsaken roads is rather dangerous, especially in the dark after a good wine.'

'Well, it was very kind of your father to invite me.'

Isabel did not reply and headed up to one of the guest rooms on the first floor.

'Go ahead,' she said, opening the old dark-wood door.

Charles looked around the huge room which was dominated by a soft double bed in the centre and an immense semi-circular window that looked out towards the mountains. He put down his case, went over to the windows and opened them wide.

'What a wonderful place,' he said in a quiet voice, looking first one way and then the other.

'It's not bad,' replied Isabel, English-style.

Charles looked at her attentively.

'Have you lived here long?'

''I don't live here, I have a place in Villarreal, where I work, but my parents moved here nearly two years ago, so in fact this has never been my home,' she said. 'It's too big for my liking.'

Charles was surprised by this. Who wouldn't be happy with such a mansion? Looking out of the window again, he could see the show-jumping arena with its pavilion, and next to it the swimming pool, which was now empty, surrounded by a more landscaped area with a lawn.

'So your place in Villarreal isn't like this?'

Isabel gave a hint of a smile.

'I'm happy with a small apartment, where I can have a bit of peace and rest in the little free time that I get; what with my job and coming to Morella at weekends to help in the hotel, I don't really stop.'

'Without wishing to interfere,' said Charles, 'why don't you get more help in the hotel so that you don't have to do it?

'Well, we'd like to,' Isabel replied, 'but it may surprise you to know that in Morella it's very difficult to find people who are willing to do bathrooms and beds. This country became rich overnight and no-one wants to do the worst-paid jobs. But of course we can't pay a fortune for cleaning rooms, either.'

Isabel took in a deep breath and headed towards a door that led to the bathroom, no doubt to inspect it.

'Normally we have someone who helps,' she went on, 'but the truth is you can't rely on anybody, so I always end up taking it on.'

Charles nodded sympathetically.

'And are you not working in Villarreal this week?' he asked.

Isabel looked away for a moment and after a brief pause, she replied:

'Well, no, I've taken this week as a holiday.'

'But you haven't taken the opportunity to go away?' Charles couldn't understand how an independent adult could devote her holidays to helping her apparently rich parents.

Isabel, who Charles reckoned must be about forty-something, looked away again and went over to the bed to straighten out the eiderdown, which had a couple of wrinkles. When she went back over to Charles, who was still leaning on the window-frame, she replied:

'Well, don't tell my father, but in fact I've taken these few days off to look at other jobs; I've got an interview at a factory in Castellón this Friday,' she said.

'Don't you like working in the tile place?' he asked attentively.

Isabel pursed her thick lips and tilted her head slightly to one side.

'The place is fine and the people are nice, but I get the feeling that things aren't going too well and there are rumours that they're going to get rid of people,' she said rather shamefacedly.

'What a pity,' said Charles thoughtfully, for she seemed to him to be a good, honest and hard-working woman. 'But I'm sure you'll find another job that's as good or better, you'll see. You seem to be very reliable, from what I've seen.'

Isabel gave a slight smile.

'We'll see, because it seems to me that this isn't the right time,' she said.

'Oh, really?' said Charles, thinking immediately of Robin. 'What makes you say that?' he asked, not giving away the great interest that he had in the subject. It wasn't a question of being alarmist, but in a business transaction such information could be useful.

Isabel gave a long sigh before going on.

'This country and especially this region have grown a lot in recent years. I've seen it clearly in the factory, where we get big-money orders from people who are having new houses built and want the best materials. You don't know what I've come across,' she said in an almost confidential tone. 'From construction workers building houses worth more than a million euros to taxi drivers who became millionaires through a couple of property deals via some shady outfit that they'd set up with a brother-in-law or a mate. Black has become white here, I can assure you,' she said looking at him directly. 'But it's been some time since I've seen orders like we had before. They're still starting new builds, the cranes are still there, but I don't see anyone buying or moving house. No-one talks about it.'

Charles remained thoughtful.

'Very interesting,' he said, stroking his chin. 'And how do you think it'll all pan out?'

Isabel gave a brief laugh with a rather nervous smile.

'Mr Charles, I'm just a simple secretary, I don't know anything about economics, and I wouldn't be so bold as to make any forecast,' she said modestly. 'I only know what they taught us in school: don't count your chickens before they're hatched.'

Charles nodded.

'The situation in England is not very different,' he said. 'We've also seen an unprecedented bonanza, but fortunately in my sector they didn't inflate the salaries like they did with the bankers, so however much we'd like to go crazy with money, we just can't afford to!' he said with a smile.

The two of them were silent for a few seconds and feeling a little uncomfortable, since basically they were two single middle-aged adults and they were alone in a bedroom. Despite the fact that he would never feel attracted by a rather ample secretary in Spain, it didn't seem proper for them to be in his bedroom, in an empty house, when her father the Mayor was about to arrive.

Looking around him Charles finally said to Isabel:

'If you'll give me a few moments to settle myself in, I'll join you downstairs in a few minutes.'

'Of course,' she said. 'Everything's ready, and please let me know if you need anything and I'll get it for you right away. I don't think my parents will be long.'

'There's no need to be so formal with me,' said Charles, feeling sorry for that poor talented artist whose father had inculcated such a servile attitude in her.

Half an hour later, the two of them were drinking coffee in the kitchen when they heard the sound of *Lo Petit* approaching the house.

'Here's my father,' said Isabel, getting up to make another pot of coffee.

The Mayor, who was dressed more informally that day, with a pair of old corduroy trousers and a baggy knitted jumper, immediately went over to Charles with open arms.

'Look who's here! My very own Englishman!' he said with a broad smile and giving him a warm hug.

Vicent looked more rested than he did on Sunday, thought Charles, although his dark eyes looked rather sunken and he had bags under them. In any event his appearance was better than the last time he'd seen him on Sunday in Colón Square, with his frockcoat tie somewhat askew and his face full of stress. Today, at least, he looked in better health, although he wasn't yet sure if he was in a better mood, too.

'Get me a coffee, my girl,' said Vicent to Isabel without looking at her.

She obeyed at once, looking at the ground.

'Come through, *Mister*, come through,' he said, taking Charles by the arm. 'Come, we're going to enjoy ourselves today. You'll see how well we live in this town.' Turning towards Isabel, he said: 'Bring my coffee to me by the fire and a drop of sherry for our English friend – the mature one, he'll love that; and a bit of ham, as well.'

Isabel said nothing and the two men sat in the armchairs by the fireplace. Vicent stoked the fire and added a couple of bits of wood, more for the appearance than the heat, for it wasn't really that cold.

Isabel brought them the drinks and the ham on a tray, which she left on a little table between the two armchairs. Vicent took no notice of her, but Charles felt obliged to comment on her contribution.

'Your daughter has been a great help,' he said, looking at her.

'Oh, really?' Vicent replied in surprise and looking at Isabel, who had remained standing next to the fireplace without quite knowing what to do while they were talking about her. 'And might I know what she has done?' the Mayor asked in a tone of incredulity.

'She's been very kind to me since the first day, and she's told me some very interesting stories about the hotel,' Charles replied firmly as he gave a conspiratorial look towards Isabel.

Somewhat alarmed, Vicent asked:

'What stories are you referring to?'

Isabel jumped in straight away.

'The one about the Seville Virgin, father.'

Vicent let out a loud laugh and picked up his coffee to take the first sip.

'And that's interesting?' he asked scornfully. 'Never mind, Charles, I've got some interesting stories to tell you, of the financial kind!'

Charles looked at Isabel, who now left with a hint of sadness.

'Try the sherry, my boy, you'll like it,' Vicent invited him.

Charles did as he was told and tried what was undoubtedly one of the best sherries he'd ever tasted in his life.

'It's exquisite,' he said, sounding like a gentleman.

Vicent smiled, leant back in his armchair and put his feet on the broad front part of the fireplace.

'Well, Charles, tell me,' he said in a paternalistic tone, 'what do you think of Morella, now that you've spent a few days with us?'

'It's a lovely town,' replied Charles, succinctly and ignoring Vicent's superior air.

The Mayor looked at him with a degree of suspicion, as if he were thinking that they weren't going to get anywhere if they spoke in monosyllables. He offered him the plate of ham, which Charles felt obliged to taste. In fact it was delicious.

'Good,' Vicent went on, playing with the thick shiny gold ring on his large, powerful hands. 'And the school, what did you think of it?'

Charles leant back slightly and crossed his legs. He linked his hands on his knees, and looking at the fire, he said:

'It's an interesting project. It's definitely a building with potential,' he said, trying to avoid committing himself.

Vicent looked at him straight in the eye.

'I know that.'

The pressure made Charles feel uncomfortable. The Mayor couldn't expect him to have made a decision to purchase after only one visit and without having studied the legal situation. He was a rational man and these decisions took time.

Vicent persisted:

'I'm only asking because there are other investors who are interested, in case you don't want to get left behind,' he said, looking at the ring he was still playing with.

Charles had never responded to threats or being rushed, especially not by a town mayor.

'Have you received any offers yet?' he asked, returning the ball to the other court.

Vicent gave a slight cough and served himself another glass of sherry.

'Well, no, not officially, but I have received serious expressions of interest,' he said, looking at his nails and his hands in a rather self-important way.

Charles found this arrogance rather amusing.

'And how much are these offers for?' he asked with a hint of mischief, but without losing his innocent and charming tone.

Vicent looked at him with his eyes wide and his brow furrowed.

'My dear Charles,' he said, 'this is a business negotiation, and if you're interested you have to say so and make an offer that we'll consider.'

Charles took a sip of sherry. The momentary silence enabled him to hear a slight noise coming from the kitchen, reminding him that Isabel was still in the large room, a broad open space that occupied the whole of the ground floor.

He observed Vicent in silence while the Mayor checked something on his mobile in an almost compulsive way. Charles didn't particularly like the Mayor, on account of his brutish, direct manner and the way in which he treated Isabel. In spite of that, he thought about the school and its possibilities and made an effort to focus just on that.

'Yes, naturally I'm interested,' he replied eventually. 'But, of course, I need to come with the boys to see if they like Morella, too, and if they'll fit in to this community.' He paused briefly. 'In addition I'd like to talk with that older lady again; I'd like to have a better idea of her reasons for being so opposed to the plan.'

Vicent sighed and leaned slightly forward, as if he was about to share something of great significance.

'That lady, Charles, is of no importance whatsoever,' he said, looking him in the eye. 'Take no notice of her, you'll be wasting your time, I'm telling you.'

The Mayor leant back again into his armchair and Charles remained thoughtful. Only the crackle of the wood in the fire and the sound of Isabel moving around in the kitchen filled the awkward silence.

It was eventually broken with the arrival of Amparo, the Mayor's wife, laden with bags from Morella's supermarket, the only one in the town. Having put the bags in the kitchen and given Isabel an affectionate kiss on the forehead, Amparo turned to the two men.

'Hello, Mr Charles,' she said in a friendly voice. 'Welcome to our home. You'll see how nice it is, and please tell us if you need anything, that's what we're here for.'

Charles looked at her in the same way that he'd observed Isabel earlier. That servility was beginning to make him feel uncomfortable, as well as Vicent's passivity in allowing and encouraging such a situation. Like Isabel, Amparo wasn't what you would call a beauty, but she had a certain air of pleasantness, she was stocky and dark like her daughter, and she gave Charles good feelings about her. With her dark trousers and long knitted jumper, which was probably home-made, Amparo compensated for her limitations with a touch of make-up which brought out her dark eyes, a neat head of hair and especially her gentle smile.

The Mayor's wife now turned to her husband:

'Vicent, I'm sorry I'm so late back,' she said, without him looking at her. 'The group of ten from Barcelona have decided to stay two more days, and they suddenly turned up to eat without warning, so I had to leave them some food ready,' she explained by way of excuse.

Vicent shook his head.

'That son of mine doesn't know how to run a business,' he complained. 'People must be asked about their plans so that they are committed in advance, and if they don't then they pay extra,' he said, furrowing his brow,

Amparo tried to be mollifying:

'I think they're having a wonderful time, looking for fossils and truffles everywhere.'

'Don't they have work to do?' Vicent persisted.

Amparo headed for the kitchen, but responded:

'I think they're celebrating the grandmother's birthday, but they're leaving tomorrow.'

As she took some of the shopping out of the bags with Isabel's help, Amparo tried to calm her husband down.

'Don't worry,' she said. 'The meal will be on time, I've got everything ready, and I've got Isabel to help me.'

Vicent looked skywards in exasperation at the mention of his daughter's name.

Charles gave a hard stare at Vicent, as he couldn't understand how a woman like Isabel, who did not appear to be a problem, could irritate her father so much. Maybe there was something he didn't know about.

'Sugar!' Amparo suddenly shouted. 'Not the water again!'

Vicent and Charles looked at each other.

'Vicent!' shouted Amparo from the kitchen, but without abandoning her gentle tone. 'They've cut the water off again. How annoying. What are we going to do? I can't cook without water. Can you call them, please? I've tried a thousand times this week.'

Charles watched Vicent get up, rush to the kitchen and whisper something in his wife's ear. That situation was starting to get a bit strange, although he knew from his own experience that the sudden loss of water or electricity was not uncommon.

Immediately after the secret family get-together in the kitchen, Isabel rushed upstairs and after a few seconds came down with what looked like an invoice that she gave to her father. He excused himself for a moment and headed upstairs with his mobile in his hand. Charles got out of his chair to join the two women, who were still standing in the kitchen, their arms folded, not saying anything and with a worried look.

'Everything okay?' he asked.

'Don't worry, Mr Charles, everything's fine, my husband will get it sorted,' said Amparo.

Isabel went over to the drinks cabinet next to the fireplace and returned with another glass of sherry for Charles.

'There's no rush,' said Isabel. 'Enjoy it, it's one of the best sherries there is.'

'Only if you join me,' replied Charles to both mother and daughter.

The two of them smiled and after a few moments the three of them were drinking a toast with the small lead-crystal glasses that Charles liked so much. It was the first object he had seen since he left England that would fit in at Eton. A thought that made him feel at home.

'Señora Fernández, do you also make Sevillian clothes?' asked Charles, causing Isabel to laugh and Amparo to look surprised.

Isabel explained.

'Mama, Charles has been in room fourteen and came across the Blessed Virgin.'

Amparo had a good laugh.

'Oh, my goodness, I'd completely forgotten that the Virgin was still there!' she exclaimed. 'Poor guests! We'll have to remove it one day. It must have given you a shock, Mr Charles.'

He shook his head slowly.

'Not at all, Señora, I found the story fascinating.'

Amparo sighed.

'That place is full of surprises,' she said. 'During the war a number of religious objects were hidden, but also in later years, including in the sixties and seventies when foreign tourists began to come.'

'Oh, really?' Charles asked. 'What did they use to hide?'

'Valuable religious objects, especially to help the church protect itself from Erik the Belgian.'

'Erik the Belgian?' asked Charles, amused by the stories of these two women.

Isabel and her mother leant back laughing and relaxed with their hands on the stove. Amparo took a swig of her sherry and went on:

'He was Belgian, of course, and filled his boots in the sixties by stealing from fountains and taking silver and gold cups from churches. Well, anything he could lay his hands on,' she explained. 'In those days the churches were always open, even if the priest was away, especially in the towns and villages, where everyone knew everyone else and no-one went in except to pray. But this chap had his eyes open and spent his time going round the province with a sack and collected a vast amount of booty. Notices were put around and everything, so when there was a rumour that he was in the area we hid some objects in the loft. The fact is that in the end they caught him in Castellote and they sent him back empty-handed to where he came from after a severe warning.'

The three of them laughed over the adventures of Erik the Belgian, whose name Charles found amusing. In fact he always remembered that story and used it as something with which to amuse his Spanish students.

The harmony of the little group was cut short, however, as soon as Vicent came back into the room looking serious.

'The water people are a group of idiots,' he said. 'There's nothing we can do, because those good-for-nothings don't know how to solve the problem straight away. But as soon as I get the chance to talk to the top man they'll remember who I am. Amparo,' he said to his wife, with the air of a commandant, 'can you cook something without using water?'

Amparo recovered her servile pose of looking at the floor and with drooping shoulders, and replied:

'I'm sorry, dearest, but I can't: cooking and washing-up use up a lot of water and it's best to leave what's left in the water tank for an emergency, or for showers, rather than waste it now on eating.'

Vicent sighed.

'Well, we'll go and eat in town,' he decided. 'That way Charles will get to know one of the best restaurants. I'll call from the car to see who's still open,' he said, looking at the clock.

The two women started to clear up the kitchen while Charles went to his room for his suitcase.

'Are you not stopping?' asked Isabel when she saw him looking just the same as he was when he arrived only two hours earlier.

'Well, if there are problems with the water and the showers, it's best if I go back to the hotel; I don't want to be a nuisance, and the truth is that I've got some work to do.'

'As you wish, but that's a shame,' Isabel replied, looking him in the eye.

That comment surprised Charles since, in truth, it was the first time in a long while that a woman had expressed interest in his company. He felt flattered by the thought, although more significantly it left him confused.

9

That leaden Tuesday afternoon hung like a millstone around Vicent's neck as he sat in front of the fireplace smoking one cigarette after another. The meal with Charles in Vinatea had gone quite well, although he would have preferred it if his wife and daughter had talked more about things to do with Morella and its charms instead of all that gossip about personalities past and present that seemed to interest Charles so much. There was this about the war, that about Erik the Belgian, the other about the chocolate maker, and more about her aunt. Such nonsense was of no interest to the Mayor, for whom the only thing was the school project, and he would have been grateful if there had been more support coming from the family. On the other hand it seemed that the two women and Charles had had a wonderful time gossiping for over two hours, all at the Town Hall's expense, of course. At least he could justify the invitation as necessary, since Barnús was the only other investor who had shown any interest in the school. What's more, the Cullera investor had only offered two million, so someone would have to be found who could put in another three to reach the five million that the Council was asking for. The investors would have to share out the proceeds, because Vicent was not in a position to reduce the price; the Council had accumulated a sizeable debt and it also had to finance the million euros that had already been invested in the Castellón airport.

Investments like the redevelopment of the Alameda, the new swimming pool or the participation in the airport had been essential to make Morella a more attractive place. But the time had come to focus on sales and income so as to be able to pay some of the suppliers whose patience was beginning to run out.

From his armchair and with his gaze fixed on the fireplace, Vicent was convinced that everything would soon sort itself out. He didn't doubt that he would get the five million for the school, although the investment in the airport had reduced his ability to manoeuvre and to bargain. He couldn't agree to any discounts if he was going to reduce the Council's debt, which unfortunately was higher than everyone believed. Public works had been paid for with loans that at the time were offered at low rates of interest, but they had ended up costing more following a general interest rate rise. And not only that, he thought in annoyance. The bank had also raised the commission that it charged on all its loans. Vicent couldn't understand why credit had become more expensive if the country was doing so well.

The Mayor took a sip of the coffee with a dash of anisette that Amparo had placed on the small table next to his armchair. His wife had gone up to the little sitting room, no doubt to watch the TV soaps or do some sewing, her favourite pastimes, the Mayor thought to himself. Isabel, still in Morella despite the fact that it was a weekday, had gone out for a walk, while Manolo had just called from the hotel.

Vicent gave a deep sigh and lit another cigarette, the fifth since the family had returned from the meal with Charles only a couple of hours earlier. Deep down Vicent knew that everything would get sorted out as usual, but that didn't remove a degree of uncertainty that would remain until all the loose ends were tied up.

On top of everything they had been left without water, and he did so like his hot bath before he went to bed. Well, he thought, that night he could use the reserve water in the tank, as he was sure that those idiots at the water company would restore his supply the next day. It was true that he still hadn't paid for the last quarter, but the invoice for five thousand euros had seemed to him so exorbitant that he was unwilling to pay it until they had come to an agreement about it. He knew they used a large amount of water to irrigate the fields and fill the swimming pool in summer; plus access turned out to be expensive since they needed to pump the water with a generator so that it would go up the underground passage that they had built from some of the farms near Morella. The suppliers were very quick to put in the installation, but dishonest about calculating the average cost to use it. At no time did they tell him that the infrastructure would cost nearly thirty thousand euros a year. In fact they had cut off the supply two weeks earlier, but fortunately they always had the use of the hotel for a meal and a shower.

His mobile rang, with its usual high-pitched and irritating sound, and it moved slightly on the small table next to his armchair. He quickly stretched out an arm and saw that it was Barnús. He took the call, hoping that it might get the project moving.

'How's the financial genius, then?' he said, regaining his assured tone and sitting up straight.

'Marvellous, Mayor, just marvellous,' replied the Cullera investor at the other end.

In this country things always seem to be going well for everyone, thought Vicent, before continuing.

'Listen, many thanks for the paella last Sunday, it was first class, and the whole town appreciated your generosity. Did you see what a queue there was to come and talk to you?' Flattery was a technique that never failed, thought Vicent, who could never understand why there were people who never used it. It was so easy...

'Well, they were queueing for the food, not for me,' Barnús replied with false modesty. 'In any case, what do I care?' he added. 'What I want is the town's school to turn into a huge casino; the idea, Mayor, has got the Marquis and me really excited,' he said, ' and that's what I wanted to talk to you about,'

Vicent smiled.

'I'm all ears.'

Barnús waited for a few seconds and went on:

'As I said the other day, they don't call me shark for nothing and both the Marquis and I need confirmation in writing that the Regional Government will take responsibility for the refurbishing. If not, the numbers won't add up,' he said.

'Yes, you already told me, Paco, I remember, and I'm on to it,' Vicent replied somewhat dubiously, as he didn't feel comfortable about pressing Roig on the matter. In any event, after the solution agreed on Sunday in Colón Square, he was sure there would be no problem. 'Don't worry, I'll sort this out in no time at all. I'll call you as soon as I have it or I'll fax it to you. Okay?'

'You're a good man, Mayor!' Barnús replied in a rather high voice. 'I knew this town had a good nose for business.'

'You'll see how fast property will go up when we've got the airport in Castellón and the school's been converted into a tourist trap,' said Vicent, believing every word he said.

'The airport, that's the key,' replied Barnús. 'In Vinaroz I also have a long list of clients for one of my towers who are just waiting for confirmation of the schedule of flights in order to set up their offices just ten metres from the beach.' Barnús paused briefly. 'This is going to bring in hordes of northern Europeans, just you wait and see!' he exclaimed triumphantly.

The two men laughed and without more ado finished the conversation.

Vicent lit another cigarette, playing with it with his fingers as he smoked it. The coffee had gone cold and there was no-one in the kitchen to make him another. With a gesture of irritation the Mayor went over to the drinks cabinet to serve himself a whisky with ice.

Back in his armchair he toyed with his mobile for a while, not knowing whether to ring Roig and ask him for the guarantee or wait until it arrived. Unfortunately he didn't have much time, especially after the payment of the million. He needed the money from the sale of the school very soon into order to justify the Town Hall's accounts. If he didn't, the opposition and the entire town would come down hard on him.

Brushing back his dark hair he dialled Roig's number. To his surprise Roig answered at once.

'Just the person I wanted to talk to, dickhead,' Roig snapped.

Vicent sat up straight and opened his eyes as wide as saucers.

'President?' he asked, as if deep down he thought there must be some mistake. 'It's me, Fernández, from Morella.'

'I know, you idiot,' Roig replied, although Vicent could hardly hear him, as it sounded very windy, almost blowing a hurricane, wherever he was. The President went on: 'Wait while I get into the boat.'

Vicent stood up and waited with his legs completely rigid. Something had gone wrong.

'Fernández,' came the voice once more, 'do you know what a deal is, or what, you clown?' said the President in a quieter voice, no doubt so that no-one could hear him.

'I don't know what you're referring to, President,' he said.

'Don't play the fool with me, I'm here in the middle of the America's Cup, I've got I don't know how many diplomats in the boat and I haven't got time to waste on a shitty school in a shitty town,' he said.

Vicent closed his eyes as if he couldn't absorb that string of insults. He listened to the popping of five or six champagne corks on the other end of the line, and also what sounded like clinking glasses. He had forgotten that this week Valencia was hosting the America's Cup, another project that Roig had poured money into and that, frankly, Vicent didn't understand. At least the Morella casino would create permanent employment, but a sailing competition was temporary and the profits would only be pocketed by the delegates of the luxury businesses that took part. The infrastructure built for the occasion would, as usual, be left abandoned and forgotten.

'What's happened?' Vicent finally dared to ask, closing his eyes once more in the face of the possible approaching storm.

'The money didn't arrive on Monday, you imbecile,' the President of Valencia replied. 'Why the hell did you go back on your word? It caused me a serious problem, because you know that the useless Mayor of Castellón wants to delay the project, because deep down he's a wimp. I told him not to worry, that on Monday everything would be sorted, and then you left me looking like an idiot. What the fuck happened?'

Vicent immediately thought of Eva. For a second he questioned her loyalty, but dismissed the thought at once. There was no way that Eva would have disobeyed, although now he thought that instead of leaving the Town Hall on Sunday night, he should have stayed to supervise the operation. But he was worn out and she had said that it would take hours to prepare a budget that would allow her to carry out the transfer. She had to redo the accounts to avoid the filters that the Town Hall had in place, precisely to prevent operations like that one.

Vicent didn't know what to say, other than to apologise and promise a rapid solution.

'President, I'm really sorry if I've caused you any problems,' said Vicent sheepishly.

'Don't come to me with excuses, just sort the thing out, damn it,' Roig interrupted.

'Of course, I'll get to it right away…' remarked Vicent, leaving the sentence unfinished.

The Mayor didn't understand why it was so urgent. If Morella was going to devote a million to a project from its small local coffers, at least they should be told why the money was required so urgently.

'President, may I ask just one thing?' he said.

'What is it?' Roig replied. 'Be quick, I've got I don't know how many businessmen wanting to talk to me. What is it now, Fernández?'

'As you know I have obligations towards my townspeople and I'd like to know exactly what our money is going to be used for. Given the urgency, it seems that it's for something specific.'

Vicent heard Roig blowing out some cigar smoke.

'What do you want to know for?' he asked.

Vicent was surprised about the secrecy, as he thought that his position gave him access to information which didn't always reach the public, but did, of course, reach him.

'Well, if we put in a million, at least we should know what it's for, shouldn't we?'

Roig gave a sigh at the other end.

'Okay, I'll tell you, but not a peep about this to your people, otherwise there could be an unholy row about it. That's why I'm not sure if it's better for you to know or not.'

'I'd rather know, President. After all these people did vote for me,' said Vicent, aware that this was a delicate moment and he had to get it right.

'It's up to you,' replied the President, apparently puffing quickly given the large amount of smoke he heard him blowing out. 'The thing is that it's the local football club that needs the money, as they'll be wearing the airport logo in order to promote the city.'

Vicent was surprised by his reply.

'I thought the football contract had been signed a long time ago. Hasn't everything been paid that was agreed at the time?'

'The bastards included a clause in the contract that we all overlooked, which said that, if they were promoted to the first division, we'd have to pay them more; and the sons-of-bitches went up,' Roig explained. 'We've spent the whole year putting them off and now they're putting us under a lot of pressure, threatening us with leaking it to the press and, of course, taking us to court. There's enough opposition to this project without having the press hounding us as well.'

Vicent remained thoughtful.

'But can't an agreement be reached with them? We could offer them free flights once the airport is built. Does the contract say that the payment has to be in cash or can we be creative?'

'That's not a bad idea,' said Roig, sounding positive at last. 'But they've also got caught out. They've built a stadium that's too big for them and have signed players they now can't pay.' The President paused. 'I think they need the million to pay the wages for the last three months.'

Vicent pressed his fingers on his eyes as if he didn't want to hear any more.

'What a fucking mess,' he said, regretfully.

'Yes, Fernández, it certainly is,' Roig conceded. 'Best to send the money now and sell your school quickly, because if the money doesn't start to shift soon, we're going to get caught out.'

'You can count on it and sorry for the delay, President,' Vicent concluded, now more concerned about the Region's finances than Morella's million.

'But don't worry, Mayor, everything will be fine and we've got good support,' he said in a brighter tone. 'This America's Cup event will bring us some good investments, just you wait.'

Vicent nodded and ended the call as quickly as he could so he could call Eva and clear that matter up.

Just as he was about to press the 'call' button on his mobile, his daughter Isabel came in at the wrong moment as usual.

'Aren't you working this week?' he asked, still on his feet, with a whisky in one hand and his mobile in the other.'

He noticed that Isabel was looking him up and down.

'May I ask what you're looking at?' he said, nervously and defensively.

His daughter took a step back in the middle of taking her coat off and fixed her gaze on her father.

'And may I ask what's the matter with you today, in such a bad mood?' said Isabel, now folding her coat carefully on one of the kitchen chairs.

Vicent put down his whisky on the side-table and lit a cigarette. After the first puff, he sighed.

'Work things,' he said.

The Mayor looked at his daughter's appearance. She was still wearing jeans, which were rather tight for her ample hips, and the same loose-knit red jumper that she had worn when they went out to eat with Charles, which made her look rather like a wardrobe. He hadn't seen her wear make-up for some time and he didn't know whether she went to the hairdresser, since she always wore her hair tied in a ponytail, sometimes with a hair band that looked more like an elastic band.

'You could do something about your appearance,' he said, scornfully. 'At least when you accompany me on work-related matters, like the meal with the Englishman today. It's important to give a good impression; you're the daughter of the Mayor and you can't dress just any old how. You look ridiculous.'

Isabel raised her chin slightly and looked at him dismissively.

'Well, I think the Englishman enjoyed himself precisely because Mama and I were there,' she responded.

'Well, if you're so good, why can't you get five million out of him for the school?' he said defiantly.

Without replying his daughter went upstairs to her room.

Give me patience, why is everyone so useless? Vicent asked himself. He was the only one who was working. While the President was on a yacht off Valencia opening bottles of champagne, his wife sewing, his daughter wasting time and his administrator missing in action, he was the one who had to get everyone off the hook. Fortunately the day was drawing to a close. He would call Eva and then take a hot bath, although to do that he'd have to get into the tank itself.

Vicent put out his cigarette, poured himself more whisky and paced up and down the room as he called Eva, who hadn't turned up in the Town Hall all day. In the secretariat they'd told him she was ill.

After more than a dozen rings, the young woman eventually answered.

'May I ask where you've got to?' he said straight off.

In a tiny voice Eva replied:

'I don't feel well, I've been having some terrible headaches.'

'Okay, but what in heaven's name happened with the transfer on Sunday? I'm told it didn't arrive.'

Eva waited a few seconds and then said:

'I couldn't do it, Mr Mayor.'

'Why not?'

'The software wouldn't let me.'

'But didn't you tell me that you'd redo the budget so it would work?'

'Yes, but I couldn't.'

'Why not?' Vicent heard Eva swallow hard three times. 'Tell me why not,' he said in a loud, commanding voice as he stretched his neck forward. Eva remained silent for a few seconds. 'Your Mayor is waiting for an answer!' he shouted, putting his whisky down on the table so sharply that a few drops spilled over on to the wood.

'Vicent, that transfer has not been approved and I cannot alter the council budget just like that.'

'Just like that? But it was your Mayor asking you, isn't that enough?' exclaimed Vicent with his eyes as big as saucers, staring into space.

'I'm sorry, Vicent, I'm sorry if I caused you any problems, but please, don't ask me to do things I'm not authorised to do.'

'I'm asking you to carry out this transfer for Morella. This investment is crucial for the future of Castellón, for the whole Region, it's the number one project for the President himself. Do you think this isn't right for Morella, eh?'

'I'm sorry, Mr Mayor, I'm sure you're right,' Eva replied in a quiet, trembling voice. 'But I'm only an employee and I don't talk with people at your level. I'm just paid to do my job, and I have to stick to the rules.'

'Well, I make the rules and I'm asking you once and for all to carry out this operation tomorrow, on the basis that we spoke about, and then I want you to tell me that you've done it,' he said in an authoritarian tone.

There was a long pause before Eva replied, while Vicent looked at the fire in the fireplace, finishing off his whisky.

Finally, Eva said: 'I can't.'

'What do you mean you can't?' retorted Vicent, more surprised than angry. Who did this wretched girl think she was?

'It's a lot of money, Mr Mayor,' Eva went on. 'Besides, every day a supplier asks for payment and I don't know what to say to them anymore. The past few months have been complicated.'

'Well, tell them if they want to sell and get paid straight away they should go to the market and sell rabbits!' said Vicent, almost shouting again. 'This is the local government here and everyone knows that you have to be patient; that's what we pay them generously for. I just can't believe it.'

They both remained silent for a few moments, exhausted by the tension that had mounted up since Sunday night.

'Please don't ask me,' Eva begged.

'But do you think you can deny your Mayor?'

'I know I can't.'

'Do you want to be able to pay the mortgage for the nice little apartment you've just bought with your fiancé, eh?' he snapped.

'I don't understand what you mean, Mr Mayor.'

'You understand perfectly well, Eva, you're not ten years old. This is a delicate situation and we need sound people who are committed to the town. People who can be trusted, like I thought you could be.'

'I'd prefer to keep out of it if possible.'

Vicent's patience was beginning to run out.

'Don't make me waste my time. You know very well that you're the only one who can make that transfer. If you don't come to the Town Hall tomorrow and bring me a copy of the transaction, I shall have to take steps,' he threatened, with more anger than thought.

After a brief pause, Eva asked in a very fearful voice:

'What steps?'

Vicent didn't stop to think about his reply for a second.

'Do you remember how easy it was for you to get the job of administrator in Morella? Fifty thousand euros a year for working nine till three in your home town, everything straightforward and without any competition or need to do the competitive tests, or maybe you don't remember?'

Eva didn't say anything.

'I always thought you were the right person,' Vicent went on. 'I knew that you'd always worked well in the hotel, you were honest and you didn't mind staying to do some more cleaning if necessary. I took you out of there to give you a nice job, didn't I?'

Eva finally replied:

'Yes, Mr Mayor, and I shall always be grateful to you for that.'

'In order to appoint you I had to pull a few strings, since the rules were against hiring someone for this job who hadn't done the competitive tests. But I managed to make it possible, because otherwise you'd have had to compete with heaven knows how many people and someone better than you was bound to have turned up.' Eva said nothing. You couldn't even hear her breathing. 'I know you like the work, and of course you've always done a good job, and you need to carry on doing so right now.' Vicent paused for a few seconds. He was nervous and didn't like threatening anyone, but he couldn't let Roig down. 'I imagine you'll have a bigger mortgage with the apartment you've just bought and I don't suppose your bricklayer fiancé will be able to pay it by himself, so if you don't want any worries, if I were you I'd make that transfer tomorrow.'

'And if not?'

'If not I shall feel obliged to arrange the competitive tests for your post and choose someone else.'

Vicent held his breath for a few seconds while he waited for a response. In any event he was sure that his strategy would work because Eva's parents were humble folk and the girl needed her salary. He knew that she had nowhere to go. As he knew from his own experience, that would force her to accept it.

Eva took her time before answering, but eventually she did so and took Vicent by surprise.

'I could explain that I was asked to transfer a million without any authorisation on the part of the full Council.'

'Well, that's up to you,' he replied. 'All I'd have to do is refer to Roig, and then see who in the Town Hall dares to confront the President of the Region of Valencia, who is a good friend of the Prime Minister.'

The two of them fell silent. With his sleeve Vicent wiped the beads of cold sweat that were running down his forehead. He almost dropped the phone from his sweaty hands. He had become Mayor in order to inaugurate walkways and swimming pools, to get out of the hotel and rub shoulders with the powerful, but also to leave the town a better place – but not to deliver bitter blows like this. Deep down he thought highly of Eva. She'd always been loyal ever since he hired her in the hotel to do the rooms when she returned from Valencia without a job and with her Business Studies degree behind her. She was a good-looking girl and recently she had got together with her fiancé, a bricklayer or decorator, with high hopes for the future. This was a difficult ordeal for her, of course, but for him, too.

'Eva, the best thing is for you to give me the confirmation tomorrow, and we'll forget about the whole thing, as well as this conversation, which is not pleasant for either of us.'

'It's really horrible, I never thought I'd be speaking with you like this,' said the young woman, now talking between sobs.

Vicent felt a stab in his chest. He didn't want to hurt anyone, but he needed the airport in order to sell the school. Without the school the hole in the council budget would engulf them all. He had to be resolute.

'Eva, my dear, let's put an end to this unpleasant episode and don't make me do things I don't want to do,' he said, as if he were trying to arouse her sympathy.

'Would you really arrange the competitive tests for my post?' she asked slowly, finding it hard to utter each word.

'I hope you won't make me do that.'

Vicent sighed noisily and without trying to hide it. He, too, had feelings.

'Okay, it'll be ready tomorrow,' Eva said finally.

Vicent took a deep breath, relaxed his shoulders and eased his grip on his mobile.

'That's what I like to hear, Eva,' he said. 'You can be sure that your loyalty will be rewarded.'

Eva ended the call without replying.

10

The last time a helicopter had landed in Morella was more than a year earlier, when an elderly man in the town needed an urgent liver transplant and they took him to a hospital in Barcelona, Valli explained to Charles while they waited in the small heliport.

They were standing next to the poplars behind the second arches – a marvel of medieval architecture still more or less intact that was built to bring water to the town– as they waited for the arrival of one of Charles' students. He had organised a trip to Morella with eight students to see whether it was a suitable place for them and also to find out what the townspeople made of them. He had liked the school in principle, but there would be no point buying a building so they could improve their knowledge of the language and the culture if the town was not receptive to the visitors.

Apart from James, who was about to arrive, the group had been in Morella for two days, staying at the hotel. As they had chosen the English half-term holidays, the hotel was almost empty and Isabel let them use the dining room to hold talks or Spanish language and culture classes. The select group of Etonians had already had a visit from the Mayor, the local historian and a well-known chef who, of course then invited them to eat at his restaurant. The boys were used to nothing less.

Some Etonians were fabulously rich, which is why they were sometimes allowed certain privileges. On this occasion James, whose arrival they were now awaiting, had been absent from the college the whole of the previous week in order to go on holiday with his family to Dubai. Initially Charles had refused to allow the student to arrive late in Morella, but the Principal of the college had overruled him since the student's father made substantial donations to the institution. Charles, however, preferred to impose greater discipline and didn't want the students to get used to seeing the world revolve around them; instead they were the ones who needed to adapt to the world, he said.

But in the end James and his family had had their way, and the boy, who was captain of the college's first rowing crew, was arriving in the special helicopter that his father had hired for him.

'I can't believe that they'd organise such an operation for a seventeen-year-old spoiled brat,' said Valli to herself and hoping that Charles wouldn't hear what she said.

Wearing a headscarf to protect herself from the wind, Valli surveyed the scene expectantly, scouring the sky in search of the helicopter. Two council workers were waiting as well, wearing high-vis jackets and holding fluorescent batons to assist with the landing. Valli looked at them suspiciously.

Charles, elegant and straight-backed as usual, with his lightweight Burberry raincoat and a pair of smart suede shoes, studied her carefully. Out of the corner of his eye he noticed how Valli had looked at his shoes with unusual interest. She was wearing some old walking boots, which surprised Charles as he didn't imagine she went mountaineering. But today he had to be nice to this extraordinary woman who had agreed to help him with the academic activity that he had organised. Initially her agreement had surprised him, after she had accused him of being classist and called his students "lords" when they had met in Colón Square.

'Thanks for coming with me, I'm sure it'll be a great day,' said Charles with conviction. Although travelling with teenagers can be a pain, the older the boys the better things work out. For that reason Charles had selected eight students from the senior school who also represented a series of different interests. Some were very academic and others were good sportsmen, but they all shared an interest and good skills in the Spanish language.

Valli, with her hands in her thick woollen jacket, looked at him with her penetrating dark eyes.

'I imagine it will be good for the people of Morella to practise their English a little, for we certainly need to,' she responded.

'Exchange always works,' Charles noted, conscious that a good part of British colonial wealth rested on this principle.

Valli did not reply and the pair said nothing until, eventually, they heard a noise that after a few moments grew and became deafening as the enormous helicopter approached. In a matter of seconds there was a huge downdraught that obliged Charles to take Valli by the arm and move them both further away. The council workers stood their ground as best they could and vigorously waved their fluorescent batons. Valli and Charles ended up behind a tree, protecting their ears from the noise and the strong wind that almost removed Valli's scarf and gave Charles a coughing fit.

After a couple of seemingly very long minutes the noise stopped. It had been a long time since Charles had collected a student from a heliport, although it wasn't the first. In England where distances are shorter he was more accustomed to seeing his students arrive at the college in a Rolls Royce.

It was a few minutes before the enormous rotor blades came to halt, during which time Valli and Charles came out from their position behind the tree and slowly approached the intimidating machine, which looked disproportionly big for the three people who were in it.

The door finally opened and James, in his unmistakeable Doc Martins, placed his foot on the steps. The son of the owner of an investment bank in the City, he was wearing a pair of torn jeans, Beckham-style, a pure cashmere jumper and carrying a leather bag in his hand. His blond hair, long at the front and short at the back, was blowing about in the wind. With a firm step, like Obama entering or leaving the White House, the young man went straight over to his schoolmaster, without the trace of a smile.

'Hello, Sir,' he said. 'Ma'am', he said by way of greeting Valli, bowing his head as if he were greeting a member of the royal family.

Charles introduced him to the old schoolteacher, who remained silent during the short journey from the heliport to the local school, where they were about to start the game of football that had been organised between the two schools. The Etonians had always been best at rugby or rowing, but in Morella the most popular sport was undoubtedly football, so Charles had to give way.

Charles drove the mini-bus that he had hired in Valencia for the whole group and in a few minutes they reached the local school, just at the beginning of the Alameda.

'This is the school?' asked James. 'Isn't it modern!'

'Of course it's modern,' Valli quickly replied. 'It was only built about ten years ago. It won some very prestigious architectural awards,' she explained proudly.

James raised an eyebrow, and still looking out the window he said:

'Well, I'd never heard of this school before.'

Charles didn't want any tension during the encounter, neither between his students and the local ones, nor with Valli. The mysterious lady was opposed to the sale of the school, and although Vicent said she was harmless, he wasn't entirely sure. He had partly organised the day in order to get closer to her; he had the feeling that it was better to have her onside.

'Come on, James. If you don't know the school now, you're never going to forget it, because we're going to spend a marvellous few days here,' said Charles as he brought the vehicle to a stop and climbed out. The others followed suit.

Valli looked the boy up and down, noting especially his scruffy, torn jeans, which he wore very low, revealing the top of his underpants. She shook her head and furrowed her brow, as if she didn't understand that fashion. She was convinced it wasn't a case of being careless.

Although James had never been there before, he moved decisively to the main door and pushed it right open. Valli and Charles followed.

'Tell me,' Valli said to Charles in a soft voice, 'why do your students go around showing their underpants?'

Charles gave a brief, discreet laugh. Turning to her, he whispered:

'They think it'll help them to pick up girls.'

Valli smiled. At last. Charles saw that gesture as his first victory. The day was starting well.

As there were only eight of them the English boys had to add three students from the town, also aged seventeen or eighteen, to their team. When they got to the ground with its artificial turf which was in excellent condition, Charles saw his students standing in a group and hardly talking to the Morella team who, to his surprise, were mixed. It was always hard to break the ice, Charles said to himself, checking that everything was ready as planned. On the table between the two benches, Charles looked at the cup and the row of medals that he'd ordered to mark the occasion. The referee for the match, the teacher of English in Morella – who was from Alicante – was dressed in black and headed over to Charles as soon as he saw him,

'*Buenos días*, Charles,' he said. 'Has the last one turned up?'

'Good morning,' Charles replied, giving him a friendly, sporting handshake. 'He's getting changed and he'll be with us in a second.'

'Well, we've got a slight problem,' said the referee. 'Nothing serious, but the Morella team has always played this sort of friendly game as a mixed team and your students are saying they only want boys in theirs.' The English teacher looked at the ground. 'If we want to avoid the girls getting angry, and justifiably so, I'm afraid your students will have to accept three Morella girls, who will certainly be excellent players,' he added.

Charles looked at the local team, which was well balanced between boys and girls, who certainly looked like good athletes. The Morella team, who were on the short side and dark-skinned, were practising taking shots at their goalkeeper, while on the other side, his seven Etonians, white, tall and thin, were standing in a small huddle.

'Don't worry, I'll sort it,' said Charles to the referee. 'The college is all-male and they're just not used to it. I'll talk to them, I'm sure they'll understand.'

Charles went quickly over to his students, who listened to him with their arms folded, but without complaining.

'Come on, lads, act like men,' he urged them.

'The girls will make us lose,' said Harry, the smallest of the group but looking very fit as he was the national fencing champion for his age-group.

'Why haven't they got a grass pitch instead of this artificial carpet?' came the complaint from William, who had recently been selected to play in the English Under-eighteen rugby team.

Charles looked them in the eye, one by one.

'Come on now, lads,' he said. 'You know that countries are different. They haven't got a grass pitch, but look at the sky and you'll see why. Less complaining now, and let's play.'

'And what about the girls?' Harry persisted. This red-head never gave up a fight as lost.

Charles would like to have given them a lesson about equality. In fact he was sure that some of the Morella girls would outplay his Etonians at football. But that was a longer and more profound conversation, so he chose to convince them by the rapid route.

'These girls are excellent athletes and nice young women,' he said, casting the bait. 'This evening, after the conversation exchange, we could invite them to have a beer in the bar before dinner if you like, and the boys as well, of course.'

The Etonians looked at each other. The tallest and most athletic one, Thomas, immediately agreed.

'Sounds good!' he said, and the matter was resolved.

With a crowd consisting mainly of old men who, with berets in hand, were watching them from the Alameda, the referee blew his whistle for the kick-off. Straight away the Morella players ran like rabbits after the ball, while the English, now looking pink from the sun, looked upon the scene with an air of superiority. It wasn't long before the first goal was scored. Charles, like his students, looked on with surprise at the extent of the Morellans' celebrations, given that it was a friendly game. He tried to spur on his players with a few claps of his hands from the touchline, but they barely had any effect.

The Morella girls on the visiting team began to chivvy their new teammates, shouting at them and asking for the ball. The three girls, who had played a lot of games before, had been holding back during the first few minutes but now seemed to be getting tired of the fact that no-one was passing the ball to them.

Segregated education had its limitations, and this was certainly one of them, thought Charles. He knew that although Eton produced fully developed men ready for the world, many of them, including himself, didn't feel totally comfortable in female company, especially in certain circumstances, including playing football.

In any event what he was most concerned about was that his boys should improve their Spanish, get good marks in their 'A' Levels and get into the best universities. That was his task; each of them could solve his own women problems, he thought.

The locals were now four goals in front at half-time when Charles had to give his first pep talk as a football coach in his life. Neither he nor his students were too bothered about that particular sport. In any case he didn't have to try too hard, because the Morella girls in his team dominated the discussion.

'We've got to press harder and play like a team if we want to get into the game,' said one resolutely.

None of the Etonians responded; only her two companions supported her. The English players continued to ignore them and started to swap jokes, speaking very quickly in a deliberately clipped English. Charles reprimanded them straight away, especially for making fun of the local number nine, a tall dark lad with particularly tight shorts, which is why they called him "twink". Such comments produced lots of laughter among the eight English students, who spent a lot of time looking at the ground as if they felt uncomfortable, while the three Morella girls looked at each other without understanding a word.

'That's enough, please,' said Charles in a soft voice, more appropriate to a library than a football bench.

Finally Arthur, one of the brightest students, found the answer.

'Guys,' he said. 'The Morella chaps just run like bulls, so we've got to fight them like bulls!' he exclaimed, to the cheers of his companions and the amazement of the girls. 'We're much smarter than them,' he went on, 'so we're going to make use of our speed. You, María,' he said, looking at one of the girls, who immediately cut him short.

'My name is Anabel,' she said.

'*Disculpa*,' Arthur said immediately with an artificial smile, before going on. 'Anabel, I think you'd be an excellent goalie in the second half. When you get the ball, pass it to me, I'll come back to fetch it. As I'm very fast, I'll do a long pass to James, who's a good forward, and that way we can cut out their mid-field, who are good at putting the boot in. Dirty lot,' he said disparagingly. 'And that's how we'll beat them.'

Charles listened to this conversation with amusement, because he had no idea about football, but at least his students were practising the language.

Anabel stared at Arthur.

'I've never played goalie in my life.'

Arthur smiled at her again chivalrously.

'But I know you have a lot of potential,' he said.

'And what do you know about it?' the girl rapped out.

Arthur looked at her, lowered his head and said:

'You've got lovely hands.'

The three girls turned to stone at this comment, which made the other seven boys look this way and that, trying not to laugh.

One of the Morella girls stood up to him.

'Why aren't you the goalie? With your head and those big ears you've got, you'll be able to stop a lot of shots.'

The whole group laughed, taking some of the tension out of the discussion. Charles had to mediate and chose the goalkeeper in a quick drawing of lots, which James won.

Feeling more confident now that she'd avoided being the goalie, Anabel persisted:

'But do you think that you're going to score with only two passes, without doing a bit more running and putting more effort into the game?'

Arthur looked at her with an air of superiority.

'Effort is for those who can't think,' he replied with a smile and a sense of self-assurance.

The second half went the same way, with the girls playing for Eton not getting a touch of the ball and the English team losing seven-nil. As Charles suspected would be the case, James only lasted five minutes in goal, since he managed to persuade George, the weedy one of the group, to take over. Probably in exchange for a small bribe, thought Charles.

After the awarding of the cup and the medals, they all sat down to eat at a large table in the yard provided by the school, where the cooks served them up a tasty paella. On the barbecue at the back of the yard they were roasting lamb cutlets that some of the vegetarian Etonians looked at with disgust.

'Don't you think that eating meat is a crime against the animals?' Arthur asked the boy from Morella sitting next to him. Charles had insisted on mixed seating so that they mingled, something that, from what he could see, wasn't happening by itself.

The Morella boy looked surprised and said:

'Yes, it's bad for the lamb, of course. But if you've nothing else, what do you eat?'

Arthur looked at him just as surprised.

'What do you mean if you've nothing else?' he asked.

They both carried on eating in silence.

Next to Charles, Samuel, the official hippy of the group, was trying to make conversation with Anabel, who was now looking very pretty and smart after her shower. She explained excitedly her plans to apply for a grant to study Veterinary Science in London.

'And what do you plan to do?' asked Anabel, looking curiously at what Samuel was wearing.

Samuel, who was the son of the family that owned one of the largest construction companies in England, was wearing a large, white Ibiza-style sports shirt that came down to his knees. On his feet he had a pair of Lacoste canvas shoes.

Sam looked skywards and stroked his blond hair, delaying his response as usual. The bucolic poet, as he liked to describe himself, knew that he would never have to work if he chose not to.

'I don't know if work, as viewed by our society, is something that interests me,' he said finally.

Anabel put the cutlet that she was about to eat back on her plate. As Charles surveyed the scene he noticed how his boys ate their cutlets with a knife and fork, something that hadn't occurred to any of the Morella people. This was the exchange of customs that he wanted his students to experience, as they were very much in need of seeing what the world was like outside of their own bubble.

Anabel, looking straight at Sam, replied:

'And what are you going to do if you don't work. I don't know anyone who doesn't work by choice. Here, the people who don't work are the unemployed.'

'That's interesting,' said Sam. 'Is there really no-one who doesn't work because of their personal philosophy?'

Anabel and her two friends sitting near her burst into laughter, which made Sam feel uncomfortable and thereafter he had nothing more to do with them. The girls didn't seem too bothered.

The conversation on the other side of the table wasn't going much better, either, from what Charles could hear. Out of politeness James was exchanging impressions with the local team's number nine, which provoked all sorts of kicks under the table and the odd serviette with the word "twink" written on it and sent in his direction. As soon as he could, James swapped places and sat next to Arthur. And between the two of them, and feeling more comfortable because they had each other's company, they struck up conversation with Ivana and Marta, the other two girls from their team. They asked them what countries they had visited, and without concealing their surprise, discovered that they'd only been to the south of France. For them that was just on the other side of the Pyrenees and not on the glamourous Cote d'Azur, where James' parents had a house with a private beach, as he explained.

The girls looked at the two boys with a degree of admiration, no doubt attracted by their blond hair and their clothes, thought Charles. He imagined that the girls would not have seen such frayed jeans and tee-shirts with large letters on them other than on Beckham or some other footballer. He had observed that his students were a more advanced version of the typical Spanish rich kids still obsessed with showing off their Lacoste crocodile logo and other similar brands. On the other hand, the British upper class went more for design than for labels. Although essentially it came down to the same thing: fashion, thought Charles disparagingly.

Arthur and James seemed quite delighted by the attention from the girls, as Charles couldn't help noticing. But it seemed pretty normal and he wasn't too worried about it. At the end of the day they were young chaps immersed in a totally masculine world and it was normal for them to do some flirting on an occasion such as this. There was nothing to worry about, since they were staying in the hotel, there were only eight of them and they were in a small town in which they were easily manageable.

Charles, sitting in the centre of the table, decided to have a coffee along with Valli, who had chosen to sit in the corner and from there hadn't missed a word of the conversations around her.

'Señora Vallivana, I imagine you're happy about Morella's victory?' Charles asked Valli politely after changing places with Samuel.

Valli gave him a long, hard look.

'What's wrong with your boys?' she asked. 'And what do they think they can learn here? It seems as though they know it all, and they're disappointed that we haven't got rowing facilities or ten tennis courts.'

'Is that what they've said?'

'The one from the helicopter did.'

Charles looked at James, still fully engaged in his efforts at flirting.

'Don't take him too seriously,' he replied. 'Like all of them, he's learning that the world is bigger than he thinks. This experience will certainly help him in that direction.'

Valli sighed, unconvinced.

'And what's this exchange going to do for *us*?' she asked.

Charles looked around the table of twenty people. Despite their great differences, the two groups seemed to have struck up an earnest conversation. So far everything had gone according to plan. Turning to Valli, he responded:

'Give them some time, Valli, and you'll see that they're really nice people. They're just boys at a difficult age and some of them have parents who've sent them to boarding school because basically they want to get rid of them. Many of them have money, that's true, but you know as well as I do that that doesn't automatically make them happy.'

Valli nodded, although she added:

'I understand what you're saying, Charles, but I don't feel sorry for them.'

A half-smile came across his lips.

'Come on, let's get on with our day, because so far it's working out just fine,' said Charles getting up. 'It's time for their guided walk, and we're all looking forward to it.'

Charles rounded up his group, who said goodbye to their Morella guests, especially to the girls, who they arranged to meet in a bar in town before dinner, with Charles' permission. As far as the boys were concerned, they said goodbye to them in an unexpectedly friendly tone after having ignored them for the whole day. This sudden change of attitude surprised the local boys, Charles noticed. It was the English coldness, which was so useful for getting out of any situation without getting your hands dirty, Charles thought – with a certain amount of guilt, because he too had had recourse to it when he'd needed to.

Having said thank you with impeccable manners for the paella and the cutlets, the group slowly followed Valli, who took them up the hill to the Fontanella, a small fountain at the entrance to a natural cave, not far from the school in the part behind the mountain. It only took them ten minutes to get there.

Puffing and panting, Valli observed the look of surprise on the boys' faces when they saw the beautiful grotto. Charles didn't know that the walk was going to start there, and he wasn't totally impressed, because it was an ideal hiding place for teenagers and he didn't want to give them any ideas. He thought that Valli had prepared a route that would follow the path taken by George Orwell through the town, although he was sure that that would be where she would take them after the grotto.

'It is said,' Valli began, 'that Orwell hid in this cave during one of the bombardments that Morella suffered in 1938. He had come here with the International Brigades, which helped the Republicans so much in the Battle of the Ebro, which took place not very far from here, just a couple of days away on foot. His division had a camp in Morella until Franco decided to cut the Republican zone in two and reach the sea after crossing the Maestrazgo. As part of that objective they bombed the area and destroyed some of the surrounding towns and villages.'

Leaning on her stick and with a scarf on her head, Valli went into the cave followed by the English students, who were listening to her carefully.

'In those days I was a trainee teacher in the school,' she told them. 'When we were in the school and we heard the sirens, I took the older ones and we ran here, where we felt safe.'

'At least,' she went on after a brief pause, 'we never went hungry, because around here we could always catch rabbits and cook them on an open fire, and we had water from the fountain. To freshen up our clothes we used to use lavender, which as you can see is plentiful around here.'

Two of the boys each went and picked a bunch and gave it to Valli.

'Our Spanish club on Tuesday evenings is called the Lavender Club,' said Harry.

Valli was surprised.

'Really? And who gave it that name?' she asked, smelling the lavender that she had been given.

The boys looked at each other and shrugged their shoulders.

'It would be interesting to find out,' remarked Charles. 'It might have been Orwell himself, an old boy of the college who often came to the Spanish club.'

Valli went out of the cave to continue with the tour which she had prepared so carefully and which the boys really appreciated, giving her a small plaque with the Republican flag on it to remind her of the occasion. Valli was very grateful for the thought, and despite the great differences that separated them, she said goodbye to the group with a kiss for each of them.

Charles could not have asked for more.

In his white silk pyjamas Charles eventually closed his eyes after midnight, lying on his bed and listening once more to the now familiar squeaking of the bed base in room fourteen. The activity of the day had made him forget for a second that when he lay down on the bed he would roll into the middle and he would need to keep still if he wanted to avoid the irritating noise. He stayed still, face up, and took several slow, deep breaths in order to settle himself after everything that had happened during the day.

The most important thing was that relations with Valli had improved considerably. What a tough woman, Charles thought, reminding himself that she was nearly ninety years old and feeling rather guilty at all the running around they had given her to do. Back at the hotel and rather anxious at how tired Valli was by the end, Isabel, as kind as ever, had calmed him down, reassuring him that that woman was frankly indestructible.

He was thinking these thoughts when suddenly he heard footsteps on the stairs. Listening carefully he could make out more than two people climbing up to the next floor with, by the sound of it, several bottles in hand. Well, he said to himself, it was to be expected that his boys would bring in some alcohol. He couldn't forbid it and, of course, when he was their age he had done exactly the same. Seconds later he heard voices in the room just above his, which was occupied by James, who had doubtless become the leader of the group as he was tall, blond and rich. That's the way the world worked, like it or not. That boy had everything going for him, but Charles wondered what would eventually become of him, because despite all the possibilities and opportunities that were open to him, very often he got stuck trying to decide which one to choose.

Charles' window was open and so he could hear perfectly well some of the boys leaning out the window upstairs. It was the end of May and a warm night and so naturally the boys had crowded around the window ledge in James' room to smoke. Charles could hear them passing the cigarettes from one to the other and asking for the lighter.

He sighed. Nothing was going on that he wouldn't have done himself, so he had to be patient and try to get some sleep. In spite of the low voices he could hear, he was just dozing off when, once again, he could hear footsteps going upstairs, although this time they were more stealthy. He opened an eye and raised an eyebrow, feeling both curious and responsible. Following two gentle taps on the door above, it was opened and the boys started to greet someone effusively. He quickly realised that he could hear two female voices.

Charles closed his eyes and sighed. It was now no longer a question of cigarettes and booze. But how could he get those girls out of that room? And what if they only came to talk? He decided to wait to see if he heard any more voices before doing anything. At that age his students, tall and handsome as they were, felt they were infallible, so to spend the night with girls was to some extent normal.

In fact their behaviour with Valli during the whole day had been exemplary. Polite and attentive, they had listened to what she had to say with interest, asking some good questions and, of course, always treating her with respect. The boys attended the best college in the world, they were his students, and so he had to trust them.

Besides, Isabel was also asleep in the hotel, in a room on the third floor at the top, which must enjoy some spectacular views, he imagined. The Mayor's daughter had been fantastically good with them. When they arrived all the rooms were ready and allocated, and the breakfasts, lunches and dinners had, incredibly, not aroused a single complaint. She sorted everything out with her brother, who didn't actually seem to do very much.

Charles heard two people return to the window upstairs to have a smoke. He lifted his head a little so as to hear better, and was now able to make out the voices of Anabel and James chatting away. He was saying that at the end of the year he was going to take a year out to travel round the world, but he had to explain to his new friend the concept of a year out before going to university, something that Anabel confirmed she had never heard of. While James ran through the list of places that he planned to visit – San Francisco, Sydney, Buenos Aires, Havana, Delhi, Beijing, and so on – Anabel made expressions of surprise at each one.

Charles knew that his students were very privileged and thought that encounters such as these would make them see a little better what kind of world they were living in. Feeling that a conversation about travel and plans, a few cigarettes and drinks didn't need to be taken too seriously, he closed his eyes once more and lay back down again. He recalled the impressive sky that he'd been looking at a few hours earlier from the castle which was beautifully lit up. Isabel had helped them to organise a night visit with a well-known local historian who, lantern in hand, had told them some fascinating medieval tales. The Mayor's daughter went with them, because she didn't want to miss it, and they had all enormously enjoyed the unusual visit, perhaps the best that he'd ever made to a castle or museum of the hundreds that he'd seen around the world.

Immersed in these pleasant memories, Charles gradually fell asleep. He didn't know how much time had passed, whether it was five minutes or three hours, but a terrific noise woke him up and immediately he jumped out of bed. He heard laughter from the floor upstairs and then remembered the party he had been listening to earlier and looked at the clock: it was ten past three in the morning. A loud male voice – he couldn't tell who it was but it was definitely an English one – boomed downstairs, followed by the crash of a door slamming. Charles was on his feet but struck dumb, listening to what sounded like a cavalry charge come up the stairs and start to pound wildly on several doors. He was just about to go out when a great crash of broken glass was followed by an enormous thud. Charles heard more laughter, a few bumps and the opening and closing of several doors.

He hurriedly put on his red velvet dressing gown and shot up the stairs, where he found the door to James' room wide open. Inside Anabel and another friend, whom Charles hadn't seen before, were lying on the bed half naked and fast asleep, one on top of the other. The windows had been shattered and were now lying on the floor.

Charles took the girls' pulse; they scarcely moved, but he was relieved to establish that they were only asleep. Back in the corridor he looked left and right. All the doors to the rooms on the second floor occupied by his students were shut and there was a highly suspicious total silence.

Until, that was, he heard laughter once more and what sounded like someone throwing up, this time on the third floor. In a fury Charles went upstairs and there in the middle of the corridor he found James and Harry, shirtless, stretched out on the floor, bottle in hand and laughing and looking goggle-eyed.

'Hi!' said James, before hiding his head under his arm.

Harry threw up once more.

They were both totally stoned.

The door of the room at the end slowly opened. Wearing an elegant white dressing gown, Isabel stepped out into the corridor and picked up two football boots that had been thrown violently at her door. Looking straight ahead she walked smartly towards Charles and the two students and without saying a word threw them at Charles' feet, looking all the while at Harry and James with goggle-eyes just like theirs. Charles was still in a state of shock but couldn't help noticing Isabel's long dark hair, which previously he had only seen tied back.

'What on earth is going on here?' she asked, serious and imposing.

Isabel looked at the two boys again, with so much contempt that the most snobbish English person would have looked like a novice in comparison.

Eventually Charles reacted.

'Isabel, I don't know how to apologise.'

'Do something,' she ordered, scarcely batting an eyelid, with her gaze fixed on the two young men.

Charles had previously had to deal with young people who were stoned and knew that the best way was not to make an immediate fuss, since this could prompt some kind of attack.

First he took hold of James and dragged him as best he could downstairs to his room and sat him in a chair as the two girls were still on the bed just as he had left them. On the table he saw the white powder that they must have taken. He went over and confirmed that it was cocaine. He sighed, took a tissue from the bathroom to wipe up the rest of the substance and threw it down the toilet. Without further ado he flushed it away.

Charles went back for Harry who was lying next to whatever he had brought up of his dinner. It stank, but Charles, still under Isabel's watchful eye, took Harry back to his room next to James', which was still open. Isabel followed him down to the second floor.

'There are two girls from the town in James' room; they need to be got home,' said Charles, feeling more ashamed than he had done for many years.

Still with her inquisitorial gaze, Isabel went into James' room and put her hand to her mouth as she saw how things were.

'Good heavens, what on earth…?' she exclaimed. She immediately went over to the girls and in turn took their pulse on their wrist. After a few seconds she breathed a sigh of relief. 'Thank heavens!'

Charles went over to her.

'Isabel, this is awful and I don't know how to apologise. I can only assure you that we shall of course compensate you for whatever damage has been caused, which looks to me as though it's quite substantial.'

Isabel examined the room with her huge green eyes that looked bigger than ever. The glass crunched beneath her slippers when she went to close the half-broken window.

She turned to Charles and with surprising speed and control she said:

'I'll go and fetch some buckets and mops. Tell the other students that they are to wash and clean up this mess straight away, and also of course leave the third floor just as they originally found it. Meanwhile I shall get dressed and take these girls home, as their mothers will be extremely anxious. They will need an explanation and for the time being it's better for me to take care of that.'

That seemed like a good idea to Charles and he agreed. Not that he had any choice; that was a moment to do as he was told.

Isabel ran downstairs and in less than a minute she was back with a number of cleaning buckets and rubbish bags that she left outside James' room. With barely a glance at Charles she disappeared upstairs.

Charles started to hammer on the students' doors and thought that only George and Arthur seemed to be waking from a genuine sleep. The others had all the appearance of having hastily hidden in their rooms when they heard him coming upstairs.

Charles was tempted to yell at his students, except for George and Arthur, although it was better not to be hasty. At that moment he needed to focus his energies on clearing up and making sure that the ones who had taken drugs didn't get any worse. In the morning he would evaluate the situation more calmly and coolly. But, of course, that sort of behaviour would have consequences.

One by one Charles ordered his students to get down to it at once and the two who protested, saying they didn't know how to clean because they'd never done it before, were on the receiving end of genuine looks of hatred. Samuel said that if there was any damage they'd pay for it between them, and he didn't see why he should be cleaning up at four o'clock in the morning. Charles made him clean up his friend's vomit.

With her coat and boots on, Isabel made her way along the corridor between the English youths, some of them still drunk but all of them holding some form of cleaning implement.

'I want this spotless when I come back,' she said looking them coldly in the eyes one by one. It sent a shiver down Charles' spine.

Isabel asked Charles to help her to get the two girls downstairs to the car in the garage. As they set to it the two adults breathed a sigh of relief as Anabel opened an eye, only to close it again straight away; at least it was a sign that she was conscious. As best as they could, they got the two girls to the garage and Isabel set off, still in the darkness of the early hours, to take them home. Charles couldn't find the words to apologise again.

When Isabel returned after about an hour, the hotel was clean, there was no sign of vomit or alcohol on the floor and the doors to all the rooms were shut. As she reached the second floor Charles heard her footsteps and immediately went to see her. It was now almost five in the morning and the first light of dawn was coming in through the windows of the corridor that looked on to the street.

'Everything okay?' he asked.

Isabel gave him a sad, tired look.

'As okay as it can be in the circumstances,' she said. 'At least the girls woke up in the car; I gave them some Aqua Libra and it perked them up a bit. Fortunately before I got them home they remembered their names, addresses and where they'd been. They told me it was James who'd given them the drugs…'

'Cocaine,' said Charles.

Isabel raised an eyebrow, pursed her lips and after a few seconds, said:

'They also told me that they had not been forced to do anything.'

Charles took in a deep breath and let it out slowly with a sense of relief.

Isabel looked up to the heavens.

'What's going to happen to today's young people?'

Charles looked at the Mayor's daughter intently. He didn't know what to say.

'You don't know how ashamed we are about all this, Isabel. But you can be sure that we will fully compensate you for the breakages and for the night we have given you.'

The two of them remained silent for a few moments.

'The girls' mothers were still up waiting for them,' said Isabel. 'I told them they'd been drinking more than they should and that's it. But I think you should go and give them an explanation tomorrow.'

'Of course,' Charles agreed. 'I'll do whatever is necessary and I'll also see to it that these girls receive some sort of compensation.'

'That's not what it's about,' said Isabel. 'Humiliation has no price.'

'I know, I know. I'm sorry.'

Isabel looked around to check that everything had been cleaned up.

'Is the blond boy's room okay? Has the glass been picked up?'

'Yes,' Charles replied. 'The bags of rubbish are in the bin on the other side of the street and the boy is fast asleep, although without any glass in his windows.'

'A bit of fresh air might do him some good,' said Isabel, finally introducing a bit of humour into a rather tense situation.

Charles didn't dare smile.

'He's the ringleader, isn't he?' asked Isabel. 'Wasn't he the one in the helicopter?'

Charles nodded. Isabel looked at the floor.

'I don't know what you want me to say. In this town young people don't go anywhere by helicopter, but I don't think they have as many vices,' she said.

Charles nodded.

'There's no doubt that the people of Morella have set us an example today.'

'But these boys of yours, Charles, they've got it all. Why do they squander it like that?'

Charles sighed and finally relaxed his shoulders after the tenseness of the night.

'I don't know,' he said. 'Maybe that's the problem, they've got the world at their feet and they don't have to fight for anything.'

He paused for a few seconds.

'This boy, James, is particularly lost,' he confessed, although he wasn't very keen on sharing details about his students. 'His father is one of Britain's most important industrialists and the boy has decided he wants to be an architect. An architect! Of course at the college we're doing everything we can to get such an idea out of his head.'

Isabel looked at him in astonishment.

'And what's wrong with being an architect? In Spain they're highly regarded.'

'Well, in England they're starving,' commented Charles.

'So what does that matter? Precisely because he doesn't need the money, why shouldn't he study what he wants?' asked Isabel directly and with a slight frown.

'Because at Eton we educate in order to produce lawyers and bankers, lucrative professions that enhance the college's reputation,' he said. 'We don't want former students who just eke out a living. It's the college's policy.'

Isabel was taken aback.

'So you don't want students in your college to be happy?' she asked, her eyes bright with vitality.

Charles didn't know what to say in reply.

Without another word Isabel went up to her room and Charles went in to number fourteen, closing the door behind him.

For the first time in a long time he wondered if he was happy.

11

The auditorium in the Young Ladies' Residence in Miguel Ángel Street was now painted in a strong but light Mediterranean blue, but the room itself, high and majestic, remained unchanged. Around the first floor it still had the elegant balustrade in white wood, which was set on a frieze of classical design that gave the room a very stately air. The ceiling had not changed; it was as high as before, and curved gradually until it touched the tops of the walls. The high wooden skirting board and the doors in brilliant white gave an air of distinction and smartness to the place, which retained the same wooden seats that were joined together as in the theatre. The old organ was still next to the main wide entrance door which was also of white wood. The auditorium was designed to seat only about two hundred people, and had therefore kept the same warm and intimate atmosphere as when Valli was studying there.

It was a lovely June evening and Valli watched from the platform as the last members of the audience hurried to their seats, silently and discreetly. They were walking on the same dark flooring over which many others had walked to listen to some eminent person like José Ortega y Gasset or Doctor Gregorio Marañón. Valli would never have thought when she was a resident that one day she would preside over an event in such a special place. Life truly brought surprises, some tragic and other marvellous ones like this, she thought.

The old clock on the wall showed exactly seven thirty in the evening and the murmur of voices began to subside. The room was full to capacity.

Soledad, the Director of the International Institute, who in the past had hired out this very room to the Young Ladies' Residence, gently squeezed Valli's hand and gave her a smile. With her eyes she asked if she was ready, to which Valli nodded. On the other side of Soledad sat Consuelo, another former resident more than ninety years old, who indicated that she, too, was ready.

The three women, elegantly dressed and made-up for the occasion, looked out at the audience in different ways. Consuelo, who seemed tired even before they started, constantly rubbed her hands and fingered the pearl necklace that she was wearing on top of a white high-necked blouse, more appropriate to the period that she had come to talk about. She shifted in her chair and looked swiftly around, although most of the time she stared into space. She appeared uncomfortable, as if she felt out of place. The Director, with a tasteful and elegant sleeveless black dress that matched her wavy hair, smiled with pride at having organised an event that already appeared to be a success. Valli, her hair looking whiter and wavier than ever, wore a navy-blue skirted suit with a bright floral blouse. With her fundraising project in mind, she had chosen to give herself an image of modernity and efficiency rather than an unfashionable old woman to whom no-one would entrust a penny. Aware that all eyes were upon her, Valli remained calm, looking in front of her, radiating a sense of assurance. She had given many lectures and talks about her life in exile and her struggle against Franco in the mountains of Huesca and Teruel. She had visited a number of schools, especially in Catalunya, to talk about her life in the resistance, her confrontations with the Civil Guard or the contact she had with the demi-monde of other exiles. But now she wasn't so much interested in sharing these stories, since she was now faced not with a group of students but with almost two hundred adults from whom she hoped above all to extract some money for her project. It's not that she was an interested party, but at such a special gathering as this, and after a life that was never what she wanted or what her time in the Residence had prepared her for, she preferred to keep her feelings to herself, since to bring them to the surface would surely overwhelm her in such a way that she wouldn't even be able to speak. It would be better to focus on the task that had brought her there and not to wallow in past struggles that had already taken their toll, she thought. Valli also remembered the words of her former teacher of philosophy, María Zambrano, who once said from the same platform on which she now sat: "Carry on doing what you are doing".

The auditorium finally fell silent and Soledad opened the proceedings briskly and with a sense of excitement. The Director had written books on the exchanges between American and Spanish women in the Residence and had been captivated, like other researchers, by the wonderful world that María de Maeztu and her assistants, as well as the residents, had created all those years earlier. Those women, she said, had a century earlier established a place that would still be considered as modern and advanced at the present time.

Consuelo spoke first, looking at the audience with a mixture of fear and surprise. As the old lady stumbled through her first few sentences, Valli gave her a long hard look as she tried to remember her when they were young, but she could barely do so, since Consuelo had a room in the building on Fortuny Street and not Miguel Ángel like her, and also she was a few years older so they didn't take the same classes at the university.

In a faltering voice and still fingering her pearls Consuelo explained how she had come from a backward Ávila in the mid-thirties to a Young Ladies' Residence which provided her with an environment in which she could do what she liked most: studying and eating well. They lived so well in the residence that even her brother, who was also a student in Madrid, started to call her "princess". While they had access to warm

133

libraries and ate with knives and forks, he – in his boarding house in Carretas Street which was in fact more expensive – complained that the food was dire and that what with the bedbugs and the noise from the street, he could hardly do any studying.

Consuelo explained that those years were a sort of oasis in her life, because afterwards everything changed. After the war the Young Ladies' Residence became the Santa Teresa Hall of Residence, directed by Matilde Marquina, a member of the Falange who gave it a radically different character. Although she completed her studies in Law, Consuelo got married to a university classmate, a liberal in what he said but a spoilt young man in the way he behaved, and she had four children, to whom she devoted herself full-time while they were little. She never practised Law and now, at her age, she had no regrets, because she was satisfied with what life had given her, essentially good health, a family and few serious problems. She didn't want to add anything further and the warm applause was thanks for her obvious effort. She leant back in her chair and finally she could relax.

After that Soledad gave an educational presentation about women in Spanish universities. It was brief but as interesting as it was amusing, as it explained how some of the first female university students at the end of the nineteenth century, such as María Goyri or Matilde Padrós, went to classes accompanied by a servant or family member, entered the classroom with the lecturer and sat apart from the other students. With the lights out Valli began to get a lump in her throat, because now in the darkness was when she could best see – and above all feel – the auditorium. The laughter of the audience, their interest in learning and sharing, the pervasive atmosphere of camaraderie and the fact that there were three women on the platform brought her some of the most beautiful memories of her life, before it came to a permanent end.

In a quiet voice and after an introduction full of admiration, respect and affection, Valli explained to her audience, although still looking into space, how she often came to this same auditorium to hear the early evening talks that María de Maeztu gave to the residents. At the height of the Republic, she said, and especially as political tensions increased, María always used as an example Erasmus from Rotterdam, the scholar accepted by Protestants and Catholics alike in an age that was also marked by tense and violent disagreements. But the atmosphere was such that the women students revolted at the mere mention of the Dutch scholar's name, Valli explained, because in *In Praise of Folly* he had written that a woman was "an inept and foolish animal" and that if ever she sought wisdom "she would only succeed in becoming doubly foolish". In the Residence we were encouraged to question everything, even Erasmus himself. Politically and socially everything legal and respectable was permissible, and on that basis everyone was free to think what they liked, Valli explained to her audience, who were listening in total silence.

After a brief pause to have a drink and clear her throat, Valli continued with more confidence in her voice. She had also learnt to read there, but to read properly. A student prepared a text and between them they broke it down, established the main ideas and analysed them ad infinitum. There they learnt to summarise, to think and to counter an argument.

Feeling more and more relaxed, Valli recounted that not everything was a bed of roses and that they suffered some harsh criticism.

'As is always the case when one has the energy and the talent to do new or different things, those who are accustomed to or who are favoured by the status quo feel unsettled, so you always get criticism,' she said, prompting some brief applause from the audience. When it stopped Valli continued with a gentle smile. 'Just think,' she said, lowering her eyes and shaking her head, 'they even criticised us for not having a chapel and because – they said – we used to go out whenever we liked, which was not at all true.'

Valli also denied any accusation of elitism. Most of the residents came from the provinces, she assured them, they were daughters of educated fathers with average means, such as doctors or lawyers, but also tailors and school teachers who worked hard to pay the one hundred and forty pesetas per month that the Residence cost. But it was also true that from time to time someone famous turned up. One day Lili, Rubén Darío's niece, came and sat at her dining table, she said, while on another occasion a new resident arrived accompanied by her chauffeur. But it was an Italian girl who caused the greatest stir when one afternoon she received a personal and private visit from Miguel de Unamuno, who apparently was a friend of her father. They never found out exactly who it was, because the Residence always considered her as just one more student, without any privileges.

Part of the audience started to applaud, but Valli wanted to finish by recalling the most important lesson that she had learnt there.

'Above all this place gave us security,' she said. 'Here we felt protected and respected. The environment gave us enthusiasm and drive and demanded that we give the best of ourselves, but without laws or norms or punishments. We thought we were going to take over the world but in order to leave it a better place'. She went on: 'María de Maeztu knew us all personally, and at least once a year we had dinner with her in groups of six or seven, when she would ask us how we were, if we needed anything and if we had any problems. The truth is that few of us dared to say anything, but when we did mention anything, María dealt with it at once, which made us feel very well protected. This was neither a convent nor a college, but a new kind of institution conceived as a motor for change in a poor and backward society. It was a genuine healthy, peaceful, social and intellectual revolution in which we all felt engaged,' she concluded.

The audience rewarded her with a long and loud standing ovation. Soledad looked at Valli with bright eyes and again shook her hand, a gesture that brought her to the verge of tears. She closed her eyes and after a deep sigh she managed to control the tears, while she repeated several times to herself that that was not her purpose. As soon as the applause had died down enough, Valli thanked those present for coming and briefly explained her plan to convert an old school into a cultural centre that would pick up the spirit of the Residence. That school, she explained, was in her home town of Morella, where the crazy Mayor wanted to convert the former school into apartments or a casino. She announced that she had left leaflets about it at the entrance and that she would be available to anyone interested during the drinks reception that would be held afterwards in the garden.

Soledad closed the moving event with thanks to the participants and sponsors, and said that the Institute would always uphold the spirit of the Residence or, as far as possible, any project that tried to emulate it. The Director warmly shook hands with Consuelo and Valli.

The *Goyescas* by Enrique Granados entertained the small reception in the garden of the Institute, although now the melody came not from the windows of the building but the loudspeakers installed for the occasion. Nevertheless Valli looked in the direction of the room that used to house an old black piano that some residents played to enliven the pleasant soirées that they often organised. While some took their turn at playing, others read, chatted quietly or studied in the large first-floor room where they gathered almost every night after dinner. It was a sizeable room, with two old chandeliers that lit the quiet reading corners, the shelves full of books or the round tables with wicker chairs. Sometimes ten or so residents crowded round a table to discuss some topical subject or other or an article in the papers. The more special soirées, when they could invite guests to the concerts for piano or violin given by some of the residents, were properly organised in an atmosphere of peace and harmony that required no monitoring or supervision.

'My dear, you were fantastic,' said a blond lady of about fifty to Valli, who was still absorbed in her memories.

With a glass of punch in her hand and looking rather tired, Valli looked at her. She was elegantly dressed in a light blue summery suit with gold buttons. As politely as she could, Valli introduced herself and deep down was pleased to see the enormous diamond that the lady wore around her ample neck and the several bracelets that announced her presence every time she moved her arm. This could be a good fundraising opportunity, she thought to herself.

'Thank you very much,' she replied with a rather weary smile after so much emotion. Valli found it tiring to be the protagonist, but today she had to be, she said to herself. 'And do you still have some connection with the Residence?' she asked.

The lady, who had introduced herself with one of those long, double-barrelled names, tossed back her blond hair and replied showing her perfect white teeth.

'Oh, yes, my three sons were at Colegio Estudio, you know, the one that followed in the footsteps of the Instituto Escuela which had strong links with the Residence and the Institución Libre de Enseñanza. We're very happy.'

'That's good. And which year are they in?' Valli asked more attentively, since basically she never stopped being a teacher and she was always interested in students.

The lady was taken by surprise and stepped back slightly before letting out a laugh.

'Oh, how funny!' she exclaimed. 'My sons have already finished university and two of them are even married,' she said, 'but you're flattering me if you think they're still at school.'

Valli observed her features. Looking more closely she could make out some wrinkles beneath her heavy make-up. In any case it used to be the case in the towns and villages that older women were big and fat with ample breasts and of course the inevitable grey hair. She wasn't used to seeing grandmothers with fabulous long blond hair, diamonds and thin waists like this lady. Well, she thought, she wasn't there to judge anyone, but to get some money.

'Thank you very much for coming,' she said, 'and I hope my school project in Morella was of interest to you. It's a great opportunity to get involved in a cultural proposal of this kind,' said Valli resolutely.

The lady, who was a bit taken aback by such a direct tone from a person approaching the end of her ninth decade, took her by the arm, showing off her perfect bright red nails. She moved closer to her.

'Yes, what a good idea,' she said, 'but I think that rather than approaching individuals, you could try approaching a foundation, couldn't you? Come with me,' she said, starting to walk, 'and I'll introduce you to my friend Cuqui, who runs one of the most important foundations in Madrid.

Valli felt a bit lost but also hopeful and as best she could she followed the lady whose name she couldn't remember, passing in front of Soledad, who was keeping an eye on her guests of honour to make sure that everything was all right. After a few minutes, having negotiated their way around about a hundred people in the garden – more or less half of the people who had come to the event – Valli and the lady reached their target.

'Cuqui, how are you? I say, you look fantastic, and so beautiful, you look about twenty,' said the lady to her friend, a tall dark woman, and apparently younger, although Valli no longer knew what to think. 'Look,' the lady went on, 'I'd like you to meet Vallivana Querol; isn't it lovely to have her with us? Hasn't it been a wonderful occasion?' she said with a toothpaste-advertisement smile.

The lady referred to as Cuqui, who was wearing riding breeches, tall leather boots and a black high-neck jumper, immediately gave her two air kisses and smiled.

'Of course, I've never been to anything like it, it's absolutely fascinating,' she said taking her by the arm and looking her in the eye. She had impressive green almond-shaped eyes.

Looking around her, Valli felt as though she'd got caught up in a parade of models rather than a meeting of intellectuals. She thought of her friends in the Residence in the mid-thirties, with their knitted cardigans and their blouses done up to the neck, long check skirts and flat, strong walking shoes. Valli couldn't understand why all these women had decided to wear such sexy clothes to attend a function that she thought had educational overtones. The old *maestra*, who barely reached the bust of the others present, looked around her feeling rather confused and sighed. "Oh, my dear," she said to herself.

'Cuqui, darling,' the first lady went on, 'I wanted you to meet Vallivana personally, because you've heard about her school project. As she's looking for funds, I thought that you, with your involvement in a foundation, could advise her as to who she could approach, or maybe you know some institution that could be of interest,' she said, while greeting someone else at the end of the garden, her arm aloft and waving her noisy bracelets once more. Turning back to Cuqui, she went on: 'We must help our new friend Vallivana, of course,' she said, putting on her professionally charming smile.

'Yes, yes, of course, what a splendid idea, let me think about it,' Cuqui replied, pursing her lips and looking at the tree in the centre of the garden which was surrounded by a small area of lawn.

Everyone at the reception was smiling, thought Valli while Cuqui seemed to be more focused on saying hello to other guests than on replying. Valli also looked at the solitary oak in the centre and felt equally abandoned. Unfortunately there was nothing left of the spring foliage that formerly covered it, attracting dozens of sparrows that spent the day singing, fighting or flirting and that she used to listen to from the library. As she recalled this with nostalgia, she said to herself that frankly she preferred the cheeping of the sparrows to the banal conversations that surrounded her. But strong and determined as she was, she sighed and set about achieving her objective, even if it meant being a hypocrite. Once and for all the time had come to be practical and follow the example of the politicians, who always came out on top. Valli had seen mayors and businessmen turn to people who were infinitely more capable than themselves, without that stopping them at the time from asking or cashing in, or feeling that they had every right to be given just because it suited them. At nearly ninety years of age Valli had finally learnt the lesson; now she was going to follow their example.

'You'll see what an excellent investment it'll turn out to be,' Valli said finally after a long pause to Cuqui, who looked at her with a slight air of surprise.

Of course, when she saw Valli's persistence, the lady with the bracelets disappeared as quickly as she could.

'Good, I'll leave you two so that you can talk about things,' she said, tossing her hair back once again and turning to Valli. 'Vallivana, it has been such a pleasure to meet you, and good luck in everything, I'm sure you'll be very successful!' she added, before disappearing among the rest of the guests and picking up a glass of champagne on the way.

Valli set about her task.

'It must be interesting to work in a well-known foundation,' she said to Cuqui. 'Do you take part in many projects?'

Cuqui smiled and looked around her as she replied.

'Well, we'd like to, but, you know, we have so many requests that we have to select very conscientiously. We study the projects carefully, which means on average they take about two years,' she said with a smile.

'Two years to decide!' exclaimed Valli, as surprised as she was disappointed, because she couldn't wait that long. She had a first sip of the punch that she'd been holding in her hands for a while, without really knowing what to do with it.

Cuqui, who was looking at the other people present and saying hello to some acquaintance or other from time to time, declined the canapés that she was offered by a waiter. She turned to Valli once more, and with a little more sincerity this time she said:

'We have to proceed with caution, because as you know things are getting ugly.'

'Ugly?' Valli said raising her eyebrows.

'Well, you know that we've had a number of boom years and I think people are starting to tighten their belts, that's all. It'll blow over,' she added, looking her in the eyes, perhaps the first person at the reception to do so, apart from Soledad.

Valli remained silent for a few moments. At last she had found someone who thought as she did. She had suspected for some time that the pace at which people were acquiring shiny new cars and houses was unsustainable.

Cuqui took the opportunity to excuse herself and to continue greeting friends and acquaintances. The attractive woman moved into the crowd, smiling and charming people left and right. She would get whatever she wanted, thought Valli, regretting that once again she had made the mistake of believing that good ideas or intentions, even hard work, were enough to achieve an objective. No, everything was – and continued to be – much more arbitrary.

Always attentive, Soledad came over to her. Valli was now her only concern, since Consuelo was worn out and had gone off in a taxi a short while before.

'How are you getting on, my dear? Are you okay?' she asked, gentle and caring as ever.

'Yes, yes, everything's fine, thank you, Soledad,' Valli replied, half lying so as not to disappoint the kind Director, who had organised the event largely to help her.

'You look a bit crestfallen,' Soledad said to her, looking at her dull eyes and her drooping shoulders. 'Are you sure you're all right? Has someone upset you?' she asked with her sensitive gaze.

Valli sighed.

'Oh, my dear girl, I don't know what to say,' she replied, becoming less tense and taking another sip of punch. 'All the work you've put into this and I don't know if I'm going to achieve anything; they all take me hither and thither but no-one seems to be sufficiently interested,' she said, looking down.

Soledad gently took her hand.

'I did warn you that it wouldn't be easy. But give it a bit more time, you never know,' she said sincerely. 'In any event everyone is saying wonderful things about you, you should be so proud of what you've achieved, of what you represent, of the great example that you provide. It's women like you that make the world go round,' she said with a frank look.

Valli looked at Soledad in a kindly way, but then remarked:

'I'm not here for tributes, Soledad, I don't want medals or honours. I just want to save my school, to give young people an opportunity to study in Morella, and for that I need five million euros and not more awards.'

Soledad looked at her with fundamental admiration and above all with understanding. The two women remained silent for a few moments, listening to the gentle notes of the *Suite Iberia* by Albéniz who had replaced Granados and provided a more relaxing tone.

Valli smiled at last.

'Just imagine, I saw Albéniz play this piece in the auditorium of the boys' residence one summer night in – I think it was 1935,' she said, looking at the sky which was now a dark twilight red thanks to the contamination in the city and not at all like the marvellously clear dusks in Morella.

Soledad realised she needed to do something.

'Come,' she said with renewed energy. 'I'm going to introduce you to one of the Ministers at the Department of Education; he might be able to help you.'

Valli turned to her with a look of complicity.

The two women crossed the patio, which was now emptying, and carried on weaving their way through the guests until Soledad started to head towards a young man who was about to leave.

'Don Jaime, don Jaime!' shouted the Director, and quickened her step until she caught up with her friend, with Valli rather left behind. 'Don't go without personally meeting out main guest.'

'Valli,' said Soledad when, rather out of breath, the old lady caught up with them, 'I'd like you to meet Jaime, Education Minister and a good friend of the Institute,' she said looking at them both proudly.

The Director's manners were exquisite, thought Valli, who had never had anyone to show her how to behave in polite company. For a moment Valli thought of her parents, who never introduced her to anyone, since they spent their days quietly and happily in their farmhouse, surrounded by goats, pigs and sheep until their peace was cut short. Valli closed her eyes for a second, but immediately came back to reality.

The affable Minister, who was wearing a narrow tie and a close-fitting one-button blue suit, kissed her hand and she felt the touch of his short but neat beard as he did so. He wore his hair on the long side, although he wasn't a pony-tail man, as Valli called them. He had style.

"Gay", thought Valli at once.

'I loved your talk; it was a great example for all of us,' Jaime said politely. 'If you don't mind I'd like to ask Soledad for your details, because we'd be very interested in organising similar events. You could inspire thousands of children who need better examples than those that unfortunately they get at home.'

Valli was pleased and surprised to find a politician with a degree of sensitivity, or so it appeared, because that was more than many of them offered, she thought. This could be a good opportunity.

'I'd be delighted to help,' she said. 'I'd also like to be in contact with you about my school, which I mentioned at the end of my talk. I left some leaflets at the entrance, I don't know if you've seen them.

The Director smiled slightly, but he answered in a respectful tone:

'We'd love to help, Señora Querol, but I'm afraid that in Spain we are still constrained by the most basic needs. There are hundreds of schools without heating, some libraries hardly have any books and many classes, more than I'd like to admit, have more than fifty pupils per teacher.' He paused briefly and looked straight at Valli. 'I really would like to help, but I'd rather be honest with you.'

Valli managed to put on a false smile, although in her mind's eye she began to see hundreds of neon lights lighting up row upon row of slot machines in her school. She pictured large luminous posters on the medieval wall proclaiming the biggest casino in Spain or in Europe. The image horrified her.

'Never mind,' she said eventually. 'I'm grateful to you for being honest. I wish that all politicians were equally clear and straightforward, instead of promising what they can't give.'

'The worst thing is when they've given what they didn't have,' commented the Minister rapidly before he left.

Soledad and Valli looked at each other in silence while some of the people followed Jaime and were getting ready to leave. The sun finally hid behind the nearest buildings and as if it were a wedding or a funeral, the two women, standing by the entrance, said a friendly goodbye to those who had attended.

Feeling worn out, they finally sat down on a couple of metal chairs, like the ones to be found on a bar terrace. There was only one other person there, sitting alone on a chair at the bottom of the garden. Valli hadn't seen her before, but she noticed her now. In the growing darkness, she could barely make out her features, but she looked like a young foreign woman, with long, reddish hair. She was wearing a short skirt and a tight-fitting top, and she had a fairly white complexion. She was holding a book in her hands and was looking at them attentively.

'Do you know who she is?' Soledad whispered quietly, for the garden was empty and still, except for the three women.

Valli shook her head and looked at Soledad with curiosity.

'It's Samantha Crane, the grand-daughter of Victoria Kent's companion.'

12

In the morning of that same day towards the end of June, Vicent left the Town Hall feeling extremely angry. Eva had continually been transferring calls and forwarding emails from suppliers who were waiting to be paid. In addition, he had just received a note from one of the world's largest credit agencies saying that they wanted to speak to him in person about some loans as soon as possible. He hadn't even had anything to do with any such agencies! What on earth did they want?

Even though he didn't much like the idea, he would of course need to prepare for such a meeting, thought Vicent, giving a flicker of recognition to acquaintances who greeted him in the street. The Mayor just smiled, with barely any eye contact as he tried to avoid having to stop. It was hot and he loosened his tie and undid the top button of his shirt. He felt a sense of relief that summer was just around the corner – it was the best time of year for the hotel, not only because of tourism but also because most suppliers, especially those claiming payment, were on holiday. That year was becoming more difficult than he had expected, although he was surprised that nobody was talking about it. The press only seemed to offer good news, about Spain as well as the rest of the world. Global finance was now so advanced that boom-and-bust cycles were history; now, they said, everything could be prevented or resolved. Morella should be no different, he thought, so after the summer things would surely return to normal.

Vicent felt a bit more relaxed as he finally reached his hotel. He just wanted to return to his daily routine of taking lunch there, having spent most days in recent weeks eating in restaurants because of so much work. But that week he was planning to eat at the hotel every day, as his daughter Isabel had taken charge of the kitchen after she had been sacked from her job. She had told him that the business was losing money and they had to cut staff, but Vicent had always had his doubts about how good she was at her job. Whatever the case, her moving into the hotel meant more maintenance costs for him, despite her claims that she could devote herself to the business. Paying his son Manolo a salary every month for his work in reception was already difficult, as their competitors had stolen some of their regular clients. The business was not in a position to employ anyone else, so he had to choose. The boy, of course, was a much safer bet and he would never leave him out on the street. A woman could always get married instead, thought Vicent.

'Hello!' he shouted after shutting the front door behind him. 'I'm here! Has the Brit arrived yet?' Vicent yelled from the empty reception area, while he put his jacket on the clothes hook.

The Mayor sighed with irritation as once again Manolo seemed to be absent from his post. Without thinking, he pressed down hard on the buzzer on the counter, causing his daughter to respond immediately.

'Coming! Coming!' she said from the floor above. As he opened the door to the main dining room, Vicent heard his daughter come quickly down the stairs and she got to him just as he went in.

Isabel adjusted her apron, which looked brand new, and the two clips that she'd put in her hair, which unusually she was wearing loose today. For the first time in a long time she had put on some makeup. Vicent was pleased to see this as, if she was to work at the hotel, she needed to take more care of her image. Vicent looked his daughter up and down.

'Aren't you going to wear the white hat?'

'It's very hot now in the summer, Father,' she replied and, without waiting for any objection or approval, she went into the kitchen.

Vicent followed her. As soon as he stepped into the room he noticed that everything had changed. There was a new oven, the preparation area had been repositioned in a corner and replaced in the centre by a large aluminium table with as many as eight burners, twice as many as before. The number of pots and pans that normally hung from the ceiling had been reduced by half and the walls were whiter than usual. Had somebody painted them?

'May I ask what's been happening here?' Vicent asked, surprised not so much by the changes themselves but more by the fact that he didn't know anything about them.

'Father, look how good and how practical everything is now,' his daughter said proudly, leaning gently on the new table, where Vicent noticed a brand new wooden knife holder, full of shiny knives that he had never seen before.

He went closer and took hold of one. It was smooth and made by Global, a brand he didn't know. After close inspection of the razor-sharp specimen, which a Japanese samurai would have been happy to have, he slowly put it back in its place. It slotted in perfectly.

'And who has given you permission to change the kitchen?' he asked. 'It was you, wasn't it? You're the one who's changed everything.'

'Yes, and look how great everything looks. Now we have the professional kitchen we really need if we want a properly functioning hotel.'

Vicent moved towards her, at the same time calculating how much everything had cost. He couldn't believe that his daughter had organised all those changes in the two weeks that she had been at the hotel. He looked around and noticed a little herb garden in a large pot on the window-ledge.

'A professional kitchen, eh?' he said in the calm tone that tends to come before the storm. 'But you're only interested in the damn plants and paintings! What a waste of time!'

Vicent took a deep breath and closed his eyes. How could this be possible? Slowly he went up to Isabel and looked at her intently, frowning, his eyes wide open.

'And how are you planning to pay for all this, may I ask?' he said, leaning his strong arms on the new table as if he was reprimanding a child.

Isabel seemed surprised by the question.

'Don't worry, Father, it's not really that expensive. The oven and the table cost the most, but everything else is purely cosmetic, just some painting, flowers and basically, my labour,' she said, proudly surveying her work. 'But there's no need for you to worry. I've spent hours and hours trying to upgrade this place, throwing away loads of old pots and pans that dated from before the war, at least. We couldn't carry on with such an old kitchen if we want this business to be profitable.'

'And who are you to take any decisions without your father's approval?' he asked, still unable to understand how all that could have happened without his knowledge.

'Father, as I say, you don't have to worry because...

Vicent didn't let her finish.

'How on earth do you expect me not to worry if you can't even hold down a job!' he said. 'God knows what you must have done to lose it!'

Vicent knew such a comment wasn't fair, but it was true. The Mayor had never thought very highly of his daughter, who to his surprise had managed to get a university degree, although he still didn't know how. He never thought of her as either clever or entrepreneurial, as she had always seemed rather clumsy and slow and never somebody with an eye for business. He had tried to dissuade her from going to university, but he couldn't fight the common front that mother and daughter put up against him. He already knew that it wouldn't work and time had proved him right. Since she graduated – a long time ago now – she had only worked as a secretary or a saleswoman, without climbing any higher, and now, on top of everything, she had been fired. The money that he had spent sending her to university in Valencia he would much rather have invested in Manolo, who lost his way at university and never graduated. Had Vicent had a bit more money in those days, he would have taken him out of the apartment where he spent too much time partying and sent him to a Catholic student residence, where they would have got him to focus more on his studies. But he couldn't. And now, after bringing his children up and paying for them through university, he had them both at home, like parasites. Not only that, but they were also taking advantage of him, spending his money on kitchen toys while the reception was left unattended. Enough was enough.

'Father, please let me run the kitchen for a while and you´ll see that things will change and clients will come back. Let me take it on.'

'How much have you spent?' he asked, staring into her eyes.

Isabel said nothing.

'How much?' he shouted, banging the table with his fist. He loosened his tie as a few beads of sweat started to run down his forehead. He rolled up his sleeves as it was quite hot in the kitchen, although he was the one who had banned the use of the air conditioning because he already had enough problems with the electricity bills.

Isabel looked away without answering, and then Vicent moved even closer towards her, with his hand raised, as if he was about to hit her like he did when she was little… and when she was not so little, too. He would readily have given her a good slap, but for once he controlled himself.

'Tell me how much, damn you!' he yelled again, his hand still raised.

On the verge of tears, Isabel finally spoke.

'Ten thousand euros,' she said in a tiny voice. 'Only ten thousand.'

Vicent thumped the table three times, his face now red with anger.

'Ten thousand?' he shouted. 'Have you gone crazy or what?'

Vicent threatened with his hand again, but brought it back down only a few seconds later.

'You will pay it back out of your own pocket,' he said. 'I swear that you will pay for all this. Right now!'

Isabel took a handkerchief out of her apron pocket and slowly wiped the tears that were rolling down her face. A few seconds later, she plucked up the courage to speak.

'Father, I've already told you that you don´t need to worry about the money. You don´t understand.'

'You can pay me with your severance money' he said. 'The whole lot. Living here at the hotel at my expense, you won´t have to spend much, so I want that money tomorrow without fail.'

'Father, you know that I didn´t get any severance money,' she said in such a quiet voice that it was difficult to hear. 'You know full well that it was a temporary contract, which they could terminate whenever they wanted. They had no need to pay me anything; all they had to do was give me one week´s notice.'

'Well, why didn´t you get a better job, damn it?'

Father and daughter lowered their heads in silence for a while.

'I've been working so hard all my life to be able to have a comfortable retirement and when I get there, look what I've got: two parasites living off me,' Vicent said to himself.

'These are difficult times, but as I say, the thing is that…'

Vicent interrupted her:

'What do you mean difficult times? You and your brother are just idle layabouts! I was here at fifteen, successfully running this business, providing for my mother and myself, and those were really hard times. Look, first I had to keep my mother, then my wife and now I even have to support my children, when they're old enough to be supporting me! Will I have to provide for my grandchildren as well? Well, I needn't worry, as my children aren't even good for giving me grandchildren,' he said, and he went out of the kitchen, slamming the door behind him.

Vicent didn't turn back to see what state Isabel was in. He didn't have to, as he was certain she would be crying like a baby, as usual, and cowering like a cornered animal, just as she did when he hit her as a child. If she would only take better care of herself, maybe she could get herself a good husband. But she can't even do that, Vicent thought. And as usual, he now had to cope with it all.

Vicent went into the little sitting room just by reception and poured himself a whisky from the mini-bar. He thought about the plants on the window ledge in the kitchen. This was not the time to start paying for ridiculous plants! Stressed and exhausted, Vicent took a handkerchief from his pocket and wiped his sweaty forehead and palms. He lit a cigarette to calm himself down, flicking the ash on the floor.

He was sitting there with a blank stare when he heard the front door open and somebody going upstairs. He hoped it wasn't the Brit just yet as that was really not the right moment.

Of course it was him.

'Well, look who's here! My favourite Englishman!' said Vicent, standing up and adjusting his tie as soon as he saw Charles. The Mayor tried to act as naturally as possible, but he found it very difficult.

The two men shook hands. Charles looked the same as usual, with his lanky frame and his pale skin, and carrying the same old suitcase. His blue eyes, however, were brighter than ever and his hair seemed a bit longer and rather unkempt. His angular features, his ironic smile and his immaculately white summer suit, made him a top candidate for the eccentric-of-the year award, thought Vicent.

'You look great!' he said, looking him up and down, noticing his two-tone shoes that only a clown would have worn in Spain. But after years in the tourism industry Vicent knew by now that these were smart shoes usually worn at cricket matches or regattas. He didn't really care; as long as he made a good offer for the school, he could wear whatever shoes he liked.

Charles left his luggage on the floor and looked at Vicent and around the reception area, where he caught sight of a bunch of dried lavender that Vicent hadn't even noticed.

'What a lovely scent that lavender has!' he said with a smile, approaching the vase on the counter. 'I wish we had this all year-round in England.'

Charles sighed and puffed out his chest, looking rather pleased to be back in Morella. Vicent had never seen him this contented; he must be looking forward to the summer holidays, he thought.

'Always a pleasure to welcome you here, Charles,' the Mayor said, going round to the other side of the counter in Manolo's absence. 'My son has just gone out to do some errands, so let me check you in,' he said as he opened the registration book. He flicked through the pages but couldn't find the entry for Charles' previous stay. Manolo had been asking for a computer for a while, but Vicent had always rejected the idea. He had run that business on paper for decades without any problem, so why spend hundreds of euros on an unnecessary machine? Manolo was just lazy and disorganised. Tired of looking through the book, Vicent just started a new page.

'I understand you like room number 14,' he said, writing down the details.

Charles nodded.

'I'm good friends with the flamenco dancer by now.'

Vicent looked down at the book as that type of humour didn´t really register with him. British humour, he thought. Moving things on, the Mayor took hold of the key and handed it to him.

'Here you are, Charles. Once again, we are delighted to welcome you here.' He paused briefly. 'Are you still okay for our two o'clock lunch, as we agreed via email?'

'Yes, of course,' Charles replied. 'I just have to drop my suitcase and have a wash and I'll be right down.'

'Great. I think Isabel has cooked that truffled lamb that you like so much,' he said, wondering how on earth he could speak well of his daughter after the row they had just had. At least it was true that she was as good a cook as her mother.

Charles went up to his room, climbing the stairs two at a time, while Vicent went back into the kitchen. He opened the door and shouted, without looking in.

'Hey! The Brit's here! I want the soup and the lamb in five minutes, okay?'

There was no response.

'Isabel! Can you hear me?' Vicent said, now looking into the kitchen.

Isabel was watering the plants.

'Leave the damn plants alone and start cooking! The Brit will be down in a minute.'

'Everything's ready,' Isabel answered icily without looking at her father.

A few minutes later, Vicent and Charles entered the dining room. Just before they sat down, Charles asked after Isabel, while still holding on to a small case that Vicent assumed contained some documents relating to the purchase of the school.

Thinking that the case was for him, Vicent reached out to take it but Charles suddenly withdrew his arm.

'It's just a small present I wanted to give Isabel, for all her help during the week my students were here.'

Vicent looked surprised.

'Oh, I see. Well, you needn't have bothered, but if this is a little something for the hotel, I can take it myself,' Vicent said, thinking that given its size, it would be a tacky English plate that he wouldn't know where to put.

Charles blushed slightly.

'It's especially for her.'

Vicent raised his eyebrows, as if that was a ridiculous idea.

'Really?'

Charles nodded.

'Yes, it's for her. Doesn't she normally get given any presents?'

Vicent realised that he had to sort things out with his daughter if he wanted to avoid a scene.

'Of course. I'll go and find her right now.'

Reluctantly, Vicent tightened his tie so as to make him feel that he was in charge, and went into the kitchen to ask his daughter to go into the dining room immediately. She promptly did so, surprised and intrigued, carrying two bowls of garlic soup that she knew Charles liked so much.

The two shook hands after Isabel had put the soup on the table that she had neatly laid earlier.

'Thank you very much for answering our letter and for accepting our apologies,' said Charles, unusually direct and taking Vicent by surprise, as he didn't know anything about the problems that Charles' students had caused at the hotel.

Isabel lowered her eyes.

'That's all right. My thanks to *you* – you're very generous.'

'It's the least we could do,' said Charles. 'I hope you can spend it on something you really like.'

Isabel looked at him with her big dark eyes, now wide open.

'I've already done so.'

Charles looked as surprised as Vicent.

'I'd love to know what you've spent it on, if it's not indiscreet to ask.'

'I've refurbished the kitchen,' said Isabel, aiming an icy look at her father.

Vicent felt as if a knife had been thrust through his heart, but puffed out his chest and concealed his shock.

'May I ask what you're talking about?' the Mayor finally asked.

After a brief silence Isabel answered coolly:

'Charles' students had a rather merry night whilst staying here,' she said, her stern gaze fixed her father. 'They didn't do a lot of damage, but they did break some glass. But since they're all millionaires, they have overcompensated for the damage, enabling me to install a brand new kitchen.'

'You've worked very fast!' said Charles, visibly pleased about the outcome of his gesture.

Vicent had to swallow hard three times and take some deep breaths as Isabel went into the kitchen to show it off to Charles. The Englishman seemed full of admiration, to judge by the 'oohs' and 'aahs' that Vicent could hear, and which he thought sounded rather effeminate. He closed his eyes. Isabel might have told him that he wouldn't need to pay for any of it. In any case, Vicent wondered who would pay ten thousand euros for four broken plates. If anything, that was a good sign as he was just about to sit down and negotiate a price for the school. It was good to know they had overpaid! As far as Isabel was concerned, maybe he should have let her explain a bit more, but she also needed to understand that he was going through a rough time. At least everything seemed to have been sorted now.

As soon as the two were back in the dining room, Charles picked up the little case that he had left by the table and handed it to Isabel before she went back into the kitchen.

'Just one last thing, on behalf of everyone, but this is especially for you,' he said. 'The boys have very fond memories of you, of your kitchen, your paintings and above all, your company. Nobody had got them to use a dustpan and brush before, and you managed to do it!'

Blushing, Isabel made as if to decline the present.

'I can't,' she said. 'Really, you've already been very generous towards me.'

'Please.'

Vicent rolled his eyes, feeling that precious minutes were being wasted. He crossed his arms and started tapping the floor with his foot, looking at the soup and thinking it must be getting cold. Still, the Mayor couldn't help leaning over to see what was inside the case.

Isabel opened the shiny, dark wooden box, whose pleasant smell wafted over to Vicent. Isabel ran her hand over the smooth wood, as if she were stroking a cat. Slowly she undid the golden lock and revealed an impressive oil painting set – with all the coloured tubes perfectly aligned and ordered according to hue. Four drawing pencils lay neatly on the red velvet, which gave the set a luxurious appearance. Inside the lid the name "Isabel" had been printed in neat, elegant, gold letters. Vicent noticed that his daughter's hands started to tremble slightly as she held the box. She didn't look up.

'I hope they measure up to the standard of the artist,' said Charles, always the gentleman, as he looked once more at Isabel's paintings that were hanging in the dining room.

Vicent looked at them as well, still unable to comprehend what it was that Charles saw in them. This was all very strange, Vicent thought; perhaps it was a strategy by the English hypocrite to try and obtain a discount in the negotiations. Well, he was not going to fall for that, Vicent promised himself.

After a brief but honest expression of gratitude for the gift, Isabel returned to the kitchen, holding the box as carefully as if it were a Picasso.

Vicent, who had had enough of it all, looked at his watch.

'Sorry, Charles,' he said. 'I don't want to rush you but I have a Town Council meeting this afternoon and, as we agreed, I'd like to talk to you beforehand. Shall we get started?'

Charles, still smiling, nodded and both men sat down.

The soup was indeed cold by now, although neither man dared to mention it. The chef seemed so excited with her gift that Vicent thought it might be better just to leave her alone for a while.

After some small talk, to which Vicent paid little attention, the Mayor saw on the clock on the wall that it was almost three o'clock, only half an hour before his meeting was due to start. He had to get a move on.

Fortunately, Isabel promptly came out of the kitchen with the lamb, which was both hot and smelled delicious. She was smiling from ear to ear. As he watched his daughter serving Charles he thought that, contrary to what he would have guessed, the two of them getting on so well could actually be good for business. After the first mouthful, Vicent went straight to the heart of the matter.

'Well, well, Charles, it's so good to see you again,' he said, leaning forward with his hands joined in front of him. 'I imagine – and I hope – that it's your interest in the school that's brought you back to Morella?' he asked, having another mouthful of the lamb, as if this was his everyday routine.

Charles placed his cutlery on the plate and gently dabbed his mouth with his napkin, which he carefully folded and placed back on his lap. He adjusted the collar of his shirt and had a quick sip of water. He looked at Vicent.

'Yes, that's right,' he said, slowly. 'That's exactly what I wanted to talk to you about.'

Vicent waited a couple of seconds, but seeing that Charles wasn't saying anything further, he tried to prompt him.

'Well, go on. I'm all ears.'

Charles looked around, as if checking that there was nobody else there.

'Here? Now?' he asked, sounding surprised.

'Of course, my friend, it's not that difficult,' replied Vicent, as he took another slice of lamb in order to make everything seem absolutely normal, and also because time was passing.

'I thought we would discuss this in your office rather than over lunch,' Charles said in a low, semi-confidential voice.

Vicent looked at him, thinking they must have hit upon some cultural difference.

'Don't you worry, my friend, in Spain everything can be settled over a good lunch and a glass of wine, man to man,' he said, pouring some wine into Charles' empty glass. 'We're safe here, nobody can hear us.'

Charles raised an eyebrow and, rather reluctantly, picked up his fork to take a piece of the lamb, which he savoured exasperatingly slowly for Vicent's liking.

'Well, what do you think about it all then?' the Mayor persisted, having emptied his plate.

'I've given this some thought,' Charles said at last. 'I've spoken with my boss and we would be prepared to make a preliminary offer without obligation. We need to do a lot of due diligence, both legal and architectural, pending our final signature. Only at that point would the offer be binding.'

Vicent shut his eyes and thanked a God in whom he had never believed. Things seemed to be starting to move in the right direction. He relaxed his shoulders.

'That's fantastic, Charles, I am delighted that you've appreciated this unique opportunity in Morella. Many investors will be sorry not to have grasped it themselves,' he said, rubbing his hands together. 'But tell me one thing,' said Vicent, looking at his empty plate, 'would it be possible to know what price have you been considering?'

Charles put his plate to one side as if he just couldn't eat and negotiate at the same time. He coughed slightly and took another sip of water. He hadn't tasted the wine yet. Vicent drank the last drop of his.

'I'd like to reiterate that no offer will be binding until our own research and due diligence have been completed; I trust that's understood? And, of course, I will send it to you in writing as soon as we've settled all the formalities.'

'Sure, yes, I understand,' Vicent replied. 'No offer is binding until it's all been cleared and signed by everybody, including the lawyers. Don't worry, we do this all the time here.' Vicent was not particularly concerned about this as, to his knowledge, the building didn't have any structural or legal problems. What it really needed was a good face-lift and a multi-million euro investment. And somebody with a lot of energy.

Charles looked this way and that and, leaning towards the Mayor, said in what was almost a whisper:

'We are considering making an offer of four million euros.'

Vicent looked at him intently. That was a substantial improvement over Barnús' offer, but still not enough.

'The starting price is five million,' he replied solemnly.

'Ours is four.'

Vicent looked at his daughter's paintings, but obviously without paying them any attention. He waited for a few seconds.

'Well,' he said finally, 'I appreciate your interest, for which I am most grateful, but I'm afraid I shall have to ask you to reconsider your offer because it's not only below the asking price but it's also lower than other offers we've already received,' he lied. Vicent knew that such tactics were not lawful, but he was also aware that everybody used them and those who didn't got left behind. He was only thinking about Morella's best interests.

'How many offers have you received, and for how much?' Charles asked directly.

Vicent leaned backwards.

'Well, as I'm sure you'll understand, this is a negotiation. These are delicate situations and every investor has a different agenda. We all want to preserve our best interests, but what I can tell you is that at present we do have better offers.'

Charles remained thoughtful while Vicent looked at the clock, which showed twenty minutes past three: an excellent excuse to leave now, saving him from having to stay and continue lying, something he didn't like doing but had now become necessary.

'What about the lamb?' Vicent asked, looking at Charles' half-empty plate.

Charles looked at one of his favourite dishes that had now gone cold.

'In England, when we eat we don't discuss money matters,' he said seriously.

'But you do when you drink, right?' the Mayor said with a smile.

'True,' Charles replied, visibly appreciating some humour.

'Well, it's the opposite here,' the Mayor responded. 'When you're a bit merry, it's better to go home, to the table or to bed. On the other hand, meat and business mix much better.'

Charles forced a smile, and Vicent took the opportunity to rush off because he was late for his meeting. Polite as always, Charles was understanding and the two men shook hands again.

'You'll let me know your thoughts over the next few days,' said Vicent.

Charles nodded in agreement.

The Town Hall meeting lasted for only as long as Vicent's patience with the opposition, which was less than an hour. His opponents kept pushing for an increase in the volume of local recycling collections but Vicent didn't really have time or inclination to discuss bin bags. He had much bigger problems on his plate and, in any case, he had always felt that people should be free to do whatever they liked with their own rubbish.

He ended the meeting as soon as he could and returned to his office to deal with his mail and a fair amount of tedious administrative work that came with the job.

Vicent was signing pay cheques when his wife suddenly called him on his mobile. It must be urgent, he thought, as he had absolutely forbidden her to call him during working hours, unless it was something both urgent and important.

'What?' he said abruptly, but continuing to sign the cheques.

'Hello, Vicent,' Amparo said with her usual affability. 'Listen, the water supply has been cut off again, and I was in the middle of a load…'

'For fuck's sake!' Vicent cut in, dropping his pen noisily on the desk. 'When?'

'It must have been an hour or so ago,' Amparo replied. 'I was half-way through two loads of laundry, so when I opened the washing machine all the water gushed out, flooding the kitchen floor. I've been mopping up now for an hour and I've got lots to do this afternoon, hand-washing everything again. As far as dinner's concerned, you could eat at the hotel, I'll just open a tin here. But you'll have to forget about the stew that you wanted me to cook.'

'Bloody hell…' cursed Vicent. 'I'll call those bastards right away. They'll find out who they're dealing with.'

'Vicent, please do something as we can't go on like this,' his wife pleaded. 'Some of the plants are already dying and the trees are thirsty. It's been a long time since it rained and we need water for the garden. What are we going to do?'

'I don't give a shit about the damn trees,' Vicent snapped back. 'But I want to go home, eat my stew and have a long, hot bath, dammit. OK, well, you stay put there, eat whatever you can find and I'll eat at the hotel or in the bar. I'll be home around ten.'

'That's fine,' said his wife, acquiescent as always.

Vicent ended the call. He leaned forward and sank his head in his big hands for a long while. He couldn't understand why things had got so bad. He had a good salary as Mayor, which only a year earlier seemed to be enough for his needs. But now he seemed to be drowning: the mortgage had gone up after a rise in interest rates, the hotel was bringing in less income and the bills were getting higher and higher. That month, for instance – he hadn't told anybody yet – he didn't have the funds to pay an electricity bill for five thousand euros. It was only twelve months earlier that money seemed to be coming out of his ears, but mostly because after he bought the house he accepted the generous loans offered him by the bank where Cefe worked. With those cash advances, Vicent bought horses, built the stables and the show-jumping arena and imported the best available Italian marble for the bathrooms. But now the bank had also raised its lending rates, while his salary hadn't gone up at all.

It had all happened so quickly that he had barely noticed, or at least could never have seen it coming. Who would have thought that the European Central Bank would raise its rates like that in the middle of a crisis? Bloody Germans, their phobia about inflation was now costing him an arm and a leg. And the hotel? Who would have thought that within the past year two boutique hotels would open in Morella, taking away his clientele? He didn´t have a penny to invest in his business, to do any advertising or to improve the facilities. His children, on top of everything, weren´t much help as they didn't bring in any money: one just about answered the phone and the other had just been sacked from her job. He didn´t have any parents to turn to and his wife's family, as far as he knew, didn´t have any savings, either. Cefe had already warned him a few times about the need to pay off some of those loans, so just asking for another one wasn´t an option. To make matters more difficult, he was also the Mayor, so he couldn´t look weak or vulnerable. He would become a laughing stock if his financial problems became public knowledge.

He rubbed his eyes and then covered them with his big hands for a few minutes. Until he found a solution.

Without giving it another thought, Vicent called Roig. After solving the President's Castellón airport troubles, it was now his turn to give him a hand.

'President, how are you?' he asked in a friendly tone as soon as Roig picked up the phone.

'A lot better since you were true to your word, Mayor,' Roig replied. 'We saved a match point there, my friend. Well, everything's going as planned.' The President paused briefly. 'Tell me, what´s up.'

'President, I'm calling because now I'm the one who´s in trouble.'

'I'm listening.'

'As you know, I run the local hotel, the long-standing family-owned business that I´ve devoted myself to since I was fifteen until I was elected Mayor a little more than a year ago.'

'Yes, yes, I know. What´s the matter with the hotel?'

'Well, two boutique hotels opened in Morella last year and they've taken our clientele away,' said Vicent. 'I'm only a small hotel owner and my father was a middle-ranking Civil Guard, who was killed by anti-Franco guerrillas, so I have nobody to turn to.'

'I didn´t know about your father,' the President said with sympathy. 'I'm sorry.'

'It´s all right, it was a long time ago,' said Vicent, thinking that pity was also a useful tactic. 'I'll be straight with you: my daughter has just been sacked from her job and my son is useless. I have them both working at the hotel, but they can´t really turn it into a profitable business.'

'So what are you thinking?'

'I thought we could turn it into one of those "country cottages" instead of a hotel, which would cut our huge tax bill and would also broaden the range of accommodation available in Morella. We could offer more competitive prices and attract younger people like students. Travelling is now only for the privileged.'

'It sounds like a good idea, but what can I do?' asked Roig.

'As I'm sure you know, the Valencia government has an assistance scheme for these "country cottages",' the Mayor replied. 'The regional government has actually financed some conversions into "country cottages" near Morella, paying as much as three hundred thousand euros to owners willing to convert their old properties. In exchange, the owners agree to manage the "country cottage" for a number of years.'

'Yes, of course, I know the programme, I have signed some of these contracts myself,' the President said.

'It would save our bacon if we could be part of that scheme, and it would also guarantee the existence of that type of popular establishment in Morella.' Vicent paused briefly, using the "pity tactic" once more. 'President, I can´t even pay a salary to my own children,' he added.

Vicent heard Roig light a cigarette.

'How much do you need, and by when?' he asked.

'Ideally the maximum allowed, the three hundred thousand, and tomorrow, if possible, as we have a big cash flow problem.'

Roig waited for a few seconds.

'You'll have two hundred and fifty thousand as soon as I can get it.'

Vicent closed his eyes, sheer pleasure welling up inside him.

'President,' he said, 'you know I am your most loyal associate.'

'I know, Mayor, I know,' Roig replied. 'This is the beginning of a great partnership.'

After the call, Vicent felt he was the most important and best supported man in the world.

13

After their introduction at the end of the function at the International Institute, Valli and Sam Crane arrived at the Embassy tea room in the taxi that Soledad had called for them. It was a warm night and the two women, with an age difference of over fifty years, were convinced that they were about to discuss matters that were as important as they were sensitive. They had both heard such a lot about each other.

As they went in and saw those carefully placed polished wooden tables, the cakes on the counter delicately arranged, and felt the inquisitive gaze of three waiters wearing black bow ties and waistcoats who were keen to attend to them, they immediately realised that they had to go somewhere else. The conversation was likely to be neither trivial nor intellectual, but rather a personal and above all intimate conversation: nothing that could be discussed in such a quiet and formal atmosphere or beneath the harsh lighting of the well-known Madrid café.

Valli suggested La Venencia, a bar that she used to visit with friends after the theatre, which she had only been able to go to when she won tickets in the monthly lottery at the Residence. For her the nights at the Music Palace or the Monumental Cinema – which were theatres, despite their names – were a luxury that she couldn't allow herself unless she won the much anticipated raffle, always organised by Eulalia Lapresta, María de Maeztu's secretary. It was in these auditoriums that she saw the first performance of Federico García Lorca's *The House of Bernarda Alba*, or *The Young Man who Married a Bad-tempered Woman* by Alejandro Casona, who was later to become her friend when they were both on a working group in the male residence. Valli thought back to these performances, with the passionate audience on their feet applauding wildly, while the authors proudly took a bow, enjoying their success at such a young age. Who knows where they would have got to if they had had the chance to develop, Valli had always wondered. Barely two years after those performances, Lorca had been killed, while Casona had to continue his life and his work in a long, hard exile.

From the taxi that was taking them down the Paseo de la Castellana towards the city centre, Valli looked out at the tall buildings, illuminated billboards and night clubs as they passed. She watched the many girls who were free to go out alone to see a show. These young women, she thought, could not imagine how in her day the fact of going out with a girlfriend to a theatre at night was to enter a totally unknown and exciting world full of colour, chaos and enjoyment. Those magical nights always ended in La Venencia, in Echegaray Street, a bar founded in 1928 and frequented by intellectuals, including some members of the male residence whom she had seen at lectures, like her English friend Tristan. La Venencia also attracted workers and labourers who she would never have met in her cultured and intellectual world in the north of Madrid. Those refined people from the Salamanca and El Viso districts of the city used to go to the upmarket Chicote Bar in the Gran Vía, where King Alfonso XIII himself had been served cocktails in their comfortable, well-padded leather armchairs. La Venencia, on the other hand, was a window on another world, with its simple wooden tables and chairs, its walls full of posters for all kinds of sherry, which was the speciality of the house. Valli got to meet a good number of workers through Margarita Nelken, a socialist Member of Parliament connected with the Residence, who defended the rights of the labourers to make life difficult even for the members of the new Republican government, like Manuel Azaña himself, who never appreciated her.

Valli smiled at the memory of The Nelken, as she was known then, a writer, politician and great art critic who, like many of the great women of the Republic, disappeared into a long and difficult exile without anyone troubling to preserve or promote her memory – not even her own party.

The taxi left them at the old wooden door, with the same green lettering of old and the white, half-drawn curtains that made it look more like the entrance to an old woman's house in a village. Nothing seemed to have changed, thought Valli.

'Have you been here before?' asked Sam, cheerily and innocently, in her strong American accent.

Valli looked at her with sympathy. She had the same self-confidence and accent as her grandmother, whom she knew well in the Residence.

'You'll like it, you'll see. Your grandmother loved it; I got to know it through her and Victoria.'

Sam went in and looked all around her, her mouth wide-open because crossing the threshold of La Venencia was really like going back into the past. Valli was encouraged by the young woman's expression; although very little surprised her these days, it inspired her to think that the younger generations still retained an interest in learning. She was now too old for surprises and new experiences, but ahead of her remained one last battle to fight on behalf of people who were very dear to her, like Sam's grandmother.

They sat down at one of the small, round, Parisian-style wooden tables. A waiter, perhaps unaccustomed to serving elderly ladies there, came over to take their order and save them going over to the counter. It was after ten o'clock on a Friday, and the place would soon fill with people out to have a good time. At least the two women had found a quiet table at the back near the toilets. They ordered two glasses of pale sherry.

Valli leant back with wide and expectant eyes. She had a good look round and it seemed as though the place had been suspended in time since the last occasion she had seen it, probably just before the war. The walls were still the same light grey, only now they weren't in such good repair as they used to be, with some cracks and patches where nearly all the paint had gone. The wooden coat stands, the earthenware ashtrays and the old green metal lamps were all unchanged. The old wooden shelves still held dozens of bottles of sherry, now no longer shiny and new but totally covered in dust. All that was missing was the tricolour flag that used to hang just above the entrance door, but was no longer there.

Sam crossed her long, shapely legs that were too big for such a small table, and leaned across to Valli with her glass of sherry in her hand.

'Cheers!' she said, and took a fairly large sip.

Valli, who for a long time now only took small sips, studied her carefully. She barely recognised in her face the pictures that her grandmother and Victoria had sent her from America before they died, when Sam was still a child and they wanted to share the arrival of their granddaughter with their friends in Europe. She hadn't seen any more photos since then, but now, with Sam opposite her, she was strongly reminded of her friend Louise by her happy and bold attitude.

'It's as if I were looking at your grandmother, with her almond-shaped eyes and her painted lips,' she said, looking at her and her surroundings. 'Just like you, she caught the eye of all the men. She was tall, slim, with reddish hair that was unusual in Spain, like yours.'

Sam blushed.

'Yes, I know, I always seem to be more attractive when I'm abroad. In the States men don't look at me so much because I'm just one more of a kind!'

Valli looked at her thinking that she was just as discreet and humble as her grandmother, despite being the heir, as was Louise, to the Crane Empire, one of the most important companies in the world in the field of banknotes, envelopes and letter paper. Millionaires from top to toe. But Valli wasn't here for her money. In fact she'd rather gone off trying to get funds for her school, at least for the time being, given the little success she had achieved at the reception only a few hours earlier. She was there because that girl represented the living memory of the woman who changed the life of Victoria Kent and, in turn, marked her own.

'I came here many a night with your grandmother and Victoria; they were always very daring,' she said. 'They were at least fifteen years older than I was, and much more advanced and sophisticated. I'm not talking about your grandmother, who was light years ahead of the Spanish women of the period. But as Victoria was my tutor in the Residence and I must have seemed to her so backward and provincial, I think she felt sorry for me and took me out to see a bit of the world.'

Valli had another sip of her sherry, this time a bit larger than before. Again she looked around, at the young people at the nearby tables. Despite the obvious difference in age she felt quite at home.

'We spent some really fun nights here,' she went on. 'I knew that Victoria and your grandmother were up to something, everyone in the Residence knew, but of course the men in the bar didn't have the slightest idea and didn't understand why neither of them ever took the least bit of notice of them. In fact I didn't suspect anything until Tristan, my English friend, explained it to me. Just imagine, how innocent I was,' she said with a smile full of memories.

'So you saw how they got to meet?' Sam asked, full of interest. 'It's awesome having a lesbian grandmother, it's supercool, you can't imagine what a buzz I get when I tell the guys at the uni. No-one believes you, especially in Spain,' she said smiling and showing her lovely array of white teeth.

'Yes, I can imagine,' Valli replied. 'You won't believe it, but in those days it was also cool, as you put it. But, no, I didn't get to see how they met each other. Rumour had it that Victoria, who was well-established as a lawyer in Madrid and well-known in the whole of Spain having been Director General of Prisons, came to the Residence a lot precisely because she had a special friendship with María de Maeztu,' she said, fingering her glass. 'I don't know if you understand me.'

The young American nodded.

'A lot of residents suspected that something was going on, but the rumours settled down at the arrival of your grandmother, who was openly gay and even more openly interested in Victoria. That's something I do remember,' she said. 'It surprised us all, but as the Americans in fact did what they liked, the surprise didn't last very long. Your grandmother and the other foreign girls had their own rooms, they smoked, they drank whisky, they played sport... They were such busy and active women!' said Valli with a smile. 'The fact is that your grandmother was very attractive, very nice and spoke very good Spanish from the outset, and as a consequence all of the residents quickly came to like her. Besides, her interest in Victoria was so natural that it didn't seem at all strange, and Victoria, believe me, welcomed her almost straight away with open arms. It was clear that the two women were meant for each other, and after a few weeks we were no longer struck by seeing them always together, laughing and sharing everything.' Valli paused briefly to have another large sip of her sherry. 'Well, María was the only one who seemed rather put out, although all three were very discreet and no-one ever said anything inappropriate. Victoria and your grandmother never did anything explicit in public, so that everything stayed very discreet. But, of course, in the Residence everything was was well-known and out in the open.'

'You were revolutionaries,' said Sam.

With a glass of sherry inside her, Valli took off her jacket and rolled up her sleeves. As the night wore on, this place had the effect of making her feel less tired, just as it did in the thirties when time flew by as they discussed divorce, the monarchy, the buying of votes by landowners, votes for women, education… Sometime La Venencia didn't close until sunrise. But more than reliving these memories, what really excited Valli was sharing a table with Louise Crane's granddaughter.

After another large sip, Valli went on:

'Yes, I never thought that that type of relationship was possible, but Victoria and your grandmother between them gradually explained everything to me,' she said. 'Victoria no longer lived in the "Resi", but your grandmother did and she was one of the regulars at the secret gatherings that were organised in someone's room after eleven at night when in theory everything should have been quiet. There people could ask or talk about anything, about sex, homosexuality or radical politics; there were no taboos. We were always the same small group, but your grandmother was, of course, one of the main rebels,' she said, making Sam laugh. 'She was fantastic, she always brought along wine and cigarettes, which of course the rest of us couldn't afford, but she was always very generous and shared everything she had with everyone else.'

Sam leant back in her chair while the waiter placed on the table the bottle of sherry that she had ordered by signalling to him earlier. They also brought some potatoes, olives and homemade sausage, the same snacks that they offered during the years of the Republic. To the surprise of the very well-mannered Sam, Valli took a couple of pieces of sausage in her fingers and wolfed them down almost without chewing them. Then she wiped her mouth with her sleeve and carried on talking with her mouth half full.

'On one occasion we spent almost the whole night spying on Marie Curie – that was funny,' said Valli, going back to a time that she hadn't thought about for ages. 'She was a really important figure, having won not one but two Nobel prizes, but she hated hotels, so she and her daughter stayed in a room in our building on Miguel Ángel Street. We watched her get changed through the keyhole; she wore some wonderful shirts and nightgowns from Paris – we'd never seen anything like them. I don't remember anything of her talk the following day, but I shall never forget the embroidery that gave the finishing touches to her sexy silks.'

'I can see that you all learnt about everything,' said Sam sardonically.

'That was the good thing about the Residence,' Valli went on. 'We weren't just studying for university, but living together like that was a school for life. We formed groups, we swapped belongings, we sold clothes, and there was even a market for knick-knacks, books and skirts or blouses on Sundays. We were pioneers in recycling!'

The two women laughed, but slowly Valli's smile faded as she recalled how all that suddenly came to an end. With a trembling hand, she refilled their two glasses before continuing.

'Things were getting complicated, as you know,' she said, to which Sam sadly nodded. 'In this very bar,' she went on, 'there were arguments and long discussions as the Republic wore on. As early as 1934 there was a lot of fuss over the rebellion in Asturias and the killings in Castilblanco, a small town in Badajoz that could only be reached by mule and where the Civil Guards killed some olive grove workers who were demonstrating peacefully. They responded by killing some of the Civil Guards, and so the fuse was lit.' Valli took a deep breath. 'There was a lot of debate here, because Margarita Nelken came to talk to the southern labourers who used to come here. I still remember how she addressed them, standing on one of the tables, shouting at the top of her voice as she reminded them of their rights. Poor Margarita, they accused her of starting those incidents, when all she wanted to do was to help the poorest and all she got was trouble. They laughed at her because she was a single mother and because they said she slept with Assault Guards, but I think that all that was just right-wing smears from people who were deeply worried and basically afraid of an independent and intelligent woman.'

'Things are still the same,' commented Sam.

Valli agreed, looking at her with growing respect. She went on:

'She always answered them, she was always ready to fire back. If they told her that women should look after their family and not get involved in politics, she asked them what family they were talking about, since Spain was a country of brothels and children without a name. For her the family of the right was a bourgeois farce. As far as religion was concerned, she said that church hand-outs covered up the legal right to protection from the State. She was a wonderful speaker, in front of large crowds in Madrid or in hundreds of towns and villages that she visited throughout Spain, always giving messages of encouragement and betterment to those most in need.'

'What a pity that such examples have disappeared,' Sam intervened, looking wide-eyed at Valli. 'In the States, at least, our pioneers have become heroes and their work hasn't been forgotten.'

Valli leaned back.

'The same has happened in England and in Germany, my dear, and across half the world, except here, where we lost everything.' Sam remained totally silent. Valli went on: 'It was a tragedy, my dear, a tragedy. The war broke out in the summer, so it caught almost all of us away from Madrid, and as a consequence I didn't get to see your grandmother again, or Margarita, or María de Maeztu, or any of them. And there was I, all ready to go to Smith College in the United States, where I had won a scholarship for the following year. But, of course, I never went.' Valli gave a deep sigh from the very depths of her lungs. 'It was terrible.'

Sam nodded, with tears welling in her eyes.

'I've read a lot about the war in Spain, so I'm fully aware,' she said sympathetically.

Valli had no wish to delve any further into a conflict that she had spent a lifetime trying to forget. She went on:

'After the war, Victoria and I stayed in touch, and in fact it was in Paris where our friendship grew, now as woman to woman rather than tutor to pupil. We had both suffered a lot to save our skin and had both independently started a new life in Paris: she as an eminent politician and writer and I as an ordinary young teacher. Your grandmother went back to America for family reasons, and during the wars – the Spanish and the World War – she couldn't get together with Victoria because the Atlantic was full of German submarines and it was impossible to get a passage to or from the Unites States. Although Victoria was saddened by Louise's absence, she was very busy working for the Republican Embassy in Paris, obtaining passports for those in exile, helping them to get work or a passport or a passage to South America, which is where many of them went. She also helped me to find a small school to the north of Paris where I taught Spanish for several years. I was on my own there and felt quite abandoned, unlike many of the sons and daughters of Republican Ministers and Ambassadors, who immediately got a good diplomatic job or a place in a prestigious foreign university. I wasn't called Zulueta, or Ortega, or Casares Quiroga, Madariaga or Zamora. No, I couldn't even communicate with my parents, since our town was in the Franco zone.'

'Morella!' Sam exclaimed, with an enthusiasm that took Valli by surprise. 'As soon as you mentioned that name in your talk earlier, I recalled the many comments that I heard at home from my grandmother about your town, which she absolutely adored,' said Sam, with shining eyes. 'She had a framed postcard in her bedroom – I imagine it was from you. It was black and white, but very pretty; you could see the houses, and above the mountains, with a castle and an impressive medieval wall, isn't that right?'

'Yes, indeed,' Valli replied, slightly emotional. 'Goodness me, I didn't know that Morella occupied such pride of place in Connecticut. I'd never have thought it.'

'Well, yes,' replied Sam quickly. 'They always explained that one summer they had visited a friend from the Residence in that town, that it took them three days to get there, and that when they were there they saw a wretched pig having its throat cut – to make sausages and ham! I don't think my grandmother ever got over the shock, because I never saw her eat either sausages or ham.'

Valli looked at her with a degree of petulance.

'Well, those who had something to eat should be thankful! But I do recall your grandmother's face...' she said, trying to hide a smile. 'The fact is that such savage killings don't happen any more,' she acknowledged.

Sam sighed with relief.

After a brief pause Valli went on:

'Don't think that life in Paris was much better,' she said. 'During the Nazi occupation, there was nothing but rationing, hunger and hardship. I'd like to have had a couple of pigs in my district of Marais, which at that time was poor and neglected, nothing like the chic area that it's become now.'

Sam smiled. Valli tossed her now rather untidy hair behind her, had some more sips of her sherry and went on:

'Things got a lot worse when, with information from Franco, the Gestapo went after Victoria, who had to take refuge in the Mexican Embassy and then in the house of some diplomatic friends near Wagram Avenue. She went out disguised as a nanny, with a white apron and cap, to get a bit of fresh air. Fortunately they had a real child in the household; it was somewhat too big to still need a pushchair but the trick worked. We arranged to meet on a bench in the Bois de Boulogne in the middle of the morning and there I passed her the clandestine publications that I received from a contact. We all wanted to participate in the Government in exile, convinced as we were that the Allies would defeat Hitler and then would get rid of Franco. We Spaniards supported each other a lot. Even the most famous of us, like Picasso, who Victoria and I visited in his studio in the Rue des Grands Augustins and then we invited him to eat at a nearby restaurant, El Catalán, which he liked very much. I remember very well how kind Picasso always was towards us and whenever he could he helped Victoria and the Republican Embassy. He always seemed very pleased to see us, in fact, since he spent most of his day on his own concentrating on his work. He gave us some of his paintings, which I believe Victoria always kept.'

Sam leant forward and said, in a quiet voice:

'Yes, of course, my grandmother and Victoria had three Picassos in the beach house in Connecticut; we were always being told off if we got closer than a few feet away and they weren't as valuable then as they are now,' she said.

'Do you know what became of them?' Valli asked out of curiosity.

'Well, my mother has them in her house in Manhattan, although I think one of them is in a safe in a bank, because an expert from Sotheby's who came to see it valued it as worth a real fortune,' said Sam, looking down. 'I told her she should give it to a museum, because I don't understand what such an important work of art is doing in a safe,' she remarked despairingly.

Valli moved on from the subject. The contact with Picasso wasn't the most important thing that happened in Paris by far, Valli said to herself.

'Through Picasso Victoria and I met Simone de Beauvoir – such an impressive woman and so courageous.' Valli looked straight at Sam, who had eyes like saucers. 'I think that Simone would have liked to have had a more intimate relationship with Victoria, but I know with complete certainty, because Simone told me herself, that Victoria remained faithful to your grandmother her whole life. And she certainly had opportunities in Paris. She was well-known, having been a leading Republican, and a lot of the American journalists and writers who settled in Paris at that time wanted to interview her… and more. Most of them stayed at the Ritz, my dear, yes, the Ritz no less, so we called this massive arrival of Americans the *Ritzkrieg*, a more peaceful version, although just as imperialist, as the German bombing over London,' explained Valli, laughing to herself. After another large sip, with the bottle now half-empty, she went on in a more serious tone: 'But Victoria always hoped to meet up with Louise, first via Mexico and then in New York, when your grandmother, tired of waiting, had already adopted your mother. What a determined woman Louise was, I always thought.' Valli paused briefly and took a deep breath. 'And you know the rest better than I do. Afterwards they spent over twenty years together, and I think they were very happy, helping the exiles in New York, publishing a journal for them and pressing for change in Spain that, unfortunately, would take a lot longer to achieve.'

Valli took another deep breath and emptied the bottle into their two glasses.

'Your grandmother and Victoria taught me a lot. They taught me how to love someone: the respect they had for each other, the friendship that bound them together, the chemistry that undoubtedly existed between them and their lifelong faithfulness to each other were a good lesson. A lot of couples today would like to achieve the half of what they shared.'

Sam agreed.

'Yes,' she said in a soft voice. 'By contrast my parents got divorced not long ago: they were always arguing, I don't think they ever had much in common. My father was always working, although it was my mother who inherited the company and she spent the day giving classes or out with her friends playing golf,' she explained sadly. 'They put up with things like that for years until my father went off with someone else.'

Valli looked at her sympathetically. She would like to have known more, but chose to be discreet. She noticed how thin she was and pushed the plate of potatoes over to her.

'Come on, eat up, my dear, you look as though you need it.'

Sam looked at the plateful rather contemptuously.

'That makes you fat.'

Valli laughed out loud.

'Oh, my dear, how fussy young people are today. Well, I'd get you a nice filet steak, only they don't serve them here and we wouldn't get one anywhere at this time of night. Come on, eat up, an empty stomach with so much sherry inside it will start to complain soon.'

Sam politely took some potatoes and ate them with obvious reluctance.

'Your grandmother was a really good eater,' Valli recalled. 'In fact she taught us to eat everything, especially when we were travelling, out of politeness. She also taught me how to travel, too.'

Sam raised her eyebrows.

'Yes, that's what I said,' Valli went on, trying to lighten the conversation a bit. 'In those days people in Spain didn't leave their towns and villages other than for funerals or emergencies. Nothing like you… My goodness, I remember the Americans sent postcards from France, Italy, Rio, Cuba, what a life! We just couldn't do that. But in the Residence we organised trips that were generously subsidised, and I signed up for as many as I could, especially if Victoria and Louise were going.'

'In Morocco, for example,' she went on, 'we behaved like country bumpkins, shouting and showing little respect for the poor local people.' Valli sighed. 'The thing is you don't realise what it was like then, Spain was such a backward country… What your grandmother did straight away was to put on the black hijab and remove her shoes to go into the mosques. Silently, discreetly and always attentive and pleasant, she made friends with a lot of Moroccans and gained respect from them as well. It was a lesson for the whole group, and by the end of the trip we were all doing the same as she did. We stopped shouting in the streets and criticising the food and instead we appreciated how exotic and different other countries were. And we learnt that from your grandmother Louise.'

Sam smiled with pride.

'Just think that in Barcelona she even learnt Catalan,' Valli went on, 'and that was another good lesson, because you know how heated the atmosphere was then on the subject of nationalism.'

'Like now,' commented Sam.

Valli agreed.

'Yes, in relation to what caused the war, the truth is that very little has been resolved. Religion, class and nationalism still divide the country. But in the Residence we were very open-minded. We organised evening get-togethers, each with a regional theme, when we would listen to music and eat some of the typical food. With Barcelona we had an annual exchange, always around Easter, which was very enriching both for the Catalan women and for us. One year Victoria managed to get us an invitation via Lorca to the inauguration of the Cau Ferrat in Sitges, a wonderful house covered in tiles, in that little fishing village that for some time had welcomed all the Catalan intellectual revolutionaries. So there we were, mixing with the crème de la crème from Barcelona. And the person who spoke most in Catalan that evening was Louise, putting the rest of us to shame.'

Sam's eyes grew wider as Valli told her stories about her grandmother, who died when Sam was little without giving her time to have a more personal appreciation of her.

'My great-grandmother travelled a lot,' explained Sam. 'That's why she sent my grandmother to study in Madrid and my grandmother always wanted her daughter to follow in her footsteps. But my mother always preferred Italy to Spain, so she went off to Tuscany for two years to study art. Even so my mother speaks and understands Spanish perfectly, because Victoria always spoke to her in her native language.' Sam paused briefly. 'By contrast, I had to learn it from books, as my mother never taught me, which is a shame.'

Valli wondered if Sam's mother would appreciate her daughter's interest in Spain, or if she would have followed her grandmother to the Young Ladies' Residence. Valli knew that the relationship between Louise and her adopted daughter had always been a delicate one, especially since the death of Victoria, when she suffered from depression.

'Does your mother know that you're here with me, or that you planned to come to the function this evening?' she asked.

'No, I haven't told her,' said Sam, thoughtfully. 'Since she divorced my father, she's been somewhat distracted; I think she's on medication, so I try not to touch sensitive subjects. Spain, which undoubtedly changed my grandmother's life, is a complex subject for my mother, because she probably thinks that if she hadn't come here my grandmother would never have met Victoria and would very likely have married a man in the States. In any event my mother loved Louise and Victoria very much, even though sometimes their relationship was complicated. I know that she had problems in school, since the boys picked on her for having two mothers. Those were different times.' Sam lowered her eyes, but then had a large sip of her drink and went on: 'However, I've had everything very easy, I know that I'm privileged, but I want to fend for myself. It's been a great help coming to Spain and setting up my own projects and relationships.'

Valli smiled.

'Oh, my dear, no-one can escape the complexities of life, not even millionaires.'

They made a toast.

Sam went on:

'I think, though, that I will tell my mother that I've met you. It doesn't make sense for her to have money just for show sitting in a safe and you're struggling to keep such an impressive legacy, to which she is also party. I'll have a word with her.'

Valli's eyes lit up until an uncomfortable thought crossed her mind. Nervously she said:

'I don't want you to think for one second that I've brought you here to ask for money. Victoria and Louise mean a whole world to me and you're the only living reminder that I have of them,' she said.

Sam placed a gentle hand very carefully on Valli's, who was now visibly worn out.

'*Por favor*,' the young American replied.

14

Charles took off his elegant white straw hat as soon as he entered the hotel at midday in the middle of July, just three weeks after his previous visit. Now, relaxed after the end of term, he was there to finalise his offer for the school and to get to know what the town was like in summer. His suitcase was full of safari shirts, walking boots and the odd walking stick. Since the first time he had visited Morella at Easter, Charles had fallen in love with the town and was very curious to see it at every season of the year. The spring had been splendid, with the green fields of wheat and the almond trees in full blossom. The summer, so he had read, could be too hot, but he didn't mind that after London's long, cold and sad winter. In any case, he thought, the breeze that he'd felt in the shade when walking along the arcade to the hotel had seemed pleasantly refreshing and much nicer than any air-conditioning.

With Manolo away Isabel came to welcome him with a broad smile. She had changed, thought Charles as soon as he saw her. It wasn't that she was thinner or taller, but with her hair loose, without glasses and wearing a skirt and blouse that were more close-fitting, her appearance had visibly improved. Charles looked at her without being able to turn his gaze away from her enormous green eyes which, unlike other occasions, seemed to look rather brighter. He hoped that the paints he had given her and the ten thousand euros in compensation for the disruption by his students at Easter had wiped out the memory of the embarrassing events of that night. Given how happy she had seemed with the new kitchen on his previous visit, he would say that they had, but he preferred not to take anything for granted. The paints, too, seem to have made a good impression, which he was particularly pleased about as he had gone to get them himself. After a lot of calls and internet searches, Charles had taken himself off to Harrods one Saturday afternoon to find the best box of paints on the market. Unable to find what he was looking for, he carried on looking all afternoon until he found it in a small shop selling games and luxury stationery items in the middle of Mayfair, just behind the Ritz. He asked them to engrave Isabel's name on it and send the package to him at Eton College. The gift didn't come cheap, but from what he had seen, it had been worth it. Isabel didn't seem to bear him any resentment, and that, of course, would help him with his offer, he thought.

'How was your journey?' Isabel asked him, kissing him on both cheeks and making him blush.

Noting his embarrassment Isabel didn't know what to say and so went back behind the reception desk to register his arrival and give him the key.

'Marvellous, I'm with my flamenco dancer, as always,' said Charles, smiling, as he took the key to room fourteen.

'She's still there,' said Isabel, as she filled in the registration card.

'I haven't dared to tell anyone in London the story about her,' he joked.

'I don't tell it much around here, either,' Isabel quickly replied.

Charles picked up his small suitcase, and as he was starting to go upstairs, Isabel said to him without looking up:

'When you're settled in, if you've got a minute there's something I'd like to show you.'

Chares turned round and went back down the three steps that he'd climbed. He put the suitcase back down and put his hands on the counter. He was impatient to know what it was.

'What is it?'

Isabel took a step back and smiled.

'But there's no rush. Get settled in and when you're ready I'll show you,' said Isabel as she put Charles' card into a folder. She turned back towards him. 'It's in the dining room,' she said.

Charles' eyes widened in surprise and he felt a growing pleasure at the thought that it could be a painting. Immediately he felt he shouldn't get his hopes up too much, but his enthusiasm took over. Apart from his students, it had been a long time since anyone had given him a present – except Robin, who always gave him books for Christmas and his birthday, although he couldn't complain, because books were all he wanted and all he had received ever since Meredith had given him jumpers and ties, but that was many years earlier.

'I can't wait, I'm dying to know,' said Charles quite spontaneously.

'Don't you want to put your suitcase in your room first and have a bit of a rest?'

'I'm fine, and I haven't just travelled from China; the journey to Valencia was very good and then I hired a comfortable car to get me here.'

Isabel shrugged her shoulders and came out of the small reception area.

'Well, come on, then; I hope you like it,' she said. 'But I warn you, it's nothing special.'

Charles followed her with child-like excitement. It had been a long time since anyone had invaded his normal life with a surprise. His activities were planned to the minute, which is how he liked it, although such an unexpected gesture had made him feel special.

They both went into the dining room, with the tables set for lunch, and Charles looked at the walls as if he knew what he was looking for while Isabel put the lights on. Straightaway he saw a new picture between the windows that looked out on to the street and Isabel immediately went over to it.

'It's for you; I did it with the wonderful paints that you gave me,' she said, directly and naturally. 'They're the best I've ever had.'

Charles looked into her large and honest eyes, but the temptation to divert his gaze to the picture was greater than the obligation he felt to look at the person who was talking to him. The power of the picture was too great not to pay it immediate attention.

It was in black and white, although with a multitude of grey tones, some of them showing great contrasts. It was medium-sized and nicely framed in clean, fine and shiny dark wood, and depicted what was, no doubt, a location somewhere in the town, thought Charles. Although he didn't know exactly where it was, it was definitely in Morella because of the paving, which looked very like the church Placet, the stone wall and the low houses close by with tiled roofs. Although in principle it seemed to be a happy place, because of the pines and the flowers that were in it, the grey tones and the large cloud in the upper part of the canvas gave it a nostalgic tone. The dark pine branch, almost in relief as if it were lit from behind, heightened the dramatic quality and made the work look almost real.

Charles took a step backwards in order to look at it from several angles. He was impressed by the power of the picture, by what it suggested. It was a location full of personality and, no doubt, of history, too, he thought.

Isabel silently shifted her position this way and that, crossing and uncrossing her arms, while she awaited a verdict.

'Well, what do you think? Aren't you going to say anything?' she said at last.

Charles didn't know how to express himself.

'Anything I say will be inadequate.'

Isabel raised her eyebrows and after a few seconds she smiled. She seemed to have understood that that was the only thing Charles was going to say.

'Thank you very much,' she replied.

'Are you sure it's for me? Such an important work?' Charles muttered eventually.

Isabel laughed.

'Steady on; I don't think it'll fetch much on the open market.'

Charles walked up and down in front of the picture, unable to take his eyes off it. He would hang it in the living room of his house in Eton, in the most prominent place, above the fireplace, where at the moment he had a boring picture of a hunt in Scotland that the father of one of his students gave him many years earlier as a gift.

'It's Morella, isn't it?' he asked after a few seconds, while Isabel looked out the window, with her hands in her pockets, unsure of what to do.

The artist swiftly turned towards him.

'Yes, of course. Don't you know the Poets' Garden?

Charles shook his head.

'Didn't my father show it to you at Easter, when he took you all over the town one day?' she asked in surprise.

Charles gave a brief laugh.

'You've got a good memory, Isabel, but the fact is that no, he didn't show it to me. Where is it?'

'Just below the entrance to the castle, by the Sant Francesc convent, among some lovely little streets at the top end of Virgen Street, very near here,' she said. 'Are you sure you've not been?'

Charles furrowed his brow and went through the places in the town that he'd explored, but he'd never come across this garden.

'No, I'm sorry,' he said. 'But I'll go up and look at it very soon. Why did you paint it?'

Isabel waited a few seconds before replying.

'It's always been a special, hidden spot and until now they've not bothered to tidy it up. They've done a few tributes to poets and it's been left as a sort of Japanese garden of Morella, a place to reflect, to find a bit of peace and quiet, to sit down with a book, far from the noise of the square.'

That came as a pleasant surprise to Charles, who was a great admirer of Japanese gardens for the tranquillity they inspired. But for a second he wondered what sort of place the world would be if even places as peaceful as Morella needed their zen space.

He looked at the clock and saw that he still had a bit of time.

'Well, I'm going up to leave my case right now, and then I'll go there while there's still some time before lunch,' he said.

'I'll come with you if you like,' remarked Isabel, quickly and looking him in the eye.

'It'll be a pleasure,' Charles responded in surprise, but deep down pleased to have struck up a friendship with Isabel. That had been a nice interchange about painting and pictures that gave a human touch to his mission to Morella.

Besides, he only had one friend, Robin, who was more given to long and ample dinners in gourmet restaurants in London than to fine intellectual conversations like this that Charles enjoyed so much. Of course, at Eton he had contact with the numerous artists and writers who often came to give talks to the students, but that conversation seemed more real and above all more interesting. Isabel was a character who intrigued him. She was not very attractive, she had a father who was abusive and who treated her like a slave in the hotel, and on top of all that she had been sacked from her job. But with her great talent that only Charles recognised, she had not gone under in such circumstances and had defied everyone, reorganising the kitchen and starting painting again, without consulting anyone about anything. That woman was worth a lot more than everyone gave her credit for, he said to himself.

Within a few minutes the pair of them reached what Isabel called her favourite spot in Morella. Wearing an orange-coloured summer dress that contrasted well against her dark skin, Isabel sat on one of the wooden benches at the bottom of the garden.

'It really doesn't surprise me that my father didn't bring you here,' she said, taking some dark sunglasses from her pocket and putting them on.

'Why?' asked Charles, sitting down next to her. From there, in the shade of an enormous acacia tree, they could see the rest of the garden, which contained some magnolias and roses open in all their splendour.

Isabel sighed.

'He probably didn't bring you here because, as you will have gathered, his cultural and poetic concerns are, to put it mildly, quite limited,' she said.

Charles turned towards her and looked at her knowingly, but without saying anything.

Isabel went on:

'Now we've got a bit of a controversy, because a local group wants to dedicate this space to several Valencian poets, like Carlos Salvador or Vicent Andrés Estellés, who was a very committed poet.'

'Committed to whom?' asked Charles, making Isabel smile.

'Committed to the language and culture of Valencia, against the evils of Franco and things like that,' she replied.

Charles relaxed his shoulders and leant back against the bench.

'What did he write?' he asked, looking at Isabel. This woman was different from the one he met at Easter, with a bonnet on her head and a mop in her hand, thought Charles. She was really an artist with a good deal of sensitivity, he said to himself.

'Well, he loved Morella and wrote some beautiful poems,' Isabel replied. 'He wrote, for example, that Morella was "a sonnet of fourteen towers, with porticoed silence, held in a stony walled embrace".'

They both remained silent for a few moments.

'In any case, he himself said that words were useless,' Isabel finally commented.

'Useless?'

'According to Estellés, words were not enough to cure the pain and all the resentment left by forty years of Franco, who also destroyed the Valencian language and culture, as well as those of Catalunya, of course.'

Charles gave a slight sigh.

'Well, yes,' he said. 'The fact is I can't imagine your father publicising such messages in a poets' garden.'

Isabel took off her sunglasses and raised an eyebrow as she looked at him. In the shade her eyes were even more green and almond-shaped.

Charles looked around the garden and picked up the scent of the roses and the surrounding pine trees. There was no sound apart from the voices of a few tourists who were having a photo taken at the entrance to the castle, just behind where they were sitting.

'It's a marvellous place,' he said. 'I expect Vallivana, who I've agreed to meet up with this afternoon, will like it, too. Do you know her?'

Isabel gave a smile that was full of tolerance.

'Valli? Yes, of course, everyone knows her. Have you become friends with her?' she asked out of curiosity.

'I know she's opposed to your father's project,' Charles replied in a conciliatory tone, 'but she was very kind to my students, giving us a lot of her time, which I'm grateful for, especially considering her age.'

'That woman is invincible,' said Isabel. 'It doesn't matter what happens to her, the next day she's always so calm and collected again as she goes about doing her shopping in the square.'

Isabel paused briefly, crossing her surprisingly slender legs, especially compared to the rest of her body, thought Charles.

Then she went on:

'I know that she and my father are not the best of friends, but she's always been nice to me. In fact I think that the poor woman has suffered a lot in her life, in the guerrilla movement, in exile, and no-one has ever given her anything.' Isabel waited for a few seconds before continuing. 'There have been a few rumours, but she's never been known to have had any relationships, at least as far as we know; she's never been seen going with anyone in the town. All alone and with no family – I just feel a bit sorry for her,' she concluded.

They both remained silent for a few moments.

'It does seem a rather solitary life,' remarked Charles, thinking that his was pretty much the same, although at least he hadn't been a guerrilla and he'd never wanted for anything.

'Yes,' Isabel replied, with a sudden energy. 'But she keeps on going with her projects, full of determination. Look how she's fighting for her school. Basically she deserves to be admired.'

Charles nodded.

'And now she wants to see you?' Isabel asked, intrigued.

'Well, yes,' Charles replied. 'The Orwell route that she organised for us was very interesting, so I asked her if this time she could show me some of the places where he lived when he was with the guerrillas, apparently not very far from here.'

Isabel gave a deep sigh.

'Yes, there was a lot of activity in this area,' she said in a resigned tone. 'It's a tragedy to end up going to war just because of a difference of ideas.'

'And it seems that no-one learns the lesson,' commented Charles. 'There are still so many wars going on around the world.'

'Wars and what comes afterwards, which is sometimes even worse,' added Isabel. 'I'm sure Valli will tell you all about that; she has spoken about it a lot in lectures and talks in schools.' Isabel crossed her legs again and turned towards Charles. 'But anyway, I hate politics.'

'Are you not interested?' Charles asked in surprise.

'No,' Isabel replied firmly. 'What interests me are people, art, plants and trees. As long as we have enough for our needs, what does it matter who's in power?'

'Hey, it matters a lot, because one lot favours their own and the same with the others.'

'I think everyone should be favoured, starting with the most needy, just out of pure logic, don't you?'

Charles looked at her thoughtfully.

'I don't know if those are the principles of your father's party…'

He felt Isabel looking him straight in the eye.

'In the first place, my father doesn't have a party, he's independent,' she replied in a serious tone. 'And in any case I have my own opinions.'

Her remark made Charles feel small, and he quickly apologised.

'I hope I didn't offend you.'

Isabel put her head on one side and smiled.

'Not at all; I enjoy talking to you. You're the only one who listens to me,' she said, putting her sunglasses back on.

For a moment Charles felt rather sorry for Isabel, but the pleasure he felt from bringing her something important was much greater. As a teacher he had always felt useful, but very rarely had he thought that his words, statements or presence could make someone feel better about themselves, especially a woman. That thought gave him a sense of well-being that he didn't want to disturb.

They both sat in silence for a long while. They listened to the sound of their breathing, the jokes of the tourists and the occasional gust of wind. They felt very comfortable with each other and didn't get up until they heard the church clock strike one. That made Isabel jump up with a start, for the first group of diners were due at two.

Charles arrived punctually at Valli's house on the Pla d'Estudi at about six in the evening when the temperature had dropped a few degrees and was now more bearable.

In his hand he carried a dozen yellow roses that he had ordered from London to send to the local florist to ensure that they had some available. It was the first time he'd seen her since he had gone there with his students in May, as when he was there in June he was told that she was away, although no-one knew where.

The fact is that, after the encounter with the students, Valli had written to Charles inviting him to have coffee with her when he returned to Morella, which Charles was delighted to accept. She seemed to be very opposed to Vicent and before committing himself to the school, Charles wanted to know if that was just the peculiar obsessions of an elderly person or if there were more fundamental reasons that he should know about. Charles had noticed that Valli had some important allies in the town, such as Cefe from the bank. If he was going to buy the school, he needed to try to get on with everyone and avoid falling out with anyone.

'I'm just coming!' shouted Valli suddenly from upstairs.

Charles shouted back, increasingly unconcerned about dropping his impeccable English manners when necessary.

'Take your time, there's no rush!'

After a few seconds Valli appeared smiling, wearing khaki trousers, an old knapsack, a pair of well-worn walking boots, a large short-sleeved tee-shirt – revealing her long, white and wrinkled arms – and a baseball cap on her head. She could have been one of Fidel Castro's band in 1959, thought Charles. As she put on her sunglasses, she said:

'Ready, comrade?'

Charles was impressed by the vitality of that woman, who was well over eighty and in fine physical and mental shape. He nodded.

'You live in a very pretty square,' he said, looking at the old wooden balconies that stood out in the huge square.

Valli, who had already started to walk, stopped after a few paces.

'This is the Pla d'Estudi, it's very old,' she explained. 'It's been called that since the end of the fifteenth century and this is where the Casa Piquer was, where they taught Latin and the Humanities, the most important subjects in those days.'

'Certainly a very appropriate address for a teacher,' he said, impressed with the academic history of the place.

'Especially for a Republican,' Valli quickly added. 'It was called Plaza of the Constitution during the First Republic and Plaza of the Republic during the Second Republic, although in 1938 they changed it to Plaza of the Generalísimo until 1985, when it was restored to its original name.'

Valli started walking again.

'Let's see what name they give it in the Third Republic.'

Charles smiled. He tried to take hold of Valli's arm to assist her, but immediately she pulled it away.

'I'm fine, thanks,' she said. 'If I couldn't even walk right outside my house, I'd have had it; you'll soon see where I'm taking you.'

'I'm very intrigued,' Charles responded.

Charles had actually been waiting for this moment with great anticipation, as apart from everything he had read about the Civil War, he had recently, out of the blue, recalled some of the memories of his father, who occasionally talked to him about the war in Spain. All Charles knew was that his father had supported the Republic because it was a democratic government and that he had been one of the first people in Cambridge to warn of the Nazi danger. Although his father was a man of few words, he had sometimes talked about the time he was in Barcelona during the war, writing news items or propaganda articles together with his friend George Orwell. Once he had told him that he'd been at the front, but Charles only remembered vague descriptions of trenches, the suffocating heat and the tinned food that they ate. Now at last he'd be able to see some of those places for himself.

Charles and Valli drove out of Morella along the Alameda in his rented Seat Ibiza, passing the old abattoir – something that made Charles feel rather queasy as he was not used to picturing animals being slaughtered. They drove slowly along the road to Vinaroz as far as the Collet d'en Velleta, a hill that offered one of the best views of Morella. They stopped and Charles took the opportunity to take some photos. While he was distracted he barely noticed that Valli had started to walk along a track that led off from there. He hurried after her.

'We Republican teachers went along these paths in a cart pulled by two old mules,' she said. 'We took along books, gramophones and even a film-reel player to provide the children with the first opportunity they'd ever had to see animated cartoons,' she explained, while walking at a good pace. 'The poor things, they had seen nothing other than these mountains, they didn't even know what a book was.'

The views got even better as they walked along the track, with the perspective over the town becoming less head-on and more interesting. The silence, the crunching of boots on the ground, the smell of rosemary and lavender, filled Charles' heart with peace and tranquillity. He became engrossed in that tough landscape, with its stones, rocks and scarce vegetation. Within a few minutes they reached a junction with a main road and they stopped for a moment to look at the views. The town stood out majestically against the blue cloudless sky that was bathed in the afternoon sun. Charles took a deep breath and looking around him caught sight of a little red flower – erect, friendly and cheerful – peeking out of a nearby rock. Valli noticed him looking at that marvel of nature and went over to him.

'Everything is a question of willpower in this world, even for flowers,' she said.

Charles nodded and looked towards the almost bare mountains around him.

'It must have been very tough living in these mountains.'

Valli sighed and looked towards Morella. The town now appeared calm, balmy, a picture of peace. The noise of bombardments was a long way away.

'Well, we survived, of course – what were we to do?' Valli replied resignedly.

After a silence Valli turned back along the path towards the car at a steadier pace.

'You see me now as a little old lady,' she said to Charles, 'but I was young for many years and full of hope. We really thought that we were going to put an end to Franco and return democracy to the country. We were convinced.' After a sigh she went on: 'And all means were justified to that end. It was an extreme situation and so we performed actions that today seem brutal but at the time were a matter of life or death.'

'That's how history advances,' commented Charles, trying to make her feel more comfortable.

They got back to the car and went on their way to their next stop, which was still a mystery to Charles. All Valli had said to him was to follow her instructions.

'You see how winding these roads are,' said Valli. 'Well, we took advantage of that to hold up all kinds of vehicles and trucks, which had to brake at every bend, making it easier to get them to stop. A lot of it took place in the small hours of the morning, when we held up drivers carrying foodstuffs and vegetables, leaving them either without cash or without goods,' she said, looking down but carrying on walking. 'We had to eat, although the money we got we gave to the families of Franco's prisoners, because they had nothing to put in their mouths. When we could, we also paid the farmers who gave us supplies, many of them because they chose to support us rather than because we made them do so.'

'Did you all have a lot of support?'

'We did at the beginning, although conditions got tougher. The farmer workers who didn't belong to the Nationalist Movement had to pay a lot of tax and sometimes they had to donate part of their harvest. They weren't allowed to work on Sundays, so they lost a day of trading. One of them was even arrested for picking four tomatoes on a Sunday, even though they were for his own use. The regime went crazy,' said Valli, shaking her head. After a few moments, she added: 'Despite that, the farms provided us with meals, hams and provisions for several weeks. In Fusters farm, for example, they gave me some sandals, while at the one at Campello my group got hold of a Mauser and in Gasulla some grenades.'

'Grenades!' exclaimed Charles, turning towards her, although immediately he turned his eyes back on the road.

Valli warned him about the turning to Vallibona that they were due to take. Charles did as she said, managing to concentrate on the conversation despite the endless tight turns on the narrow road. Valli went on:

'The men looked after the grenades,' she said. 'I was the only woman in my group, although throughout the Maestrazgo there were ten of us women fighters. I spent a lot of time in the camp, because I was in charge of the publication *The Guerrilla Fighter* that I wrote to keep people informed and basically to encourage our comrades. It came out monthly and we printed about a hundred and twenty copies.'

'Where was it printed?'

'We had a little press given to us by a sympathiser. You'll see where we set up camp – it was like a village. Conditions were very hard, but we had everything we needed.'

They two of them eventually reached Vallibona, a very small town strung out in the mountains, with streets and stone houses that were very similar to those of Morella. The doors, windows and balconies were also almost all of wood, in keeping with the style of the Maestrazgo.

They parked at the entrance to the town and immediately took a small path from behind the church. The open land soon gave way to a dense pine wood which the two of them walked through at a good pace until they reached the limestone rock at the base of the mountain. From the road Charles had made out some almost vertical high walls of virtually bare rock that gave some protection to the town; but now, from the valley, he could hardly see the tops. It was a pleasant walk among the increasingly dense pines, oaks and cork trees. After about twenty minutes they reached the meeting point of two large rocks and between them there was a small run of steps, clearly cut into the rock by hand. After crossing the narrow pass, the path, which was covered in pine-needles, continued through a wood and then made its way round a mound of huge stones that in places formed a small gully. The track became more and more unclear because the junipers and thickets along the path were getting taller and making it increasingly difficult to see where to go.

'Look,' said Valli, a bit out of breath, 'these pines and shrubs gave us the name "*maquis*", from "*macchia*" in Corsican which means "thicket",' she explained. 'This type of land was perfect for us, because no-one ever found us here. And the rocks, which are full of nooks and crannies, are so well integrated with the landscape that they conceal all the hiding places.'

Charles was wide-eyed as he followed Valli, engrossed in this totally unfamiliar and increasingly dense world. From where they were they could scarcely see more than two or three yards, although from time to time they came to a small clearing from where they could see the mountains opposite, but without any sign of the town. After crossing more gullies, now reddish in colour, and a pine-grove that seemed to be fairly new, they eventually reached a large clearing very close to the summit, having walked for about an hour. Charles was surprised that Valli didn't seem to be at all tired, for her cheeks were barely pink and there was scarcely any sign of perspiration on her forehead.

'You're in good shape,' he said.

'I know these paths like the back of my hand; if I walked along this stretch once I did it over a thousand times during the ten years that I lived in these mountains.'

'Ten years?' exclaimed Charles in surprise. A decade was a long time to live in hiding. It must have left its scars.

Valli sat down on a boulder and slowly ran her hand over the small knapsack that she carried with her and was now lying in her lap.

'This is one of the few things that I have left from that time,' she said, stroking it with her strong, thick hands.

Charles went over to have a better look at the small bag, which was dark green and quite frayed, with the remains of a republican flag sewn on the front.

They both took advantage of the silence to take some water out of their respective bags and have a drink. Charles took off his hat to wipe his brow and sat down on a rock in the middle of the clearing opposite Valli.

'I'm too old to go up to the lookout,' she said after a few moments, 'but you're still young enough to climb the steps over there behind that rock,' she said pointing to a large boulder. 'The twenty of us who lived here chiselled them out with hammers so we could set up a lookout post at the highest point of the mountain. Go up if you like, because there are some impressive views,' she said.

Without giving it a second thought Charles left his knapsack next to Valli and, with his camera in his hand, followed her instructions. When he reached the top, less than a hundred metres from the clearing, he saw a long, regular and continuous range of mountains that stretched so far into the distance that you could not see where they came to an end. There was no sign of the town and on both sides there was only sky and more mountains covered in pine trees and rock. The only sound was that of the birds, the scurrying of some animal in the undergrowth and the gentle whistling of the wind. Charles closed his eyes and breathed in the pure mountain air. He looked up once more and in the sky there were no planes and no clouds. It was clear, blue now tinged with red as a sign that dusk was approaching. He felt a bead of sweat running down his chest, that now felt strong and healthy and more masculine that ever. That warm climate, he thought, was like a torch of life that made him feel more alive, more strong. He looked at his shirt in surprise, because he barely noticed it on his skin.

Charles looked around him several times. There he was in the middle of nowhere, with an elderly lady he scarcely knew, far from his regulated life at Eton, with its constant comings and goings. He could think or do what he liked, because there, at the end of the world, no-one would know. He felt he was free, just as he did on that journey to India after university, when he sat by himself beside Lake Pichola in Udaipur, to watch the sunset. He thought about his father and wondered if he would have felt a similar sensation there. Perhaps that's why he had been so insistent that he learn the language. Maybe his father had it in mind to explain everything he did in Spain during the war when Charles was older, but when he died that was no longer possible. Now he had so many questions.

Charles heard a slight cough and thought that he shouldn't leave Valli on her own in that place. He took some photos and went back to join his guide, who was still sitting there quietly stroking her knapsack.

'There were some nice views from your place, then?' he said, making her smile.

'You don't know how many Civil Guards I shot up there, and they weren't all beneath a reddening twilight sky in summer like today, I can tell you,' Valli replied. 'Winters here were very hard, with the temperature more than ten below and sometimes there was even snow,'

'How did you all survive?' asked Charles, feeling cold just at the thought of it.

'With a lot of blankets, sleeping bags, huddling against each other and tucking ourselves well in between the rocks,' she replied. 'And, of course, with several fires burning all night. That's why, when we went to the farms, apart from food the thing we needed most was matches.'

'You were saying that many of them helped you.'

'Yes, yes, especially the farm labourers, although they had to be very careful because if they were discovered they could be killed or put in prison,' Valli explained. 'The regime was very cruel and they soon came up with the Law of Fugitives, which legalised the assassination of guerrilla fighters. In fact the Guards received awards, medals and even double pay for every dead *maquis*.'

'Were many killed?' Charles asked as delicately as he could.

'Well, according to one study, in the Province of Castellón alone and in the ten years of struggle between the mid-1940s and the mid-1950s, there were seventy-nine *maquis* killed and eleven Civil Guards died. And over six hundred sympathisers detained.'

'Did you personally know any of those killed?'

'Yes, yes, of course, I lost a lot of friends and comrades,' Valli replied, with a sadness that until now she had managed to keep well hidden. 'I knew most of them. After I entered Spain through the Aran Valley in 1944, I never operated on my own. I always shared the organisation of assaults, sabotage, robberies and hold-ups with others, and I spent hours planning these attacks with them. And as it was usually my job to drive the truck and collect the spoils, I also spent long hours waiting and chatting to my comrades. I knew them well.'

'Sabotage and hold-ups?' asked Charles, finding it difficult to imagine this amiable old lady in action.

'We had to live and we wanted to help the families of the prisoners and those in exile. We took potatoes, oil and flour from the farms and brought them up here on our backs in sacks weighing twenty or thirty kilos. They also gave us – or we took – knives and watches. We paid them when we could, but if not, we always said that we were doing it for Spain and not for ourselves.' Valli took a sip of water and went on: 'This camp was very active, it was part of the Union of Guerrilla Fighters of the Levant and Aragon. It was under the command of El Cinctorrà, which was, of course, just his nickname.' Valli paused briefly. 'I was called The Maestra, of course. The fact is that El Cinctorrà organised a number of actions. He and I stopped a Ford truck coming from the Castell de Cabres mines at five in the morning and we got over five thousand pesetas from that. We also got into those coal mines, thanks to the collaboration of the company accountant, and we came away with most of the profits from the Cedrillas market in Teruel when we stopped the trucks that were loaded with the takings. When we could we also took their shotguns off them.'

Charles fell silent, finding it hard to believe everything that Valli was telling him. She carried on talking as she walked between the pine trees, stroking them gently as if they were old pieces of furniture, which they probably were to her, he thought.

'But, of course, the most useful thing was the banks,' she said. 'For example, we got a hundred and thirty-five thousand pesetas from the one in Villafranca.'

'What did you do with so much money?'

'We gave it to the families that needed it,' Valli answered quickly. 'We weren't thieves or criminals or outlaws, don't ever forget that. We were fighting against a fascist dictatorship.'

'And you were saying that you had popular support?'

'Yes, but everything got more complicated as the years went by, because the Civil Guard, who found it hard to track us down, eventually got themselves organised and even disguised themselves as *maquis* in order to try and trick the farm workers and so expose our network of sympathisers.'

'Did the farm workers recognise them?'

'Of course. Just think, the farm worker is a man of the fields, sharp and very familiar with the people of the mountains. He's easily going to spot a Civil Guard who generally comes from the other end of Spain, who hasn't a clue about the area and doesn't even have rough hands from working in the fields.'

Charles said nothing while Valli sat down again on a tree trunk. He didn't want to interrupt that remarkable flow of memories.

'The fact is that El Cinctorrà also changed and some of his last actions did damage to the civilian population,' Valli went on, speaking with some regret. 'Once we blew up the railway line between Valencia and Barcelona, but no-one was hurt, and another time we kidnapped the Mayor of La Llècua, a village very near Morella. The man was in his late thirties and was liked by everyone. That was a mistake, since we killed poor Ramonet, and what's more we left ourselves without a sympathiser in the whole area.' Valli took a deep breath. 'The grenade that we set off in the electricity sub-station didn't help, either, as it cut off the power to Morella right in the middle of the six-yearly festival.'

'Why did you sabotage the festival if it was one of the few things that people could enjoy?'

'Because the Civil Governor and countless bishops took part in the carrying of the Virgin of Vallivana to the town and we wanted to show them that not everyone in the country was as happy with Franco as they claimed. It was the only way to get a message across to the military and the church who came from Castellón, Tarragona or Valencia for the festival, because we hardly had any activity in those places. The terrain was so flat there that there was nowhere to hide, so the guerrillas concentrated on the mountains around Teruel, Castellón and Cuenca, and in some areas of Asturias or the Sierra Nevada in the south.'

Charles couldn't take his eyes off that woman, although she, with her haunted gaze, was hardly aware of what was happening around her.

'Then, things started to go wrong,' she went on. 'The first kidnapping that we carried out went well. That was Salvador Fontcuberta, owner of a textile business in Beuicarló, and we got two hundred and fifty thousand pesetas from him. But the following year, they caught La Pastora and her companion, Francisco, in the house of Los Nomen, in Els Reguers in Tortosa, and that started to undermine our confidence. In addition the orders that came from Santiago Carrillo in France were not very clear and gradually a lot of the *maquis* began to see that the great operation that was supposed to get rid of Franco wasn't going to happen. In the end many fled to France, including me.'

'On foot?'

'Yes, of course. From here to the Ebro, then Montblanc in Tarragona and going up via Lérida to Prats de Molló over the border, like everyone else. Crossing the Pyrenees in the middle of winter.'

'Didn't they keep a close watch at the frontier?'

'They certainly did,' Valli replied, turning to look at him. 'But remember, the Civil Guard was not like Scotland Yard. One night, with a comrade, we pretended to be drunk in a town quite near the border, which fortunately was holding its local festival. So, we held on to one another, staggering around with bottles in our hands, and told them we were heading for France, which was more than ten kilometres away and just the other side of a very high mountain that we had to get over in order to get there, in the middle of the night and drunk as they thought we were. The men who were at the control post and half-asleep let us through, thinking that they'd probably have to pick us up from some ditch or other the following morning. As soon as we had left them behind us, we threw away the bottles and dashed off as fast as we could, getting to France at dawn.'

Charles felt a shock go right through his body as he pictured Valli blowing up sub-stations, crossing the Pyrenees or killing mayors. He looked at her in some confusion, something that Valli seemed to sense.

She got up and in silence slowly moved to the centre of the clearing. She looked up at the sky and then at Charles.

'I never killed anyone,' she said. 'Although I took part in the kidnapping of Ramonet of La Llècua, I was always against killing him.'

Charles said nothing, trying not to let his face reveal the doubts that he felt about that assertion.

Valli went over to him and stood closer than he felt necessary. Very solemnly she said:

'I never killed anyone and everything I did was for the sake of democracy. I just want you to remember that. In the end we lost, but I fought to the end.'

Charles nodded, fascinated by the dark eyes of that impressive woman. Her face was tired, lined, hardened by terror, cold, struggle and fear. But her eyes were still lively, human, looking at the world with the wisdom acquired over nearly ninety years, but still with the eagerness of a young woman. Charles had never seen a pair of eyes like them, so full of wisdom and passion.

After a few moments he had to look away, unable to cope with such intensity. He felt small and insignificant beside such a character. What had he ever fought for in this life?

The last rays of the sun disappeared from the clearing and Valli and Charles looked at each other in mutual understanding. They picked up their bags and started to return along the path, which didn't seem to Charles to take very long, because his mind was dealing with a torrent of ideas, questions and thoughts.

Amid his confusion and as they left behind them crests and gullies covered in scrub oak and gorse, Charles recalled Isabel's painting, which portrayed a dramatic quality similar to that which he had just felt listening to those hair-raising stories. Spain was a cheerful, sunny, wonderful country, with spectacular scenery, but still being eaten away from inside by a dark, dramatic and tragic history.

As they went along Charles thought about Isabel and wondered whether she was not the opposite to her country: tragic externally but balanced and at peace internally. He was still amazed at the confidence with which Isabel ordered his students to clean up the hotel when they'd never held a mop in their lives before and were not used to taking orders from a woman. Charles smiled at the thought that Valli would also have made them get to it straight away. He was curious to know what the relationship was like between the two women.

'I imagine the poet Estellés would be inspired by this sort of place,' he said to make their return walk more interesting.

Valli, who was walking in front, turned round.

'How do you know about such a splendid poet? I didn't know he'd been translated into English.'

'Unfortunately I've never read him,' Charles replied, adopting his refined tone and his upright posture as usual. 'I was in the Poets' Garden this morning with Isabel, the Mayor's daughter, and she told me about him.'

Valli stopped and looked at him in surprise, thereby making Charles say something in order to avoid any questions:

'For reasons too lengthy to explain I brought her some paints from London and she gave me a lovely picture of that garden in return. Have you seen her paintings?'

Valli, for whom his explanation seemed to have stirred up more questions than answers, replied:

'Yes, I have seen the ones in the hotel; they're not bad.' After a brief pause, she added: 'Have you become friends?'

Charles nodded and started walking again, with Valli following. He explained how much he liked Isabel's paintings, since they revealed the strong personality of Morella, which had undoubtedly fascinated him. He walked and spoke quickly and happily while the twilight breeze gently wrapped itself around him. He felt happy among the mountains listening to Valli's stories.

Before they realised it they'd reached Vallibona and Charles was surprised to find that the only thing he'd talked about was Isabel and her paintings for a good part of their return walk.

As they got into the car and could finally take a rest, Valli looked him in the eye and said to him in a very serious tone:

'I know that girl isn't to blame for anything. She's always been very pleasant to me. But don't trust her, Charles, because her family is the devil incarnate.'

Charles turned off the engine that he'd just switched on and looked at her in great surprise. Valli went on:

'That picture could be part of their scheming to do with the school.'

Charles, who was enthusiastic about the picture, felt wounded by those words.

'How can you say that, Valli? Isabel is a wonderful girl.'

'I'm not saying she isn't, Charles,' Valli replied. 'I'm just warning you not to trust her. That family is possessed by the devil.' Valli paused briefly, looking ahead all the while.

Charles was about to respond when Valli got in first:

'I'm very tired now, Charles. I've talked a lot today, but if you like we can continue another day.'

Out of respect Charles acceded, although he felt an obligation to defend Isabel's honour. He had been deeply affected by her painting, because it was a gift that was filled with feeling and thoughtfulness. It was a long time since anyone had given him such a gift – perhaps never.

Without a further word he started the car once more and they returned to Morella in silence. That conversation would have to be continued, Charles thought to himself.

15

Valli spent more time at home during the following days than usual, in the company of her plants and the dozens of books that filled the old wooden bookcases all around her apartment. She was quite a solitary person, although she also went out for a walk almost every afternoon with Cefe from the bank or with a neighbour. Now, however, she had spent two whole days not going out other than for bread or some vegetables. It was a shame, she said to herself as she looked out the window of her small living-room, as the streets were busy and the weather was nice, although fortunately it was nothing like the stifling, intense heat of August. That was when Valli went out of town to a small house on the beach that her neighbour Carmen had in Benicarló. Morella was unbearable in August, with hundreds of tourists and holiday-makers, and the noise of three days of the bulls that completely took over life in the town. She was too old now to run with the young bulls that were let loose in the streets and to take part in the huge fiesta that was organised every year.

Valli sat in her old armchair in her small apartment on the Pla d'Estudi. She put down the quilt that she had started to knit in May, just after meeting the English students. That visit had left her rather confused since, on the one hand, she didn't want to make any deals with the most elitist college in the world, but on the other hand she didn't want to do any harm to Charles, who seemed to be a decent person who was genuinely interested in Morella and in Spain. He even knew who the poet Estellés was, she said to herself as she picked up her needles and wool once more. She still had nimble enough hands to be able to knit quilt after quilt which she then sold to the shops in the town that were mainly for tourists. The income and her tiny pension gave her sufficient to maintain the same frugal lifestyle that she'd always had.

From her armchair next to the window Valli looked at the plants on her balcony and the mountains beyond that were bathed in the pleasant summer afternoon sun. She knew that she could not stop the sale of the school, since the Mayor could count on the support of a lot of people who owed him a favour. Politics really was awful, she thought, looking at the clock and putting away her things in a little cloth bag that she had made many years before.

With a certain solemnity, as if she were going to do something important, Valli took off her housecoat and put on a dark green dress that she herself had made the previous year. She tidied herself up and, knapsack and stick in hand, she headed off to the Sant Mateu gate, one of the five entrance gateways in the town wall. Walking at a good pace and with the aid of her favourite stick, Valli negotiated several inclines before arriving with English punctuality at the Hotel Cid where she had arranged to meet Charles. It wasn't that she was very keen on stirring up the past or reliving some of the worst moments of her life, but the meeting was necessary. Charles needed to know who he was dealing with before taking a decision. Rather than oppose his interest in the school head-on, Valli had decided to explain to Charles who Vicent really was and let him decide for himself.

Charles was as punctual as she was and arrived a few seconds later with a more elegant outfit than the one for hiking that he had worn two days earlier when they visited the *maqui* camp at Vallibona. Today they were only going for a walk to the arches of Santa Llúcia, although Valli had also thought about going over to her parents' old farmhouse that was now in ruins.

With his panama hat and a pair of pleated cream-coloured trousers that matched his fine-check shirt, Charles greeted Valli with a smile which she returned. They both seemed to have found a certain balance in their relationship, which was now free from the tension that had marked their earlier conversations. Charles also seemed to be more open and interested in her.

'Good afternoon,' she said in English.

Charles slightly raised an eyebrow.

'I didn't know that you spoke English with such a good accent,' he said.

'Never underestimate an old woman like me!'

'Where did you learn?' Charles persisted out of curiosity.

'It's a very long story, but remember that exile took me to many countries,' Valli explained. 'In fact I learnt it in the Young Ladies' Residence in Madrid, where I lived and studied while I went to university. It was the Oxbridge of Spain.'

Valli saw a look of surprise and admiration in Charles' bright eyes.

'What did you think – that I'm a poor working-class old woman?' she said in a genial way.

'No, no, of course not.' Charles blushed as he hastened to reply.

The pair of them made their way along the wall towards Sant Miquel. After a few minutes they stopped at the public wash house, now turned into a kind of museum that Valli wanted Charles to see.

'Would you believe it?' she said, leaning on the sloping stone where the clothes were scrubbed alongside a small sink. 'During the dictatorship this was the only place in Morella where there was freedom of expression.'

'Here?' asked Charles as he looked around the shed-like building that was open on two sides. The echoes in the small building, now white and empty, bounced off the totally bare walls.

'Yes, here,' said Valli, her eyes fixed on one of the sinks. 'In the middle of winter, with the temperature at five degrees below zero, the women used to come here to wash and rub and scrub until their hands practically froze. But the good thing was that here they could say everything they couldn't say in the square or sometimes not even at home.' Valli paused for a moment. 'While I was in the *maquis* this was the only place where I could talk with my mother,'

Charles looked at her in surprise.

'I thought your parents lived in a farmhouse and not in town.'

Valli tightened her lips and swallowed before replying.

'Yes, yes, I'll explain later,' she said, looking around her. 'These wash houses were the only things I saw of Morella for years when I came to see my mother or to exchange information with our sympathisers.'

'That must have been very dangerous.'

'It was,' Valli replied. 'But the Civil Guards never realised and the women who came here never betrayed us. I don't know if any of them recognised me, because I was always well wrapped up, but if they realised who I was at least they didn't denounce me, or my mother either.'

'How brave of you to come from the camp to the town.'

'What choice did I have otherwise? Not seeing my mother?'

Without waiting for a reply Valli took hold of her stick and continued towards Sant Miquel. The towers that flanked the main entrance to the town rose majestically as always; their medieval stone contrasted well with the radiant blue sky, with the castle in the background. After going up a small slope Valli and Charles sat down on one of the benches just outside the wall to look at the views of the countryside.

'These roads are very modern,' said Valli, pointing with her stick towards the new junction that separated the traffic heading for the town from the road that carried on towards Zaragoza. 'Before, the roads were covered in dust, there wasn't any asphalt. In fact they were made of tarmac, a type of crushed stone, rolled flat and covered in gravel and dust. The few cars around had to go so slowly that sometimes the farm workers' mules were faster.'

Charles smiled.

Valli turned towards the towers of Sant Miquel and gave a small sigh.

'This is where they came in, right here,' she said, without saying anything further.

'Who, Franco?'

'Well, the Nationalists,' Valli replied. 'It was 1938, and in March they began the offensive across the whole of Aragón. On the tenth they took Belchite, a town that was left completely destroyed, and after about ten days they started the campaign across the Maestrazgo. In April they took Gandesa and Lérida and on the fourth they reached Morella,' she said, breathing deeply after that.

Charles said nothing.

'A lot of Republicans had escaped, since on the radio they'd said that they were coming,' she went on. 'I'd always been with the Republic but I didn't run off because at that time I was still a Catholic and the whole town knew that I went to Mass every Sunday; poor thing,' she said, giving a cynical laugh. 'Plus, I was only a trainee teacher so my name didn't appear on the blacklists of teachers who were signed up to the Republican cause. Poor things.' Valli observed a few moments silence before going on. 'The day before they entered we saw from the Sant Francesc convent a Nationalist column, with their red and yellow flags, coming along the Cinctorres road at dawn. As they advanced towards Morella we could make out the single column more clearly; it was so long that it seemed as though it was never going to come to an end. There were so many of them and, of course, they were highly organised. It took three hours for them to get to Sant Miquel and they came in through this very gate. The majority of them were Red Berets from Navarre, the Carlist militia.

'Wasn't there any resistance?' asked Charles.

'None at all, because by then all the Reds had escaped; but there wasn't any welcome, either. People were very afraid and didn't come out of their houses, although everyone was peering out from behind their net curtains. Just as the Reds had done when they entered the town, the Nationalists cut off the electricity and immediately took control of the Town Hall. The town was silent; well, apart from the troops singing their almost ancestral hymns, like the Carlist anthem, the Oriamendi. Everything was for God, the Fatherland and the King. Just imagine, those people from Navarre, who thought they were going to get a king…'

'Everyone was fighting for something different,' Charles commented.

'Yes, unfortunately for everyone,' Valli conceded, before continuing her story. 'The sympathisers of the new regime started to come out of their hiding places where they had taken refuge during the war while Morella was still in the Reds' zone. Some families that ran sheep businesses, for example, had all hidden together in a farmhouse in Xiva, sleeping up to twenty in a single hayloft. The priest also emerged from another farmhouse and they all returned to their posts.' Valli paused briefly. 'The war changed everything so that everything would carry on the same. Whoever had had power before the war kept it afterwards.'

'And what about you and your family?'

'You'll soon see,' said Valli, getting up from the bench with the aid of her stick and setting off for the arches of Santa Llúcia, by that time a brilliant golden colour from the setting sun.

Charles and Valli crossed the old medieval arches that used to bring water to the town from the well at Vinaròs, as she explained. The two of them continued along the narrow, deserted road towards Xiva, and took a turn off along a little track after the junction towards the cave paintings of Morella la Vella, that Charles promised himself he would visit another day. After a pleasant walk along an earth track they reached a path that led them to a half-ruined building, although it still retained some walls and part of the roof.

Valli went over to the building and, with a firm, sharp blow with her stick, opened what remained of the heavy, dark wooden door. Charles followed Valli into the large room in which the only thing left was the still blackened stone fireplace that was set into the wall.

She turned towards Charles.

'This is our farmhouse,' she said, nodding her head. 'I can still see my father sitting there in his wooden chair after spending all day in the fields. His name was José and he always wore his black beret, even indoors,' she said, with a nostalgic smile. 'He always wore a long black shirt buttoned to the neck, and a pair of old, well-worn trousers, full of patches that my mother sewed on. When it was cold he wore a cloth jacket, his Sunday best one, which lasted him all his life. At the end it almost fell apart.'

Valli went over to the fireplace and looked up at the roof, where there were still some half-broken wooden beams.

'My mother worked here,' she said, 'in what was the kitchen. There was a wooden table where they skinned and prepared the rabbits and birds that my father brought in from the fields or that we kept in the yard behind the house. Everything had to be done in daylight because we didn't have any lighting, only an oil lamp that hung from the ceiling and attracted all kinds of moths that died in the flame, poor things. Sometimes in the morning we found a bat that had got trapped.' Valli paused briefly to smile, looking at the ceiling as if she were seeking or seeing those moths. After a few seconds she went on: 'The two bedrooms, mine and my parents, were upstairs, and they were only lit by candles that we always kept inside glass bottles, in case they fell over. In winter when it was very cold, we brought our two mules inside and let them sleep next to the fire on a small bed of straw that my mother and I made for them.' After a pause Valli remarked: 'The truth is they stank.'

That made Charles smile.

'Did your parents have any land?' he asked.

'You must be joking,' she replied. 'They worked for the Marquis, like most farm labourers. Only the merchants and the Marquis himself were landowners, generally of very large tracts – and they still are. There were no small farmers here, and there still aren't, just like in Catalunya. Here we worked for the master, who required the same amount from our harvest even if we'd got less because of rain or storms. It was an almost feudal system.' Valli looked over at the fireplace once more. 'My father, who never learnt to read or write, never looked the Marquis in the eye. I think he spoke to him once in his life after breaking his back year after year cutting down wheat by hand.'

'By hand?'

'Yes, with a sickle,' Valli quickly replied. 'Although in fact I have good memories of those times, because when I was little my father put me up on the thresher so that I could use the whip on the mule, who went round in circles on the grain. It was great fun; fortunately I never fell off!'

'The stones of the thresher could have crushed you…'

'We took risks then; nowadays children just play around with cuddly toys.'

They both laughed.

'Then we left the wind to separate the grain from the straw and put the dried wheat into sacks that we gave to the Marquis. We always had some left that we exchanged at the Saturday market for a skinny chicken with large feet, which was very tasty; nothing like the frozen birds that you get nowadays that don't taste of anything. Those were real chickens!'

They left the farmhouse and after showing Charles what used to be the back yard, Valli sat down with him on a natural stone bench that was near the front door. All they could see from there was mountains and the odd farmhouse that was as remote as this one.

'After the war why didn't you stay in the town with your parents?' asked Charles out of curiosity.

'Because I didn't want to give in to Franco and say amen to everything, as everyone else had done. In the Young Ladies' Residence they had taught me to think and to fight, not to give up at the first hurdle,' she said assertively. 'Besides, the Second World War began not long afterwards, and we Republicans were convinced that the British and the French would get rid of Franco after they'd finished with Hitler.'

'*Disculpa*', he said in a quiet voice.

'Yes, yes, *disculpa*,' said Valli, looking at him with a rather superior air. 'A bit of a dirty trick.' She went on: 'The fact is that there were a lot of changes. One day my father, who spent the war carrying sacks of wheat on his back to the Marquis' house like a donkey, overheard a telephone conversation which would change his fate. It turns out that the Nationalists set up a single currency in the areas they were taking over, because the system of currencies in Spain had become chaotic; practically every town had its own, which created an economy based above all on bartering. As the Fascists advanced, people wondered what would happen to Republican banknotes, since the Nationalists didn't exchange them all for the new currency; they only exchanged those that belonged to a particular series, of course, in order to favour their own and to leave the other lot without anything. My father heard the list of numbers, since someone called to pass them on to the Marquis, who repeated them out loud as he wrote them down and meanwhile my father was unloading some sacks of wheat in the next-door room in the Marquis' house. My father was illiterate but he could retain numbers in his head as he was used to counting wheat and calculating prices and amounts all his life. With the help of another farm labourer who could read, they just held on to the notes with those serial numbers and they ultimately became their savings.

'And did the Marquis launder his as well?' asked Charles, who gave the impression that he didn't believe what he was hearing.

Valli looked at him rather condescendingly as if he was just a novice in the business of living.

'The Marquis... the Marquis...' she said, nodding her head before giving a clear explanation: 'The Marquis was stoned to death by another farm labourer just before the end of the war, when the tension with the oligarchs was at its height. Everyone who worked for him was delighted, because he was a real tyrant.'

Charles furrowed his brow as he tried to understand the situation.

'Was your father delighted, too? What did he do with the money they obtained?' he asked.

'My father was a good and honest man,' Valli explained, 'but that money and that death opened doors that had always been closed to him. He wanted to leave the farm and go to the town to give my mother and me a better life rather than being here all day on our own surrounded by pigs and mules.'

'But you were in Madrid by then, weren't you?'

'Yes, I went almost as soon as the Republic was declared, but I think my father always thought that I would return to Morella to teach in the school and live nearby. The fact is that when the Marquis died, some of his sisters inherited the hotel that he had in the town...'

'The religious sisters!' Charles exclaimed, fondly remembering the flamenco dancer in the hotel and the story about one of the sisters going to Seville to get married after the war.

'That's right. How do you know?'

'Isabel told me about it.'

'Oh,' said Valli, rather disappointed. 'Well, you'll know that one of them left to get married and the other one stayed, but she didn't know how to run a business. My father put money on the table, and that's how he took over the hotel.'

'The hotel belonged to your family?' exclaimed Charles in surprise.

'Of course. It was an entirely legal purchase, all done properly with deeds and everything; I was here to help my father and to check that everything was in order. We moved in and my mother and I between us painted four or five rooms with the money we had, and fixed up the kitchen that my mother took charge of. She was an excellent cook, which meant that we could immediately make a living from providing meals. All those who used to patronise the Casino Republicano and were not radical enough for someone to report them started to come to the hotel, as well as some soldiers and Civil Guards who were living away from their families and had nowhere to go.'

'And that was enough?'

'We managed. At least we were eating and living under a roof that we didn't have to share with mules, and my parents were much less isolated in the town.'

'How did the hotel end up in the hands of the Mayor's family?'

Valli was slightly taken aback but recovered herself and placed her hands on her knees. Once more, with the help of her stick, she got up and looked around her. The sun was now quite low in the sky and there was barely an hour of light left in the day.

'Come on, let's head back and I'll tell you along the way, before it gets too dark.'

Charles followed.

'It was a case of a murder and a robbery,' said Valli, going straight to the point as they set off.

Charles looked at Valli out of the corner of his eye, raising his head but not saying anything. Valli went on:

'After helping my father with the purchase, I went off to France, as I told you the other day. I spent some years in Paris, but then I moved to the south, to the Pyrenees, where most of those living in exile were. We were convinced that we could get rid of Franco. But the years went by without anything happening, and in 1944 when De Gaulle made us move away from the frontier, it became clear that we would have to sort it out ourselves if we wanted to restore democracy. After a lot of dithering, Santiago Carrillo and La Pasionaria eventually came up with a plan, but it ended in tragedy, because it was carried out badly and late.' Valli paused briefly to take in some air after going uphill. After a few moments she continued: 'They called it Operation Reconquest of Spain, with the entry through the Arán Valley in the Pyrenees of almost five thousand guerrilla fighters, who were ready to take over the country town by town and throw Franco out.'

'With only five thousand soldiers?' Charles asked, incredulously.

'Not even that,' Valli replied. 'We were just a poor mislead lot who were starving hungry, with rope sandals and the odd rifle, convinced – or rather deceived – into thinking that in Spain thousands of people were waiting for us and keen to join our army. But all we found was a sedated population that had been hypnotised by the Franco machine and his policy of faits accomplis. Collaboration was punished by the death penalty.' Valli stopped as she reached a level path after the hill. 'The majority died in the first few days of the attack, because Generals Moscardó, Yagüe and

Monasterio were waiting for us on the other side of the Pyrenees. It was horrible, but together with a comrade, who later died, I escaped and we walked three nights in a row through the mountains towards Aragón; fortunately it was summer. There we took refuge in Tramacastilla de Tena, a little village hidden right in the mountains very close to the border with France, near Biescas.

'Was it safe, right on the border?'

'Not at all,' Valli replied.' Franco had built countless guard posts, real bunkers about two hundred metres long, with lengthy stone walls containing viewing points and openings for rifles. They built them right in the mountains, sometimes nowhere near paths or roads. The bastards – and please forgive the expression – watched us more closely than they did rabbits. I don't know how much Franco spent on all those posts, but the fact is that he scattered the Catalan and Aragonese parts of the Pyrenees with those constructions, always among trees so that they were very well hidden. The great bast...' Valli didn't want to be vulgar again. 'They didn't know how to run a country, but in matters of war they were certainly not novices.'

'How long did you stay there?'

'Not very long,' said Valli, as she started walking again towards the first set of Santa Llúcia arches. 'Only a few months, but enough to plan the blowing up of a local electricity station. We organised it with a group of guerrillas we met in Tramacastilla, who we knew about thanks to La Pirenaica.'

'Who was La Pirenaica?'

Valli smiled and looked at Charles.

'It wasn't a woman, it was a radio station that the Communists, or so we thought, operated from the Pyrenees but which we discovered later broadcast from Moscow and Hungary, From there La Pasionaria and other leaders encouraged us to fight, of course, while they lived like kings in such friendly places.'

'Always the same,' commented Charles.

'*Verdad,*' Valli replied, giving Charles a wink, while he gave her the look of a co-conspirator. Valli went on: 'The thing is that via the radio, which sent messages in a secret code, we got in touch with a cell of the Spanish Communist Party that was planning an attack on the Biescas electricity station,' Valli explained, slowing down a bit as they were reaching the town.

'Why did you want to blow up an electricity station?' asked Charles, evidently not very knowledgeable about warfare.

'You always have to weaken the enemy,' Valli explained. 'Leaving the town without power was a good way of annoying the Civil Guard, which was clearly our main enemy,' said Valli, although Charles didn't seem too convinced. Valli went on: 'The fact is that before setting the dynamite, we studied the area carefully, and that's how I met Vicent's father.'

Charles stopped at once and Valli did the same. They both looked directly at each other.

'I assumed that your relationship went back a long way,' said Charles.

Valli sighed and looked towards Morella, now bathed in the reddish light of dusk. The path along which they were walking was practically empty and silent; the only sound was their footsteps on the ground. Valli leant on her stick, ready to say something more before they climbed the steps to Sant Miquel.

'It really was a long time ago. It was 1944, when I was only about twenty-five; I was still a child,' she said. 'But I was convinced about what I was doing. In Biescas my job was to spy on Vicent's father, who was a Civil Guard, and tell my comrades about all his movements so that we could draw up a good plan. And that was very successful.' She paused for a moment. 'It wasn't difficult to see that almost every night, after one o'clock in the morning when he was on watch, some tart came to visit him in his guard house, which wasn't far from the electricity station. So we took advantage of that, and of course he didn't realise when a group of comrades went in to prepare everything and blew the station up.'

'Were there any casualties?' asked Charles with a shocked look.

'No, none at all. But Vicent's father did suffer the consequences; I think they reduced his rank or something like that, since they blamed him for not keeping watch. They said that they even caught him with the tart during working hours. The fact is that he ended up in Morella, where no-one wanted to come because the fight against the *maquis* was a must-win for the Civil Guard. They had neither the training nor a plan to track them down, but even so getting rid of the guerrillas was Franco's number one preoccupation and any mistakes were punished severely.'

'And, of course, you met up with Vicent's father again in Morella.'

'Correct,' said Valli. 'Guard Fernández turned up in Morella two years after I arrived, in 1946, after spending a couple of years in Madrid, I think, or somewhere else, by way of punishment. I had arrived at the end of 1944, after the Biescas event, to join up with the guerrilla groups of the Maestrazgo, which were the most active in the country.'

'But did he know you?' asked Charles, just as they reached the Alameda.

They entered the walkway that was to take them round the back of the town. They were walking slowly, without noticing the magnificent sunset as they were concentrating so much on their conversation.

'No, I never spoke to him directly,' said Valli, looking at the ground as she walked. 'Otherwise he would have finished me off on the spot.' She sighed as she looked straight at the Mola La Garumba, an impressive tall, flat mountain high above that stretched away, dark and imposing, just a few kilometres from Morella.

'But he knew my parents, because he went to eat at the hotel every day,' Valli went on. 'As for me, my mother brought me food at the farmhouse that you've just seen, which they kept after moving to the hotel so as to house some animals and maintain a small kitchen garden. They also left me photos or letters that I or my comrades picked up at night. To put the Civil Guard off the scent my mother said that she went to the farmhouse just to take a walk or to feed the chickens, but the wretch must have suspected something and one day he followed her. There had been a rumour in the town that I was in France, so Fernández knew there was a good price on my head.'

Valli closed her eyes and although she tried to keep control of herself a tear rolled down her cheek, followed by another and another. Charles took her gently by the arm.

'Don't say any more if you don't want too, Valli,' he said softly.

Valli opened her dark eyes again, that were now full of spirit.

'No, Charles, I want you to know,' she said. Still calm and leaning on her stick, she took a deep breath and continued. 'Well, he killed them, just like that. One Sunday afternoon my parents went to the farmhouse, as they did almost every day they had off. From our lookout we saw, as soon as they arrived with the packages, that the bastards were waiting for them inside and they told them that collaboration with the guerrillas was a crime. My parents begged them, but after a few seconds they riddled them with bullets, both of them.'

Valli closed her eyes once more, unable to stop the tears that silently ran down her face. She heard Charles' deep breaths and felt his strong but gentle hand take hold of hers and stroke it. She also felt him place his arm gently and lightly round her shoulders and give her a firm squeeze.

Valli sat up after a few seconds and dried her tears.

'Don't worry, these are things that happen,' she said. 'This country is full of stories like that. I'm not the only one, far from it.'

Charles nodded, unable to say a word, but without taking his eyes off Valli.

At that moment the lights on the Alameda came on and so very slowly they started walking again.

'Very soon after,' Valli went on, 'the council took over the hotel. After a few months they put it up for sale and Vicent's father, with the money and the prestige that he had acquired killing the *maquis*, bought it for next to nothing, although they probably gave it to him. In any event I know that he also got some money on the black market, since we watched him day and night and on one occasion we saw him in the small hours exchanging sacks of flour or jars of oil, the great bastard.'

Charles, who was still holding her by the arm, asked:

'And that's how they came to own the hotel?'

'That's it. Just like that. Vicent's father killed my parents and then ended up with their business,' replied Valli. 'That's how Spain worked for over forty years.'

'And what did you do?' Charles asked, almost in a whisper.

Valli sighed several times, as if all of a sudden her years of struggle and exile weighed more heavily on her than ever.

'As you can imagine, it took me a long time to get over it, because I saw what happened with my own eyes,' she answered. 'I saw that bastard shoot my own parents, I saw their bodies fall to the ground, shot to pieces, and I suffered from nightmares for many years.'

'I can't imagine anything more terrible,' Charles muttered.

'Nor can I,' Valli responded. 'At least La Pastora was in the area – I suppose you've heard of him.'

Charles nodded.

'He was a wonderful man,' she went on. 'He looked after me a great deal, we spent a lot of time together, a lot of it in silence, but it was his support that enabled me to carry on, at least for those three years until 1953, when Carrillo finally recognised that the battle was lost and ordered the retreat. A lot of comrades had already deserted, but I stayed for a while with La Pastora. In the end, like everyone else, I went to France.'

They reached the Pla d'Estudi and slowly headed towards Valli's front door, while she said hello to a neighbour or some elderly folks who were also returning from a walk.

'So the hotel is yours,' said Charles. 'Have you never reclaimed it?'

Valli shrugged her shoulders.

'I did try when I came back at the end of the seventies, but the papers were all in order, and in fact they had bought it, so legally it was theirs; there was nothing more to be done.'

'Does the Mayor know what his father did?'

Valli's eyes narrowed, lynx-like, as she looked at Charles.

'Don't be deceived, Charles,' she said, 'that family is pure poison. Of course they know how their father earned a living: assassinating guerrilla fighters.'

'But do they know about your parents?' Charles persisted. 'Isabel, as well?'

'Well, of course they know. Everyone knows everything in towns like this.'

Charles looked down, visibly disappointed.

'I accept that you've struck up a friendship with that woman, Charles,' said Valli. 'I can assure you that she has never done me any harm, but don't trust her an inch; that family is capable of the worst atrocities. Believe me, steer clear of them, they're the devil and they may be deceiving you.' After a pause, Valli moved towards Charles, leaving very little distance between them. 'It wouldn't surprise me if the Mayor were using his daughter as bait. She gives you paintings, she befriends you and then she has you on board over the school. Don't believe a word of what they say to you.'

Charles took a step back and looked at Valli with a feeling of rejection. That warning didn't go down at all well, thought Valli, but she had to be honest with him.

'I can see that you have feelings for the girl,' she went on, 'but it may well be that the feelings she shows towards you are false.'

Charles gave her a cold look, full of contempt, which Valli felt like a sword slowly sinking into her heart. She had already suffered greatly in her life and now, at her age, she didn't want to hurt people who were innocent to boot.

'And what do you know of feelings?' Charles spat out in her face. 'When you've never had a relationship or your own family.'

Valli stood there staring at him for a few moments and used the last drop of her courage not to fall apart.

'I know much more than you think,' she said, and disappeared inside her front door, leaving Charles stunned and highly confused outside. She could stand no more stress.

As best she could she climbed the stairs to her small apartment and once inside, she fell exhausted on the bed, burying her head in her wrinkled hands, feeling confused and scared. Her breathing was rapid and she was having palpitations. She had never imagined that things would come to this.

16

Two days later Vicent arrived home after a ride on *Lo Petit* around the Torre Miró pass. During the long summer evenings, he loved to ride to the delightful village of Herbeset, which like Morella was also on a mountain, following the stony paths, crossing oakwoods, going past crags and hills and stopping to rest in one of the stone huts that were still used by the shepherds. Vicent knew these paths well, for his father, who had spent half his life hunting down the *maquis* in these parts, showed him all the hideouts that he would later use in his youth when he reached the age to get up to mischief. He remembered how he used to hide in those old stone buildings to smoke and drink with a school friend, whom he hadn't seen since the boy's family moved to Valencia. Vicent had never been a man with many friends, especially since his father died when he was fifteen and had to take over the hotel. The age of forbidden games and smoking and drinking in those inhospitable parts of the Maestrazgo had barely lasted a year or two.

Vicent now rode through these lands with pride, thinking that in fact it was better to enjoy life when you were older rather than younger, since you were more aware of things and you also had some money. Having left behind the farmhouses of Giner and Darsa, he reached the Pereroles Mountain, one of his favourites, for as a boy he had played in the shade of its tall pine trees. In a clearing he stopped in front of an old stone house where once he spent the night with his father and other Civil Guards, without food or drink or fire to keep them warm. That freezing night seemed so long ago, for the house had been converted into a fully-fitted comfortable mountain refuge, to judge by what he could see through the windows.

With his head up Vicent headed for home with *Lo Petit*, who was now very tired, stopping only at the Boca Roja. The beautiful views from that height, from which he could make out several hills, one after another, had always helped to make him feel calm at difficult times or when he was beset by worries, as now.

Slowly and with many a sigh, man and horse descended along the path that led to the farmhouse and headed straight for the stables, where Vicent fed his horse, now visibly worn out. He took off his riding hat and stroked *Lo Petit* gently on his mane, with the thought that he was finding these rides more and more difficult. Vicent looked at the other four horses that he had in the stable, thoroughbreds that he hardly ever used, because *Lo Petit* was the only one he felt confident about. The others were more fiery and unpredictable; they didn't seem cut out for the rocky ground of the Maestrazgo and in any case they only obeyed their handlers. By contrast *Lo Petit* knew the area so well that he was almost part of the scenery.

The sun was going down when Vicent went into his house by the back door – in fact, it was the one he preferred because it was smaller and more intimate than the main one. There was also a small room there where he could leave his riding boots and put on his slippers that Amparo always left ready for him. Without going into the kitchen to say hello to his wife, he let her know with a short, sharp shout that he was back and that he was going to have a shower before supper.

In his large, carpeted bedroom – something that he couldn't stand in the middle of July because of the heat that it gave out – he went into his bathroom with its white Italian marble, now bathed in the twilight that filtered in through the large windows. Wearing his white, brushed cotton bath robe Vicent waited for the hot water to come through. After a good while he turned off the tap and tried it again without success. Irritated, he went to the top of the main stairs and shouted to his wife:

'Amparo! Are you using the washing machine or the dish washer?'

'No!' she replied at once.

'There's no hot water!' he shouted back from the top of the stairs, leaning on the old wooden bannisters that they had kept when they refurbished the house.

'We haven't had any hot water for days!' his wife replied.

'Fucking hell!' said Vicent, more to himself than to Amparo.

He had never taken a shower every day, because he learnt from his parents that it was an unnecessary luxury. Showers were more for relaxing or for cooling down from the suffocating heat. But when he returned from one of his horse rides Vicent liked to get under a strong, constant stream of hot water, as if to give a final touch of luxury to the equestrian outings that he enjoyed so much.

Having had a wash in the bathroom as best he could with cold water, Vicent dressed quickly in a recently ironed designer shirt that his wife had left on his bed, together with his folded and perfumed underwear, and his trousers with waist pleats that he wore for important but informal occasions, such as the one that night. He had a shave and finally went downstairs, with the smell in his nostrils of the bread that his wife was cooking in the oven.

'And what, may I ask, have you done with the hot water?' he asked Amparo as he entered the kitchen.

Amparo did not turn round to greet him.

'I haven't done anything,' she said. 'I rather thought that you had called the electricity people to sort it out, because we've been like this for several months and my patience is starting to wear thin.'

His wife, who was wearing a black knee-length skirt and a pink fifties-style blouse, finally turned round to face her husband. She had put her hair up and the bags under her eyes were more pronounced than usual. Vicent thought that his wife had aged several years in just a few months.

Leaning her arms on the kitchen table, Amparo stared at him with her dark eyes.

'It's very difficult for me to prepare these dinners without hot water,' she said firmly but gently, as always. 'I've been up since early this morning boiling water in saucepans so that I can cook the blasted lobster and the fish stew that you asked me to do. It's impossible doing things like this, Vicent; if we don't get the electricity and the water sorted out, we'll have to eat in the hotel every day, because I can't go on like this.'

She looked at the floor without moving, while Vicent looked at her in surprise; this was the first threat she had made in over forty years of marriage. He remained still and closed his eyes, clenching his fists behind his back so that Amparo wouldn't see. The wretched transfer of two hundred and fifty thousand euros that President Roig had promised him hadn't arrived yet and he didn't dare interrupt his holidays to urge him to do so. With his salary he could barely cover his mortgage, food and some basic expenditure in the house and the hotel, and Manolo and Isabel, working full-time in the family business, hadn't been paid since June. At least he could say to them that he was providing their upkeep, because the boy lived in the hotel and Isabel had settled in the farmhouse since she lost her job. But in fact the situation wasn't good. In contrast to other summers, that year Vicent and his wife would not go and spend a week on the beach at Benicarló, where they stayed every year in a nice hotel. Using the sale of the school as an excuse, Vicent had told everyone that he didn't have time to take a summer holiday, although the reality was very different: his bank account had been in the red for months. However, Vicent believed that everything would be resolved as soon as he received the money for the conversion of the hotel into a country holiday cottage – which he would use entirely to pay off debts. In addition the sale of the school could be completed soon, so he would also be able to borrow part of that amount and pay it back after the summer, when the hotel made most of its income. Eva, his personal assistant, would surely keep the secret, because she wouldn't want to put her job at risk. Besides, it would only be a matter of a loan for reasons of liquidity and not of solvency.

Everything would work out fine, it was just a question of patience and getting a move on with the sale of the school, said Vicent to himself.

Eventually he moved towards his wife, who was still looking at the floor, waiting for a reply. When he got next to her, he put a hand on her shoulder and said to her what he told himself every night:

'Don't worry, Amparo, everything will get sorted out very soon.' Vicent paused briefly. 'I'm just waiting for a couple of things, but I'm sure everything will be resolved by August, so we can still take a few days to go to the beach. But first I have to sell the school. What do you think, eh?' he said, as if he were talking to a little girl.

His wife nodded.

'Can we still go to the beach?' she asked, her eyes brightening up a little.

'But of course,' said Vicent with a forced smile. He headed over to the fridge to get a beer, opened it there and then and drank it straight from the bottle. 'And if we sell the school to the foreign chap before he goes back to London,' he went on, 'we could even go and stay in a better hotel to celebrate. What do you say?'

Amparo nodded and turned back to the sink, where she had left some half-peeled potatoes.

'I don't know what to think, Vicent.'

The Mayor went over to his wife again, who remained with her eyes fixed on the potatoes, and put his hand on her shoulder once more.

'What you have to do is to cook one of your delicious meals and that's how we'll get the Englishman on board; you'll see, we may even seal everything tonight.'

He was going to say some more, but he was interrupted by a ring at the door. He looked at the kitchen clock and saw that it was twenty minutes to eight already.

'Why is that woman so late?' he asked his wife, who didn't answer.

A few moments later Isabel entered the kitchen, gave her mother a kiss, greeted her father with a blank gesture and placed a bag on the table containing four bottles that Vicent quickly inspected.

'Damn it! How can you be so stupid?' he said to his daughter, furrowing his brow and looking her in the eye. 'Didn't I say I wanted champagne and not cava?'

'It's cheaper,' was all Isabel said.

'And who told you that you can take decisions, eh?' he spat out. 'It's not your problem, that's why I gave you my card, so that you can pay with it, or don't you even understand that? I'm not surprised they gave you the sack.'

'The card you gave me they gave back due to lack of funds,' his daughter replied with an icy look.

Vicent had never got on well with either of his two children. It was tragic that neither of them had been born with some special talent, he said to himself. Why had he been given two parasites whom he had to support even though they were both over forty?

'There must have been some mistake, the stupid fools,' he replied. 'Didn't you protest?'

'The card wouldn't work, there weren't any funds – it was obvious,' Isabel answered quickly, 'so I had to buy some cava from what's left of the small amount of severance pay they gave me. You owe me thirty euros,' she said.

Vicent looked her up and down with displeasure written all over his face.

'I owe you what?' he asked, threateningly, his body leaning forward and his voice high and sharp.

'Thirty euros,' Isabel repeated defiantly, as she undid her small ponytail and let it fall gently on to her shoulders.

Vicent moved towards her and from only two paces pointed his index finger in her face.

'And what do you owe *me*?' he asked in a loud voice. 'I've been keeping you for two months, and your brother as well, because the two of you are incapable of supporting yourselves, because you're useless.'

'We're working in the hotel, we've a right to a salary, and there's no sign of it,' Isabel said in her defence, her voice much higher than usual, something to which Vicent was not accustomed.

For more than forty years no-one in this family had raised their voice in the slightest, nor had they challenged an order. And that's how it's going to stay, he said to himself. He could not allow his children and even his wife to undermine his authority.

Vicent looked his daughter up and down with an expression full of hatred. Raising an eyebrow with an air of superiority, he studied her short, thick legs beneath a light, old dress in a horrible brown colour. Her stocky arms made her bracelet look ridiculous, as it was clearly designed for a more stylish woman. Her thick lips and her snub nose made her frankly quite unattractive. She had small, extraordinary green eyes that seemed to reject everyone and everything.

'You've no right to anything,' he said. 'When you have your own house, if you're working in the hotel, I'll pay you, but while you're living under my roof, you'll do what I tell you.'

Isabel moved towards her mother, and like her, leant her arms defiantly on the kitchen table. Amparo watched the scene in silence, without getting involved, as Vicent had always told her to do.

'What do you mean I have no right to anything? Are you saying I've no right to a wage for working?' Isabel replied, her eyes full of anger.

'I'm your father and I make the decisions.'

'Do you think, just because you're my father, you have authority over me?'

'Yes,' Vicent replied without hesitation, thinking how his father would have given him a good slap if he had taken that position.

'Well, being my father doesn't give you the right to mistreat me!' his daughter said.

Vicent gave a little chuckle, and then in the face of the silence from the two women, he burst out laughing.

'But what mistreatment are you talking about; I've hardly ever touched you,' he said, taking a sip of the beer that he hadn't yet finished.

Isabel firmly pursed her lips and went out, heading for her room.

'Thanks for your support when I was made unemployed,' she said sarcastically, putting a foot on the stairs.

Vicent turned towards her.

'Don't mention it,' he replied. 'But if you want to make yourself useful and make me grateful to you for something, what you need to do is smarten yourself up for the Englishman who's about to arrive. Then, hurry up and set the table in the dining room, because we're having an important dinner to close the sale on the school.'

'I *am* smartened up,' Isabel replied drily. Mother and daughter exchanged glances of mutual understanding.

Vicent laughed.

'With that cheap dress that doesn't hide those fat sausage arms of yours?' he said with a malicious smile. 'Go and cover yourself up a bit more; I'm ashamed of you, you look ridiculous!'

Isabel came back down the only step she had gone up and gave her father a nasty look. Vicent had never bothered much about what his daughter thought of him, but that look was full of fire and he had other battles to fight that evening, so he couldn't take on another front.

Without saying another word Isabel went upstairs and slammed her door after her.

Charles arrived with typical British punctuality at precisely eight o'clock, wearing corduroy trousers, a short-sleeved check shirt and a slim tie. He gave Amparo and Isabel each a bunch of flowers, telling them that he had picked them himself on a trip to Toll Blau at the source of the river of Les Corces that Isabel had recommended to him.

Vicent gave his daughter a threatening look, hoping that she wouldn't spoil the night or disrupt his business dealings. The stubborn woman hadn't got changed, which made him really annoyed, because both he and Amparo has smartened themselves up for the occasion and even the Englishman had made himself half decent. His daughter's appearance really made him feel ashamed, especially on a night in which the atmosphere had to be right in order to close a deal with Charles. He had made an effort and Amparo had spent the day in the kitchen only for his daughter to appear sloppily dressed. She would pay for this, he thought to himself.

Charles had already buried himself in a conversation with Isabel that Vicent couldn't hear, as Amparo was asking him in what order she should serve dinner. After a few moments the four of them headed for the sitting room and sat next to the fireplace, which in summer was decorated with red and yellow flowers. Amparo served everyone a glass of sherry and Vicent straightened his tie in readiness to start speaking.

So as not to interrupt, Vicent waited for a natural pause before he began, but to his surprise the moment never came, because Charles and Isabel carried on their conversation, which had moved on to his trip to Toll Blau. He was describing in minute detail his three-hour hike there and three hours back which he had recorded by taking countless photos that he was now showing Isabel on his smart phone, thereby excluding Vicent and Amparo from the conversation. This scenario went on for some minutes, in which Vicent and his wife observed with some surprise how much Isabel was laughing and revealing an affability they had never seen in her at home. Vicent looked hard at his daughter, as she stroked the ends of her long, dark, loose hair while looking at the photos, with her shoulder up against Charles'. He had never seen Isabel so close to a man, although he didn't think she was capable of attracting anyone, either. He was alarmed at the thought that Isabel might abuse his trust and in desperation go after a foreigner, having accepted her lack of success with Spanish men. The time had come for him to interrupt, for an excessive interest by Isabel, who had already given that stupid picture to the Englishman, could put paid to the school plan. There was no way he was going to allow his daughter to give Charles cause to leave Morella in a hurry.

'Well, Charles, let's leave all that and go and eat; we've got important matters to discuss, and I've got some news,' Vicent said finally, putting his sherry glass down on the side-table and getting up.

The rest of them did the same.

'Amparo and Isabel,' he said, 'please go ahead to the table, and while you get everything ready, Charles and I have a few "man things" to discuss.'

The two women did as they were asked, although they had barely had two sips of their sherry.

'Man things?' Charles asked in surprise. 'I'm amazed that Isabel didn't come out with some feminist remark at such an expression,' he said, with a smile that Vicent managed to force in return. Vicent waited for the two women to leave them on their own.

'Don't take too much notice of my daughter, Charles, and apologies if she doesn't behave properly with you,' he said, lowering his voice. 'You know that she's out of work and it's affected her a lot; she's going through a bad time,' he said, pretending to feel sorry for her.

'Well, I think she's a splendid woman, who's great fun and above all very talented,' Charles replied, without beating about the bush.

Vicent stood there looking at him, as if he didn't understand what he was saying.

'You're too kind to her,' he said.

'I think she deserves all the kindness in the world.'

Vicent put his head on one side and looked at him questioningly once more. He didn't know if he was saying such things out of good manners or if that enigmatic person really had an interest in his daughter, something that he found it hard to comprehend, unless English women were really hideous and the man was desperate, or he was gay. Everything was possible, he concluded, as he gave out a small sigh.

Picking up Charles' glass and also his own, Vicent served them both some more sherry, as he knew how much Charles liked it.

'Well, let's get down to business,' he said, confidentially placing his hand on Charles' arm. 'Since we last talked about the school nearly a week ago there have been some developments.'

'It was only a few days ago,' said Charles in surprise. 'What's happened?'

Vicent turned to look away towards the fireplace, avoiding Charles' bright and intelligent eyes. His own were dark and not very transparent, something that at that moment suited him because, although he had never liked to lie, now he felt he had to.

'There have been other expressions of interest and some have offered the asking price, even more,' he said, still looking at the fireplace.

Charles leaned back slightly and took a sip of sherry.

'Good heavens, in the middle of July?'

'The early bird catches the worm, they say,' replied Vicent, now looking at him full on. 'It's an asset with a lot of potential and investors have picked up on that.'

'I see, I see...' said Charles, more to himself.

Isabel interrupted the conversation just when Vicent was about to say something, which made him turn red with anger.

'Dinner is served,' she said to the two men, with a false smile.

Vicent raised his eyebrows and looked at his daughter.

'Don't interrupt us, Isabel.'

He turned to Charles and carried on, leaving Isabel speechless, still looking at the two men.

'As I was saying, there are other people...' he started to say, but Charles, looking at Isabel, prevented him from continuing.

'Please don't interrupt us at all, Isabel, if you wouldn't mind,' said Charles to Isabel, his eyes fixed on her. 'May I say how well you're looking today; not like me – I just go red in the sun, but never tanned like you.'

Vicent raised his eyebrows, finding it hard to believe what he was hearing. He would never have thought that that skinny posh Englishman, who was dedicated to educating the richest, most refined and privileged boys in the world, could look favourably – as Vicent could now confirm – on his daughter Isabel, who neglected her appearance and who had grown up in a Spanish town in the middle of nowhere. He looked in amazement at how his short, plump daughter, with ordinary black hair and barely any sense of style, exchanged a long, intense look with the most confident posh person he had ever met in his life. Distrustful of what he saw, he was taken aback at the sight of the two of them raising their glasses in a toast and laughing at something that he hadn't managed to understand.

Feeling confused he passed his arm across his forehead and closed his eyes, squeezing them hard… until a thought occurred to him. Perhaps he should encourage that ridiculous situation and use it to his advantage. Who would have thought it, but Isabel could become the perfect snare with which to trap Charles and finally get him to put five million euros on the table. It couldn't be four million, because that amount would barely cover half the Council's debt. The extra million was necessary and urgent to cover the amount recently invested in the Castellón airport.

He smiled at the two of them just as Amparo came in to remind them that dinner was served and the lobster was getting cold. Charles excused himself to go to the bathroom and Vicent took hold of his daughter's arm.

'Listen, Isabel,' he said in a quiet voice, but now suddenly being friendly. 'I don't know what sort of relationship you have with the Englishman, but you know that he has to raise his offer to the five million that we're asking for, and that he has to sign quickly because the town's accounts need the money like flowers need the rain.' Vicent paused briefly and looked his daughter in the eye, treating her as an equal perhaps for the first time in his life. 'I've never asked you for anything, Isabel,' he went on, 'and I've given you everything.' His daughter looked at him sceptically, something that deep down he found hurtful, as he had worn himself out working in the hotel for the sake of his family. But now wasn't the time for sentimentality. 'If this school project doesn't work out, we're all sunk: the town, the hotel and us as well,' he said. 'All that's a secret, of course; you mustn't tell anyone.'

'Well, what sort of mayor are you?' his daughter replied. 'I don't understand why you've allowed this situation to arise. If things are so bad, why have you wasted money on the Alameda and the swimming pool? And on this house?'

Vicent looked at her with a blend of anger and hatred. What he needed now was support, not more problems.

'Look, my girl, don't interfere in my work, because you don't know what you're talking about,' he replied, reverting to his threatening tone.

'I'm no girl,' Isabel answered, placing her hands on her hips.

'I can see that you're no longer a girl,' said Vicent. 'And that's what I want to talk to you about.'

'What do you mean?' asked Isabel, looking surprised.

'Don't pretend or play the innocent; I can see what you're up to with that poor Englishman.' Vicent sighed and finished off his glass of sherry in one go. 'I don't know what you've done or why, but the fact is that you've got the foreigner in the palm of your hand and that might be very useful for us.'

'I don't know what you're talking about.'

'You know perfectly well, Isabel, and don't make things more difficult than they already are. I'm just going to say this once, because Charles will reappear at any moment, so listen carefully.' Vicent lowered his head and spoke to his daughter while looking at the floor. 'There's no time to waste, so after dinner your mother and I will go to bed, saying that we're very tired, because we are. You'll stay up with Charles having coffee and pastries and use all the charms that he sees in you to tell him to put another million in, because we must get to five; if not, he'll lose the sale. You're grown up enough to know how to do it, but use all your feminine charms, because we need them right now.'

Isabel took a step backwards while her father remained looking at the floor.

'Are you really asking me to do that?' she exclaimed in a fairly loud voice.

Vicent looked up and put his finger to his lips to make her be quiet.

'Shhh,' he said. 'Are you crazy? He'll hear us!' He waited for a few seconds. 'It'll be worth your while.'

Vicent felt his daughter's gaze, filled with venom, hit him straight in the eyes.

'I can't believe you're asking me to do that, Father,' she said. 'Do you take me for a whore?'

Vicent looked at the floor and put his hands on his head.

'Of course not, you idiot!' he exclaimed. 'You just don't understand anything.'

Isabel stayed silent, forcing him to explain himself.

'I've just noticed that the chap looks at you as though he's interested in you – I don't know why! But the fact is that it could work in our favour. You understand me now…'

'You're asking me to go to bed with him and ask him to put his offer up to five million?'

Vicent didn't know what to reply, because if he said "yes" a family row would break out at a most inappropriate time, but nor could he deny that it was a perfectly good idea. Besides, the two of them seemed to like each other, a situation that was too good to waste.

Since silence means consent, Vicent stayed silent, with his eyes fixed to the floor.

Isabel turned round just at the moment when Charles came down the stairs and smiled at her. Isabel crossed his path without looking at him or saying anything to him. He raised an eyebrow and looked at Vicent, who had observed the scene with a feeling of panic. He had to rescue the situation as best he could.

'Come, my friend, let's go to the table, there's a lobster waiting for us that'll make your mouth water.'

Charles did as he was bidden and the four of them sat down at the round dining-room table; it had been perfectly laid by Amparo with the best dinner service, which was white with delicate hand-painted little flowers. The wine glasses were of cut-glass and the silver cutlery lay on the perfectly ironed white linen table cloth. The bunch of flowers that Charles had brought for Amparo was the centrepiece.

The two men, sitting opposite each other, started to eat and were followed by the women. Initially the atmosphere was cold, with a lot of uncomfortable silences that were only amplified by the sound of the knives and forks on the plates. Amparo, who had always been a slow eater, tapped on the table with her fingers as she looked at the other diners, waiting for someone to say something.

'Amparo,' said Vicent to his wife, trying to change the atmosphere. 'Could you put on that CD of Spanish guitar music that we like so much?'

Amparo got up and immediately did as she was asked, something that made Vicent feel more comfortable, for he knew that a bit of music would improve the atmosphere, and as wine makes everything more relaxed he filled everyone's glasses almost to the brim.

Isabel didn't even try a sip of the excellent Galician wine, although she tucked into her lobster, which she finished almost without raising her eyes from her plate. Charles had tried to re-establish contact with her, asking her if she had plans for any more paintings, to which Isabel had replied with a monosyllabic: "No".

Amparo remained silent, realising that something had happened with Isabel but not daring to get involved. Charles looked from one to the other without understanding. Vicent began to get exasperated, but fortunately the guitar music calmed him down.

'This is really very tasty,' he said to his wife, giving her a half-genuine smile.

Amparo gave a pleasant response.

'Thank you,' she said. 'I hope that Charles likes it, too.'

'It's delicious,' he said, his eyes fixed on Isabel and her empty plate. 'From what I can see,' he said, 'Isabel likes it as well.'

Isabel said nothing, her head bowed.

'Isabel,' Vicent almost shouted. 'Charles is speaking to you, do me a favour.'

Isabel slowly raised her head and opened her enormous intense green eyes, which were full of anger towards her father. She closed them for a second and said, without looking at anyone:

'The lobster was very good. Thanks, Mama.'

The three other diners all leant back together, feeling uncomfortable. After a few moments Amparo started to collect the plates and having made several journeys to the kitchen, brought in the seafood stew.

Given that no-one was talking Amparo broke the silence by explaining that she had gone early in the morning to fetch the seafood from a fishmonger in Vinaroz, the same one that her mother had used, and even her grandmother. Despite the fact that no-one was listening to her, Amparo carried on talking about her food shopping while the rest of the table concentrated on eating. Soon they had all finished apart from her.

Vicent lit a cigarette and, looking at his silent daughter who did not return his gaze, explained to Charles some aspects of the school that he wasn't yet aware of, like the possibility of building a terrace or the plan to install fibre optics throughout the whole building.

Charles indicated an interest only out of respect, because in fact he hadn't taken his eyes off Isabel, as Vicent had noticed. Charles' eyes, which at the beginning of the evening were happy and sparkling, were now dull and all thanks to Isabel's tantrum, which she would be made to pay for, Vicent said to himself.

He gave a long sigh and stubbed out his cigarette in the ashtray that Amparo had put out, despite not even having smoked it half way down.

'Right,' said Vicent, looking at Charles and Amparo. 'The young ones can stay here, while we old ones take ourselves off to bed.' He looked at his guest. 'Charles, my daughter will show you where the drinks are, although you know yourself where the cabinet is, next to the fireplace. Please, make yourself at home and help yourself to whatever you fancy or ask Isabel,' he said, turning his eyes to his daughter. 'I'm sure she'll stay and chat with you for a while.'

Isabel immediately got up from the table.

'No, I'm going to bed, too,' she said drily.

With his hands pressing down heavily on the table, Vicent stood up and responded straight away.

'No, you're staying here, as one of the young ones,' he said with an icy smile.

'I'm going to bed,' Isabel repeated, heading towards the stairs, her mother and Charles looking on in astonishment.

'Isabel!' said Vicent, almost shouting. 'Don't be rude and have more consideration for our guest.'

His daughter turned and looked at him with fire in her eyes.

'You don't tell me what to do,' she said. 'I'm old enough to know what I have to do.'

Vicent did not reply, but he looked at her with both pleading and hatred. He couldn't believe that his daughter would do the dirty on him at such a delicate moment, just when he needed her.

'You know what I expect of you,' he said, threatening her in front of Charles, who looked on in astonishment.

Isabel, who had already gone up a couple of steps, came back down again.

'Oh, yes? Are you threatening me, Father?' she said. Advancing towards him, she went on: 'Well, just let me tell you that you, your fucking school and your evil lies can all go to hell.'

Isabel's face was livid, her eyes wider than ever and her frame seemed taller and stronger than Vicent had ever seen. For once he felt smaller than his daughter and his heart seemed to miss a beat.

Isabel hadn't finished and now gestured at him with her finger, which both took him by surprise and made him feel even smaller. It was as if his own daughter were bringing him to justice.

'You mean nothing to me,' she went on. 'I'm not getting involved in your battles and there's no way I'm prepared to help you in what you're cruelly asking me to do.' His daughter looked him up and down with the utmost contempt. 'You've stooped so low that you make me sick,' she spat out.

A moment later, without being able to utter a word, Vicent sat down again. He would like to have got up and given Isabel a great slap, but he couldn't even do that. Her poisonous words had left him turned to stone, for he would never have expected to hear them from his own daughter.

'Isabel, my dear…' Amparo started to say, with tears welling in her eyes.

But Isabel didn't let her go on and turned towards Charles.

'And you, little Englishman,' she said, to Charles' surprise, 'you can clear out of this wretched country, where you've only come to toy with us.' Isabel's voice broke as she uttered these last words and tears began to appear in her eyes. After a deep sigh she went on: 'You can go back with your spoilt little rich boys, who only come here and upset other people. We were living peacefully here until you arrived, with your platitudes and your contrived interest in my paintings.'

'That's not true!' Charles said quickly as he got up, but without being able to get Isabel to calm down.

'You can all go to hell!' shouted Isabel, who was now out of control. Without looking at anyone else, she ran upstairs, leaving Vicent, Amparo and Charles stunned in the dining room. There was a funereal silence.

After a few interminable seconds, Amparo started to clear the table without saying a word.

'Can anyone tell me what happened?' asked Charles with his eyes popping out as he turned to Vicent.

The Mayor sighed.

'Forget about my daughter, Charles,' he said, still sunken in his chair. 'She's useless. Let's carry on talking business. I'm very sorry about that sad spectacle.'

Charles looked at him with suspicion.

'I don't know, Mayor, I don't know if I want to do business with you,' he said, now addressing him more formally.

Vicent closed his eyes and cursed his daughter. As soon as Charles left, he would go up and horsewhip her out of the house that very night. His own father would have killed him if he had behaved like that.

'Don't take any notice of her,' Vicent repeated. 'She'll get over it.'

'Of course she won't,' replied Charles, who had now dropped his civilised tone and had his shirt half out and his tie undone. 'I don't want anything to do with you, Vicent,' he repeated. 'In any case, I've been told that your hotel is tainted, that the business was stolen and belongs in other hands.'

Vicent raised his head in great surprise, but Charles went on before he could intervene.

'The sale of the school is tainted, so is the ownership of the hotel, and you treat your daughter worse than an animal,' he said. 'I'm going; this place stinks.'

'Wait, wait!' Vicent said quickly, taking hold of Charles' jacket that he had left on one of the armchairs when he arrived. 'The hotel legally belongs to my family. Who says otherwise?'

Charles pulled the jacket out of his hands towards him.

'What does it matter to you?' Charles replied. The important thing is that it's true.'

'Such a lie can only have come from that old woman you've got so friendly with, the red *maestra*, for sure!'

'And so what if it was her?' Charles shouted. 'The whole town knows, but you've got them all to keep quiet by abusing your power.'

'You don't know what you're talking about,' he replied in a voice that came out weaker than he had intended.

Vicent felt bombarded from all sides, including now from Charles. He felt worn out, demoralised, as if he no longer had any strength to fight.

Stooping and sweating, he watched Charles leave the house through the open door and heard him drive off in the car, its sound growing fainter as it sped away. After a few moments everything was calm and silent, except for Amparo moving around as she continued to clear in the kitchen.

Vicent closed his eyes and thought about going upstairs to throw Isabel out of the house, but he felt that the surprisingly imposing figure of his daughter would stand her ground in a way that he wouldn't be able to deal with. Wearily he loosened his tie and lit another cigarette, going through the evening in his mind so as to understand what exactly had caused that disaster. He closed his eyes and recalled Charles' words about the hotel, to which he had devoted so many hours and years of effort in order to support his mother and his family. Who could say that it wasn't his?

It must have been that damned old woman, he thought.

Vicent turned his cigarette over and over between his fingers.

'That old bitch will pay for this,' he said to himself aloud. 'I swear she'll pay for this.'

17

Only a few days later Valli, with her basket in her hand, left her house in the Pla d'Estudi to do her weekend shopping. As usual she had put on her comfortable black sandals and one of her favourite blue overalls that was simple and practical and full of pockets, which she liked. Her neighbour Carmen told her it made her look like a mechanic but Valli took that as a compliment. All her life she had rolled up her sleeves to tackle hard work, so what was wrong with that?

With the aid of her slender stick of light-coloured wood, Valli headed off early to the square when the street cleaners had barely started their work. As usual there were the remains of glasses and bottles outside the nightclub, but fortunately the cleaning machine was already at work along the street with the arcades. With a sigh, and glancing at the closed door of the Bis which had been the local nightclub for decades, Valli walked swiftly to Carceller the printer's, where the friendly proprietor was already putting out magazines and newspapers on several display stands in the street.

As usual Valli bought the *Mediterráneo* from Castellón, because it was the one that gave most news about Morella. She used to read *El Imparcial* and the *Revista de Occidente* edited by Ortega, but she was less and less interested in the great ideas that shaped the world and its leaders and more on what was happening in her own town. Even so she glanced at *Hello!*, which she'd never allowed herself to buy however much she would have liked to. A Republican like her could not bring herself to finance European royalty, especially not the Spanish royal family, which she already supported through her taxes. She refused to give them a single penny from her meagre income.

Valli carried on down the street with the arcades at precisely her favourite time of the morning. It had just gone eight o'clock and only the traders were out in the street, which was still quiet and calm under a clear, fresh sky. As she was walking she looked at the columns of ancient stone; some were round, others square, some of light-coloured stone and others darker. But they had all been there for as long as she could remember, supporting the street's white houses, which were no more than three or four storeys high and which had small, black iron balconies, mainly used for hanging out the washing. In a few weeks' time these columns, now so peaceful and silent, would support a series of tree trunks placed horizontally between one column and the next, where groups of friends would gather to protect themselves from the young bulls that were let loose in the square for the fiestas. Sitting on the tree trunks and eating the local stewed peach dish *préssec amb vi*, the young men spent all afternoon singing and chatting except when they got down to run in front of the bulls. The noise from the music, the shouting and the fiesta during those days was horrendous, which was why Valli preferred the relative calm of July, particularly at this hour of the day. In August, especially during the fiestas, she went with her neighbour to the beach at Benicarló.

Feeling contented with her purchase of the newspaper, Valli continued walking under the arcades before going into the bread shop of her friend the baker, who at this hour was in the middle of making her loaves and rolls that were tasty enough to whet anyone's appetite. After saying hello and exchanging remarks about the magnificent weather they had had that week, Valli bought a small stick loaf and carried on under the arcades, observing how the shops and restaurants were getting ready to welcome another lot of Saturday tourists. The day before she had heard in the butcher's that today they were expecting up to seven coach loads of visitors, which was why she had got on with her shopping early and so avoid the crowds.

Valli said hello to her friend the photographer, who at that moment was putting out two stands of postcards on the pavement, and walked past the Blasco bar, where the first group of old men were having their usual breakfast of omelette and brandy. Wearing their customary berets and with their dominoes at the ready, the small group of seven or eight men proceeded with their daily ritual, always at the table by the window. They greeted her with a friendly wave.

It had not been easy for Valli when she returned to Morella from exile, but that was now thirty years earlier. Valli had always worked with the school and taken part in all of the fiestas and six-yearly festivals that had taken place, always with good grace and a smile, thereby regaining local acceptance. In addition the older members of the community had never forgotten that her parents had been farm labourers, good people who never deserved such a tragic end. Of course, Valli had always received more sympathy on the part of those who had suffered most during the war, but now, after so many years, everyone in the town loved her and respected her. Except for the Mayor.

She went past the hotel, which generally she tried to avoid, before going into her favourite butcher's to buy a couple of freshly cut veal steaks. The meat in Morella was frankly wonderful, she said to herself, recalling her recent visit to Madrid and the pallid colour of the steaks that they served there. In Morella the butcher's shops smelled of meat and not of plastic, and the produce had a splendid red colour.

A bit further down the street Valli went into the bank to collect her pension, as she always did in the middle of the month. It was a ridiculous amount, since having spent half her life in exile there were many years when she did had not pay contributions. Fortunately she also received a small amount every month from France for the nearly twenty years that she worked in Paris before returning to Spain after the death of Franco. In any case she didn't spend much, she didn't want any luxuries and her income even gave her enough to save a bit. Nor did she have any dependents: she never had any siblings and all her cousins were now dead except one very distant one who lived in Valencia, but with whom she hardly had any contact.

'Good morning, Cefe,' she said to her friend as soon as she saw him on the other side of the counter.

He immediately responded with a smile.

Fortunately banks were no longer the bunkers that they had turned into in the Eighties, with their reinforced glass between the staff and the public that prevented Valli from hearing what they were saying. Now they had been modernised and you were dealt with at a separate desk, although Cefe always invited her to come to his office so that she could be more comfortable. However hard Valli tried to reject any special treatment, that soft leather armchair in Cefe's office was the most comfortable seat in the whole of Morella.

'Oh, my dear…' Valli sighed, putting her basket with the bread and the meat on the floor. 'How are you, Cefe? Aren't you going on holiday?'

Tall and slim, Cefe had been the manager of this branch since shortly after Valli returned from France, nearly three decades earlier. She had taught his father to read and write during the Republic and had always insisted to her friendly farm neighbour that if one day he had children he should get them to study and not work in the fields. Apparently he had followed her advice and Cefe was able to build a better future for himself. The banker had always been very grateful to Valli for what she had done for his family, but leaving that aside, the two of them shared a natural friendship.

'Not quite yet,' replied Cefe, who was wearing a purple tie with a blue shirt. He had always liked to look smart, although with a touch of modernity and avoiding looking like the typical banker in a white shirt and black tie. Valli had always thought that was a sign of having a personality.

'We're going off to the beach at Alicante for a week towards the end of the month,' Cefe replied, closing some folders that he had in front of him. After a pause, he asked: 'Have you come for your usual monthly pension, Valli?'

She nodded and looked at the office walls, which were functional but warm and pleasant, with a few sprigs of thyme that he had no doubt picked himself in the mountains, frequent rambler that he was. He also had some old photos of Morella and of his parents, posing with the traditional black farm labourer's smock, the sash, the baggy trousers and a beret with a stalk in the middle.

Valli smiled.

'Ah, the beach. How your father would have loved the beach,' she said affectionately.

Cefe quickly looked up and smiled at Valli as he briefly interrupted his search for her account on the computer.

Valli went on:

'But seeing how nice it is here now, feeling so fresh, why go to the stifling heat of the beach, which will be plagued with tourists?'

Cefe laughed.

'Because you can lie on your back and you don't have to do anything!' he said.

Valli shrugged her shoulders.

'Well, I love Morella in July; the other day I went out to Torre Miró for a walk, a long one, as long as I could fit into an afternoon. Now, with so much daylight, I walked and walked as far as Herbeset, and my neighbour's son had to come and fetch me, you know.'

'Herbeset!' Cefe exclaimed, looking at her in surprise. 'Goodness, Valli, you must be good and fit, but did you go on your own?'

'Yes,' replied Valli, as if there was nothing to it.

Cefe shook his head.

'But that's not good at all. Call me next time and I'll come with you. It's not good for you to go on your own on those paths.'

Valli raised an eyebrow.

'Do you think you know those paths better than I do?'

Cefe looked at her knowingly. She had never told him in any detail about her life in the *maquis*, but in the town it was widely known that Valli had been hiding in those parts with the guerrilla fighters for almost a decade.

Suddenly Valli remembered something that made her give a little jump in her chair.

'Oh!' she exclaimed, causing Cefe to look at her as he took a sheet of paper from the printer. 'I was walking between Herbeset and Torre Miró, and suddenly I found myself on a path that I hadn't taken for a long time, maybe years, and I came across the old shack of the Messeguers, do you remember?'

Cefe lowered his eyes and turned back to the printer.

'Yes,' he replied, hardly looking at her.

Valli went on:

'Well, I don't know why we'd call it a shack, because it had always been a very large house, although I only remember it as being half ruined. I think a family of farm labourers occupied only a part of it.'

Valli paused while Cefe, who was somewhat distracted, put her pension money and a receipt in an envelope. Valli, however, leant forward with her head to one side.

'Well, what a surprise I had,' she went on, 'when I saw that that shack had now been turned into a great mansion. It was totally refurbished, I couldn't believe it! It looked so tall, with windows and balconies made of beautiful wood, all varnished, and there was even a show jumping arena there!' Valli exclaimed.

Cefe said nothing as he watched Valli with interest. She went on:

'Well, I don't know who in the town could afford something like that; I don't even want to think about how much the refurbishment must have cost.' She paused. 'Surely the owner isn't from the town...' Faced with silence from Cefe, who was staring at the envelope, Valli saw that she had no option but to persist.

'Hey, Cefe,' she said, not liking what she was thinking, 'you don't know who it belongs to, do you?'

Cefe stared at her and let a few seconds pass. He swallowed hard and all he said was:

'The Mayor'.

Valli raised her eyebrows and leant back, before moving forward again a few seconds later.

'The Mayor Vicent Fernández? Our Mayor?'

'That's right,' Cefe replied, crossing his hands on his desktop, playing with his fingers, but looking calmly at Valli.

'But it can't be,' said Valli emphatically. 'A mayor's salary isn't that much, the hotel has never been a great business success and his family couldn't leave him anything, because his father was a middle-ranking Civil Guard. And Amparo's family, as far as I know, lost everything they had when the chocolate factory closed.'

Cefe said nothing, although Valli looked at him as though she was expecting more.

'You know I can't talk about customers,' he explained.

Valli, sitting on the edge of her seat once more, persisted:

'But the hotel is always empty, especially after Moreno opened his little place.'

Cefe finally moved back, crossed his legs and leant back in his chair.

'It seems that they have plans for the hotel,' he said. 'It's clearly no secret, because the money comes from a public grant, but they're going to turn it into a country cottage.'

Valli furrowed her brow.

'Into a country cottage? Why?'

'You know there are public grants for conversions in order to stimulate rural tourism,' he explained. 'Well, they've received one of those grants. I'm sure it's all clearly set out in the Town Hall.'

Valli narrowed her eyes for a moment and sat up straight.

'Well, I'm going there right now to check it out, because I don't know to what extent a mayor can request funds for local development, if he's the mayor!'

'It was the son, Manolo, who requested them,' Cefe clarified.

Valli looked incredulous.

'You can't be serious…'

She picked up the pension envelope and her shopping. She went over to Cefe, who had also stood up, gave him a firm hug and a kiss on both cheeks, as she always did.

'Take care of yourself, Valli,' he said, 'and do call me when you want to go for a long walk, and I'll come with you.'

After saying goodbye, Valli headed straight down Segura Barreda Street towards the Town Hall. She was in so much of a rush with her stick and laden with her purchases that she scarcely acknowledged the usual friendly greeting she got from Conxa, the one from Casa Masoveret. Just before nine o'clock Valli went into the Town Hall, which she knew well, and left her basket beneath the skirts of the well-known festival "giants" that guarded the entrance area, so that she didn't have to carry it upstairs. She had always used that little hiding place.

Valli was panting a little when she got to the first floor where the door to the offices was half open, and she stopped for a few seconds before knocking in order to catch her breath. As she was taking some deep breaths and straightening her hair with her hand, Valli heard a conversation in English that surprised her. As she listened more intently she realised that it was Eva, one of her favourite students, to whom she had taught English as soon as she got back to Morella, when she was barely ten years old. She was the daughter of the owners of an old textile firm, but the family had suffered from the crisis in the sector and having been the industrial motor of Morella for almost a century it had now become part of the craft tradition and a hobby of the leisured classes. Valli knew that the family had made a great effort to send her to school, although the time came when they couldn't manage it any longer and when she was fifteen they got her a job in a workshop, making one blanket after another. When the business went under in the mid-eighties, Eva had to take on countless manual and domestic jobs until eventually she got this good job in the Town Hall. Recently she had also met a nice lad and they had even bought a nice new apartment in the town. Such a struggle had won Valli's heart, which was why she was always pleased to see her.

Out of curiosity Valli wondered who she could be talking to, but at the same time she wanted to find out how much of the English she had taught her she still remembered.

'We're not responsible for what happens in the world, nor can we be influenced by baseless rumours,' said Eva in a loud, clear voice and in good English. 'What is unacceptable is that suddenly, because of a rise in the pound, a room for one night in a small hotel comes to five hundred euros. Don't you understand?'

Valli looked up with interest and remained silent while the person Eva was talking to must have been answering her.

'Look, don't talk to me about American banks at risk; I've got enough problems with the accounts in my own town…'

Eva was silent again, just saying 'yes, yes' now and again.

Eventually she hung up, and that's when Valli knocked at the door.

'Come in!' her former pupil responded.

Eva was surprised to see Valli and got up straight away to greet her warmly with a firm hug and two kisses. She took off her glasses and looked at her with her attractive green eyes.

'What a lovely surprise!' she said. 'What brings you here?'

Valli smiled and looked her up and down, noting that as usual she was wearing something simple but elegant and comfortable.

'I just came to look at something,' she said, 'but I heard voices in English and, please forgive me,' – Valli lowered her voice – 'the truth is I was curious to see what your English was like.'

Eva laughed.

'Well, I certainly need it, especially now,' she said, putting her glasses back on. 'It turns out that the value of the pound has gone up a lot, because there are rumours that some American bank or other is about to collapse, so the dollar is falling and people are taking refuge in the pound, which is sending it through the roof.'

Valli, who knew nothing about international finance, looked at her attentively but didn't understand very much.

'And does this really affect Morella?'

Eva smiled.

'Well, believe it or not, it turns out that it does, because we have to repay London for the rooms of the English students who came and, of course, it's working out a lot more expensive.'

Valli recalled the figure she had heard on the phone.

'But five hundred euros per room in Morella?' she asked, still not understanding. 'The pound might have gone up, but not that much.'

Eva looked both ways and closed the door before going back to Valli.

'Well now, I think the foreigners were charged a bit too much in the hotel,' she said in a quiet voice.

'A bit too much?' shouted Valli, who lowered her voice when Eva put a finger to her lips to ask her to be more discreet. 'In any case,' she went on, 'I thought the

English had paid for their visit and not the Town Hall, because they came at their own expense, didn't they?'

Eva said nothing, but Valli put her head on one side to indicate that she was waiting for a reply. Eva looked one way and then the other once more to check that the small room where she was working was still empty, and replied:

'There were instructions to pay for the trip as an incentive to encourage the sale of the school.'

Valli was taken aback.

'I don't believe it,' she said in a low voice, but with her eyes wide open.

Eva said no more and covered her mouth with her hand, as if she was starting to wish she hadn't said anything.

'And that brute of a Mayor charges five hundred euros per room in the hotel for the Town Hall to pay?'

Eva remained silent, her eyes glued to the floor.

After a tense silence that Valli had never experienced with her former pupil, the girl said eventually:

'Well, that figure has been pushed up by the value of the pound.'

'There's no way the pound could have gone up that much.'

Eva did not respond.

'The Mayor's a thief!' said Valli in a quiet voice, more to herself than for Eva to hear. 'I suppose soon there'll be a council session that explains why it's necessary to pay for the visit and what the final bill came to, won't there?' asked Valli, this time in a rather inquisitive tone.

Eva took a step back and after a few seconds went back to her usual place at her desk.

'I have a lot of work to do, Valli; forgive me, but I must get on.'

'But you'll know…' Valli started to say.

Eva cut her short at once.

'I don't know anything,' she replied drily.

She looked straight at her computer screen, moving the mouse under her hand. Valli continued to look at her and realised that she couldn't put the young woman in such a predicament. She sighed and headed towards the door.

'We must finish this conversation another time,' she said, with her hand on the door and looking at her former pupil.

Eva turned round and looked at Valli, tight-lipped and with pleading eyes.

'Thank you, Valli,' she said. 'It's been good to see you.'

And with that Eva turned back to her computer, while Valli went out of the room without closing the door, still lost in surprise. That was theft, she said to herself as she went down the stairs, determined that one day soon she would be able to ask the Mayor what was the point of the visit and why he had paid such an excessive amount for it. When she had almost reached the foot of the staircase that took her down to the ground floor, she remembered Vicent's mansion in Torre Miró. Her heart started to pound so strongly that she felt rather startled. Now she understood everything: those excessive prices charged by the hotel and financed by Morella taxpayers had provided the funding for such a large house. Valli grabbed hold of the iron knob at the bottom of the stairs because her legs were starting to tremble. She thought of the council projects like the new swimming pool and the Alameda and its grand inauguration. She wondered if anyone had seen the detailed accounts and if there were surcharges similar to the one at the hotel.

Valli clenched her fists and promised herself that she was going to get it all out in the open; she would make herself responsible for putting the relevant questions to the local council. Confident about what she was going to do, Valli dabbed her forehead with a handkerchief, picked up her basket and headed off to Casa Masoveret, where she would have a much-needed drink of water.

She walked slowly until she eventually reached her friend's place, where the tourists were starting to arrive, asking for ham and wine for breakfast. Valli looked at them sympathetically, aware of the importance of being nice to visitors, for in the absence of any industry the town depended on them.

When her friend saw what Valli looked like she served her a glass of water and a small black coffee, for she knew her well enough after nearly thirty years. Conxa, the daughter of farm labourers who were friends of her parents, had also been a teacher, although she was a lot younger. They shared some wonderful years together when Valli returned from France, and between the two of them they set up the municipal school that the town needed after the Escuelas Pías nuns left Morella. For the first time since the Republic, the school organised assemblies where the pupils elected their representatives through a proper electoral process, with campaigns and everything. The two teachers re-established festivals, like the floral games, and designed inspiring projects that the town welcomed with enthusiasm. Unfortunately the school was not the same after the two of them retired, Valli because of her age and Conxa out of necessity, as the farm did not provide them with enough money and the family had to open their business in town. With a lot of hard work and some sound decision-making the little business had had considerable success, serving good food and selling good quality traditional products that delighted the tourists.

Valli drank down the water almost in one go and went to sit down to have her coffee near the entrance at one of the high tables, which were almost in the street since in summer the doors were wide open. She remained standing, however, because she had never liked sitting on those high chairs and because she saw that her friend was very busy selling shoulders of lamb to some German tourists. She was also keen to get home.

There she was in the middle of drinking her coffee when Manolo, the Mayor's son, came in. The lad, who was not very athletic but was a good eater, drinker and smoker, couldn't be blamed for whose son he was, Valli said to herself. She even felt a certain soft spot for him because he always seemed rather cowed as a consequence of having an authoritarian father. She had taught him English, with not much success, but he was a nice boy at school, always sharing his sandwiches, footballs and whatever else he brought to class. He had constantly lacked confidence and because he always thought he was going to fail, in the end on most occasions he did. Valli tried to be fair with him and gave him the same attention as she gave to everyone else, trying to ignore their families' past. He was grateful, especially as an adult, and had always been pleasant and respectful towards her. Every time he saw her with a heavy bag he offered to carry it home for her, something that Valli only accepted when really necessary, which was more and more often.

'Hey, Manolo, how are you?' Valli said as she saw him come in looking preoccupied.

'Hello, Valli,' he replied with his usual smile. He hardly stopped at Valli's table. 'I'm in a bit of a hurry; my sister has sent me out to get some ham, because we've run out and twenty people have just arrived for lunch.'

'Twenty!' Valli exclaimed. 'But that's good, isn't it? Business must be booming.'

Manolo gave a nervous laugh.

'Well, we do what we can, Maestra,' he replied, looking at the floor and giving his head a bit of a scratch.

Of course, the boy was still single and had never dealt comfortably with social relationships other than with his long-standing friends, with whom he spent most of his spare time. There were rumours in the town that he was gay, something that Valli suspected ever since she had him in her class as a very small boy, as he always latched on to his closest friends in search of physical contact, although at that time only in a very innocent way. Basically, it had always made Valli sad to think that, if her suspicions were correct, the boy was still living hidden away in a reality that would never make him happy.

'Congratulations on the conversion to a country cottage,' she said, always with an interest in the goings-on at the hotel, but also with the hope that the boy would finally have good reason to feel proud of himself.

Manolo looked surprised.

'What country cottage?' he replied honestly.

Valli pursed her lips.

'I was told that you've plans to convert the hotel into a country cottage and make some major investments.'

Manolo raised his eyebrows and looked incredulous.

'Well, it's the first I've heard of it,' he replied, as if it were simply town gossip.

'How strange,' Valli answered, without understanding what was going on. 'Your father probably hasn't had time to explain to you, seeing how busy he is,' she said, although she remembered perfectly well Cefe telling her that the grant came in Manolo's name.

He smiled at her and placing his hands on Valli's table, he said:

'Well, I don't think so, because I see my father every day now. As they have no hot water they come to take a daily shower at the hotel.'

Valli had picked up the small cup to take a sip of her coffee but put it back on its saucer.

'What do you mean they've no hot water?' she asked, increasingly puzzled.

Manolo adjusted the collar of his shirt and replied with all the naturalness in the world:

'They've got such a nice house and yet they have to come and shower in the hotel. You obviously can't have everything!'

He sighed and apologised for being in such a rush, saying that Isabel was expecting the ham right away. Valli said a friendly goodbye to him and watched him go, the ham under his arm, running up the street to the hotel.

She took a deep breath, and for the first time in many years sat down on the tall chair, which took quite an effort. She needed to rest and, above all, to process the series of facts she had learned. Everything seemed very suspicious and she had begun to think the worst. Not only was the Mayor using money from the people of Morella to pay himself highly inflated prices in the hotel, but she was also suspicious about a public grant received by the same hotel, in the name of his manager, Manolo, who knew nothing about it. And as a background, the Mayor was living in a mansion that no-one seemed to know about, that for some strange reason had no hot water and that Valli wondered how he had managed to pay for. Perhaps there was a simple explanation behind it all: Vicent could have won the football pools or his wife had some family money tucked away somewhere. But as a minimum those facts required some investigation.

Having got her breath back and with her mind made up, Valli went back up along the street with the arcades to her house, this time having to work her way around the groups of tourists who were filling the streets and the shops buying jumpers, blankets, cheeses and cured meats in industrial quantities.

Valli walked as fast as she could until she reached the Colón Square, where she had to stop to rest for a few moments. Feeling a bit calmer she went on up to the Pla d'Estudi, which was now bathed in bright, even stifling sunshine, in which Valli had no desire to remain.

As soon as she entered the front door, she saw a large, blue, very thick envelope just above the three letterboxes. Neither Valli nor her female neighbours received much post, apart from letters from the bank or invoices. However, that envelope was different and, full of curiosity, she picked it up. To her surprise she saw that it was for her. On the back, on a golden sticker with elegant oblique writing, was the name and the address of Samantha Crane: Plaza de Santa Ana 4, 28012 Madrid.

With much excitement and forgetting everything that had happened that morning, Valli went up to her apartment and felt the pleasant summer breeze as soon as she went in. As she had hardly anything of value, she always left all the windows open to let the air through. Breathing rapidly, she left her shopping in the kitchen and quickly went to sit down in the armchair next to the window. It was many years since she had received a letter like that.

Madrid, 2 July 2007
My dear friend Valli:

I hope you are as well as you were when I met you just a few weeks ago in Madrid. The time you spent with me in La Venencia – where I now go almost every weekend – was wonderful, one of the most special conversations of my life. I felt privileged just to meet you and listen to your memories and reflections, not only about my grandmother and Victoria but also about the history of this incredible country that has stolen my heart.

I've seen on the internet pictures of Morella that reminded me once more of the photo that my grandmother and Victoria had in Connecticut. How wonderful! Since I met you and after looking at those pictures, I haven't stopped thinking about your project and wondering how I might help. I have rarely felt as excited as I do now.

Well, my dear friend, I have some good news: I spoke to the Principal of Vassar College, my American university, and she assured me that there would be no difficulty in providing grants for ten American students to go to Morella every year to study Spanish. I was lucky, because she told me that they've been looking for such a project for some time.

So we've got ten students already!

I also spoke to my mother, who as you know is coming out of a difficult time following her divorce, and she told me that one of the Picassos in her house in Manhattan is for me. Well, I want this picture to help to finance your project and I've been in touch with Sotheby's, the auction house in London, for them to value it. I think an expert came once and valued it at one million dollars. I know that's not enough to save your school, but unfortunately my mother refuses to donate any more paintings. But at least this is a good start.

I've thought a lot about this decision and all I can say is that I've never been more sure about anything. All I ask is to be involved in the project, which I believe can change the lives of the American girls who go to Spain, just as being away from home this year is being so helpful to me. Suddenly I feel like a strong, new woman who is capable of striving after my dreams and succeeding in fulfilling them. And this project is, of course, one of them.

One more thing. I had occasion to go to Yale two weeks ago for the wedding of a friend who studied there. I took the opportunity to consult the Victoria Kent archive that my grandmother donated to them and I discovered a script belonging to La Barraca theatre group signed by Lorca to his friends Louise and Victoria, "whose love is more true than the laws that shackle it".

Can you imagine what it's worth now? It's a pity that such an item is in a box in an American university when there are still so many countries where a dedication like that could set a great example. I have started formal contacts with Yale, and as the work is so clearly dedicated to my grandmother and to Victoria it shouldn't be difficult to reclaim their property. I'll keep you posted.

I shall also try to get my mother to come to Spain to visit me, firstly because being so far away has made me appreciate her and understand her better, and because taking a trip plus spending some time with me could help her to feel better after the business with my father. It will no doubt all turn out positive, as I can get closer to my mother, who I miss more than I thought, and besides, we could involve her in the project.

I'll keep you informed of everything.

Are you planning to return to Madrid? I'm dying to share another bottle of sherry with you again; that night was undoubtedly one of the happiest – and even most important – of my life. Although it may sound corny to say so, for the first time I feel in charge of my own destiny.

Thank you very much for being such an estimable example.

With much affection and all my admiration.

See you soon,

Sam Crane

Valli sighed and pressed to her chest the three pages written in such a fine, clear and elegant hand. Although she did not have much strength left she had to continue her fight for the school; if not for her, then for everyone else.

Lying back in her armchair, Valli raised the blinds a little and could see the long stone wall and the dry countryside beyond. It was there that she had played, had fought and had seen people killed. That fight for justice and freedom had been the driving force in her life and she wasn't going to give up now at the end. With the letter still pressed against her chest, Valli closed her eyes and felt young again for the first time in many years. She had to go on with the project, whatever it cost, if only as a moral obligation.

18

That same Saturday, while the people of Morella were taking refuge in their houses from the mid-afternoon heat, Charles was sitting by himself on one of the benches in the Poet's Garden, looking at the surrounding houses and the silent hills. He had been there for about an hour, shifting his position from time to time, with an unopened newspaper in his hand. With drooped shoulders and head bowed, he closed his eyes and tried to breathe in the pure Morella air that he had found so alluring, but he couldn't. He just felt overwhelmed by the suffocating heat that was typical of inland towns at three in the afternoon in the middle of July, when everything was drowsy, weary and silent. He felt as if he were in a De Chirico painting, alone, lost in a play of light and shade created by the stifling air. Quite the opposite to the fresh air of Eton or the cold of winter that kept teachers and students awake and that deep down he found really pleasant. Charles hated that general sleepiness of southern European countries, which is why in fact he wanted to return to London the very next morning, first thing on Sunday. His suitcase was almost packed and he had the car ready for an early departure.

He adjusted his Panama hat, by which everyone in the town now knew him, in order to keep the sun off his delicate, white face. Only a week earlier he had arrived in Morella full of high hopes of converting a rural school into one of his more interesting projects in recent years. After ten years of work with hardly any breaks or interruptions, Charles had hoped that the development of a satellite centre in Morella would have given him a second flush of youth. At the age fifty-four he didn't want to give up on living, and that challenge had been his most exciting one in many years. Barely seven days earlier he could scarcely have imagined that the week would end like this.

What with the remarks from Valli, the Mayor's shady business deals and his way of pressurising him in such an informal manner – through lunches or dinners at his house, rather than through formal communications or meetings – Charles didn't trust the people of this town. He could no longer see things clearly. Even Isabel, who he had come to feel so close to, had literally told him to "go to hell" during that very unpleasant Wednesday evening, just three days earlier, from which he was just beginning to recover.

It had been a long time since anyone had shouted or spoken to him in that tone. Charles had always been surrounded by impeccably well-mannered people, who, if they had anything unpleasant to say, did so with kid gloves. For years no-one had confronted him in such a full-on and direct way as Isabel did that night. And he found it hurtful. He had tried to be nice to her, appreciate her paintings – which, in spite of everything, continued to impress him – and had tried to get to know her beyond her outward appearance with which, it is true, she was not exactly blessed. But he was different and looked at people for what they were and not for their appearance, as half the world seemed to do, or at least the men with whom he had established a friendship. For that reason he had found it painful when Isabel had called him "little Englishman" and accused him of being interested in her paintings so as to get close to her father. Him!

Charles sighed and shook his head as he remembered her words and the scornful tone with which she had spoken them. He was used to being treated with respect, which was why he felt so wounded by her contemptuous tone. The last time someone had spoken to him like that, he recalled with sadness, was in Oxford, where some students laughed at Old Etonians like him, because they were seen as spoilt, not very sharp and socially inept. It was true that the Etonians used to form a closed group which no-one from outside was allowed to join, but he had always tried to avoid being so closed-minded and to make friends with students from all sorts of backgrounds. Through his travels he knew that what was different and exotic generally turned out to be more attractive, although in fact his life remained as comfortably monotonous and Etonian as ever.

With women Charles had never managed to feel comfortable either, perhaps because he did not have any sisters nor even a mother. Brought up by his father and always living in boys' boarding schools, his only experience with a woman, when he got married, only served to confirm to him that women were not his thing, but not because he didn't like them or desire them. In Oxford, he recalled, there was a fellow student, Laura, with whom he fell in love, perhaps for the only time in his life, but he got so nervous when he was close to her that he couldn't even speak. If she was in the pub that he used to go to on Friday nights, Charles couldn't cope with the thought of going up to her for a chat, so, without talking to anyone, he ordered two pints at the bar and took them to his room to drink them on his own. When he'd finished he repeated the operation, again crossing the pub without saying a word to anyone and being given all kinds of strange looks. A friend tried to help, but he never let him. He felt more comfortable that way.

Charles took a deep breath thanks to a breeze that he finally managed to catch. English and rational as he was, he did not give in to panic or sadness, and he turned his thoughts to returning the following day to his beloved Eton, where life would continue as always in its calm and orderly fashion, with its classes and its students. He felt his shoulders relaxing as he thought about the majestic trees that lined the Thames beside his college surrounded by green meadows. The image filled him with a sense of calm.

Just as he decided to glance at his newspaper, he heard a familiar voice that surprised him and pleased him at the same time.

'I can see that you liked this place,' said Isabel, walking over the gravel to the bench where Charles was sitting, and where she sat down, crossing her legs under the blue smock she was wearing.

She looked at him, taking off her sunglasses and waiting for a response from Charles that wasn't forthcoming. Isabel pursed her lips and lowered her eyes. Since Wednesday, they had barely exchanged a word that wasn't to do with breakfast, lunch or dinner.

'I'm sorry about the other day, Charles; it wasn't your fault,' she said, looking up at him and protecting her eyes from the sun with a hand on her forehead.

With so much light and with Isabel's eyes half covered by her large hand, Charles could not see the beautiful green of the gaze that had charmed him just a week earlier. Although it seemed as though the world had changed, it was only seven days before that Isabel had shown him this marvellous corner which she had painted in the picture she had given him.

That very morning, in spite of what had happened at the dinner, Charles had wrapped the painting as if it were a Picasso, and planned to hang it above his fireplace to give it maximum visibility. He looked hard at Isabel, recalling that that woman, who had literally told him to go to hell, had also painted a lovely canvas, just for him.

'I'm not used to witnessing live scenes from *The House of Bernarda Alba*,' he said with subtle British irony.

His remark brought a smile to Isabel, who now felt more relaxed than when she first arrived. She leant back on the bench and looked around the garden. After a few seconds she turned towards Charles.

'I really am sorry; you have always treated me well and you didn't deserve to be involved in such a bust-up,' she said, her eyes now wider and more expressive, enabling Charles to see how honest she was being. 'My family is a bit special, my father is difficult and right now we're going through a bad patch, as I'm sure you'll have realised.'

Charles nodded.

'But I don't want you to have bad memories of Morella,' Isabel went on. 'I don't want to interfere in your business affairs, I just don't want you to leave here with a bad taste in your mouth.'

'There's no chance of that,' Charles replied, now a little more well-disposed and less on the defensive. Just as her comments during the dinner had wounded him, that full and sincere apology had made him feel more positive towards the town. Besides, he knew that Spanish people were not much given to apologies, which made him appreciate Isabel's gesture all the more. The direct and transparent look in her eyes also made him feel that her words were sincere, certainly more than the constant and continuous apologies of the English, which were often mere euphemisms to disguise something hurtful that had been done very intentionally. That woman was honest and the look on her face seemed to come directly from the heart, thought Charles.

They both remained silent for a few seconds.

'I've kept you a bit of Morella soup, because I've noticed that you haven't eaten today,' Isabel said finally.

Charles was pleased by the gesture and tried to show his gratitude:

'That's very kind of you,' he said. Looking at his watch, he added: 'I could have it for dinner.'

'Actually we'd planned not to open this evening,' Isabel replied. 'My brother only has Saturday nights off and we only have a couple from Barcelona who've said that they're going to eat at the Daluan. In fact they've come especially to try it.'

Charles looked curious and put his head to one side.

'Daluan?'

'Yes, the best restaurant in town. It opened just a few months ago and caused a sensation; people come from Barcelona and Valencia just to try it out. It's both traditional and modern at the same time. Have you not been?'

Charles thought back through the restaurants he'd been to, especially with Vicent, and shook his head.

'I don't think so. Where is it?'

'In a little street just behind the Town Hall; it's a very narrow street between two inclines. Do you not know it?' Isabel asked again in surprise.

Charles again shook his head.

'Well, you must try it,' said Isabel, putting her hands on her knees in decisive fashion. 'You can't leave Morella without having been. You're leaving tomorrow, aren't you? When are you coming back?'

Charles looked at her for a few seconds. He loved the positive energy and determination of that woman.

'Yes, I'm leaving first thing tomorrow morning and I don't know when I'll be back; I suppose it depends on what happens to the offer, although, of course, I don't know what to think any more after everything that's happened.'

Isabel lowered her eyes, but immediately raised them again.

'Well, if I were you I'd get a move on before I go. That place is really worth it. They've even had reviews in the national press.'

Charles stared at her while she put her sunglasses back on, as if she had decided that the conversation was at an end after he had indicated such uncertainty about his possible return. Everything was definitely up in the air, thought Charles: the offer, the school, even his interest in Morella. He no longer knew what to think. In any event, dinner in the best restaurant in town seemed a splendid idea, as well as a good opportunity, if she accepted, to get to know better the woman behind those marvellous paintings, and without the presence of her father.

Charles didn't know how to formulate the invitation, fearing that she already had other plans or that she simply didn't fancy the idea of spending time with a boring foreign teacher like him and one who had filled the hotel with teenagers who thought they ruled the world. He picked up his newspaper firmly but nervously as Isabel got up and indicated that she was leaving.

'Well,' she said in a fairly quiet voice. 'Tell me if you'd like the soup tonight, or if not I'll see you in the morning for breakfast. I'll have it ready for you for half-past six, as Manolo told me.'

Charles nodded, still not knowing what to say and recalling how in the Oxford pub he walked back to his room carrying two pints that he would be drinking alone. As he walked across the old wooden floor he saw out of the corner of his eye that his so-called friends were laughing at him because, out of nervousness at walking on his own in front of Laura, he always spilt some of the beer from the two very full glasses. He was horrified by the memory and thought that a refusal would always be better than to relive that feeling again. The last thing he wanted was to find himself dining alone in the Daluan with two beers.

When Isabel was almost at the bottom of the steps that led from the garden to the street Charles finally plucked up sufficient courage to ask a woman for a date in more years than he cared to remember. Apart from a couple of not very serious flings, all of the relationships he had had with women since the divorce from Meredith had involved paying, once a month, on a regular basis, like many of his colleagues. Why make things more complicated?

This time, the fear of finding himself alone in the restaurant, having a hard time just like at university, finally made him say something.

'Isabel,' he said.

The Mayor's daughter, now almost on the slope, barely heard him.

Charles jumped up and rushed after her.

'Isabel,' he persisted in a louder voice.

Having caught up with her, he finally said, looking at her in her sunglasses:

'If you're free tonight we could go to the restaurant together; as you said, I can't leave without having been there.'

Isabel did not take her glasses off, but Charles noticed that she did slightly raise an eyebrow. Without giving it much thought, she replied:

'Well, I'll mention it to my friend Ana, because they're usually fully booked; if they've got a table free I'll let you know.'

Charles gave her a full and open smile.

'Okay,' he said.

Isabel walked off happily down the hill, turning along Virgen Street to get back to the hotel. Charles didn't move for a few seconds, unsure about what to do or where to go, but filled with a sense of pride that he hadn't felt for a long time.

At eight o'clock on the dot Isabel came down to the reception area of the hotel where Charles had been waiting for more than ten minutes, checking his nails, adjusting the belt of his impeccably ironed, pleated white trousers, and making sure that all of the buttons on his red and white striped shirt were done up. He stroked his closely shaven jaw and smoothed the little hair that he had, now more grey than black. As soon as he heard a pair of heels he stopped looking at Isabel's painting in the small room next to reception and turned to welcome her.

Charles was surprised by Isabel's appearance, which was radically different from how she looked the first day he met her a few months earlier with a mop in her hand. Although her profile was still as round as ever, she was wearing a summery red dress this time which, for better or for worse, revealed her curves. "That woman doesn't hide herself away," thought Charles.

Isabel went over to him and greeted him with a smile, which showed off her thick, red lips that contrasted with her perfect white teeth that Charles hadn't noticed before. Black eye-liner ran round her large green eyes, while her black hair, which had more body and waves than ever, cascaded over her majestic, proud shoulders.

'Are you ready?' she asked, as casually as you like.

Charles tried to hide the surprise that he felt. Behind that rather awkward artist who only three days earlier had told him to go to hell there was a surprisingly attractive woman who was coming to dinner with him. Charles felt how lucky he was, lifted up his head and went down the stairs alongside Isabel, looking left and right as if he were looking for his Oxford friends, convinced that they would now look at him with envy. They would now be in their Victorian houses protecting themselves from the rain, sitting next to their white, boring and skinny English wives, he said to himself, making his smile stretch even wider. Who would have thought that years later he would be going out to dinner with an attractive artist in such a marvellous town?

Charles looked at Isabel out of the corner of his eye as the couple crossed the square heading for the restaurant. He was thinking that, while his friends would have wolf-whistled at her, especially for looking so attractive in that red dress, what really impressed him was her paintings. They walked in comfortable silence, until Isabel gestured to the hill that they needed to turn down. He followed her, feeling very happy. Deep down Charles was enjoying his unexpected adventure in Morella, which was so different from his life in Eton. He felt like a character from one of Lorca's plays involved in a great drama and it not only amused him but also motivated him.

As they went down the hill, they passed a few people who said a friendly hello to Isabel and didn't hesitate to look him up and down as well. Given his surprise Isabel didn't stop to talk to any of them, no doubt to avoid town gossip, Charles thought. He felt increasing respect for that strong and independent woman who had no qualms in setting about cleaning rooms when necessary or going out to dinner with an unknown foreigner in front of the whole town.

Before long they came to a small, narrow street with forward-leaning white houses that were supported by wooden beams that looked as though they were about to break. A few young cats dozed on the large, irregular stone slabs that gave a certain character to this hidden corner. On the right-hand side there was a modern building, evidently nicely refurbished and recently painted, with the name "Daluan" above the door.

They went up to the first floor, where they found a dining room with about ten tables, all still empty. The orange chairs and lamps of Danish design added charm and originality to the place.

'Come in, you're the first,' said a pleasant lady, wearing a modern black dress, as she came out of a door at the end of the room.

Isabel went over to her at once.

'Hello, Ana – thank you very much for doing us this favour.' Isabel turned to Charles. 'We're in luck,' she said, looking again at her friend. 'This is my friend Ana, the owner. We were at school together.'

Charles leant forward and kissed the hand of Isabel's friend, which prompted a little laugh from the women, no doubt unaccustomed to such manners.

'Charles is from England and is in Morella looking at the issue of the school,' Isabel explained.

'Yes, I know,' said Ana, indicating that it hadn't gone unnoticed in the town. 'I've given you a table here, next to the window.'

Ana had put them at a large table for four, which was still lit by the clear, calm light of the evening. It was perfectly set out, elegant and modern, without any more frills than necessary, all of which pleased Charles, who was not at all fond of unnecessary trimmings.

After she had seen another couple of diners to their table, Ana brought them the menu and the wine list, with more than seventy to choose from.

'I can recommend the truffles menu,' said Isabel, leaning over towards Charles and showing him the option. 'You know there are a lot of truffles in Morella and here they've developed a special menu of dishes with truffles. It's really more for winter than summer, but as it's become so popular they offer it all the time,' she said leaning back in her chair again.

Charles needed to give it no further thought and closed the menu.

'Well, that's what I'll have,' he said, to Isabel's surprise, as she hurried to make her choices. 'The mushrooms and the fish,' she said to her friend, while Charles chose a nicely aged Ribera del Duero that he had picked out from the long wine list and that only cost fifteen euros. Such a dinner would have cost him three times as much in London, he said to himself looking around and hardly believing his luck. He hadn't expected a last night like this. He was in a very good mood.

'Where do so many truffles come from?' Charles asked Isabel while Ana served them the wine, which felt smooth and pleasant to Charles' palate.

Isabel smiled at him with her green eyes from behind her wine glass.

'I remember very well when it first started,' she replied, gently putting her glass down on the table. 'When I was very little and Spain opened up to tourism, the hotel immediately started to fill up with tourists, especially from France. But suddenly groups of men started to arrive, without women, and that made us start to get suspicious,' she said, causing Charles to smile. 'They didn't say what they were coming for, and nor did we see them visiting the sights around the town. What's more they wore hiking boots and carried spades and sticks, but they weren't hikers, either. It was all very mysterious.'

Isabel paused briefly to take another sip of her wine and lean back slightly, while Ana put the cold appetisers from Charles' menu on the table: truffled sausage and an empty egg-shell filled with truffles, plus a pâté of foie gras with truffled bread, as Charles read in the menu. He was also served mille-feuille with soft cheese and truffles with winter miniatures, which was like a feast for his eyes because the aroma that they gave off was different and strong and very unlike anything he had tasted before. Ana refilled their glasses.

'The thing is that one day my mother,' Isabel went on, 'noticed a horrible smell that was coming from under the bed of one of these men and after a few days, when she'd had enough of the stench and thinking that it might be something that could be bad for us, she decided to open the bag where the smell was coming from and she got a bit of a shock when she saw so many tubers: they were truffles.'

'Well, this smells wonderful,' Charles commented, taking a bite from all of the starter dishes but still looking at Isabel or at least paying attention to her.

She smiled while at the same time nibbling at a piece of sausage.

'Yes, of course, in the fridge or when they're cooked there's no problem, but in summer after a few days under the bed, it's certainly more than a bit whiffy,' she replied, taking another mouthful. After she had cleared her throat she went on: 'The thing is that in the hotel they'd set up a kind of truffle black market and people started to arrive offering huge sums of money for what they called the "black diamond" of cooking.'

'How much do they cost?' asked Charles, who had heard that they were quite expensive.

'Well, one about this size,' said Isabel, making a circle with her fingers the size of a large strawberry, 'could fetch up to three hundred euros.'

Charles put his knife and fork down on the plate.

'Good Lord! More than the wine!'

Isabel laughed.

'In England you only have eyes for alcohol, do you?'

'Well, just look at Spain…' he replied quickly. 'But I'm not surprised; with such magnificent wine, even I would be an alcoholic. I'll miss it after I've gone home!'

Isabel's eyes narrowed and she looked at him with interest.

'Is anyone expecting you in England?' she asked directly, which hardly bothered Charles at all. He even liked her self-assurance and confidence. What was the harm in asking? He wished that he had the same courage.

'Well, more than a hundred students will be expecting me in a couple of weeks and more parents than I'd like to count will want to talk to me at all hours about their offspring,' he said, with modest pride.

'Don't you have family expecting you?' Isabel persisted, taking the last piece of truffled sausage.

Charles leaned back slightly. He didn't feel at all threatened by that conversation, far from it. The table didn't have any candles or any unnecessary decoration, the evening light still illuminated a good part of the dining room and the meal seemed more like a dinner with a glamorous friend than a formal date, as would be the case in England. Their get-together was much more entertaining than boring dinner-dates in London, where every movement was programmed and conventional, and where he had always felt trapped.

'Well, no,' he said, leaning his elbows on the table, something that he would consider too ill-mannered to do in London, but which felt really comfortable here. 'I was married once, a long time ago, but it wasn't my thing,' he said, coming straight to the point.

'Why?' asked Isabel, being equally direct.

Just when Charles was about to answer a waiter came to take away the plates so that he could serve Isabel's sole and Charles' scallops and the little-known Iberian dorado with pumpkin puré and julienne truffles. Charles sat staring at his plate and was on the point of taking a photo for his friend Robin, who he would see the following day in London.

Isabel was looking at him.

Charles noticed and after he had tasted the first mouthful, which made him close his eyes with pleasure, he went on:

'I don't think we knew each other well enough before we got married,' he said with his mouth half-full, something he would tell his students off about but which he now felt as something like a liberation. He was also surprised by the ease with which he was dealing with a subject that he had scarcely talked about in years, but which now seemed almost unimportant. He went on: 'We got married quickly, shortly after I returned from India where I spent three years travelling and studying after finishing university.'

Isabel looked at him with interest as she tucked into her fish. Better to be hungry than not to have an appetite, he thought, daring to look at Isabel's neckline for the first time as she leaned forward slightly to serve him more wine. Her red dress had a v-neckline that dipped provocatively between her breasts. Charles averted his gaze at once, for he noticed how her pale skin started to redden. Even so he could not help appreciating the woman who was sitting opposite him. He looked at her arms, her face, her neck, her whole body with its olive-brown, delicate, and well-cared for skin. Charles looked at her eyes and felt curious to know her past. At that age everyone had a history behind them. He decided to finish his own story as quickly as he could and then focus the conversation on Isabel. If he wanted to know, he had to give a little first.

'The thing is that she was very young,' Charles went on. 'She had been brought up to be a good wife, but she hardly had any life of her own. I worked in the City leading a life that I didn't like; everything was very easy and seemed to be written just for me; it was like being part of a predictable script in which I felt trapped. So I went back to Eton to teach, taking refuge in my books and my students, and that's how I've spent the last twenty years, quietly and happily,' he said, smiling and with conviction.

'Happily?' Isabel asked, putting her knife and fork down on her empty plate.

Charles took a deep breath and looked around him; the restaurant was beginning to fill up now. He took the opportunity to pour some more wine and in so doing finished the bottle, so he signalled to Ana to bring another one. He didn't want to spare any expense, for he was enjoying that easy-going, comfortable meal, for once with an attractive, talented woman.

'Well, you're happy until you ask yourself why, isn't that right?' he replied at last, fingering the base of his glass while he waited for the second bottle of wine. 'What about you?' he asked directly.

Isabel sighed and leant back in her chair, shaking her head.

'I was happy in Vinaroz, where I worked until recently,' she said with a certain nostalgia. 'I went for a walk along the beach every morning, winter and summer, I had a very nice apartment, that I rented on my own, and after work I had the time and the peace to paint, which is what really makes me happy.'

'You have a lot of talent,' Charles interrupted her. 'You ought to think about turning professional at it.'

Isabel laughed.

'No,' she said roundly. 'It's my passion, I don't want to make obligations for myself. I want to live quietly and free.'

'So family isn't your thing?' he asked with interest.

'No, when I say I don't want any obligations I'm referring to painting; I don't want to have deadlines or paint out of obligation or for money.'

'But don't you have a family?' Charles persisted, surprising himself for breaking the most basic rules of discretion.

Isabel put her elbows on the table and looked him in the eye. Charles couldn't help studying her green eyes, now more noticeable and imposing as the sun went down.

'No, I've never had one,' she replied. 'I was about to once, with a boyfriend I had in Castellón, but he went off with someone else,' she said, lowering her eyes.

'I'm sorry,' said Charles, who was about to extend his hand towards hers, but in the end held it back. It pained him to think that someone could have hurt such a creative and generous creature with whom he felt so comfortable.

'Never mind, it was a long time ago,' replied Isabel, with a rather forced smile. 'Besides, he would probably have turned out to be a rogue. For a start, he didn't like my pictures.'

Charles was taken aback.

'I can't believe it,' he said, almost angry.

Ana came and took the plates away, and after a pleasant interval, served the dessert, a *carpaccio* of pineapple and a capuchin tart with champagne and truffle ice-cream, which captured the two diners' full attention. Isabel was the first to attack the plate that Ana had placed in the middle of the table with two spoons.

They both finished the meal with a feeling of contentment, but continued with their animated conversation that Charles did not want to spoil by mentioning the dinner the previous Wednesday or talking about Isabel's relationship with her father.

This was an evening full of positives and Charles didn't want to ruin it by making an out of place remark or bringing up a delicate subject.

The restaurant was beginning to get animated and the diners had to keep raising their voices to make themselves heard. There were people waiting their turn on the stairs, something that had always made Charles feel uncomfortable. The noise partly broke the magic of the evening, making it more difficult to continue with their muted and intimate conversation that Charles had no desire to abandon.

'Do you feel like taking a walk to stretch our legs?' he asked, once more overcoming his timidity and his fear of rejection. The sense of victory that he had felt as he walked across the square with Isabel had left him with such a good feeling that he just wanted to experience it once more before he left the following day.

Isabel was looking out of the window just at that moment and answered him with a gentle smile as she turned towards him:

'Okay,' she said.

Two and a half hours after they went in, the two of them left the restaurant feeling happy and having had one glass too many, with Charles helping Isabel as she went down the stairs and adopting once more his elegant Etonian manners that his new friend welcomed with pleasure.

With the steady, clear sound of Isabel's heels marking their steps, she led Charles up slopes and into places in the town that he barely knew, or didn't remember, no doubt to avoid meeting people, he imagined. Their steps echoed along the quiet streets that were now dark and only lit by the charming old black streetlamps. Voices could be heard in the houses and the sound of families moving around in the kitchen as they prepared their evening meal. The smell of chipped potatoes frying or the sound of a fork beating an egg were clearly distinguishable, as were the shouts of a mother to her son, telling him to set the table or reprimanding for getting home late. That quiet, domestic simplicity on a summer's night made Charles feel part of the Morella family for the first time since he arrived in the town at Easter. He breathed calmly and he stole a glance at Isabel, who was walking on confidently towards Sant Miquel. Leaving the two towers behind them, they went into the Alameda, which was dark and still and lit only by a starry sky that was bright and clear, something very rare in London where the sky was always covered with clouds and pollution.

Charles and Isabel walked slowly and silently, but this did not make Charles feel at all uncomfortable. He didn't have to do, say or show anything, because the following day he would return to London and he wouldn't have to come back to this place if he didn't want to. But the idea of not returning to Morella now seemed ridiculous.

'And are your parents expecting you in London?' Isabel asked out of the blue.

Charles was surprised by the question. Only in Spain do people give such importance to the family. In England, by contrast, and especially at Eton, the school quickly becomes the first point of reference and parents are just two adults with whom you exchange a few superficial thoughts for a few days during the year.

'Why do you ask?' he asked, as they continued their almost solitary walk along the Alameda, while the majority of the people of Morella were still eating their evening meal.

'Just out of curiosity,' said Isabel, looking at him. 'But you don't have to answer if you don't want to.'

'It's not a problem,' he hastened to reply. 'Not at all. In fact, it's such a short story that it's of no importance,' he said, pausing briefly before continuing. 'My father was a Hispanist at the University of Cambridge, which is why he always spoke to me in Spanish. He was fanatical about Spain; he only read and wrote about Spain, its history, its writers; he even came here during the Civil War.'

'Oh, really?' exclaimed Isabel in surprise.

'Almost five thousand Englishmen came to support the Republic, including my father and his good friend George Orwell, who had also studied at Eton.'

'Good heavens!' said Isabel, stopping for a second, looking at him with wide eyes.

Charles felt flattered by such interest, even though it was about his father rather than about him. Even so, it was the first time that he had impressed a woman in many years.

'Well, I think they all knew each other,' he said with typical, and false, British understatement. 'The fact is that he returned to England after Franco won, but he devoted himself to writing about Spain after that.'

'And what about your mother?' Isabel asked.

At that point Charles stopped, for no-one had ever asked him about his mother, as far as he could recall, and he had hardly ever thought about her. He realised that it wasn't easy for him to reply, perhaps because it was something he still found hard to accept. He wasn't sure.

He started walking again and said:

'Well, the truth is I don't have a very clear picture about my mother; my father never spoke to me about her.'

Charles noticed that Isabel was looking at him out of the corner of her eye.

'And are you not curious to know?' Isabel asked gently, without looking up.

Charles pursed his lips and crossed his hands behind his back. He was past the age of thinking about his mother like a needy child.

'Well, no,' he said. 'I know it sounds odd. Maybe I thought about her more when I was little, but as the college becomes your family from such an early age, the fact of not having a mother doesn't matter so much, because your life is in the college. I only saw my father once a month, or once every two months,' he replied.

'English boarding schools…' remarked Isabel, without finishing the sentence.

'Yes, I know they're not exactly fashionable in Spain.'

'No, they're not,' Isabel replied. 'Sorry to go on,' she said, 'but don't you want to know who she is and start looking for her?' After a pause she added: 'Forgive me if I'm interfering too much.'

'No, no, it's not a problem,' he replied. He remained silent as they came out of the Alameda and entered the Pla d'Estudi, which was well-lit by some strong lamps that put paid to the intimacy of their conversation.

'I think I'm too old for that now,' was all he said.

Isabel did not reply.

The two of them continued in silence along the street, which became more lively as they approached the arcades, which were now full of people eating on the terraces and enlivened by upbeat, relaxed music. Charles and Isabel caught the mood and they stepped up their pace without realising it, looking this way and that, both happy to be part of that pleasurable scene.

Charles, however, regained his serious look as they approached the door of the hotel. He was suddenly invaded by a mixture of sadness that the evening was over and uncertainty, following thoughts about his mother for the first time in many years. He was also aware that the following morning he would leave this special corner of the world, where that night he had been so happy.

He looked straight at Isabel, who still looked as fresh as a daisy, with her wavy hair now pushed back and her eyes sparkling.

'There's one thing,' she said, when they were outside the hotel door.

Charles looked at her with interest. That woman was a box full of surprises.

'What I'm going to tell you is confidential and you must promise that you will not say you heard it from me.'

Charles nodded, feeling surprised and a little worried.

'You have my word.'

'Do not trust my father, Charles,' she said in a serious voice. 'He is deceiving you. He only has one offer for the school, just one, and it's for two million, not the five that he has told you.'

She looked straight at him with her green eyes that were full of honesty and concern.

Charles was slightly taken aback.

'How do you know?' he asked.

'Because though I hate to admit it he's my father and I've heard several conversations he's had.'

Charles let a few seconds pass while he processed that unexpected revelation.

'Why are you telling me? Such information is obviously damaging to him.'

'You're an honest man and he's not, that's why I'm telling you,' Isabel replied, her eyes still firmly fixed on him.

Charles felt confused talking about the school and about Vicent at such a special moment after a wonderful evening, but also after having thought about his mother, which had upset him a bit. He was not very used to surprises and shook his head several times. Suddenly he felt all his defences rise to the surface. For a second it went through his head that Isabel had been manipulated by her father and could be trying to convince him so that he would lower his offer and thereby lose out, a device by Vicent to get himself out of a hole. He would never have thought it of Isabel, especially after the marvellous evening they had just shared, but nor could he get his head round such a betrayal of her father. Valli's words about the family were still echoing in his head. From what he could see they were capable of anything, at least Vicent was.

'And suppose what you're saying isn't true? Why should I trust you?' he said defensively, regretting his words as soon as he saw the sadness that came from Isabel's eyes.

'You'll see,' was all she replied.

Without saying another word, Isabel went into the hotel and disappeared upstairs, leaving Charles rooted to the spot.

That vague reply left him feeling even more confused. He remained on his own in that position for a few minutes, once more feeling those two pints in his hands in Oxford.

19

Barely two months later, the world had changed with the fall of two investment funds with Bear Stearns, one of the big American investment banks. The news sowed panic in the international markets and prompted the immediate intervention of the central banks. It was the first prick of a financial bubble created during two decades of overindulgence; a clear sign – although many chose to ignore it – that the spending spree that politicians, regulators and ordinary people had enjoyed so much had come to an end.

But at that time world finance and the financial catastrophe were still a long way away from Morella, where events were considered from a distance, without them being fully understood. In September the town was quiet after a good summer and the gentle, calm days of autumn followed as they did every year. No-one in the town knew yet what risk premium was or Standard & Poor's.

Vicent had to look up on the internet what the agency with the long name was, because nobody in the Town Hall had any idea. The week before he had received a letter from an Anne Thomson, head of the agency, asking for a meeting. He had replied cordially, fixing the interview for that very morning. Now, five minutes before her visit, he still didn't know what the lady wanted, since according to what he had read the agency graded debt and Morella had never issued any bond or instrument of public debt. The fact is that the English name of the agency and its representative had put him on his guard, but thinking about Charles and the sale of the school, Vicent had decided that it would be better to cooperate and get it sorted out. If a positive report came from the meeting, Vicent could then pass it on to Charles and any investors he knew. He hoped and was convinced that everything would start to be resolved in a positive way very soon.

At home things had improved to some extent, since he had finally received the two hundred and fifty thousand euros from Roig – in payment for the conversion of the hotel into a country cottage – so that what he owed the power suppliers had been sorted out, as well as other matters and outstanding debts. He had finally been able to pay his son and daughter at the hotel, although after Isabel's horrendous rudeness in July, he had only given her a monthly salary of eight hundred euros, half of what her brother got. Fundamentally he knew that Isabel put in many more hours in the hotel and that if the meals' side of the business had improved substantially it was because she had fully devoted herself to it since she had lost her job. But he couldn't forgive her for the scene she created in front of Charles in his own house in July. Since then Vicent had had no news of Charles and had barely exchanged a word with his daughter. He was on the point of throwing her out of the hotel but clients had said how good her cooking was and she even brought in guests from neighbouring towns to have a meal. For the time being, he thought, it would be better to leave things as they were until the sale of the school had gone through and he could breathe again.

While Vicent was absorbed in these thoughts there was a knock at the door and he immediately invited whoever it was to come in. Eva came in first, speaking in English, which he did not understand, to a tall, slim young woman with blue eyes and long, dark hair. She was impeccably made-up and wore an elegant navy blue dress and a pearl necklace, while on her arm she carried a Burberry raincoat; all very British.

Vicent thought that she would do better for herself as a model than as a city analyst and couldn't help looking at her remarkable figure. Her legs were so long that he had to move his head up and down as he looked at them. His gaze, which he barely disguised, seem to make her feel uncomfortable, and immediately she looked at him coolly and directly in the eye.

'Come in, come in,' he said, getting up and taking the lady by her arm to her chair. She quickly shrugged off any such assistance. 'Thank you, Eva,' he said to his assistant with barely a glance towards her. 'You can leave us now.' Discreet as ever, Eva left the room.

'Good morning,' said Anne with a marked American accent, as she crossed her legs in front of the Mayor's impressive polished wooden desk.

Having sat down again in his large red velvet chair, he looked at her with a smile from ear to ear. In his period of more than twelve months at the head of the mayoral office, this was undoubtedly the most pleasant visit that he had received. A nice bit of skirt, he thought to himself, although without hiding his admiration.

'Isn't Eva in charge of technology in the Town Hall?' the American woman asked? 'Wouldn't it be better if she were present at our meeting?'

Vicent was surprised at the suggestion but calmly leant back in his chair and gave out a brief laugh. He was in command in his office and with such a fine figure of a woman in front of him, why would he want to share the moment with an ordinary young girl?

'No, my dear, no,' he replied, picking up a packet of Marlboro that he always kept on his desk. 'We're fine as we are,' he said, lighting a cigarette and blowing out the smoke to one side.

Anne began to cough and to look at him with her eyes almost popping out of her head, as if she were looking at a madman. Her gestures to get rid of the smoke were so exaggerated that it looked as though she must be suffocating. When she eventually took in a breath after a few seconds, she said:

'Would you mind putting out your cigarette? It's really bothering me.'

Surprised at such refinement, Vicent reluctantly agreed as he wanted to avoid any trouble.

After a brief pause, and realising that maybe the visit wasn't going to be as pleasant as he had imagined, Vicent decided to get straight to the point.

'Please tell me how I can help you, Miss,' he said, placing his elbows on the desk and his hands in front of his face. With his tie nice and neat and sitting behind his mayoral desk, Vicent felt himself to be invincible. He would soon deal with this foreigner and get on with his work.

'Mrs, not Miss, if you don't mind,' the American lady commented.

'Well, tell me, Mrs,' said Vicent in response, now getting rather tired of this woman. 'Tell me what brings you here.'

Anne placed a crocodile-skin briefcase on her impressive knees and from it took out some documents that were protected by transparent sleeves. She placed them on top of the desk.

'As I said to you in the email, I am the specialist for Spain from Standard & Poor's in London.'

'Fine,' Vicent replied, somewhat exasperated, since as far as he was concerned her role was less relevant than that of the representative of the Morella farmers, who really could bring him problems. That woman, who looked as though she'd come straight from a leading Madrid catwalk, didn't look as though she was going to cause him any great difficulties.

'I wanted to talk to you because we're a bit worried about Spain,' she said in a serious voice.

Vicent lay back in his mayoral chair, still trying to work out what the devil that woman wanted.

'Well, there's not a lot we can do in Morella to save Spain,' he said sarcastically.

Anne didn't appear to appreciate his remark, and with the energy and firmness that were more typical of a man, she placed her crocodile-skin briefcase on top on the desk and gave Vicent a penetrating stare.

'We believe that a very dangerous real estate bubble is developing in Spain and we're examining a few cases,' she said.

'Well, everything's very quiet in Morella,' the Mayor replied quickly. 'There's nothing being built because we've got some very beautiful walls that restrict our growth. I think there are better places to start your investigation, Miss,' he said, correcting himself immediately, since the fierce American lady was already about to protest: 'Sorry, Ma'am.'

'I know there can't be any building in the town, but I've noticed that Morella has invested three million euros in Castellón airport, which isn't up and running yet, and since I can't see any such item in the council's budget I've come here to find out what's happened.'

Vicent immediately felt his shoulders and the muscles in his face tense up. Who the devil was this woman and why had she chosen his town if they were all the same? He crossed his legs and joined his hands together on his knees. He made an effort to appear normal. Basically he knew that he had nothing to fear from that Yank.

'And may I ask how you know about our investment? As far as I know it doesn't appear in any of the airport's public accounts nor in any of ours, simply because it's very recent and as you know things in Spain move very slowly, especially in summer. Only just now I was talking to my personal assistant, Eva, about the need to start working on the end-of-year accounts, where of course the item will appear. I don't know what you're really looking for. What I don't understand is how you know about our investment.'

'Don't forget, Mr Mayor, that behind the Castellón airport there are foreign investors who have bought bonds and they don't go on holiday in the summer; they always want prompt information, which of course is what they get.'

'Right,' said Vicent. After a brief pause he tried to put an end to the conversation. 'If there's nothing more I can do for you, I'll be getting on with my work.'

The American lady looked surprised.

'I don't think we've finished yet, Mr Mayor,' she said. 'Spanish law states that town councils must present their accounts four times per year or every three months. According to my information the investment of three million in the airport dates from after Easter, so it should already have appeared in July's accounts, but it's not there. I wanted to ask you why not.'

Vicent began to feel uncomfortable in the presence of that woman, who now seemed to him more like a robot that a model.

'As I told you, Ma'am, things move more slowly in Spain and there was nobody around here in July and I doubt that investors spent the summer months reading my accounts. And if they weren't on the beach, then they should have been; everybody benefits from a few weeks' holiday,' he said, letting out a brief laugh, which he immediately stopped when he saw that Anne was not amused.

'I am not the regulator,' said Anne. 'All I know is that my clients, the investors, will be very surprised if they see that the party that has committed three million to the project cannot show them in their next accounts, which we are expecting in October, about two weeks away. I assume they'll be out by then, won't they?'

Vicent felt a slight tightening in his throat. Of course he had no intention of damaging the council budget and revealing such an investment, at least not until the school has been sold for five million and until the airport is up and running and he can take part of the credit. Until then discretion is the word.

'I didn't know that the investors in London were so dependent on Morella's accounts,' he replied. 'But if they're so interested in our town, they should come and see me, for we have excellent investment opportunities here,' he said with the smile of an American politician.

'That's not the point, Mr Mayor, but the three million.'

'But three million is no big deal for an airport! Why is there so much interest in us?'

'As I've said, it's a small example of something that could be much bigger and could be affecting the whole of the Region of Valencia and Spain in general,' she replied, sounding cold, calculating and distant. 'Besides, you must have seen the news; tough times are approaching.'

Vicent put on a poker face. It was obvious that he couldn't tell her that he was waiting to sell the school and for the airport to be operational in order to include the item in to the council budget. But if the problem wasn't just his, but the whole Region's, he could call Roig to ask for help.

'And you say you're looking at the whole of the Region of Valencia?' he asked, seeing a way out.

'Yes.'

'Right, well, you can calmly go back to London and tell your investors that there's no problem here, that everything's fine and there aren't any ghosts. Our accounts will be straight from the next quarter, and if they have any doubts, they should come here, and in addition we can offer them some good opportunities.'

Vicent got up nervously, anxious to put an end to that unexpected and uncomfortable conversation.

Without another word Anne gathered her papers, her briefcase and her coat, and before she left she reminded him:

'My clients and I will look forward to receiving your accounts. You will know that the international community is used to a very high standard of information and transparency and if they don't get it they will not hesitate to go to court,' she said, just like that, but looking him straight in the eye.

With the same style and arrogance with which she entered, the American left without closing the door behind her.

Stupefied, Vicent hurried over to shut the door and went back to his desk, where he sat down at his laptop for a few seconds, nervously rubbing his hands. He had never received a threat like that before, especially not from a woman and a foreign one at that. Without knowing what to do, he got up and stood next to the large stone window in the shape of a gothic arch, through which light poured into his office. From there he could see the roofs of the town's houses and the surrounding fields. It was a pleasant, sunny day bathed in a soft autumnal light. That meeting, however, had left him feeling unsettled. He would have to add the wretched three million to the budget, but that was impossible at the moment, no-one would understand and the hole it would create would be inexplicable for many and fodder for the opposition. The only thing left was to call Roig.

After fiddling with his mobile phone for a couple of minutes, Vicent eventually tapped in the number of the direct line to the President of the Region of Valencia.

'And what does the most verbose mayor in Valencia have to say for himself?' asked Roig as soon as he picked up the phone.

As usual the President was surrounded by noise, something that Vicent was beginning to find annoying because he could never have a quiet conversation with him. With Roig everything took place in a rush. Maybe that was the way to manage so many activities, or rather to bury yourself in them, thought Vicent.

'Everything's fine,' the Mayor replied as usual. As a politician he had learned that he must always, but always, say that things are fine.

'And that's what you've called to tell me?' replied Roig, rapidly as usual. 'I've only got a few seconds, I'm just going into a meeting in a bank.'

'Well that's precisely what I wanted to talk to you about, President,' stammered Vicent, believing that with Roig the best thing was to go straight to the point. 'I've just had a strange visit from a woman from an American agency, I can't remember what it's called, Standard something or other… The thing is that some investors in the Castellón airport from London are clients of theirs and have seen that our investment of three million doesn't appear in the council's accounts. They suspect that it's another example of the real estate bubble that has been created in the Community and in Spain in general…'

'Is this the pompous American broad who's drop-dead gorgeous?' Roig cut in.

'That's the one!' exclaimed Vicent. 'Do you know her?'

'No, I haven't had the pleasure, but another mayor has told me something similar. It seems that she's going around with the same story. Bah, let her get on with it.'

Vicent didn't feel that the matter was quite as insignificant as the President made out.

'The fact is that she told me that she's expecting the item of the three millions to appear in our accounts next October and that if it doesn't the investors will take legal steps.'

Roig remained silent for a few seconds.

'You're not telling me that the fucking American or English woman or whatever she is has threatened you?'

'You heard what I said.'

'Well you're fucked, my friend, because that agency is important. I've got a meeting right now with a bank that's complaining that another agency has lowered their rating and so their debt is now much more expensive.'

'What do you suggest I do?' asked Vicent, who didn't know anything about agencies or credit ratings.

'Well, you put the item in the budget and you tell your council that when the airport starts to function, the investment will more than repay itself. That it's the best investment that Morella ever made.'

'I can't, President, the opposition will eat me alive.' After a few seconds Vicent loosened his tie and continued nervously: 'I thought that maybe we could move the item to the Regional Council. We would pay it, of course, but if at least it could appear in the Region's books, it wouldn't be noticed so much.'

'You're crazy, old chap,' Roig replied straight away. 'Don't you realise I've got elections in only five months? That's impossible.'

Vicent felt the weight of the world on his shoulders.

'Isn't there anything you can do to help me?'

Roig remained silent.

'Yes, of course, and I've already done it and I'll continue to do it. I'll pay another visit to your town – or even two – just before the elections. I'll support you, we'll hold some joint event and I'll talk about how important the airport is for everyone, especially Morella, which has always been left behind when it comes to communications. Motorways, trains… they've always passed Morella by, but not this time.' Roig paused briefly. 'Listen, my meeting's about to start. Put the item in, and you'll see how everything will come out just fine in the end. Do you think that a dumb American broad can interfere in the historical development of our Region which, thanks to politicians like you and me, is emerging from a rural economy to position itself as a centre of world development?'

'Of course, of course, President,' was all that Vicent could add before Roig abruptly ended the call.

The Mayor sat down again in his chair and covered his face with his hands. After a few seconds he noticed the diary on his desk; he had barely two weeks to present the third-quarter accounts, so he would have to get a move on. With Eva expecting a baby, so he had been told before the holidays, they would have to get started on it since she would now take more time over things. Vicent took a deep breath, because another unpleasant conversation with Eva would only make things worse. Especially right now, after he had finally managed to improve their relationship following their bust-up when he made her make an urgent transfer of one million euros. Vicent hadn't yet told her that he had committed a further two million – only a verbal commitment, which, it would appear, hadn't stopped Roig from adding them to the airport accounts, raising the total to three. That was the amount now included in the airport accounts which, according to the agency, were in the hands of the international investors. Vicent wiped a hand across a now sweaty brow.

Although he had a plan all worked out, Eva represented a serious problem. He intended to delay the investment of nearly two million euros for the installation of a new heating system in the nursing home, which was needed because the one they had at the moment was very old and had stopped working. That investment was already budgeted for, so they could redirect those funds to the airport, although without making any mention of it, of course. It would just be necessary to give the item a general name, without specifying what it was, for it all to fall into place. He would tell the agency that that item included the investment in the airport, and he would assure the opposition that it referred to the work in the nursing home. Besides, the nuns and the old people surely wouldn't complain, or if they did he could put them off, delaying the works until the funds became available again after the sale of the school. It would only mean one more cold winter. As soon as the airport was up and running and generating more income for the council coffers, he would add the investment in the infrastructure, which would end up totally accounted for.

After thinking about it and chewing it over for about an hour, Vicent adjusted his tie once more and asked Eva to come in.

The young woman came in rather nervously. Since the discussion about the transfer, they had hardly spoken to each other more than necessary. He didn't want to have threatened her, but that's how the world worked: as he supported her and chose her for the job, thereby releasing her from one or two years' study for the competitive tests, she now owed him a favour. He's not asking for more than he should, he thought. The worst thing was that there was more to ask for, which made him feel uncomfortable. But it was something he had to do. Anyway, he said to himself, he would try to be gentle and kind, because no-one wanted any nastiness.

'Eva, my dear, come in, come in. How are you? Okay?' he said to his assistant, who was in her fifth month of pregnancy and was now starting to show a bit of a bulge. 'Please, sit down,' he said in a paternalistic tone while accompanying her to her chair, as if as well as being pregnant she has some kind of disability. 'It's getting close to the end of the quarter and we've got to get the accounts ready,' he began.

'I've nearly finished them,' Eva commented in her efficient manner. 'I've added the item for the refurbishment of the nursing home, which is the largest one, and also the ten thousand euros for the poster competition and the five thousand for the wire fencing for the Querol farmhouse, now that their cows are part of the town's meat consumption plan. There isn't anything else, is there?' she asked, biro and notepad in hand.

'There is one more thing, Eva,' Vicent said, leaning back in his chair and crossing his arms. 'It's to do with the Castellón airport, which until now has been a secret and an investment planned at the highest level. But you already know something about that, after the investment of a million that we made a few months ago.'

Eva lowered her eyes, just as keen as the Mayor not to be reminded of that unpleasant episode again.

'The thing is that this project is crucial for the Region and for the future of our town, which has always been passed by when it comes to infrastructure. We shouldn't miss this opportunity.'

'I'm listening,' said Eva, without looking at him.

'I have agreed with President Roig, who I speak to almost on a daily basis about these plans and who's fully behind us, that Morella will, in fact, invest a total of three million in the airport, of which we have already paid one million, as you know.'

As he expected, Eva left her notepad on her knees and raised her big, wide-open eyes that were full of surprise and incomprehension.

'Three million!'

'I know that for our budget it seems like a very significant sum, but it has to be added. In any case, we have to think strategically and not focus on the details.'

'But don't we need the approval of the full council?'

'I've agreed it with the President of the Region.'

Having been put in her place, Eva started to take notes in her notepad, but abandoned them almost at once. After a few seconds, she stammered:

'But we can't afford it, Mayor, with the debts that we already have…'

'I know, Eva,' he said. 'I'm doing it for the good of Morella.'

'But where are we going to get the money from?' she asked, fiddling nervously with her biro.

Vicent cleared his throat before answering:

'From the nursing home, but only by way of an advance,' he said, noting how Eva had already started to shake her head. 'Don't worry, it'll only mean a short delay. As soon as we have the money from the sale of the school, we'll start work on the nursing home; it'll be the first thing we do,' he said decisively. 'I'll explain the details to you, don't worry.'

Eva looked at him in silence, without batting an eyelid; she had stopped playing with the biro and her fingers were now firmly gripped around it.

After a tense silence, when Eva was about to get up, Vicent added one more thing while pretending to sort out his papers.

'There's something else,' he said, making Eva turn round as she was heading for the door. 'I'd also like you to add to the budget an item of income of five million for the school, as we're definitely about to tie things up.'

Eva dropped her arms by her side and leant forward slightly.

'I beg your pardon?'

'As I just said,' he replied, moving some piles of papers from one side of the desk to the other. Showing himself to be busy was another technique that never failed.

'But given that we haven't sold it yet...'

Vicent leant his large hands firmly on one of the piles that he was moving and looked at Eva in exasperation as if she was making him waste his time. Basically he didn't like to treat Eva like that, but he had to get over this hurdle. At least with women it was easier, since they gave in more easily than men, thought Vicent. That's why he had always hired women, and in addition they worked more and cost less, he said to himself.

'I know we're very close to completing the sale with the Englishman,' he said looking her straight in the eye. 'But this is, of course, confidential. Please keep it between ourselves.

Eva looked at him in bewilderment.

'Well, I wanted to tell you that just this morning we received a letter from him,' she said, taking out a folded envelope from her notepad. 'He brought it, but with so many things going on I forgot to tell you. He says he's reducing his offer from four million to two and a half.'

Vicent felt as though he'd been stabbed in the heart, but he tried to pretend otherwise. With a poker face he got up and went over to Eva, who was still standing there stroking her belly with one hand while holding the letter in the other with a look of astonishment. Vicent suddenly seized the envelope and having nervously opened it he glanced rapidly at the letter. It was short, direct and definitely said what Eva had just told him, without any explanation. That wretched Englishman, he said to himself, immediately thinking of his daughter, Isabel; he was sure it was her fault. With the letter in his hand, Vicent headed over to the window, where he looked over the town that he was finally in charge of after so many years. He wasn't going to allow himself to be defeated by an effeminate Englishman, nor by a stupid American woman who knew nothing about Spain and even less about Morella.

'Take no notice,' he said finally to Eva. 'I've got it all under control, it's only business tactics. The bastard only wants a discount, but he's not going to get one. We'll give him some kind of tax incentive if he gets tiresome.' He looked firmly at his personal assistant. 'So, you just stick to what concerns you and make sure the airport and the five million figure in the accounts.'

Eva raised a hand to her mouth.

'But, Mr Mayor, you know that's illegal, the sale hasn't yet taken place.'

'Believe me, the operation will have been carried out before those wretched accounts reach the investors, so there's nothing illegal here, do you understand?'

Eva stayed silent.

'And get me tickets for London, will you, for tomorrow morning? I'll go personally to close this deal with the Englishman. And make it business class. Come on now, let's get on,' he said, sitting back down at his desk and staring at his laptop. His hands were trembling.

Eva didn't budge an inch. After a few tense seconds, Vicent shouted:

'What's the matter? Didn't you hear me? Come on, there's lots to do. Get hold of those tickets and get a move on with the accounts.'

Eva said nothing and Vicent noticed that she seemed to have tears in her eyes. He sighed in irritation. He didn't have time for the emotional upsets of pregnant women.

'What the fuck's the matter?' he spat out.

'I can't do it, Mr Mayor,' Eva begged. 'You can't ask me to do something illegal.'

'It's not illegal, damn it; I'm telling you that by tomorrow the deal will be closed.'

'Well, when it's closed and signed off I'll adjust the accounts, but not before.'

Vicent dropped the pencil that he had nervously picked up a few seconds before on to his desk. He looked Eva up and down, pausing to observe her developing bump, which she continued to stroke as if trying to protect it.

'I think, Eva, that you're not in a position to refuse,' he said. 'Am I right?'

The young woman looked at the floor and then back at him. Now she did shed a tear.

'Please, Mr Mayor, I beg you, don't ask me to do something like that.'

Vicent looked at Eva and felt a degree of pity for her, now pregnant and without a penny to her name. Her partner was a bricklayer and the family depended on her, so she had nowhere to turn. He didn't like putting her under pressure, but basically thanks to him the girl had done well and could now start a family. He wasn't a bad man. In reality she owed him everything.

'Eva, please, don't make me do what I don't want to do, and in saying that I've said everything,' he said. 'I know that right now you need stability and I'm prepared to give it to you. But this has to be done,' he concluded, looking down at his computer.

Eva got the message and left the office in silence, dragging her feet and with her arms by her side. At least she shut the door behind her.

As soon as he was on his own Vicent struck the desk with both hands. He couldn't understand how a morning that had seemed so glorious and calm when he took his daily morning ride with *Lo Petit* could have become so complicated.

He thought about his horse and counted the hours until six o'clock in the evening when he would go out again, just for an hour, to ride along the paths of Torre Miró on the back of what was undoubtedly his best friend and his greatest confidant. Today he needed him more than ever.

Vicent turned towards the window and looked at the terracotta roofs that covered the town's white houses that rose in tiers up the hills as far as the wall. He opened the window to breathe in the pure air of the Maestrazgo and the smell of the first home fires of the winter. Deep down he was proud of having fulfilled his duty. He wanted to be popular in a town that had always treated him as an outsider. He wanted those farmers to know that he could bring Morella wealth, development, casinos or English colleges, and even the benefits of an airport, while all they had thought about was their land, maintaining the status quo for centuries and putting a brake on any progress. The battle was tougher than he'd imagined it would be and he'd been through some unpleasant moments, but he was sure that one day in the not too distant future he would be in the front row at Castellón airport alongside President Roig welcoming the first tourist flight. Morella was finally going to occupy its rightful place in the Region and in Spain. Even in the world.

Vicent was engaged in these daydreams when the Bang & Olufsen telephone rang. He had had it installed as soon as he became Mayor almost two years earlier. He looked at the receiver with its elegant, modern design and hesitated about answering it. That morning had brought so many problems with it and he didn't know if he could cope with any more. At least a little red light indicated that it was a call to his direct personal line. Although the transfer from Roig had now solved all his domestic problems, Vicent thought that it was Amparo and answered it.

'What do you want?' he asked before letting out a snort.

'Mr Fernández?' asked a voice that he immediately recognised because of the unmistakeable Catalan accent.

'Jaume! From the detective agency?' asked Vicent in a soft voice. It was two months since he had spoken with him.

Vicent straightened his back and raised his head solemnly, as if he were expecting an important verdict. Having listened to the speaker at the other end for a few seconds, he said:

'That's fine, Jaume, but tell me: what exactly have you found?'

He remained seated, listening attentively in silence, the receiver firmly clasped to his ear. In a while a smile began to appear and he opened his eyes as wide as he could, then squeezed them shut and raised his tightly clenched fist as a sign of victory.

Without saying a word he continued to listen with pursed lips until finally he burst out.

'And you've found it in La Pastora's documents, like I told you?' he asked.

Vicent nodded as he listened to the reply and started to take notes.

'Are you absolutely sure? The name is the same, right?' he said a few seconds later.

Vicent carried on listening, his eyes sparkling. At last, at last the moment had arrived for him to obtain justice, for himself and his father. Not only would he avenge his death, but he would also give a boost to the sale of the school. Right now.

When he had hung up he almost ran out of his office, hurriedly putting on his raincoat as he went down the Town Hall steps two by two. He didn't even pause to greet the people who tried to ask him where he was going in such a hurry. In order to avoid bumping into people he didn't go up towards the Pla d'Estudi along the street with the arcades, but headed uphill towards the church to get to the Colón Square via Virgen Street. From there he went up to the beautiful square where Valli lived and arrived at her house. He knew the place well, because he'd gone to fetch his children after their English classes that Valli gave them when they were little.

He replied straight away when Valli's calm voice asked who it was via the intercom.

'Vicent Fernández; I need to speak to you urgently,' he said strongly and firmly.

Valli hesitated for a few seconds and then replied:

'Is it so urgent? Can't we meet in your office?'

'No,' Vicent replied categorically. 'It's better for you for it to be in private.'

'I don't believe you, Mayor.'

'You'll believe me when I tell you that I know precisely what you deposited in Cambridge in 1955.'

After a long silence, the door opened.

Vicent, who had waited for this moment for many years, thought of his father, picturing him proudly looking down on him somewhere. His father had told him that one day Valli placed a bomb in the power station at Biescas, when he was in charge of its security and its demolition almost cost him his job. Although they might not have caught them, the Civil Guard had hundreds of *maquis* on file and kept very detailed records of the actions that they carried out. After that event, the Benemérita (as the Civil Guard was then called) sent – or rather condemned – his father to a dingy office in Madrid, with hardly anything to do and on half the salary. Two years later, they sent him to the Maestrazgo and gave him the force's worst job, the one that no-one wanted and that none of the guards up until then had managed to carry out: to find the most legendary of all the *maquis*, the one that had tricked the Civil Guard and slipped through its fingers for years: La Pastora.

Of course his father, like everyone else, failed in the attempt, and cursed the years wasted on an impossible objective that finally ended his life. If it hadn't been for that power station that Valli blew up under his nose, his father would no doubt have had a peaceful life in Biescas, where he had some family and where he himself would have grown up in better surroundings and greater acceptance than in Morella. Now finally he was able to avenge the memory of the former Civil Guard and put up against the wall the woman who changed his destiny and who was part of La Pastora's group who killed his father.

Vicent listened to Valli's breathing through the door and felt that he was being observed through the spyhole.

'Vallivana, for Heaven's sake, I'm not going to eat you, come on, open the door,' he said impatiently.

Gradually the door opened, but only as far as the safety chain would allow.

'What do you want?' asked Valli sharply, revealing her large, dark eyes which no doubt looked terrified by the unexpected visit.

'Don't be afraid, Vallivana,' said Vicent in a soothing tone. ''Of course I have something to tell you, but I'm not going to do you any harm. I'm the Mayor of this town and not a murderer, for Heaven's sake, so please let me in.'

Valli undid the chain and finally let him in to her small apartment.

Vicent took a step forward and without waiting to be told where the sitting room was he found it himself by following the narrow dark passage until he got to the small but warm, sunny room.

'Please sit down,' Vicent said to Valli.

'You, too,' she replied at once, gesturing to one of the four chairs around the round table in the middle of the room. She didn't offer him anything to drink and watched him in silence, her fingers drumming nervously on the cloth that she herself had embroidered.

'Go ahead,' said Valli.

'Yes, Vallivana, yes, I shall,' Vicent began, without even having taken off his coat. He cleared his throat: 'As you will doubtless remember, I always followed the comings and goings of La Pastora, even after he went to prison, because I always wanted to know what exactly had happened to my father. I wanted to find someone who knew what he said or did in his final moments, someone who had witnessed the scene. I've always wanted to show that he was a hero, although I've not been able to.'

Vicent paused to look Valli straight in the eyes, while she remained cold and silent.

'The fact is that recently I've been searching in La Pastora's archives, and to my surprise I found a reference to you, who he spent a good amount of time with.' Vicent looked at Valli again, but she hardly batted an eyelid. He went on: 'In my searches I followed up a comment that La Pastora made about a trip to England to deposit something surprising in a large house very near Cambridge. Are you with me?' he asked Valli directly.

'Tell me what you want,' she answered directly.

'I'm glad we understand each other,' he said. 'That's good news. So after tying up some loose ends and doing some more checking, I came away very surprised on realising that that magnificent house is precisely where our friend Charles grew up and the deposit was made in the name of his father, a well-known Hispanist at the university.'

'Tell me where all this is going,' insisted Valli, growing more pale.

Vicent noticed that gradually Valli was looking increasingly sad. She really was very old and he didn't want to cause any kind of attack or illness; he just had to be practical and get what he really needed. He couldn't waste time on melodramas.

'All right, I'll be frank,' he said. 'As you know, we need a substantial offer for the school and Charles has come up with the highest bid so far of two and a half million, but it's not enough. We need five.'

'And what do you want me to do? Pull five million out of a hat?' said Valli defensively. 'All I have is a miserable pension, as you know.'

'Yes, I know, Vallivana, don't worry,' said Vicent with a false smile. 'I need you to talk to Charles – I've seen you chatting to him in a very friendly way; show him you support the sale of the school and help me to get him to put up his offer to five million. We can invite him again, have dinner and let him see that now you support the project. You've been so opposed to it that his offer might go out the window.'

Valli lightly bit her lips and looked at Vicent in silence.

'You know that you're asking me to go against my principles, don't you? And if I don't do it?'

Vicent looked at her again eye to eye, leant forward and put his elbows on the table, taking control of the situation.

'If you don't do it, my dear, I'm afraid I shall have to tell Charles what was deposited from Morella in that house in 1955. I think he'd like to know,' said Vicent, pronouncing his last words very slowly.

Valli kept her eyes shut for a long time. Initially Vicent felt satisfied that he had delivered the killer blow. At last he had nailed that interfering old woman who had caused him so many problems and who was capable of organising a local revolution to prevent the sale of the school, the project on which his entire plan for the development of the town depended. Now he had her in his grasp and she would have to cooperate with him. This feeling of power made him breathe deeply, puff out his chest and look her in the eye. It was precisely that feeling of being in control that he enjoyed most about the post of mayor. After a life feeling inferior to the people of Morella, he now had them at his feet, starting with this old woman. Vicent looked at her tired, wrinkled face, her trembling hands still holding on to the tablecloth, the bunch of dried flowers in the centre of the table that until now he hadn't noticed. While he was waiting for a reply, he looked around him. The room was small and attractive with many books and photos. It was certainly true that that woman had had a full life. But this wasn't a courtesy call and he was starting to get impatient.

'Vallivana?' he said as he shifted his position and crossed the other leg.

She remained motionless and completely silent, which started to worry Vicent. He only wanted to put her under pressure to accept the deal and help him to sell the school. Frankly it would be a catastrophe if he made her have some kind of attack, since he would be fully implicated. Nervously he got up, went round the table and put his hand on Valli's shoulder, on top of the black smock traditionally worn in Morella and that she almost always put on.

'Vallivana, are you all right?' he said in a soft voice.

Valli immediately shook his hand off her shoulder.

'Don't even think about touching me, you snake,' she spat out.

'Sorry, it's because you were so quiet…'

'Shut up and get out of my house, you revolting rat!'

Surprised by such a verbal attack Vicent took a couple of steps backwards.

'Vallivana, this doesn't have to get nasty. All we have to do is reach an agreement and carry out the plan,' he said in a condescending tone.

'I said get out of my house, you evil blackmailer; you're as cruel and as stupid as your father,' she said, looking him in the eyes.

'Vallivana, I think you're suffering from emotional stress; maybe it's best if I leave, you can think things over and we'll talk again tomorrow,' said Vicent, trying to salvage the negotiation. 'Will you be in at the same time?'

Valli got up and crossed the room as fast as she could to take hold of her stick, which was leaning against the shelves. Seizing it firmly she raised it aloft and threatened Vicent with it.

'I said clear out,' she said in the most powerful voice she could muster.

Vicent didn't move.

'Out, I said, you nasty piece of work!' shouted Valli, this time in a very loud voice.

To prevent things from getting any worse Vicent got up, although he didn't want to leave with his tail between his legs. After crossing the passage and heading for the front door, followed by Valli, who still had her stick in her hand, Vicent said before leaving:

'I hope you reconsider and we can come to an agreement. If not, I don't know how you'll be able to justify such a criminal act. Oh,' he added, as if he had suddenly remembered something, 'I've also found out that your little friends in Paris…'

'Out!' Valli shouted once more, threatening him with the stick and preventing him from going on. 'Get out of here, you nasty, poisonous weasel! You're worse than your father, although I thought that was impossible!'

Vicent turned round in fury.

'Leave my father out of it,' he said, very seriously.

'Your father was a numbskull whose only objective in life was to kill people, or am I wrong?' replied Valli with fire in her eyes.

'I said leave my father out of it,' Vicent repeated, with his teeth firmly clenched to control his nerves.

'I'll say what I like about your father, because he did enough damage to my family. He was a murderer.'

'And you're a whore and a lesbian!' Vicent spat out, raising his arms in the air, red with anger at the remarks about his poor father. 'A whore and a lesbian!' he shouted again. 'That's what you are!'

Valli went over to him and was about to use all her strength to hit him with her stick when Vicent scrambled away and rushed down the stairs. When he got to the entrance door, panting, he looked up and saw Valli's face, red with anger, looking at him from the first floor.

'You're a poisonous rat!' she shouted.

Vicent took a step towards the door but turned round and looked up.

'I'll be back tomorrow, Valli. You can shout all you like but you've no way out. We'll talk tomorrow.'

Without giving her a chance to reply, Vicent went out into the street and gave a deep sigh. He was convinced that on the following day she would have no option but to come to an agreement with him. He had her cornered.

20

Valli spent the next three days in bed, hardly touching the boiled rice that Carmen, her neighbour from upstairs, made for her. She had found Valli lying on the sofa, unable to speak, just after the visit from Vicent. Since being widowed ten years earlier, Carmen had looked out for Valli, never missing an occasion when she went out or when she came in, and especially not a visit from the Mayor himself. Out of curiosity – or nosiness – Carmen had tried to listen to the conversation between Valli and Vicent, although she could only hear the insults, shouts and threats at the end. Having waited a few minutes after Vicent's departure, Carmen rushed down to Valli's apartment, but she didn't let her in. Carmen was worried, didn't hesitate to use the spare key that Valli had given her for emergencies and went straight in, shocked by such a commotion. Apparently Carmen had found Valli virtually lying on the sofa in a semi-conscious and unresponsive state. After a good dose of smelling salts, which for ladies of that generation cured everything, Valli eventually came round. Since then her neighbour had been very kind to her, looking after her and bringing her something when she felt like eating. Valli had been very grateful, but now that she was beginning to recover her strength, she preferred to be on her own. She had to sort out a lot of feelings and make decisions about what action to take.

With her eyes closed and sitting at the round table in the dining room, Valli tried to take advantage of a quiet moment while Carmen had gone shopping. Pen in hand she had started writing the same letter more than ten times, but all her efforts had ended up in the waste-paper basket.

The telephone rang again – it had been ringing for days – although once again she didn't answer it, convinced that it was the Mayor. She didn't want either to see him or talk to him ever again. The blackmail to which he had subjected her was cruel and despicable, and now, despite her desire for revenge, she had decided her first priority was to have the conversation that she felt she owed Charles. But she didn't know how to begin.

Looking at the waste-paper basket full of false starts, Valli put her hands to her face and dropped her shoulders. Maybe she'd never be able to win that battle. Maybe she'd already lost everything. But far from giving in, she felt that her duty was to try until she could do no more, so she went to the cupboard in the sitting room and took another piece of paper from the box. As she was about to sit down again, the intercom buzzed. She wouldn't have bothered to answer it were it not for the fact that Carmen often forgot her keys, although Valli had always thought that she did it on purpose so that she could have a chat. Carmen had never got used to being a widow and it was clear that she needed to talk even if no-one was listening.

'It's open!' she exclaimed as she pressed the intercom button to open the door downstairs.

'Thanks!' replied a voice that wasn't Carmen's.

Valli thought she recognised Cefe, but she quickly put the security chain on the door in case it was Vicent or someone trying to break in. Just in case, she grabbed her stick which she now kept in the hallway and waited by the door, almost holding her breath.

Cefe's slow pace and heavy breathing after years of smoking were unmistakeable, thought Valli, putting her stick back in its place. Her friend's arrival took her by surprise and she quickly looked in the mirror in case her appearance immediately suggested something was wrong. She quickly did up the top button of her housecoat and arranged her hair with her hand. Just as the bell rang she was dabbing on a touch of perfume that she always kept in the hallway cupboard so she could put some on before going out. She had always used 1916 by Myrurgia, which was created in that year, mainly because she had given classes in Paris to Esteve Monegal, son of the Catalan industrial chemist Raymon Monegal, who founded the company. Valli had very fond memories of the young heir who, far from settling down into his role, took to Paris full of curiosity and enthusiasm before transferring what he had learnt to the family firm, which he managed until it was bought by Puig.

Despite the fact that she was expecting them, the two loud knocks on the door made her jump.

'Valli?' came Cefe's loud, husky voice.

Valli breathed a sigh of relief on confirming that it was indeed her friend, although she was surprised by his visit. Cefe certainly came to see her sometimes at weekends, but never during working hours. She opened the door and produced a faint smile for the first time in three days.

'What a pleasant surprise,' she said, kissing him on both cheeks. 'What brings you here? Isn't the bank open?'

Cefe went in and as usual almost hit his head on the hallway light, which was too low for a man of his height. Leaning on the cupboard Cefe looked Valli up and down, examining her closely.

'I'm delighted to see that you're all right,' he said in a serious tone. 'I was worried.'

'Well, of course I'm all right, Cefe,' Valli replied at once, trying to feign normality. 'Why wouldn't I be?'

'Because I've been ringing you for three days, and you haven't once picked up the phone and in the bread shop they told me they haven't seen you since Monday.'

'Oh, right!' she said, as if she had suddenly remembered something and making it out to be of little importance. She gestured to Cefe to go through. 'I just had a bit of a headache and I spent a few days in bed, but I'm all right now, as you can see,' she said, heading for the kitchen.

Cefe followed her.

'You go in and I'll make you a coffee,' she said in a friendly way to Cefe, who accepted. 'Thank you very much for your concern, although there's no need to bother yourself. But now that you're here, it's always a pleasure to see you. Are you on your mid-morning break?'

'Yes,' Cefe replied, looking around the kitchen as if he were looking for signs of something suspicious or as if he were trying to prove that all was not well in that household.

Valli got out the same metal coffee pot that she always used, the kind that whistled, despite having been given numerous electric percolators or cafetières as birthday or Christmas presents, which were all still in their boxes, abandoned at the back of a cupboard. Valli was a loyal person even with her coffee pots.

'Well, tell me, my dear Cefe, how are things? How's everything in the bank?' she asked while she was preparing the coffee, spoonful by spoonful.

'I'm fine, Valli,' he replied, leaning against the doorway to the small kitchen. 'I'm just concerned about you.'

Valli looked at Cefe with tired but alert eyes, and then she turned slowly to light the cooker. She sighed. It was clear that her friend knew her well and she didn't want to lie, but she really didn't know where to begin. She looked lost in thought and watched the small coffee pot in silence until it began to whistle. Slowly she set out two small cups and saucers on the table, and with the aid of an old kitchen cloth she served the coffee and sat down.

'Well, I must say I am a bit anxious, yes, and I'm upset with the Mayor, as well,' Valli said eventually, before taking her first sip of coffee.

Cefe looked her in the eye as he held the delicate little cup in his large, dark hands on the table.

'And what are you anxious about?' her friend asked.

Valli took a sip of coffee and lowered her eyes. As she played with the small coffee spoon, she said:

'You told me that the Mayor was going to use public funds to convert the hotel into a country cottage and that his son, Manolo, was leading the project, didn't you?'

Cefe nodded.

'Well, just after you told me, I bumped into Manolo and congratulated him, but it turns out he didn't know anything about it,' said Valli in a confidential tone. 'And it's not as though he didn't see his father, because – fools that they are – having bought such a large house, it turns out that in the summer they had problems with the water and had to go to the hotel to take a shower. Look what you have to put up with if you're country yokels, eh?'

Cefe smiled.

'In the summer, before you went on holiday,' Valli went on, 'I also found out that the council paid for those privileged snotty kids from Eton to stay in the hotel, apparently as an investment towards the project of selling the school, since Eton is a possible buyer.'

Cefe raised an eyebrow.

'I didn't know that. How did you find out?'

Valli shook her head.

'I'm not naming names… But believe me it's the truth, Cefe, I wouldn't lie to you. I know they paid a real fortune, some five hundred euros per room per night – and in that hotel!' Valli exclaimed with a sense of shock. 'Can you believe it?'

Cefe pursed his lips and adjusted the knot in his woollen tie that he always wore.

'Are you sure?' he asked.

'Completely, although I think that in part it was because the pound went up or something like that, but in any case five hundred pounds is a lot of money for a room in a small-town hotel.'

Cefe nodded, looking concerned.

Valli leant her elbows on the table and moved closer to her friend.

'Cefe, this has to be looked into. There's something here that doesn't smell right.'

He lowered his eyes and stirred the sugar in his coffee more times than he needed to.

'I can trust you, Valli, can't I?'

'Of course,' said Valli emphatically. She sat up. 'Why do you ask?'

Cefe sighed.

'This must remain between us, because I'm breaking professional secrecy, but I'm doing it for ethical reasons,' he said.

'Go on.'

'I've also been surprised by certain things,' Cefe said eventually. 'I can suspect a lot of things, but what I know for sure is that Vicent received a large sum, two hundred and fifty thousand euros, all of it public money, to convert the hotel into a country cottage, although I'm sure that he's used that money to cover debts on his own house and that at the moment there's no plan to change anything at the hotel. I also know because I see Manolo almost every day.'

Valli leant back in her chair.

'I'm not even surprised,' said Valli coldly, looking her friend in the eye. 'That scrounger is capable of anything.' She paused briefly. 'He's a thief!' she said after a few seconds with a look of disgust.

'You could say that, yes,' Cefe acknowledged.

'We must act straight away!' Valli almost shouted, bringing both hands down hard on the table.

Cefe put a hand on top of Valli's.

'Take it easy now, Valli, take it easy; this has got to be well planned. We don't want to make fools of ourselves, because Vicent will pull another rabbit out of the hat and put one over on us. We've got to gather evidence,' he said in his usual calm way. 'First, I'll find out a bit more about the laws concerning these funds for country cottages. Maybe there are clauses that would make this transaction illegal, such as incompatibility with holding public office, for example.'

'Or maybe there's a maximum time limit on carrying out the work,' Valli added.

'Exactly. But we have to go bit by bit, you understand?'

Valli nodded and looked at her friend, who smiled at her. At last she had got someone to help her. At last justice was going to go her way, having eluded her all her life. She had always felt safe with Cefe, who was so tall, calm and clever. She looked at his impressive, green eyes, his thick eyebrows and his tough features that reflected more hours spent in the fields than in the classroom, until Valli, with a great deal of effort, convinced his father to let him study. From that moment their destinies had been tied together for ever. Cefe had always been grateful, for her persistence had allowed him to have a comfortable life and a much more healthy and secure one than farming would have done.

'Of course I understand,' she eventually replied. 'We're in this together, as usual.'

Cefe looked at her with a smile, finished his coffee in one go and got up.

'I'm late, so I must be off,' he said and he moved along the hallway to the door. As he got there he turned to Valli: 'But don't do that to me again, eh? Always pick up the phone, otherwise I'll be worried. Understood?'

'Okay,' she replied resentfully, as if she were defending herself from an attack.

Cefe smiled and gave her a firm hug before he left.

As she shut the door Valli felt more calm, although not entirely so. She didn't like to deceive anyone or hide the truth and hers, she was convinced, would come out sooner or later. She had to think very carefully about how, with whom and when she was going to talk.

Valli sighed and undid the top button of her blue overalls; she was still using the lightest-weight one, because that September day had started off very warm. She needed a bit of fresh air and so she raised the blinds and for the first time in three days she opened the window to let in a bit of a breeze. It felt good, she thought, going out on to her little wooden balcony, which was just like all the others on the square. It perked her up to see her plants again, some lovely spider plants and geraniums that seemed to be shouting for a bit of water. She hurried off to get them some.

Back on the balcony and feeling more energetic and able to do things, Valli looked out at the square thinking that Carmen, who had looked after her so well, would be arriving soon. But to her surprise it wasn't Carmen who was coming up so early from the Colón Square, but Eva, the Mayor's personal assistant. Valli looked at her in surprise, because once again someone was out during working hours. But more than that, what really caught her attention was the sad, dejected way she was walking. As she approached, Valli looked at her more closely and when she caught sight of her in profile she saw that she was expecting. That made Valli very happy, because she had always liked the girl since she gave her English classes many years earlier. Valli knew that she had bought a new apartment and that she lived with her fiancé, who was a bricklayer, if she remembered correctly. She had a good job and now she was expecting a baby. Valli felt proud of the girl's progress, the daughter of labourers who could barely read and write.

'Hello, Eva!' she called when the young woman passed close to her house. Valli's mood had at last brightened up.

Eva looked up wondering where the voice was coming from and then saw Valli on the balcony.

'Hello, Valli,' she replied with barely a smile and with her body looking rather listless.

Valli was surprised, conscious of the last conversation she had with her, when she told her about the large payment from the Town Hall to the hotel for the visit of the English students. Valli recalled that their encounter had ended by agreeing that they needed to talk some more and that maybe this would be the right time. She hesitated for a few seconds because of dealing with delicate questions with someone who was pregnant, but then she thought that it would be better to do it now before her pregnancy got too advanced. She felt that Eva knew more than she let on, so Valli decided to go ahead.

'Eva, come up and have a coffee. I can see you're looking different!' Valli said with an ironic little smile.

Eva didn't answer but she came closer to the balcony with her shopping bag in her hand.

'I can't, Valli, I'd love to but I've got a lot to do.'

'Aren't you working in the Town Hall?' Valli asked, leaning on the railing and looking down from her first-floor level.

Eva looked around the square, which was empty.

'No, I've asked for a day off, because I've got a lot to do.'

'Do come on up!' Valli persisted.

Eva seemed to hesitate but finally agreed.

'Just for a short while, okay?'

'Of course, whatever suits you,' Valli replied quickly, hurrying off to open the outside door downstairs.

Valli waited for her impatiently for two long minutes while Eva climbed the stairs, which she found surprising as it was only up one floor.

Valli was even more surprised to see the girl's sad face when she got close to her on the landing. She tried to make her feel at ease and took her by the hand before leading her through to the sitting room, where Eva sat down heavily on the small sofa. Valli went to the kitchen to fetch a couple of cups and the left-over coffee which was still warm.

She served Eva a small coffee with a dash of milk and another for herself, which she sipped as soon as she sat down in her favourite armchair next to the window.

'How nice to see you, Eva; it's been a while since I bumped into you in the street.' Valli looked directly at her tummy. 'I can see you're very well,' she said with a smile.

Eva returned the smile.

'As you see, Vallivana,' she said, with the usual respect that she had always shown towards her. 'I'm five months gone now – how time flies!'

'Congratulations,' Valli said quickly. 'What a great joy for you both. I'm really happy, Eva, about the apartment, about your partner and the family you're about to start. I'm so proud of you,' she said, speaking from the heart.

Eva, however, kept her eyes lowered for a long time. Valli said nothing, not knowing quite how to begin.

Finally, Eva looked up at her old teacher, forthright and direct as ever. Her eyes were normally full of life but now seemed vacant, as if nothing was worth bothering about. It truly pained Valli to see such a dispirited look.

'Tell me, my girl, are you all right?' she asked, leaning forwards. Why pretend to have a trivial conversation, she thought.

Eva lowered her eyes again, moved her body forwards and buried her face in her hands. A few seconds later she began to sob.

Valli got up immediately and went to sit next to her on the sofa, putting a hand on her shoulder and stroking her gently while she calmed down.

'There, there, Eva,' she said. 'It's not as bad as all that. Everything has an answer, I can assure you. Old as I am, I know what I'm saying.'

Eva remained with her face in her hands, but was now quiet. After a few moments, that got Valli really worried because she was afraid that the girl might be suffering from a serious illness, Eva finally sat up and leant back in the sofa. She gave a deep sigh.

'There, that's better, it's over now,' said Valli. 'You know I'm here for whatever you need.'

Eva gave her the same look that she used to give her as her teacher when she was little, full of admiration. With no-one at home who could teach her anything other than how to handle a loom, Eva had always been fascinated by her English teacher because she was the first and perhaps the only person in her life who had opened her eyes to the world. Valli remembered not so much Eva's questions about English grammar but about London and English people, their customs and their politics. In fact she had helped her to get enough money to fulfil one of her dreams and spend a summer in the capital of England. Eva said it had been the best summer of her life.

'I don't know where to start,' Eva said eventually, as she took a paper handkerchief out of her bag to dry her eyes.

Valli quickly got her a glass of water from the kitchen and when she came back she sat down next to her again.

'You know you can confide in me about anything you like.'

Eva nodded.

'But please swear to me that you won't do anything without telling me beforehand.'

Valli nodded.

Eva leant back in the sofa and, feeling calmer now, gave a big sigh. She took three deep breaths and finally turned to Valli.

'That day in July, when you overheard that conversation in English about the rooms in the hotel, I think you suspected that there was something there that didn't add up, didn't you?' she asked Valli.

'Indeed I did,' she replied.

'Well, I thought that things would end there, although I also know that there's a lot of pressure over the school and that Morella has gone way over the top as far as expenditure is concerned, as I suppose you can imagine.'

'You only have to go around the town to see that everyone, starting with the Town Hall itself, is living way above their means,' Valli responded.

'I'm the same,' said Eva with a sigh. 'I bought an apartment which may have stretched me beyond my limits, which I now regret. I'm trapped now.'

Valli raised an eyebrow.

'Tell me, my dear, tell me what you know, and maybe I can help you.'

'I felt excited about life with Pablo, you know, my fiancé who works as a bricklayer, and with my good salary from the Town Hall, we went crazy for one of those new apartments that they built near the wash-houses. It's on the top floor with a large terrace and wonderful views… Well,' she said, feeling rather ashamed, 'the thing is everything was fine in the beginning, but now interest rates have shot up and we're really struggling to pay the mortgage.'

'But you still can, can't you?'

Eva nodded.

'Yes, we can at the moment, but that's not the issue,' she said, and paused a moment. 'The thing is that I need to leave my job, but I can't; with what's about to happen,' she said, gently putting her hand on her tummy, 'and the mortgage, I'm completely trapped, and I can't leave my job, even though I ought to. And I'm really worried about it.'

'Why do you want to leave your job if you like it so much?

Eva looked into her eyes and bit gently on her bottom lip before replying.

'Valli,' she said completely openly, 'I think I get on with the Mayor as well as you do.'

Valli smiled.

'Listen to this,' said Eva, sitting up. 'The thing is, if I don't tell you I'm going to explode. I don't know how to deal with it, who to talk to or what to do, all I know is I can't sit here and say nothing faced with a situation like this. Although, as I say, I'm trapped.' She paused. 'I've been grabbed by the short and curlies, as they say.'

'Tell me,' Valli urged her, never having heard Eva say a rude word before.

'Vicent has been blackmailing me for a long time. A few months ago, just after Easter, he made me transfer one million euros to the Castellón airport project, without the transfer having been approved by the council. He just told me that it had the blessing of Roig who, as you know, came to Morella in Holy Week.'

Valli nodded, looking very serious.

'But what's he got over you that he can blackmail you with?'

'You know that I didn't take any competitive tests to get the job when I should have done. I suppose Vicent chose me and skipped protocol because he knew that such a favour would give him control over me, and without a rich or powerful family, I wouldn't have many places to turn in case of need.'

'I can believe anything to do with that snake,' said Valli, looking into space. 'Go on.'

'I made the transfer a long time ago, thinking that one day it would come out in the council and that everything would get sorted out. But that hasn't happened. What's more, the other day, first I received a letter from the Englishman, Charles, saying that he was reducing his offer for the school to two and a half million. Well, then the Mayor asked me to redo the council accounts to include a further investment of two million in the airport, taking the money from the repairs to the nursing home. That takes Morella's investment in the wretched airport to three million! Three!' Eva stressed.

'Three!' exclaimed Valli in astonishment.

'That's what I said. And things don't end there,' Eva commented while Valli, not knowing what to do, sat back and put her hands to her face. 'He also asked me to show a credit of five million for the sale of the school.'

'I don't believe it,' said Valli in a whisper, as if it surpassed her worst expectations. 'I just don't believe it.'

'That's what I said,' said Eva, now feeling more angry than sad or depressed. 'I told him that very morning I'd received the letter from Charles reducing the offer, but he replied that that was just a negotiating ploy, that everything was under control and that I should put in the five million.'

'What did you say to him?'

'That I couldn't, that it wasn't ethical, to which he replied using blackmail. Either I put it in or I lose my job... now that I'm pregnant, I've bought an apartment, the mortgage is crippling me and my fiancé, the bricklayer, well, you can never be sure, as you can imagine. But of course I'm the main breadwinner.'

Valli looked her in the eye.

'You're a very brave woman, Eva, very brave,' she said admiringly. I'm very grateful that you trust me. We will get this sorted out, you'll see. You've done well to tell me, because this is a very serious matter.'

'I don't think we're the only ones who are on to the case,' Eva remarked.

'Oh, really?' asked Valli in surprise, but thinking of Cefe.

'That same day,' explained Eva, 'last Tuesday, an American lady came from one of those credit agencies asking more questions than was comfortable. It was after that conversation that Vicent asked me to change the accounts.'

'Last Tuesday?' asked Valli, deep in thought. 'Are you sure?'

Eva nodded, surprised at Valli's interest in the exact day.

Valli pushed her head back on her neck as she tried to sort things out. How strange that that same day he should have come to blackmail her as well. Obviously the pressure from the agency was greater than he realised and that would have made him pressure her to persuade Charles to increase his offer.

Valli gave Eva an understanding look. Eva's eyes were watching her expectantly, as they did when she was little and expected her teacher to have all the answers.

'It's okay,' she said, putting a hand on Eva's for a few seconds.

After a few moments Valli got up and looked through the window towards the fields of wheat, shining bright and golden in the sun. Those fields and her wonderful town deserved a mayor who was so much better than the one they had. He had to be got rid of straight away, before he blackmailed any more people, especially vulnerable, old or pregnant women. The great bully. But fortunately Valli now had a piece of information that would get rid of him ipso facto. She would now be the blackmailer.

She turned towards Eva, who was still looking at her expectantly.

'Eva, my dear, would you be prepared to say this in court?'

'Valli, for heaven's sake!' Eva replied with a frightened look. 'I've told you that this is between you and me.'

Valli went over to her and sat next to her again on the sofa.

'I know, Eva, but we have to act, things can't go on like this. Do you want that swine to carry on blackmailing you all your life?'

Eva shook her head.

Valli bit her lip before she spoke again.

'You know?' she said thoughtfully. 'I don't think it's even going to be necessary. You leave it to me and you'll see that by tomorrow we'll have got him off our backs. There won't even be any scandal and it won't be done in public.'

'How?'

'We'll tell him to resign, to find a dignified way out, or we'll take him to court and cause a scandal,' said Valli with determination.

'Are you sure, Valli?' asked Eva in a whisper. 'I'm really afraid. I'm pregnant and I've got a crippling mortgage.'

Valli reached out for Eva's hand once more, giving a tight squeeze.

'Don't be afraid, my dear, don't ever be afraid of anything. You get rid of fear through bravery, like you did just now. With this information you've just saved the town and that rat will have to run for his life. You'll keep your job and let's hope they can organise elections soon so we can have an honest mayor.'

Eva nodded.

'And if it works out badly?'

'Trust me, like you always have.'

Eva smiled.

'If you don't mind, I'm going to get going right now,' said Valli, getting up briskly. 'You must go home and don't leave it until I tell you. The clock's ticking for that rat.'

21

Feeling happier than usual, Vicent went into the Town Hall through the main door, whistling and greeting everyone left and right. Having waited for a reply from Valli for three days, he was getting ready to meet her at lunchtime to give her an ultimatum. The time had come to take action, because regrettably he could not wait any longer. He needed to sell the wretched school for five million and the sale would start to fall into place at once, since Valli would have no option but to call the damned Englishman and convince him to increase his offer. If not, she knew what to expect.

In spite of not being in very good shape Vicent went up the stairs to his office two by two. The information that the private detective had given him had turned out to be expensive but crucial, as proven by Valli's silence. She had not been in touch with him since his visit to her the previous Tuesday, which no doubt indicated that she was either terrified or else trying to find a solution. If the latter was the case, it was obvious she hadn't found one, because he'd heard nothing from her.

Until he saw her.

She was sitting by his office door waiting for him, wearing her dark blue suit and with her head and back held upright. It didn't surprise him that she wanted to see him, indeed he was rather expecting it, he said to himself, although the fiery look that she gave him didn't augur well.

He went over to her and leant over her diminutive figure to show her who wielded the power.

'At last you've come to see me; I've been expecting you,' he lied, as he began to feel his heart beating faster. 'Come in,' he said drily.

She got up without taking her eyes off him, which made Vicent feel rather uncomfortable. He moved away from her burning gaze and entered his office when the clock on the wall was showing exactly ten, which was the time he usually arrived. Feigning normality he took off his smart autumn raincoat and hung it on the coat stand as Valli came in, and without any invitation she sat herself down in the Mayor's desk chair, all the while giving him a piercing look.

Vicent arched his eyebrows, but preferred to close the door before proceeding.

Once they were alone, he went swiftly to the other side of the desk, leaning his arms on it in an authoritative way and preparing to address Valli, who over time had given him so many headaches. He took a deep breath and reminded himself that there was nothing she could do to him; on the contrary, she was at his mercy. She might well get angry, and so he promised himself not to create any scandal in the Town Hall that might compromise him. Whatever he felt about Valli, the objective was to sell the school and to get her to help him do so. However tempting it was to defeat her, right now he needed her.

'Did you sit in my chair so you could call Charles?' he asked, without feeling the need for any preamble.

Valli continued to look at him with great intensity and hatred. She still did not say anything, which made Vicent feel more uncomfortable than it should have done. That witch had set more booby-traps for him and his father than anyone would ever have thought possible, and in principle that was from a teacher who was committed to serving the people of the town. Bloody hell! Vicent said to himself, trying unsuccessfully to hide his thoughts.

Tired of waiting and sensing that the balance of power was shifting towards Valli, Vicent banged his fist on the table.

'Valli, say something!' he spat out. 'Otherwise, why have you come?'

Valli sat back in the Mayor's red velvet chair and crossed her legs with the offhand manner that power usually brings. Vicent, who was still at the other side of the desk where normally his guests sat, rolled his eyes in exasperation.

'I've come here so that you can return to me what is rightfully mine,' Valli said at last, with a calm that began to make Vicent feel anxious.

'What the fuck are you talking about?' he asked immediately.

'I would advise you not to use macho, unpleasant or vulgar words,' she replied, equally quickly.

Vicent's shoulders dropped. That old woman was a tough nut to crack.

'You're not in a position to dictate terms, Valli; if I remember correctly we had an agreement. If you don't call Charles right now, I'm going to call him myself with a piece of information that will rather change his opinion, to put it mildly, and the opinion of the whole town, too,' he threatened.

With these words Vicent's confidence returned, and standing up straight he began to walk round his desk towards his own chair with the intention of taking it back that instant.

'Not so fast,' said Valli, raising an open hand with sufficient determination to stop Vicent before he could reach her.

Vicent looked at her but said nothing.

'I'm telling you in all seriousness, Vicent, that I'm the one who's come to collect, and you can put your blackmail where you like,' said Valli, letting fly.

Vicent looked at her in amazement. Whatever he thought of Valli, the fact is that his threats weren't getting to her. There must be something else.

'What are you up to, Vallivana?' he asked in a rather paternalistic tone.

Valli got up from the chair and put her hands on top of the desk with the same determination and aura of power that Vicent had displayed a few moments earlier. He listened, more surprised than intimidated.

'I'm the one who's going to start spreading information around the town, Mr Mayor,' she said, looking him straight in the eye. 'I'm going right now to the local radio station to announce that the taxpayers in this poor, small town have already given, in cash, one million euros – one million,' she repeated in a louder voice, 'to an airport that not only means very little for them but isn't even in operation. And that's not the only thing, because apart from being small in number and not very well off, they've also committed themselves to give two million more. As if we had too much.' Valli paused briefly to take in some air, but then carried straight on. 'And on top of that the people of Morella are treated like idiots. Apparently their Mayor expects to sneak into the accounts the sale of the school for five million euros before it has happened and when it is still far from being agreed.'

Vicent looked at her in astonishment and immediately thought of Eva, the traitor to whom he had let the cat out of the bag, the only person who knew this information. He clenched his fists as he thought about the young woman who he took out of the hotel one day to give her an opportunity in the Town Hall. She was going to pay for this. That young whipper-snapper would now find out what it was like to have to struggle in life. Now she would see what it was like to have water up to your neck and to have to go from town to town like his father, dragging his family with him, trying to make a living. Always an outsider, always a stranger; now she would learn that life isn't all about favours from kind people like him, who gave her a good job. She would pay for this.

Valli had carried on talking, although Vicent hadn't heard her last words. He wasn't bothered about the details, because what he had heard was enough. That old woman had got him by the balls, the bitch; who would have thought it possible?

He undid the knot in his tie, went back to the chair on the other side of his desk and flopped down into it. He looked at Valli with small, narrow eyes; she had sat back down again in the large chair and remained silent, looking at him with those big, wide, dark eyes full of mystery. That damned lesbian now had him like a hostage in his own office. He leant back in the chair and looked around him. He had spent some of the best years of his life in this room. He had organised fiestas and directed council projects and had left the town in better shape than ever. The charming new Alameda, the new school, all the streets nicely paved. So much work, consultants, architects' and engineers' plans – for what? To end up sunk by a Republican fossil who, to make matters worse, had ruined the life of his father, and was now ruining his. That woman should be behind bars.

Vicent sighed and looked round the walls of his office, with their well-ordered stonework and decorated with countless photos of his works and those of his predecessors. His gaze stopped at one picture in particular, with President Roig, at the fiesta they organised in the Colón Square at Easter. That's where everything started. Maybe he should have declined to invest in the airport, since he'd had a bad feeling about that from the start. In particular he'd felt uncomfortable about the commission he'd agreed to pay to a company in Roig's wife's name in the Cayman Islands. But he hadn't dared refuse, and was attracted by the President's gamble. In the photo the two of them appeared smiling and triumphant, bursting with power and dreaming of further successes. Who would deny themselves that?

Valli suddenly raised her voice, engaging Vicent's attention once more.

'I haven't finished yet,' she said. 'I also know that you've stolen more money from the taxpayers of Valencia by receiving a substantial sum to convert the hotel into a country cottage, a project that no-one knows about and whose funds have been used to pay for your hugely extravagant house.' She stopped for a second to take a deep breath. 'You're totally shameless!' she said after the brief pause. 'You're a crook! A thief!' she yelled, banging her fists down on the table.

Vicent stared at her wrinkled, worn hands. He didn't know what to say; all he wanted was to find a rapid solution. Could he buy her off? He could always arrange that and re-mortgage his house to pay her with. Or else he could call Roig; no doubt the first thing he would do would be to help him get out of this mess.

'What do you want?' he asked, knowing that there was no point in countering her accusations.

The old busybody had good friends who had no doubt confided in her. He now realised that he was the one who didn't have any good friends. He wondered who could have informed on him regarding the country cottage. His first thought was Cefe, but he rejected that straight away, because he couldn't imagine that such a good man would betray a professional secret in such an obvious way. It must surely be down to a piece of investigation, because the allocation of these grants was made public. The informers could also have been the electricity company, who no doubt would not have missed the chance to do him down after the amount of time it had taken him to pay them. They were definitely a pack of thieves, he thought.

'If it's money you want, Vallivana, we can discuss that,' said Vicent at last, breaking a tense silence.

'You and your money can go to hell!' Valli replied straight away. 'Do you think you can buy me off? You can go and buy your corrupt friends, as you've done already, but you can't buy me. Show some respect.'

'Tell me what you want, then,' he said with a defiant air. What had he got to lose? His father had always told him that things were not over until they were over and that you had to hold your head high and stay hopeful until the last moment.

'I want you to put a stop to the sale of the school immediately,' Valli replied firmly. 'I don't want any casinos or elitist colleges in this town. For the good of the people of Morella we have to start some useful projects that will improve the quality of our community and that, of course, is not going to be achieved with a casino, and even less with an elitist college which will come to take advantage of us and our services, without giving anything back to the town.'

'That's what you think, Vallivana,' he replied. 'They're only boys, and look how good the conversation was when they came, and how well they got on with the boys from our school.'

Valli looked at him in disgust.

'Oh please, please, don't waste my time, Mayor. Those toffs went away with their tails between their legs and you know that as well as I do; gossip travels fast in a town like this.'

Vicent said nothing for a few moments.

'I can't put off the sale, because the town needs it.'

'There'll be more worthwhile offers; the process can be started again from scratch.'

Vicent thought it over for a few seconds.

'Okay,' he said. 'I can start the process again.'

Valli gave a cynical laugh.

'No, no, Vicent, not you,' she said. 'As I'm sure you'll understand, after such corruption and embezzlement, the only thing you can do is resign.'

Vicent felt a stab in the heart. After two years, this could be his last day as Mayor, all because of that evil old woman. His shoulders dropped and he put his head in his hands while placing his elbows on his knees. The bitch had sunk him. In the face of such easy-to-prove accusations, he had nowhere to go other than prison, most likely. If only she wanted money…

The Mayor – at least for now – raised his head and stared at Valli. For a second he felt like jumping on her and pummelling her into the ground, but that would only make things worse.

'Tell me what it is you want,' he persisted, his only aim now to save his neck.

'I've come to get you to write your letter of resignation right now, and to get you to give me back the hotel that your family stole from my parents. And I want that right now, too.'

'But they bought it,' Vicent said at once.

'For a song,' Valli replied quickly. 'You know that as well as I do. It was a reward for murdering them.'

Vicent closed his eyes as he felt his heart freeze over. In spite of his power, the hotel was all he had. It not only gave employment to his two children, but if he had to hand it over he would also have to give back the two hundred and fifty thousand euros from the grant that he had almost completely spent. If he lost his job it would mean selling his house, the crowning glory of his life, his greatest success, the symbol of a life of struggle. He leant forward and almost buried his head between his knees.

'I want an answer right now,' said Valli, drumming her fingers on the desk impatiently.

'There's something else,' she added, creating yet more fear in Vicent, who couldn't think what else there could be. He looked up at her, his face almost without expression.

'As you will understand, and much to my regret, I don't want a local scandal either, although I'd give my right arm to see you in prison,' Valli began.

Vicent tightly gripped the armrests of his chair. She was the devil incarnate, that woman, and he had to be prepared for anything. He remained silent while she went on.

'I say that because I think that there's something going on between Charles and Isabel. Out of respect for them and their future, I don't want them to be affected by your scandal,' said Valli, who was being more practical than Vicent would ever have imagined. 'For that reason, and only for that, I'm offering you my silence in exchange for your withdrawal from the school business, your resignation and the return to me of the hotel with all the legal papers signed. And, of course, the return of the grant for the conversion to a country cottage; I can't inherit a lie that has cost the taxpayer thousands of euros, as I'm sure you'll appreciate.'

Vicent sighed deeply. Given all the evil that could befall him, that wasn't the end of the world, he thought. At least he would retain his honour, although, depending on which way you looked at it, much good would it do him. In fact, he would prefer to keep the house and his job more than his honour, but he wasn't in a position to choose. In any event he still had one last bullet left, he said to himself hopefully, in the shape of Roig. As his father had always taught him, Vicent would fight until the last moment.

A few seconds later he thought of another possibility.

'What about if we both keep quiet?' he asked. 'I say nothing about your issues and you say nothing about mine, and everything stays as it is.'

Valli looked at him in astonishment.

'You're crazy,' she said, looking at him and shaking her head at the same time.

Well, it was worth a try, he thought.

'You'll give me some more time,' Vicent finally agreed, as if it was a right rather than a favour.

'No,' Valli responded forcefully.

Vicent gave a long, deep sigh.

'Every accused man has the right to his defence,' he replied. 'Vallivana, I gave you three days; do the same for me. Or at least one.'

Valli looked him up and down with contempt, but she agreed.

'All right,' she said. 'You have until twelve o'clock tomorrow. I'll come here at that time, and for the good of the whole town I expect you to have your letter of resignation ready.'

Vicent got up as if he had just managed their meeting, as if the ball was in his court rather than hers.

'Okay,' he said with authority, wanting to terminate this disagreeable visit and set about finding a solution.

Valli, somewhat surprised, got up and without saying a word, headed towards the door without taking her eyes off Vicent, as if she still didn't trust him.

'I shall be here tomorrow at twelve,' she said to Vicent, who was increasingly sure that he would find a solution.

Valli walked out of the office with her slow, tired and heavy gait. As soon as she was out of sight, Vicent sighed, locked the door and anxiously went to his chair. He sat down at once, surveying the pleasant room that he himself had furbished, with new modern lighting, paintings, the desk where Eva sometimes worked and a soft carpet that he had had brought over from Istanbul. He turned to the window, looking with pride at the town, the stone walls and the fields. This was his empire and would continue to be so. That old woman would have to shut up for good.

Without losing a second, he took his mobile out from his sports jacket pocket and called Roig. He adjusted the knot in his tie when the phone started ringing.

The President picked up immediately.

'What's up, you asshole?' he said, using his usual greeting once more.

'Hello, President, how are you?'

'I'm fine, Mayor, but cut the crap and get to the point, because I'm fucking well on a yacht in Mykonos with a couple of blondes and I don't want to waste one second. Boy, you'll have to come on the next trip. It's amazing. But tell me, what's up?'

Vicent put his hand to his forehead. Even he found it difficult to understand such behaviour. Not that he'd always been faithful to his wife, far from it, but at least he was more discreet. Anyway, he wasn't there to judge anyone, especially not now, as he had infinitely more urgent needs.

'President, I have a problem,' he said frankly.

'Damn it, Vicent, you've always got problems. What's the matter now? Get to the point, my son.'

'Well, some clever clogs has let slip that we've paid a million for the airport and that two million more will follow.'

'And what's the problem with that? Isn't that what we agreed?'

'It hasn't been discussed in a full council meeting and with our small budget the whole town will come down on me.'

'But, my friend,' Roig replied, 'for heaven's sake, what are you thinking of? Don't you know the secret of democracy is to gain everyone else's confidence? Who on earth tries to plough ahead without the people? But, okay, it's not a problem, you explain it to them, you tell them it's the best investment Morella has ever made and Bob's your uncle.'

'I can't, President, they'd never approve it. This isn't the Region, it's a town and it's more difficult to hide. Plus, they're also accusing me of trying to include in the council budget the sale of the school for a rather optimistic sum of money, if I can put it like that, before it's actually happened.'

'Have you gone crazy or what?' President Roig spat out. 'You don't do that, you idiot.'

'President, there's no other way if that amount is going to go to the airport; it was the only way we could invest three million.'

'Listen, old chap, I've never asked you to do anything illegal, have I?'

Vicent waited for a few seconds.

'Well, President, with all due respect…' he started to say, but stopped for a brief pause. He didn't know whether to continue or not, until he saw clearly that his priority at that moment was to save his skin. He went on: 'If I remember correctly, on one occasion you asked me to send the commission for assistance with the reconstruction of the school to a company in the Cayman Islands in your wife's name.'

The President remained silent for a few seconds that seemed like an eternity to Vicent. He never thought that he would end up threatening the President of the Region himself. He felt a mixture of power and terror.

'Listen, you moron, you're not threatening me, are you?' replied the President, sounding very serious. 'That transfer never happened and you, you idiot, can never prove it. But what kind of politician are you, you good-for-nothing? I'll simply deny it, and what's more, I don't even know what you're talking about.'

Fear started to run through Vicent's whole body. Fear of losing everything, even the support of the person who had got him into this mess. If it hadn't been for the wretched contribution to the airport, he could sell the school for two and a half million and get on with other projects. But that investment forced him to increase the sale price for the school, and that's where the problem with Eva and the lies started. And it was the oh-so-clever President Roig who had made him invest in the airport in exchange for a commitment to pay for the refurbishment of the school, which was essential if it was to be sold. The bastard had kept the money but had got rid of any responsibility. And now Vicent was in his hands, heading like a lamb to the slaughter. Despite the rising anger that he was starting to feel, he tried to focus on staying calm and finding a solution. Experience had taught him that he who kicks up a fuss usually comes off worse.

'President, President,' he said in a conciliatory tone. 'Please, let's not go that far; up until now we've had such an excellent cooperative relationship.'

'What do you want, Mayor? I don't know that I can do anything for you,' said the President, sounding very distant.

Vicent had to try the impossible.

'One solution would be for the debt, the three million, to be moved to the Regional coffers.'

'I've told you that's impossible; there are elections coming up.'

Vicent closed his eyes, beginning to despair.

'The solution, my political novice,' said the President, 'is to do what everyone else does, but which you are too stupid to do and it hasn't even entered your head to do.'

Vicent hated being subjected to such abuse, but his hands and feet were tied. He hated it with all his might, because the Civil Guard command had done the same thing with his father: making him feel small and treating him like dirt, just because he couldn't catch the *maquis*, who everyone was chasing but no-one could find.

'I'm all ears,' he said, finally, swallowing hard three times.

'Set up a new company in your wife's name and outside the framework of the Town Hall you get a loan from the local bank that covers the three million. So you won't have to explain anything to the town. And when the investment starts to become profitable, you pay back the loan and that's it: no-one is any the wiser. Get it?'

'Perfectly, President,' replied Vicent, feeling hopeful. 'Can you suggest which bank I should ask? Maybe with your endorsement…'

Roig interrupted him:

'I can't endorse you for anything; I'm surrounded by loans and businesses everywhere. But it's okay, it'll all get sorted. Just go to your local bank.'

Vicent thought of Cefe.

'I can't. I don't know if I can trust them.' He paused. 'I'm sure you understand.'

Roig gave out a long sigh with a mixture of irritation and exasperation.

'Well, my son, you're going to have to sort that out all by yourself,' he said sharply. 'You should know that the first obligation of a mayor is to get on well with everybody, especially with bankers. If you have to lick their arse, that's what you do and that's that. You follow me?'

Vicent closed his eyes once more, squeezing them hard. He didn't at all like the idea of depending on Cefe or having to ask him a favour.

'Of course, President,' he said finally.

'Off you go then, good luck, old chap,' said Roig. 'I must go, they're waiting for me.'

'Have a good…'

Vicent couldn't finish his sentence, because Roig had ended the call straight away.

Vicent stood up and went over to the window. The sun that came in in all its splendour was so high and strong that he had to draw the taffeta curtains that were typical of Morella, making the room quite dark. Having thought for a few moments he realised that he had no option but to call Cefe and try to carry out the operation that the President had described. Vicent now understood how the debt companies, that were simply front organisations to conceal more debt, had financed all the Valencian pomp of recent years. He had always wondered how the Region, where there were so many people still living off the land, could allow themselves such extravagance; because they were really show projects, like unnecessary suspension bridges, sporting events that left no legacy or museums that were as spectacular and modern in form as they were empty in content. At least he had built a swimming pool and a state school, and a walkway that older people enjoyed.

Vicent hurried back to his chair and felt that he had no time to waste. He had to look for Cefe's telephone number in his diary, a sign of his bad management. As Roig had warned him, he should have spent these past two years establishing a better relationship with the banker; he should have known his number off by heart.

Eventually he dialled the bank's number. They put him through to the manager straight away; he was not the Mayor for nothing.

As Vicent half expected, Cefe said a firm "No" to the proposal. Clearly but concisely the manager explained that council projects had more than surpassed the maximum financial risk permissible and that it was therefore impossible to set up a new credit facility, even though it involved a new company.

Vicent pushed as far as he could, and out of desperation suggested taking him out to dinner, but Cefe declined. The bastard was good friends with Valli and they were clearly in cahoots, thought Vicent.

He walked up and down again in his office. He only had one possibility left: he could call Charles himself and propose an incentive for him to increase his offer.

He set to it straight away and had the good fortune to find Charles at home during his lunch hour. After the usual preliminaries, Charles wanted to get on with it and go straight to the point.

'So tell me, Vicent, is there any news about the school?'

'Yes, yes, that's what I was calling you about,' Vicent replied.

Charles said nothing, obliging Vicent to continue and carry the burden of the conversation.

'We got your letter reducing the offer,' he said. 'We were surprised because it was a considerable reduction.'

'It corresponds to our valuation,' said Charles, short and sharp, without giving a fuller reply.

'It was about the price that I was calling you, Charles, on a personal level, because of the fondness I feel towards you and the affection that you feel for our town,' said Vicent, hoping to sow a small drop of understanding or agreement.

Charles said nothing. Vicent realised he would need to explain himself.

'I'm calling you in confidence because, as you know, we have made some major investments to improve the town and make projects like the school attractive to investors.'

Charles still said nothing, which made Vicent feel uncomfortable, so he had no option but to continue despite sensing a clear lack of support. It was like heading for a waterfall but in addition having to row in order to get there, he thought. But he remembered his father and repeated to himself that it was his duty to carry on fighting.

'As I say, the town needs funds so that our administration can carry on and produce the benefits that we are all hoping for.' Vicent paused. 'The thing is that we need to sell the school for the five million we asked for and no less. That's how it is. It has occurred to me that I could offer you a small personal incentive if you wish to accept it. If you settle the purchase at five million, I can offer you a personal cut of two per cent.'

Both men remained silent.

'I don't know if you understand me...' Vicent started to say.

'Of course I understand you,' Charles cut in sharply. 'But the answer, of course, is no. And I shall ask you for a bit of respect, Mayor. If that's how you operate in Spain, that's up to you, but this is England and we are the most prestigious college in the world. How dare you propose such a thing to us? I find it most offensive.'

Vicent did not know what to say.

'Okay, okay, Charles, don't be offended, and forgive me if you didn't like the idea...'

'The answer is no and there's nothing more to talk about,' Charles interrupted with annoyance in his voice.

Vicent quickly played his last trick before the irritated Englishman hung up. He would have preferred to avoid mentioning Isabel, but after the commotion on the occasion of the dinner at his house, the stupid girl had managed to get her way, thought Vicent. He added:

'I just thought that it might be of interest to you, especially in the light of the friendship that you seem to have with my daughter…'

'Leave you daughter out of this; she has nothing to do with it,' Charles replied firmly. 'I have nothing more to say to you. I have made an offer and I expect a response. Although I must add that I do not like these practices at all. That's all. Goodbye.'

Charles placed his phone down so suddenly and forcefully that Vicent's receiver carried on emitting strange sounds for some while afterwards.

Vicent flopped down into his chair without knowing what to do, nor where to turn. He was sunk. There was only one place for him to go: his own house. He knew his wife had inherited some money, but Amparo had never told him how much. Today, after years of not giving her a crumb of attention, the moment had come for him to ask.

Without acknowledging anyone he left the Town Hall with his head down and headed for home, the only place where he would be welcome.

Barely half an hour later he went into the house without calling out and to his surprise he found his wife sitting quietly in the lounge, as if she were waiting for him. She looked at him intently and immediately got up, kissed him on the forehead and hugged him in a way that he'd forgotten.

'Everything okay?' was all Vicent said, looking straight ahead, but still surprised by his reception.

'Everything's fine, better than you can imagine,' Amparo replied with a gentle smile.

'I'm not up for playing games; I'm in a terrible mess and I'm not in the mood,' he said as he took off his jacket and threw it on the sofa. Vicent turned to his wife, because basically what he needed was a firm hug, which she gave him.

He was now feeling calmer and was about to speak, but his wife got there first with unusual determination and confidence.

'I know everything,' she said, in an understanding voice and looking him straight in the eyes. She took his hands and pressed them against her chest.

Vicent took a step back and raised his eyebrows.

'What do you know?' He was almost at the end of his strength and his wife seemed to have noticed.

Amparo moved towards him again and put her hands gently on his shoulders. The gesture helped him, albeit only slightly, to reduce his tension.

'Valli called me and told me everything, woman to woman,' she said.

Vicent stepped back once more and looked at her in astonishment.

'I'm going to kill that witch!' he almost shrieked, feeling great tension throughout his body once more.

His wife placed her gentle hands on his shoulders again, stroking them in order to calm him down.

'I just need to know one thing, Vicent, and whatever you say I shall still go on loving you and supporting you, but I need to know the truth,' she said, looking him in the eye. 'Is it true what she says?'

Vicent lowered his eyes, unable to speak. He was ashamed. He had ended up at the mercy of an ordinary old woman, his daughter and now even his wife. They all held sway over him, the Mayor. How had it come to this?

He couldn't hold back any longer and covered his face with his hands to hide the tears that were welling in his tired eyes. It was the first time that his wife had seen him cry in over forty years of marriage, but now he couldn't hide his swollen red eyes that were more troubled and ashamed than ever.

She realised that silence was the best response.

'Don't worry, Vicent,' she said, taking hold of his hands. 'I have been with you, I am still with you, and so I will remain.'

Vicent uncovered his face and looked her in the eye. That was the first sincere look that they had shared for many years. He closed his eyes once more, feeling that at such moments of maximum darkness, incredibly there was a part of his heart that was swelling with pride. He would never have imagined that his wife would react that way, which is why he didn't dare to ask her about her savings as he had planned to do. He had implicated the town, even his own daughter, and he wasn't going to do the same thing now with his wife, who wasn't to blame for anything.

'Vicent, listen,' she went on, with a determination that Vicent hadn't come across before. 'Valli is right and hers is a good proposal. It saves you from public disgrace and opens the doors to our daughter's future.'

'Isabel?' Vicent asked in surprise.

'I don't know how things are exactly between Isabel and the Englishman,' Amparo explained, 'but I've been told in the town that they were seen having an intimate dinner together one night and that then they walked along the Alameda.'

'Oh, really?' asked Vicent in some confusion. 'Well, I knew nothing about it.'

'Of course you knew nothing about it, because since that horrible night you haven't spoken to your daughter, and that's not right.'

Vicent lowered his eyes. Deep down he knew that as usual his wife was right. Amparo went on:

'I don't know how things are, but I do know that if you put too much pressure on Charles, everything could go down the drain and you could end up without the school and in addition be gambling with our daughter's future.'

'But do you really think there's something going on?' Vicent persisted incredulously.

'Because of course I'm in touch with her as she's my daughter, I can see that she has her hopes up for the first time in a long time. Especially after they dined together that night.'

Vicent raised his eyebrows. He was surprised that so many things were going on around him without him realising. He looked at his wife, who was looking prettier than usual. He looked at her more closely, because she had put on some make-up and was wearing a blouse that she had bought on a trip to Paris many years earlier and that he had always liked. That woman had supported him unconditionally for over forty years without any obligation and in exchange for almost nothing.

He didn't deserve her, he thought. She was the only person that he had in the world. His wife, his house and his horse, the only things that he had.

'What should I do, Amparo?' he asked, maybe for the first time in his life.

She looked at him and smiled.

'I don't need to tell you, you already know,' she replied.

22

La Fonda
Calle Colomer, 7 y 9
Morella (Castellón)
October 2007

My dear Charles,

I hope that this letter finds you well. I picture you engrossed in your affairs, surrounded by your students in their black jackets, as I've seen on the internet. Eton seems like a special place, so I'm not surprised that you've made it your home.

I'm okay, although I'm writing to you now to tell you about some things that have happened lately, and there's quite a few. Some weeks ago my father resigned as mayor. I'm not exactly sure what happened, only that he had a big argument with Valli and that in the end he didn't get any help from the Regional President, who was supposed to be his friend. There's been a lot of talk and rumours in the town, but I don't know what to believe. The thing is that there's no longer any talk about the school and I think they'll put it out to tender again. Maybe someone's been in touch with you, but I wanted to let you know as well because, as you can imagine, things are a bit upside down and at the moment the town is without a mayor.

I can't say I feel sorry for my father, because I'm sure he got what he deserved, but the atmosphere has become strained and we have to make an effort to carry on with a normal life. In that respect I'm finding painting helpful. In fact yesterday I finished one that I think you would like. I could send it to you if you wish, because it's not very big.

I've also got a new job in Castellón, in an art shop where they needed an assistant and where they'll let me use all the materials I want for free. I'm very happy about it and hoping to start in a couple of weeks.

There's nothing more to tell you, except that a lot of people ask me about you, because you left a very good impression in the town. People here like

you, Charles, in case you ever want to forget about the school and come
back to visit us. You know that Room Fourteen is always there for you.
    Affectionate greetings,
    Isabel

Leaning back in his leather chair Charles left the letter on his lap once more and looked at the fire that was burning in the sitting room hearth. He tried not to think about the letter any more, nor about Spain or anything to do with it while he was waiting for his friend Robin. In spite of his intentions he raised his eyes and looked again at *The Poets' Garden*, the picture that Isabel had given him that summer. Still wearing his uniform of black jacket and bow-tie, he looked back at the fire and then at the letter that he had read several times since receiving it in the middle of the week.

Charles gave a deep sigh and loosened his bow-tie as he listened to the gentle crackling of the firewood. That sound and the heat from the fireplace brought him some calm, although since he had received the letter he hadn't slept well even for one night. On the one hand the school business had disappointed him, as he had had high hopes for that project. Not only had he had to deal with the local chaos in Morella, but the recent crisis in the international credit markets also meant that it was much more difficult to get funding. He followed the economic news from the shelter of the security and the detachment of Eton, but he sensed that the problem had barely started.

The return to school after the week in Morella in July had also been difficult, as he hadn't adapted as well as usual to the monastic and scholastic life that he had enjoyed so much for many years. He had started this academic year with less enthusiasm than usual, now that Eton, despite its long and splendid history of taking in some of the brightest students in the world, no longer seemed anything like the centre of his life.

Charles couldn't stop thinking about the starry sky above the Alameda, as he walked silently along listening to Isabel's footsteps and her deep breaths. He recalled tales of markets for illegal truffles or of figurines of flamenco dancers that lived secretly inside a wardrobe in hiding during the war. The same war that had apparently changed the life of his father and even that of George Orwell. Charles, with his eyes fixed on the picture, wondered if his own life was about to change, for it had not been the same since his return. As he walked around Eton's pretty surroundings and alongside the gently flowing Thames, he remembered with nostalgia the bundles of rosemary growing between the steep, dry rocks of the Maestrazgo. The Morella countryside was more honest and direct that these subtle British curves that hid everything. That characteristic was also reflected in its people, Charles thought. Spain seemed to expose its inhabitants and its visitors, revealing you for what you are; just the opposite of what happens in England, where people cover themselves with a socioprofessional layer mainly designed for self-protection. In fact in Eton they taught all the students to behave in the same way, because it was frowned upon if you stood out too much. You made your moves wearing white gloves, without any fighting or getting your hands dirty, always without putting your cards on the table, something that a good Etonian would never do. Students were always told that the last thing you should do in life was close off options.

Things had not been the same for him, either, following the conversation he had with Isabel about his mother. Since then he had looked differently at mothers visiting their sons at Eton or, with evident pain, leaving them at the boarders' house on the first day of term. Having met Isabel he no longer saw these women just as wives of influential men, brought up to serve – like his Meredith. Now he knew that these women could be concealing talents that often the world knew nothing about. During that first term, Charles had given these women a lot more time, surprising them by his sudden interest after having ignored them for so many years. He saw in their eyes a great appreciation for the attention he gave them, and at the same time they showed no resentment for his previous disdain. How could he have disregarded those women for so long?

Charles thought about his mother again, just as he had since Isabel had asked about her. Over recent weeks he had wondered about the image that over the years he had formed about her: a tall, sweet, smiling English lady with blue eyes and lovely, long blond hair. But he knew that that was all stuff of imagination. He had started to hunt among his father's papers to find some traces of his mother, but he found nothing. He had even gone to the old house in Cambridge where he had grown up and that he himself sold after getting divorced and moved permanently to Eton. The owners, still the same family who had bought it, allowed him to search in the basement, which they hardly used, in case some object or other had been left behind in the move.

He didn't find anything, but in the hallway of the house he did see a photo of old Morella, framed in plain pinewood. The owners told him that they had found it in the basement and they had brought it up because the town looked lovely and because they wanted to keep something from the history of the house.

Charles picked up the frame that now lay on the wooden side-table next to his armchair. It was a very old photo, rather scratched, in which there were no houses to be seen outside the wall and where the castle and the wall itself seemed to be in more of a state of ruin than they did now. The roads coming into the town were very narrow and unpaved, and some of the houses looked as though they were about to fall down. Charles stared hard at the photo until the main doorbell rang, loud and long, almost making him jump out of his chair.

When he heard Robin's voice, he pressed the button that opened the door downstairs and immediately took off his jacket and bow-tie and put on his red velvet dressing gown, with his father's initials still sown in fine golden thread. It was one of the few objects that his father had left him and that Charles hardly used until he discovered the photo of Morella. Since then he had felt much closer to his father, perhaps closer than he had ever done in his life.

Robin, stocky and with his usual loud voice, came into Charles' flat like a whirlwind. He usually came on Friday nights, as Eton was on his way to the Cotswolds, where he had his weekend retreat. That region of innocent little villages built of golden stone, in which you could only see smiling, white-haired little old ladies, was in reality inhabited by bankers and investors, the only people who could afford the house prices, but who were never to be seen. While the little old ladies filled the local tea rooms, the residents in the large houses with thatched roofs stayed in their drawing rooms, popping champagne corks at private parties. Robin was one of them, although a little less social. In fact, Charles' friend, a banker in the City since he left university, hardly accepted any of the many invitations he received, for everyone wanted to be associated with an ex-Harrow, ex-Oxford banker. All Robin wanted to do was to spend the night with his on-call prostitute, who he changed about every two months.

'Cheers, Comrade!' said Robin, giving him a firm hug as soon as he saw him. 'How's George Orwell's disciple? I'm afraid he's about to start another war in Spain – but this time an economic one!' he said.

Charles smiled. His friend was a professional provocateur who was never afraid to give his opinion. What's more, that's how he had managed to amass a nice fortune: Robin bought when everyone else was selling (cheap) and then sold (dear) when everyone was buying. He had always said that other investors were basically stupid.

'I'm not bad, thanks,' said Charles, looking at the floor with the British false modesty that he always used, a great technique for diverting attention.

Robin flopped into the armchair next to Charles' which were both facing the fireplace, while Charles served him a glass of sherry that Robin quickly tasted.

'Aah, I love what you bring back from Spain. Wonderful,' he said, placing the glass on the side-table where Charles had left Isabel's letter.

'A friend called Isabel?' he asked out of curiosity.

Charles blushed slightly and quickly put down the bottle of sherry in order to pick up the letter that he had forgotten to put away before his friend came in. He folded it carefully and put it into the pocket of his red robe under Robin's watchful eye. Robin, well-settled in his armchair, looked at him slightly amused. As he did every Friday he was wearing smart casual clothes that in fact were more expensive than his City suits. He had on a pair of cream-coloured pleated trousers and a white shirt with designer buttons beneath his black cashmere jumper, which suited him perfectly and hid his large paunch.

'How's the crisis?' asked Charles, sitting down and leaving the bottle of sherry on the side-table between them.

Charles and Robin had kept up a close friendship since they shared rooms in Oxford. However, it had been years since they discussed their love lives, and not just because Charles was fairly impenetrable; Robin wasn't much given to talking either, especially after his wife left him some years earlier and moved to a house in central London with their three children, whom he now hardly ever saw. Charles didn't dare ask him either, because he knew that deep down it had broken his heart, however much he tried to pretend by saying that the divorce was the best solution and that the relationship had been dead for years. Since then Charles had always seen a hint of sadness in his friend's eyes, which he had tried unsuccessfully to deal with through alcohol and women.

'Goodness me, the crisis,' replied the banker, resting his feet on a nearby footstool. Without taking his shoes off, of course. Robin lit a cigarette, knowing that Charles wouldn't mind, and noisily blew out the smoke. Then he said: 'You've no idea what's brewing.'

Charles raised an eyebrow in expectation.

'The financial situation is full of shit, we're all up to our eyes in it and the politicians, of course, don't know anything about it. But, well, at least I'm surviving, because what I lost I've recouped by reckoning that things are going to get worse. And the facts are proving me right.'

They both remained silent for a few seconds, until Robin went on, in a more serious tone:

'I don't want to talk about this, Charles, because I've been living and sleeping with this subject for a month. Since the thing with Bear Stearns I've not been to the Cotswolds nor seen my girlfriend; as you can imagine I'm going up the wall,' he said with a nervous laugh.

Charles, who sometimes thought his friend a bit vulgar, didn't respond.

Robin looked around him and stopped to look at the picture.

'Is that new?' he asked. 'I like it! You've finally abandoned Scottish hunting scenes and chosen something a bit more modern. Charles, I'm delighted to see it.'

Charles hesitated before replying, but he felt he had nothing to hide.

'It's a gift,' he said eventually.

Robin looked at him in surprise.

'Ah!' he exclaimed. 'A gift from whom?' he asked in a jovial voice, leaning over towards Charles.

'The artist gave it to me,' he answered quickly, while he refilled the two sherry glasses.

Robin tilted his head to one side as a faint smile spread across his lips.

'A Spanish painter?'

'Well, yes,' Charles replied.

'Ah.'

After a brief and uncomfortable silence Robin returned to the attack, making Charles regret having started the conversation, because he knew how keen his friend was on gossip.

'Is the artist also the writer of the letter?' he asked, now with his lips pursed and a smile in his eyes.

Charles looked at the fireplace and got up to throw on another piece of wood and give the fire a stir, as it was starting to die down.

'Well, Charles?' Robin persisted in a markedly pointed tone.

Charles went to sit down again.

'She's only a friend, Robin; don't look for things that aren't there.'

Charles had managed to say the words while sounding convincingly calm, but the blush in his cheeks gave him away.

'Well, don't tell me anything if you don't want to,' said his friend, now without poking fun at him. 'I'll just say to you that if you've found a lover in Spain, I think that's great and I would just encourage you to carry on. Life's a bitch, Charles, and getting close to someone can be fantastic. We've got to make the most of the bit of youth we've got left, because soon we won't be up for it!'

Charles shook his head.

'Don't be vulgar, Robin,' he said. 'Besides, there's nothing going on. She's a good friend who runs the hotel where I stay in the town where I want to buy the school, but it's all ground to a halt because the mayor turns out to be a crook...' Charles paused briefly to have a sip of his drink. 'Anyway, it's too long a story to explain, but the fact is that it's all come to a halt, so I don't know if I'll see her again.'

'I *told* you that the real estate business in Spain is sitting on a time bomb,' commented Robin.

'Robin, please...' said Charles, rolling his eyes. That wasn't the right time for any of his 'I-told-you-so's'.

His friend seemed to understand and now looked at him with genuine interest.

'But Charles, do you really want to see her again? Is she really worth it?' After a brief silence, Robin added: 'You know that we're too old in the tooth now for self-deception.'

Charles pursed his lips and moved his fingers nervously on the arm of his chair. Robin sipped his glass of sherry as he patiently waited for his reply.

'I suppose I do,' Charles said finally, staring into space.

He surprised himself with this confession, which maybe he had also tried to hide from himself, taking refuge beneath the mountains of work that he had to deal with or the non-stop activity at Eton. In spite of his efforts not to think about Morella, he had spent his time when dining alone looking at the painting of the garden and recalling the moment when he overcame his fear and invited Isabel to dinner. But unfortunately, despite the success of the dinner and the walk afterwards, things had ended up rather uncomfortably, after he had questioned Isabel's motives when she revealed that her father was deceiving him by exaggerating the rival offers for the school. No doubt prompted by Valli's warnings, Charles had asked why he should trust her, something that he now deeply regretted. Since then he didn't know what to think and nor had he dared to get in touch with her again. This week's letter had filled him with a mixture of happiness and fear, causing him to start telling himself that for his own good he ought to start to admit what was really happening to him.

Charles eventually looked up at his friend, who was still waiting, glass in hand.

'Why don't you go and see her again?' he asked, lighting another cigarette.

Charles said nothing for a few moments.

'Good question,' he said finally.

Robin crossed his legs and leant towards Charles.

'My dear friend,' he said seriously. 'I don't know what you're up to here, but you look pretty preoccupied to me and, of course, keen on a woman who writes to you and gives you paintings; for me, frankly, that's a clear invitation.'

Charles shook his head.

'It's more complicated than it looks, Robin,' he said, interrupting him. 'Her father is the town's crooked mayor, or rather former mayor now.'

Robin quickly cut him short.

'I don't care what her father does, or about her past or what the circumstances are,' he said. 'All I know is that these things are never perfect and there's no point in waiting until everything's in order before making a move.' Robin paused briefly in order to swig down the rest of his glass of sherry. 'Believe me, my friend, because I spent twenty years making a fortune, thinking that when I'd got it and retired I'd be happy with my family, but that moment never came, because they grew tired of me before then. So here I am, up the creek.'

Charles looked at his friend and felt sorry for him.

'Don't make the same mistake, Charles,' said Robin, looking him straight in the eye. 'If that's what you want, go for it right now and don't waste any more time. Why wait? In this life we only seem to think in the short term, where we all take refuge: me with my three-month investments, you with your academic terms. The short term is fine for keeping ourselves occupied and distracted so that we don't have to think, but it doesn't make us happy. Believe me, life is a long-term investment; that's what I never understood and what has sunk me.'

Charles said nothing while the most sincere words that he had ever heard his friend utter echoed round his head.

'Well,' said Robin after a few seconds, 'maybe I've said too much, and drunk too much, too, and I've still got to get to Burford,' he said, getting up.

'Yes, drive carefully,' Charles reminded him, his head buzzing with countless thoughts, images and memories. He couldn't take in anything else.

Robin had put on his coat and gave Charles a farewell hug. It wasn't a typical man-to-man squeeze but a long and meaningful embrace that Charles felt had a special significance. It had been years since he had experienced such human warmth.

The two men said goodbye and as soon as Robin had left, Charles leant his back against the door with a deep sigh. Moments later he went over to the fireplace where he took a cigarette from the packet that his friend had left behind and lit it. He hadn't smoked since he was at university.

With his arm resting on the mantelpiece Charles looked once more at the old photo of Morella and also his painting, almost without blinking an eye. After only three puffs Charles threw the cigarette firmly into the fire and went to sit in his study. With trembling hands he switched on his computer, went on to the internet and typed: "British Airways".

In mid-afternoon the following day Charles arrived at Valencia airport with only a small backpack for luggage. He felt the same enthusiasm as he had landing in Bombay more than twenty years earlier when he was setting out on a long stay in India. As he started the Seat Ibiza that in just two hours would get him to Morella, Charles felt on his own and with the rest of his life in front of him.

Although he had put his foot down rather more than he should in order to get there as soon as possible, Charles stopped in Collet d'en Velleta to take in the air and to look out over the town that had also captivated his father. Morella had won his father's heart to such an extent that he had kept a photo of the town his whole life and one that, surprisingly, Charles had never seen. Perhaps life held such incredible coincidences that linked people's existence in mysterious ways. Charles carried on towards the town with pride and with his heart beating fast. Having parked in the Alameda he almost ran through the streets, without noticing the two or three people who said hello as he passed, so as to get to the hotel as quickly as possible. He hadn't brought a present and he didn't know what he was going to say. He just wanted to get there. To see her.

'Well! This is a real surprise!' exclaimed Manolo when he saw him and dropped the biro he was using to do a crossword on the counter. 'I didn't know you were coming. Did you let Isabel or my father know? I must have forgotten,' he said, feeling rather worried.

'Hello,' Charles replied, looking around at the dining room, the kitchen door, the stairs, in case Isabel might appear at any moment. 'No, no, the fact is I forgot to call,' he said, blushing like a poor liar. 'I've just come to spend a couple of days to tie up a few things to do with the school, you know,' he said.

'Ah.' Manolo looked at him with a frown. 'I imagine you'll know that things have got a bit stuck. They still haven't elected a new mayor and everything's a bit... delicate.'

'Yes, yes, I can imagine,' replied Charles, who didn't want to lose a second. 'I hope your father and your sister are well,' he said. 'Are they about?'

Manolo, who had already got the key to room fourteen ready, got out the registration book and wrote Charles' name in it at his customary slow speed, which Charles found exasperating.

'Well, my father isn't, he's at home. He doesn't come into town much these days, and my sister's gone to a lecture,' he said, handing him the key.

'Oh, really? A lecture? Who's giving it?' asked Charles, trying to hide his personal interest beneath one that seemed a bit more intellectual.

'Huh,' Manolo replied rather scornfully. 'Some ancient Catalan politician who apparently was one of the people who wrote the Constitution or something like that. I'm not sure what you'll have missed.'

'How interesting!' Charles exclaimed with clearly false and exaggerated enthusiasm. 'And where is it? I wouldn't like to miss it,' he said. 'Maybe I can still get there.'

Manolo looked at him in some surprise, no doubt because that impulsive and decisive side of Charles contrasted with his usual restrained character. Manolo looked at the clock on the wall.

'Well, I think it started at six, and it's now nearly twenty past, so if you get a move on you could still catch some of it. It's in the Casa Ciurana, you know.'

Charles' face lit up as he nodded, for he knew that the venue was barely two minutes away on foot, which was all that it would take for him to get to see Isabel.

Manolo offered him the key.

'Here you are, number fourteen as usual, Charles.'

Charles didn't take it and all he said was:

'As I've got so little luggage, would you mind if I left my backpack here and I'll go to the lecture, too? I'll pick it up later.'

Manolo agreed and was left staring at Charles as he started to run downstairs. Suspecting that something was going on, Vicent's son leant over the counter to watch the Englishman run out into the street without shutting the door,

Exactly a minute and a half later a rather out of breath Charles entered the beautiful building that had been standing on that same corner for over five centuries.

After crossing a small but welcoming lobby, where two young men were sitting next to a coffee machine and a small cash box, Charles burst into the lecture room, without realising that he had to pay an entrance fee. When the students reacted and stood up to stop him, Charles was already in the room, his eyes wider open than ever as he tried to catch sight of Isabel. Some people in the audience turned round at the sudden noise made by the door, but turned back to the lecturer after giving Charles a look of disapproval. He finally realised that he was not alone, so he closed the door carefully and entered on tip-toe. It was a beautiful room, crowned by a stone gothic arch and softly lit by some old Morella-style black lamps. The plain stone floor and the tranquillity of the event and the people in general finally filled Charles with a degree of calm. He cast his eye over the thirty or so people present until eventually he caught sight of Isabel, on her own, sitting in the middle in the second row. Slowly he moved up the side aisle to a position where he could see her in profile. There she was, with her dark hair loose, her straight nose, her thick lips, her calm gaze fixed on the speaker.

Charles sighed and closed his eyes, feeling the welcoming warmth of the room on that cold autumnal day. Aware of his own, rather dishevelled appearance, Charles secretively tucked his shirt into his trousers and adjusted his high-neck black jumper – an article of clothing that made him feel safe and protected.

Leaning against the wall, Charles gulped as he looked at Isabel, whose attention did not stray from the lecture for a second. He must be patient, he said to himself resignedly. After a few minutes, to his great surprise, Isabel raised her hand when questions were invited, and hers was the first. Charles opened his eyes as wide as he could to take in the scene. He now thought everything Isabel did was perfect. Even the large and rather unattractive Fairisle jumper she was wearing now seemed like a symbol of personality and talent, since she had no doubt knitted it herself.

'Good evening,' said Isabel in a loud, clear voice, since the room was too small for a microphone. 'Señor Roca, thank you very much for your presentation; what you told us about how the Constitution was written is certainly very interesting,' she said. 'But I often wonder if we have succeeded in this country in getting those democratic ideas that you speak of really embedded in our society.'

Charles was surprised by the comment, as he was unaware of Isabel's speaking skills, never having heard her express herself in public. He carried on looking at her, although now in a less engrossed way, as he paid greater attention to what Isabel was saying.

'Well, of course Spain is a fully democratic country,' this Señor Roca replied in what Charles thought was a rather snooty tone. 'I don't know what you're referring to,' he said drily.

Isabel seemed to hesitate for a few moments, but went on:

'Sometimes I think that in this country it's always the same people in power, or at least members of the most powerful families. In fact,' she went on, 'recently I read a book in which it said that Spain is in the hands of about a hundred families. I haven't counted them, but personally I think that there's not much social mobility in this country, and as for women, I don't know where to start,' Isabel concluded, looking at the speaker with her large green eyes, always open to the world, thought Charles.

By contrast Señor Roca's eyes were neither as pretty nor as honest as Isabel's, and he cut a pinched, gaunt figure with a long face that was too serious and morose for a man of his age, Charles said to himself. He believed that older people have lived long enough to be able to laugh a bit more at life in general and themselves in particular. The speaker, in his smart suit and with a Montblanc ballpoint pen in hand, eventually replied to Isabel.

'Look, Señorita,' he began in a paternalistic tone, 'what you say is totally wrong and I'll tell you why.' Roca made one of those irritating pauses that politicians do when they want to attract greater attention, but the only thing they achieve is to waste the time of those who are listening to them. He went on: 'I can tell you that we have in this country many people who have risen to the top and who don't come from powerful families.'

'There are always exceptions,' commented Isabel quickly, despite the speaker not yet having finished his reply. 'Let's not waste time talking about exceptions, which take us away from the idea that I asked you about,' Isabel concluded, to Charles' surprise and admiration.

This Señor Roca appeared rather indignant at having been interrupted and carried on as if he had not heard the comment, which Charles thought was rather rude.

'If you'll allow me to speak, Señorita,' the politician remarked in a haughty tone, 'this is a country in which many people from a humble background have achieved success. What's more, I will tell you that real power, which you attribute to people of privilege, lies in the hands of the small business people, at least in Catalunya. They're the ones who are running the country; they have the tenacity to keep it going.'

Isabel was not convinced and made another comment:

'I know that they work hard, but in fact they are not in control at all. I'm talking about positions of political, social or intellectual power that are still closed to people without any connections,' she said, with a nervous cough at the end.

Her remark provoked laughter from the audience and exasperation from the chairperson for the session who was sitting alongside the speaker and who said:

'That's enough now, Isabel, don't go on.'

Such a remark annoyed Charles, who was not going to let anyone prevent from having her say the person who he admired so much and the woman – as he now recognised – who he had thought about night and day almost since he first met her. He jumped to her defence:

'She's not going on, she's waiting for a speaker of his standing to give her an intelligent reply, and frankly, to say that there is social mobility in Spain I think is an insult to the intelligence of those present, including me,' said Charles, causing everyone to turn round in surprise.

Charles felt his cheeks quickly redden, not because the whole audience and the speaker were staring at him in silent amazement, but because Isabel had also turned round towards him and her full red lips gave him the smile that he had dreamt about for months.

'Well, yes, of course, it's true,' the speaker said eventually, looking at Charles in a conciliatory and respectful way. 'Of course, things are never perfect, and it's something that we're working on,' he said.

Charles, who was making an effort to concentrate on the words of the speaker, of whom he had never heard, felt even more provoked when he thought about the reply he had just given him.

'I don't understand,' he said, 'why you are agreeing with me if I've just said to you the same thing as the lady who has just asked you the question.'

'It's just that she's such an aggressive woman!' the politician replied almost without thinking, leaning back and stretching out his legs.

His words amazed Charles, who felt that such a remark in England could put an end to a politician's career for being such a male chauvinist. Such a lack of consideration would leave any English representative, however popular he might be, without a single female vote for life.

'Next question?' asked the chairperson, as if nothing of significance had happened.

To everyone's surprise, including Charles, Isabel charged in again:

'Aggressive woman? If a woman asks you something uncomfortable she's aggressive, but if it's a man, then he's listened to and seen as someone independent and intelligent?'

Señor Roca lifted his eyes in a sign of desperation, gave a loud sigh and put his pen on the table. As if he were doing her a favour, he replied:

'I'll have you know, Señorita, that you can't get more feminist than me; my daughter is the main heir to my legal practice and when I retire she'll be in sole charge of the two hundred-strong legal team we employ.'

'But she's your daughter!' exclaimed Isabel, visibly annoyed. 'What I'm saying is that it's all but impossible for men or women who don't have the good fortune to come from families just like yours.'

'That's not true; there are a lot of women in banking and other sectors,' the speaker replied. 'Why, every bank I go into I'm served by a woman. And I'm not surprised because women are so much more hard-working and efficient than men,' Roca added. 'As you can see, I'm a real feminist.'

After a long pause, he added:

'Come on, let's see if there are some more interesting questions.'

Charles, who couldn't believe what he was hearing, was able to react in time before anyone else raised their hand.

'I'm sorry, Sir,' he said, making everyone turn round again. 'The lady is asking about access to power, not about shop-floor jobs, and I'm wondering about the same thing,' he stated confidently.

Charles kept looking steadily into the eye of the speaker, who meant nothing to him but who dared to ill-use his Isabel. He felt comfortable and secure and noticed how the politician was gradually losing his composure. Señor Roca scratched his head nervously, coughed and took sips of water, because clearly he didn't know what to say. But Charles knew how to go on and to do so effectively. Eloquence and verbosity were the best things taught at Eton, where seventeen British prime ministers had been educated on the basis of teaching them how to attack and to defend themselves in the cauldron of the English parliament, where everything was a question of argument and counter-argument.

'Please can you give us an answer to the question?' he persisted.

A murmur went round the room that stopped when Señor Roca started speaking again.

'Look, Sir, I don't know you and I don't know which country you're from, but you sound English to me.'

Charles nodded with pride.

'Well, I suggest that before you come here and have a go at the problems of this country, you go back to your own and sort out your own affairs, for you've got plenty of them and they're greater than ours.'

Charles didn't believe it. As well as being an unreconstructed male chauvinist, this man was xenophobic.

'Next question?' asked the chairperson straight away in exasperation.

Charles and Isabel looked at each other intently, with a mixture of indignation and passion.

A young man spoke next and in a trembling voice spent four minutes saying that Spain had lost its values, that the only thing that seemed to matter was consumerism and people only wanted cars and new houses. At the end of his speech he asked the speaker, who must have been at least fifty years older than him, what had happened to its values.

In a calm and gentle voice, Roca replied:

'That's a fantastic question, young man,' he said decisively. 'It's precisely those values that we need to reclaim. And for that we need young people like you to get involved in politics. But I warn you, you have to be prepared to earn very little and for people to attack you all the time; you can see what sort of thing you get subjected to everywhere,' Roca commented, glancing over at Charles and Isabel.

The young man, who looked at the speaker admiringly, nervously fingered the ring he was wearing and nodded repeatedly when Roca was addressing him.

Isabel felt irritated at the fact that the difficult questions were criticised while the easy, adulatory ones were commended – a common occurrence nowadays – and once more to everyone's surprise she stood up and went over to Charles, who only had eyes for the imposing figure who came towards him, full of life and energy.

'Shall we go?' Isabel whispered so close to his ear that Charles could almost feel her lips. Or maybe he was dreaming, he thought.

Charles took her by the arm and the two of them left the Casa Ciurana, to the astonishment of everyone present, who took a few seconds before carrying on with the meeting. But Charles and Isabel didn't care. As soon as they got outside they both laughed out loud and gave each other a long, firm embrace.

After a few minutes of confusion, during which Charles muttered some patently false excuses about the reason for his visit, they looked at each other without knowing what to say. He felt his throat drying up and his stomach tightening, just as if he were with Laura in Oxford. He made a great effort to avoid finding himself left on his own in the street as Isabel had done the last time they saw each other and quickly helped her to put on her coat as if they were getting ready to go somewhere together. Charles looked at her but couldn't find the words. There was hardly anyone else in the street; the only sounds came from a football match being broadcast on television or cars going through the square.

'Come on,' Isabel said eventually. 'I'll get you some dinner in the hotel.'

Charles dutifully accepted, as if he were walking on his own in the pub in Oxford with two pints in his hands. Breathing deeply as they went up the hill, he told himself that on this occasion everything was going to be different. The worst that could happen was a rejection, but at least he wouldn't spend the rest of his life regretting the simple fact of not having tried. As was the case with Laura.

Laughing and talking about his journey and the lecture, Charles and Isabel arrived at the hotel, where Manolo seemed pleased to see them as he was hoping that Isabel would take over from him in reception. After a brief conversation, as pleasant as it was trivial, Isabel asked Charles to follow her into the kitchen.

'Come on, Charles,' she said. 'There's no-one in for dinner tonight; we've only got two couples staying, but they're in the Daluan, so we can get a bit of ham out and some wine and make ourselves a nice meal – does that seem okay?' she said.

Charles looked at her wide-eyed and with such a broad smile that his cheeks were beginning to ache. With his stomach inside out and uncertain as to whether he was hungry or not, he continued to look at Isabel, with his nervous hands hidden in his pockets.

When he got to the kitchen Isabel had already put her hair up and her apron on, but without taking anything away from the magic of her appearance. Without even thinking about it Charles took hold of another apron from the door and put it on.

'What can I do?' he asked.

Isabel laughed, not only at the question, but also at the effect of her old and rather large apron on Charles' slender and gangly figure.

'Go and open the wine,' she replied, taking hold of a bottle from the rack. 'Pour us a couple of glasses and leave the rest to me.'

'No, no, I want to cook as well. What shall I do?'

Isabel stood looking at him with interest and curiosity, and eventually agreed.

'Well, here are six eggs; you can break them and start beating them, because I'm going to make you a nice omelette. If I remember correctly, you quite like them, don't you?'

Charles nodded enthusiastically.

To see Isabel in her apron cutting potatoes into small cubes, while he was beating eggs in the kitchen of a small hotel, seemed to Charles to be one of the best moments of his life. He never shared anything with Meredith, not even cooking a simple omelette. It was precisely that domestic simplicity that Charles had never had and had always wanted. Now finally he was preparing a family meal, but a real family meal: it wasn't with his childhood nanny, nor with the cooks at Eton or Oxford, but with the woman with whom he wanted to share dinner day after day for many years. He saw it all clearly now, he thought, as he leant on the kitchen table with a glass of Somontano wine.

Laughing and joking the two of them put together the salad, omelette and some bread with ham and tomato that Charles had prepared, because as it was one of his favourites he had learnt how to make a good job of that.

'If I'd have known I could have sent you a ham with the letter,' said Isabel when they sat down at the old round table at the back of the kitchen.

'Well, not to worry, I've come to fetch it,' replied Charles ironically, having taken a mouthful of the soft, yellow omelette with its taste of pure olive oil that swept over his palate.

'Well, if you've come back to Morella just for a ham, it'll work out quite expensive for you,' said Isabel with a mischievous smile.

Charles stopped eating for a second that seemed to him like an age. With a piece of bread still in his hand and a mouthful of omelette, it occurred to him that it had been a long time since he had felt such a close connection with anyone.

'If the ham's worth it, it doesn't matter,' he said, raising an eyebrow and hoping that that was all he had to say for her to understand.

'Well, I'll tell them at Casa Masoveret,' replied Isabel seriously. 'I'm sure they can prepare a package with two hams filling the space of just one.'

Charles looked at her in surprise, although he recalled that Spain was not a country renowned for subtlety. At some point, he said to himself, he would have to put his cards on the table – a thought that suddenly made him feel afraid of failure. Charles lowered his eyes and carried on eating his omelette, one mouthful after another. Isabel spoke first.

'Thanks for your support this afternoon,' she said. 'Without your help I'm sure I wouldn't have pressed that idiot so hard.'

'But I didn't do anything!' replied Charles quickly, feeling a bit more secure. 'You did it all and with incredible courage. You were an example to everyone. You put up a fantastic fight!'

Isabel smiled.

'No, Charles,' she said after a few seconds. 'Believe me, without your help I wouldn't have persisted, but with your support I felt safer.'

Charles raised his head from his plate when Isabel said those words and looked at her in a way that possibly he had never looked at anyone before: his blue eyes that were more transparent than ever, his strongly beating heart that had opened up to her, his hands stretched out on the table, every part of him leaning towards her.

'Thanks,' he muttered in a voice that came out lower that he intended because of his nerves. The time had come, he said to himself; he couldn't go through life with those two pints of beer in his hands. Eventually, he went on: 'This dinner reminds me of the really pleasant evening we spent in the Daluan,' he said, now in a clear and sincere voice.

Isabel's eyes opened wide and she leant towards him.

'Have you seen it yet?'

Charles was surprised by the question.

'Seen what?'

Isabel looked amazed.

'Didn't my brother give you room fourteen?'

'Yes, of course,' replied Charles, confused. 'Why?'

'Haven't you been in?

'No, I went straight to the lecture, because…' Charles realised that he had reached the point of no return. He felt a lump in his throat and his heart missed a beat. But he had to go on. 'I went straight to the Casa Ciurana, because your brother had told me you were there.'

Isabel sat up and raised her eyes to look at him. She had a slight blush in her cheeks, which gave Charles some encouragement.

'Why do you ask? What's in the room?' he asked, slowly and with more confidence.

Isabel swallowed hard before going on, but relaxed her shoulders a little and pursed her lips. More calmly than he had anticipated, Charles stretched out his hand, resting it on hers, which felt large and warm; it was a touch through which passed a current of humanity and intimacy that he had never felt before.

'What's in there, Isabel?' he asked rather awkwardly.

'It's a new painting,' she replied eventually in a timid voice.

'One of your paintings?'

'Yes.'

'Can I see it?'

Isabel raised her eyes to his and waited a few seconds.

'Yes, of course.'

'Now?'

Isabel didn't answer.

Without any hesitation Charles stood up and waited for Isabel to do the same. He took her by the hand and headed decisively for reception, where the key to room fourteen still lay on the counter. The pair went upstairs in silence to the first floor. Calmly and in spite of how nervous he was feeling, Charles opened the door and switched on the soft, yellow lights that he liked so much. Opposite on the wall between the two windows there was indeed a new painting that Charles quickly went to look at. Isabel followed him in silence.

He held his breath when he saw that it was the narrow street where the Daluan was, with the restaurant visible on the right, the houses supported by ancient wooden beams on the left and even a little cat in the centre. It was a very elaborate picture, in a nostalgic, warm autumn colour that created an air of peace as soon as you looked at it. In one corner there was a little dedication: "For Charles" it said, plus the signature of the artist.

After a few seconds and with his tears in his eyes, he turned to Isabel.

'It's wonderful,' he said with a tremble in his voice.

'I put it here because I didn't know if I would see you again,' replied Isabel, lowering her eyes. But after a few seconds she added: 'Between the flamenco dancer and the painting, this could have been turned into a museum.'

Charles smiled.

The raised pulse that had made his heart race all day was slowly turning into strong, regular and steady heartbeats: a sign that the moment had arrived. He took Isabel by the hand and with the other gently lifted her face, to lose himself in the enormity of her green eyes that were now shining and radiant, giving out as much happiness as he was feeling. Slowly Charles approached her and kissed her, at first briefly and lightly, until the two of them fused together in a long and passionate embrace, the like of which neither of them had even dreamt of before.

After a few minutes, when both of them could no longer contain their desire, Charles put out the light and let himself be carried away by his feelings, perhaps for the first time in his life. Between love, confessions and laughter, the two of them stayed awake until the first light of dawn began to appear.

23

Monday afternoons were the gloomiest times in Morella, because businesses closed in order to recover from the hustle and bustle of the weekend when the town was full of tourists and Sunday visitors. Autumn was increasingly making its presence felt; the leaves in the Alameda were starting to fall and the temperature dropped rapidly after the sun went down.

Nevertheless Valli went out for her usual evening walk to stretch her legs and take in a bit of fresh air. Since the Mayor's resignation she had been very busy organising meetings in the Town Hall, because she wanted to be sure that the replacement of the Mayor was an open and participatory process. The Town Hall was about to call new elections, because as Vicent had stood as an independent candidate there was no immediate successor.

Valli was delighted with the results of her actions, although the thrill of her victory – at least for the time being – concerning the school was mitigated by the uncertainty about the final matter – and the most difficult one – that still had to be resolved. Valli owed it to Charles to have a talk with him, but she had avoided doing so during the almost six months that she had known him. Now she could wait no longer, once the matter of the school had been resolved, but above all because she had seen him around the town with Isabel. The day before in the market everyone was talking about Charles' intervention at the lecture, his support for Isabel and how the two of them had left together wreathed in smiles. Valli had once harboured the hope that Charles' visit to Morella would be brief, but she now realised that he had been captivated not just by the town but also by Isabel. This circumstance meant that it would be increasingly difficult for her to stay silent. Charles had the right to know what Valli had to tell him, so while he was there she had approached him in order to arrange a meeting. As polite as ever, Charles agreed without question or query. The last time they had seen each other on their own in July, the afternoon hadn't ended very well because Charles had not liked Valli's warning about the Mayor's family. But now Vicent's resignation had proved her right and Charles seemed more receptive to the idea of re-establishing a good relationship with her. The fact that Charles was in a very good mood when she saw him in the hotel also helped to make it easy to set up a meeting.

Valli was immersed in such thoughts as she sat on one of the stone benches in the Alameda, next to a fountain where they had agreed to meet at about four in the afternoon. As she was feeling on edge, Valli had set off quite a while beforehand and had walked through the town for about half an hour in order to calm her nerves. Sitting on the edge of the seat, her back tense and playing nervously with her fingers, she saw Charles appear through the entrance to the walkway. He approached with huge strides, whistling and with his hands in his pockets, an unusually relaxed air for him but which Valli immediately interpreted as a clear sign of love reciprocated. A slight smile came over Valli's face, for however much Isabel was Vicent's daughter, deep down Valli was pleased for her. Who said that love is only for the young, she thought.

Charles greeted her with a sincere smile and kissed her on both cheeks for the first time. Valli was at once pleased at the gesture and also intimidated by it. She wasn't sure that at the end of their conversation Charles would say goodbye to her in the same affectionate way.

'Hello, Valli, you're looking younger than ever,' he said, perfectly mannered as always.

In any case Valli knew that such remarks were typical of boys from private schools who learnt how to please older people, teachers, superiors and people in authority, so as to gradually win their confidence and to rise up the hierarchy of the company, the family or the association. A lie was well worth it for a bit of credit.

Too committed to the truth, Valli immediately corrected him, frank and unequivocal as ever.

'You know as well as I do, Charles, that life goes forwards and not backwards,' she said.

Charles looked at her in surprise, perhaps not accustomed to his smooth words being rejected, especially by such an elderly woman. In any case this was not a day for wasting energy on trivialities, for she had enough to do with what she had to tell him, she thought.

Valli stood up and proposed a walk as far as the arcades of Santa Llúcia, which Charles readily agreed to. As they walked they exchanged opinions about the weather, the beautiful autumn light and Saturday's lecture, which everyone was talking about.

'I couldn't believe that in the twenty-first century someone could come along and lecture to people in such a paternalistic way,' said Charles. 'In England it would be impossible.'

'Oh, my dear,' Valli lamented, as she took his arm. 'That's what we get every day here. But in any case I'm glad you defended Isabel.'

Charles kept quiet as soon as he heard her name mentioned.

'She's a great woman,' he said, his eyes firmly fixed on the ground. 'I remember very clearly what you said about her family and how they took the hotel away from you,' he went on, now looking at Valli. 'But she can't be blamed for being the daughter of Vicent.'

'True,' Valli replied in English, after a brief sigh.

Charles smiled.

'I keep forgetting that you speak English,' he said.

Valli adjusted the scarf that she wore round her neck, protecting herself from the strong wind that had taken them by surprise as soon as they reached the towers of Sant Miquel. They continued towards Santa Llúcia accompanied only by the occasional car or small groups of elderly folk who, with stick in hand, had gone out for some fresh air.

'I had an excellent teacher,' Valli said eventually.

'Oh, yes? Who?' asked Charles, always curious.

Valli took a deep breath and carried on walking slowly.

'He was a very young man, just over twenty, who went to spend two years in Madrid in the Students' Residence, where I also studied, but in the ladies' part, the Young Ladies' Residence, which was very close by.'

'I didn't know you'd studied there; it has a great history and a very good reputation abroad,' said Charles, looking at her with admiration and surprise.

Valli nodded and continued her story, her head lowered, not looking at Charles.

'That young man always fascinated me; he was gentle, gracious and caring and very different from the typical Iberian chauvinist to be found everywhere in Spain then and now. We got on straight away and we started to go to each other's classes; I taught him Spanish and he taught me English. We became good friends. When the war started he joined up as a volunteer in the International Brigades and came to Morella with them, which is where we saw each other again.'

Valli paused briefly and headed towards a small flat stretch of ground on an abandoned plot next to a deserted road. She sat down on an old tree trunk to rest and to take in the beautiful views of the town, the castle and the wall. Charles followed. The air was no longer so intense and everything seemed calm and peaceful. The only sounds were birds singing and a few rabbits hopping about and jumping in fright whenever a car passed in the distance. Valli picked up the conversation again.

'The thing is, Charles,' she said, 'I didn't see him again until I went to London in 1953, three years after my parents were killed. I already told you about that.'

Charles nodded. Valli noticed that Charles was looking at her with understanding and affection, which instead of giving her more confidence only increased her fear. In any event she was determined to continue, because she felt she had to. She went on:

'I decided to go to London after those three awful years,' she said. 'I only survived thanks to La Pastora, who looked after me and who made sure that they didn't kill me as well, or that I didn't kill myself, something that did occur to me more than once. It was all very hard.'

Charles closed his eyes for a moment.

'The situation became unsustainable,' Valli went on, with her eyes fixed firmly on Morella. 'The *maquis* weren't getting anywhere, many comrades had died or deserted, and on top of that the Communist Party had called on everyone to evacuate the year before. We had lost the war. In spite of everything I had stayed in the mountains just to avenge the death of my parents, although by now it was very difficult because there were very few of us and we didn't have much equipment. I was also getting weaker.' Valli paused briefly to catch her breath. Leaning her hands on the trunk on which she was sitting, she continued: 'I knew that in London I had friends from the days of the Residence who had offered me help and somewhere to stay as soon as the war broke out. It took me over ten years to accept the offer, but in the end I went, with an urgent need to start a new life. I went across Catalunya and via the Pyrenees I got into France and managed to stow away in a boat to Dover, where I was met by the Madariaga sisters, who were good friends from university days in Madrid. They were daughters of a famous intellectual and professor and they lived in great comfort, which they allowed me to share. They were very generous.'

'The daughters of Salvador de Madariaga? The Oxford Professor?' asked Charles in surprise.

Valli nodded.

'Their father was a friend of my father,' said Charles. 'They often met at conferences and I think they even wrote articles together. What a coincidence!'

Valli bit her lip as she looked at him. She went on:

'The thing is that the daughters put me in touch with my good friend from the Residence who taught me English and who they also met in Madrid, and I visited him in London a few days after I arrived.'

Valli stopped for a few moments and lifted her hands to her face. After a long silence and with her eyes fixed to the ground, eventually she continued:

'My friend, who had never married and had only sought the company of his books and his studies, was very welcoming. The bond of friendship that had brought us together twenty years earlier had remained unbroken and we began to spend many evenings together. At the age of thirty-six I had never been with a man, Charles, but I fell into his arms one cold, dark night in London. I don't know how to put this, but I had never particularly liked men, and I hadn't had much time to think about them, either, because the Republic, the war and the *maquis* had left me very little time for such matters. But once the war had been lost, and without being able to return to my country, with no parents or family, I fell into the arms of someone who offered them to me with affection and honesty.'

'Why didn't you stay in England?' asked Charles, his brows furrowed and his face more serious.

'The weeks went by and I didn't feel comfortable with such an easy life. I had a commitment to my country, which was in the hands of a tyrant, and I couldn't forget the death of my parents; I still had nightmares about it every night. So I decided to return in order to avenge them. It broke my friend's heart, but although I liked him very much I was not in love with him. I would have made him very unhappy. It was very hard, but another destiny awaited me.'

Charles said nothing, while Valli went on with her story.

'I went back to the mountains, and after spending many nights alone I eventually found La Pastora in one of our most inaccessible hideouts, in Tinença de Benifassà, not far from here. There were other comrades who came back and forth from France and between us all we survived. After a few weeks,' said Valli breathing deeply, 'after a little while,' she repeated, 'I discovered that I was pregnant.'

She gave out a sigh and glanced at Charles, whose head remained bowed.

'Go on,' he said drily.

Valli closed her eyes and squeezed them tight, but did as he said.

'I couldn't have a child in the *maquis*. First, because it wasn't allowed, and second, because it was really dangerous, for if it cried it could give us away and that would be the end for all of us. They offered to help me get rid of it, but I refused, pointing out that I had a right to choose, something that they respected. Of course, I thought about going back to England to be with my friend and start the life of a married woman with a stable family. But deep down I knew that that would never make me happy. I had spent ten years in the mountains and that was where I belonged, fighting against those who had stolen my country and killed my parents and many comrades. I couldn't fold my arms and go off to England to pretend to be happy with a man I respected and liked, but who I wasn't in love with.'

She paused again briefly and turned towards Charles, who now covered his face with his hands.

With a great effort Valli went on, recalling the only phrase from the Bible that she valued: "The truth will make you free."

'Through a British secret agent who I'd met in occupied France and who always helped Spaniards, I was able to organise a contact. I met up with him in Prats de Molló, just this side of the border, and there I gave him the child when he was just a few weeks old so that he could be taken to be with his father. I also gave him a letter, in which I explained that he could give him a much better future than a mother holed up in the mountains, fighting against a dictatorship which had no end in sight.'

Valli covered her face, because however hard she tried she could not hold back her tears. After so many years of life-and-death struggle, she no longer had the courage to look at her son.

He, too, had covered his face with his hands, sitting upright and tense. Valli began to tremble all over, but despite that managed to find sufficient composure to finish her story.

'Don't think that I haven't regretted that decision, but I had to think about what was best for that child and not for me, and that was a life in England and not in the mountains with a fugitive. Supposing something had happened to me; what would have become of the child?'

Valli took a deep breath, and felt a bit calmer before she went on.

'I stayed with La Pastora and the other comrades, and we planned the revenge of my parents, which happened a few months later. The Civil Guard Fernández, who by that time had eliminated many of our comrades, always went into the farmhouses at midnight to search them. After a lot of preparation we set up an ambush that got rid of him and the guard who was with him.'

Valli shook her head several times and watched as Charles eventually took his hands from his face and turned towards her. His eyes had lost all the vitality that they had shown only a short time before; now they looked completely horrified. His face was pale, his fists pressed against the trunk, his lips tight and tense.

Valli looked away; she couldn't stand it. She just wanted to finish her story and leave, and allow life to decide her fate, as it had done thus far. She never seemed to have had control.

'Once my parents had been avenged,' she went on, 'I went off to Paris, because even La Pastora had grown tired of our struggles. Everything was getting more and more difficult and I didn't know where I belonged in the world. Spain had turned into a country of sad, silent pilgrimages, of black suits and dresses, and a lot of three-cornered hats. From our hideout we saw processions with barefoot men dragging chains, women with coffins on their heads or young men dragging heavy wooden crosses or wearing crowns of thorns and bleeding. That was not the happy, open and intellectual country that the Republic wanted to build, but it was what it had ended up with. Having just turned forty, I realised that I had left my youth behind and I had abandoned a child for what was now a lost cause. I needed time to think, to rebuild my life.'

'In Paris?' Charles finally asked, sounding more like a policeman than someone trying to understand or take a genuine interest.

Valli felt hurt by his curtness, but felt he had every right to question her and to reject her.

'I had spent some good years there with Victoria Kent just after the war, and left many friends behind. They helped me to settle in and find a job teaching Spanish in a school. I set myself up in a small apartment in the Marais district, when it was still a very deprived neighbourhood, and I got to know and work with a lot of people living in exile.'

'Did you get married? Did you have any more children?' Charles asked in an increasingly inquisitorial tone.

'Of course not, Charles,' Valli replied, leaning towards him. 'But I did have a good long relationship that made me happy. It was the only time in my life that I knew happiness.' Valli paused before going on, 'Her name was Natalie and she was a French artist, a sculptor. We were together for nearly twenty years, until she died of cancer in 1976. Then, after the death of Franco, I decided to go back to Spain.'

There was a long, tense silence between them.

'And did you never think about going back to England and getting in touch with your friend again?' said Charles finally.

'Of course I did, I thought about it every night. I was on the point of going many times, especially when I got to Paris, but by then the child was five years old and I thought it was too late. I thought my appearance would only unsettle his life.'

'Do you know what happened in England?' asked Charles, his brow furrowed and looking straight at Valli.

She turned towards him openly.

'Yes. I corresponded with Tristan from Paris, because I wanted to know how they were. Later, when he died, a friend of his wrote to me to give me the news, something that he himself had asked to happen when he fell ill. His friend told me that your life was taken care of financially and that you were a boarder in a very good school, where you were living healthily and happily.'

Charles looked at her, his eyes burning with anger, with incomprehension, with utter rejection.

'Even without my father, you never thought to contact me? I was only fourteen years old.'

Valli closed her eyes to stop the tears from coming back but she did not succeed. After a few moments and with a bit more control, she replied:

'Of course I was on the point of doing so many times; there was nothing I wanted more in the world. But you were in a very good environment that assured you of a good future, and I had nothing to offer; my life had just been a waste. I hadn't got a penny, I was a fugitive from my own country and lived with a woman in France. You wouldn't have liked it; you would have been ashamed of me. Life has been much better for you this way, however much it saddens me.'

Valli felt her whole body going weak. She leant forwards, propping her elbows on her knees, burying her head in her trembling hands. Despite all her experiences, she had only felt the world falling on top of her on a very few occasions, and this was one of them.

Charles punched his own leg so hard it made him shout out loud, startling Valli to such an extent that she almost fell off the trunk they were still sitting on. Flushed with anger, Charles stood up and leant over her, pointing at her with his finger.

'What you are telling me is a pack of lies. It's not true!' he shouted. 'I don't know who you are and this is just a shit town and I'm never coming back.'

Valli remained silent. It was better not to say anything. Charles had the right to reject her.

'You and this town only want my money, that's why you invented those dreadful stories. They're just lies!'

Valli shook her head.

'I shall go to England and prove to you that it's not true, I swear! And you'll have to eat your words.' Valli's trembling was getting more pronounced and plain to see. 'I don't care in the least if you're a defenceless old woman! As far as I can see, when it comes to accusing, swearing and lying you're not as feeble as you make out, are you?' Charles yelled.

'Everything I've told you is true, believe me,' said Valli, almost in a whisper.

Charles was still standing and threw his arms in the air as he took a step back.

'Believe you? Why would I want to believe you?'

'Charles, it's your story, whether you like it or not,' Valli replied, speaking to him from the heart. 'You have the right to know, even if it hurts you.'

'Look, you mad old woman,' Charles answered back, pointing at her with his finger once more. 'My father was a Hispanist at Cambridge with a very good reputation, and you, you're just an old town gossip, a lesbian to boot, and on top of that, a murderer!'

Charles waited a few seconds, during which he continued to look at Valli with fire in his eyes.

'Why would my father want to go with a woman like you?'

'We were very close friends, Charles,' Valli replied. 'We lived through some very special times and circumstances. The lives of all of us were marked by them.'

'My father would never have got mixed up with a woman who should have ended up in prison or in a lunatic asylum,' Charles, now cold and cruel, added quickly.

Valli looked at him with such a deep pain in her eyes, which Charles seemed to notice, for he sighed and turned towards the town, with his shoulders slumped in defeat. He was still breathing heavily.

Eventually he turned round.

'You just want my money,' he said.

Valli shook her head.

'You know perfectly well that I'm old and I have everything I need. I don't want anything from you, nor do I expect anything. I just thought you had the right to know the truth. And better that you should hear it from me than from anyone else.'

Charles looked surprised.

'Who else knows this pack of lies?'

'They're not lies, but Vicent found out.'

'Vicent?' exclaimed Charles, now overcome by confusion.

'He hired a detective to see what skeletons he could find in my cupboard and through a confession that La Pastora made in prison it was established that he had helped his comrade Vallivana to take a child out of Spain to be taken to England. He investigated further and confirmed that the destination of this mission was Cambridge, at the same address where you grew up.'

'That's impossible. Who could have provided him with the address?'

'I gather that the British Secret Services open up their archives after a number of years, so that the report from the contact I used must have come into the public domain,' explained Valli.

Charles furrowed his brow and put a hand on his forehead. After a few seconds he straightened up again and replied:

'You'll have to prove that in court.'

Valli said nothing, her head bowed once more.

'You only want my money,' Charles repeated.

'I've already told you that I have everything I want and I don't need anything from you.'

'Then you want the money for the school.'

'Right now I don't care about the school at all. This is much more important. Besides, as you know, I'm not at all in favour of a private college buying my old Republican school. I'm a supporter of state schools.' Valli paused to take a deep breath. 'I don't want your money, Charles,' she went on. 'How can you think that after the life of struggle and commitment I've had?'

Charles looked at Valli, this time without frowning.

'So what do you want?'

'That you should know the truth.'

Charles looked down and walked a few paces up and down.

'Give me an example, something that shows that you really knew my father,' he said finally.

Valli looked to the heavens, as if she were asking for help from a God she had not believed in for decades. After a few seconds she replied confidently:

'I have some photos of the trip we took to Las Hurdes.'

'Where?' asked Charles, pushing his hand across his head with growing incredulity.

Valli sighed.

'I know, Charles, that this is very difficult for you; it is for me, too, believe me,' she said.

Charles ignored the remark.

'What trip are you referring to?'

'Las Hurdes, near Salamanca, is one of the poorest regions in Spain and Luis Buñuel was making a documentary about it called *Land without Bread*. He often came to the Residence to consult and exchange ideas with Doctor Marañón and other intellectuals, who provided him with historical and sociological information. Tristan, who was also involved in the project, helped him with the English version of the documentary, as Buñuel, who was now in Paris, wanted the film to be shown as widely as possible with the aim of collecting funds for the Republic.'

'My father once told me that he had worked with Lorca and Buñuel,' Charles admitted.

'Yes, everyone at the Residence knew everyone else,' Valli remarked. 'The thing is that Buñuel liked your father straight away; he was always such a gentleman; he was refined in a way that everyone aspired to be. Plus your father was very practical and he also had a car, so Buñuel asked him to help move cameras, tripods and spotlights to Las Hurdes. And your father, who by then had shown an interest in me, asked me to go with him on the trip. I spent the week practically acting as their secretary.'

Charles closed his eyes.

'I know it's hard to believe, but I have photos of Las Hurdes, with your father and with Buñuel. I recently reclaimed them from the archive of the Young Ladies' Residence, which fortunately survived the dictatorship hidden in the basement of the building we occupied in Madrid. Those photos were there because I left them in my room in the Residence in the summer of 1936 together with all my things, thinking that I would return in September. But of course when the war broke out I never went back. Someone must have put them in the archive so that they didn't get lost.'

'Do you have them at home?' asked Charles, in an enquiring tone once more.

'Yes, Charles, you can come and see them anytime you like.' Valli waited for a few seconds and then went on: 'That trip brought us close together, and what we saw marked us forever – Buñuel, your father and me. That was where I decided to become a teacher, where I saw that education was the only way to get Spain out of poverty. Your father understood that, too. In the Residence, Ortega and Doctor Marañón told us the same thing, but we saw it there with our own eyes.' Valli shook her head. 'You just can't imagine it, Charles. We saw children abandoned in a town of barely two hundred inhabitants who were dying from a disease that no-one recognised. After lying sick for three days out in the street, a little girl died, completely alone, right in front of us. We saw people and animals sharing a stream for drinking and washing and picking up all kinds of diseases; we saw people with no food to eat or clothes to put on, wearing the same rags, day and night for years, until they fell to pieces. We brought crusts of bread that we distributed in the school opened by the Republic just the year before, but we quickly realised that if we gave the children bread, we had to watch them eat it in front of us, because otherwise some parents stole it from them. We saw a woman who looked eighty years old, the mother of nine children, her face wrinkled, her expression pained and weary, and we discovered that she was only thirty. We saw a primitive, benighted, illiterate man who lived more like an animal than a human being.' Valli paused before continuing: 'We were touched by it all to the depths of our being and it changed my life for ever. That was where I made my commitment, and although I know that my life is full of things that are hard to explain, at least I can say that the only thing I have is the dignity of never having stopped fighting for justice. Even in the twenty years I spent in Paris, I never stopped collaborating with the Republican Government in exile, especially the one from Catalunya, which was the most organised. In my free time and at weekends I taught Spanish language and literature to the children of exiles, who were now more French than anything else. But I never stopped trying. Like now with that wretched town school. All I've done is to try and avoid losing another battle, because I've already lost enough things in this life: I lost the war, I lost my family, I lost a son and I also lost Natalie, the only person I ever truly loved.' Valli took a very deep breath. 'Now, when I don't have many years left, I didn't want to lose this last battle and leave this world having sacrificed everything, for nothing.'

Valli gulped and buried her face in her old and wrinkled hands once more. She was exhausted and Charles was still nervously walking up and down. The sun had gone down and it was starting to feel cold, although Valli didn't care anymore. She felt that her life had been a real failure and she was now even ashamed to be facing her son, in whose upbringing she had never been involved and who now, understandably, rejected her. Why should he treat her any other way?

Charles eventually turned towards her, and in a cold and distant tone – the one that the English adopt when they want to show displeasure or discomfort – he said:

'Let's go, it's getting cold.'

Valli got up like a robot, her head bowed, and followed him on the road back to Morella. They moved slowly and in total silence. All Valli heard was the tapping of her stick on the road.

As soon as they reached the towers of Sant Miquel, Charles said goodbye. Looking straight at Valli he said to her:

'I don't know who you are or what you want. But you can be sure that as soon as I return to England I shall start to investigate, and if you're lying, it will be of no consequence to me that you are an old woman when I consider what reprisals to take. Is that clear?'

Valli's heart sank, although she scarcely felt it.

'I am your mother and I won't lie to you, don't ever forget that,' she replied, looking him in the eye and speaking with a firm voice.

Charles shook his head, and without another word, turned and set off down the street.

Valli felt exhausted and looked around her without knowing what to do. Out of mere habit she headed slowly towards the Alameda in order to return home, dragging her feet as she went. In silence and with the sky now dark, Valli went along the walkway without being able to hold back her silent tears. Nothing had any meaning; her whole life had been in vain. At least, she thought, she had fulfilled her duty and had revealed the truth to the person who deserved to know it, even though it made her heart ache. But Valli was sure that eventually he would be grateful.

She was worn out when she got home. She could hardly climb the stairs up to her apartment and had to hold on firmly to the bannisters. Once she was inside she closed the door behind her and hurried to her room. All she wanted to do was to go to bed and never wake up again. This life of hers had not been worth it and now she had carried out her final duty, what was the point of going on living?

A little red light on the telephone next to her bed told her that she had a message. She wasn't going to listen to it until she remembered that her neighbour Carmen had been ill. Maybe she needed her. With a sigh she pressed the button.

'Hi, Valli!' said a cheerful voice. It was unmistakeably Sam Crane, Valli recognised immediately. She hadn't heard anything of her since July when she had written her that lovely letter.

Now she was calling full of enthusiasm, to explain that the booklet of a work of the theatre company La Barraca, dedicated by Lorca to Louise Crane and Victoria Kent, "whose love is more true than the laws that shackle it", now belonged to her. The young woman had won a hard-fought battle against Yale University, where the script had ended up with the whole of Victoria's archive, which Louise donated to her alma mater when Victoria died.

Sam explained it all enthusiastically in a long message in which she told Valli that she had been in contact with Sotheby's in London for them to auction it. She also told her that the funds would, of course, be directed to the Residence project in Morella.

But Valli didn't bat an eyelid when the message came to an end. Poor, innocent young woman, she thought. Life would teach her that in the end things usually end in the same way: badly.

24

Three weeks after that revelation, Charles was about to light the fire in his sitting room. In England winter had now set in, the temperature had fallen and the days were growing shorter. The streets of Eton had taken on their winter appearance and were almost empty of the American tourists who filled them in summer either before or after visiting Windsor Castle, and were empty, too, of the English upper classes who filled the bars and restaurants in the autumn after attending a regatta on the Thames. By mid-November, students, parents and masters had returned to their responsibilities and were ready to spend the winter getting on with their own affairs, while almost saying goodbye to their social life until the following spring.

This state of hibernation, which left half the English nation feeling depressed, was a blessing for Charles this year. He had barely stopped thinking about what Valli said since his conversation with her made him want to get back to England as fast as he could, without saying goodbye to anyone – not even Isabel. Valli's words had turned his life upside down, when it had been so ordered and predictable, and had created a state of nervousness, instability and uncertainty that he had never previously known. Charles had never had any problems sleeping, but now he got up in the middle of the night with a dry mouth, sometimes interrupting a nightmare that included bombs and trenches. Having spent his life in the neat and exclusive quadrangles of the most select schools and universities in the world and in the best areas of London or Cambridge, he now found himself trapped in a past full of murderers, lesbians and barren, remote villages.

He got the fire going and sat down in his leather armchair in front of the fireplace and raised his hands to his face. He just wanted time to pass quickly and for it to be Monday morning again without him realising it. But whether he liked it or not, it was Friday evening after dinner, and he was faced with two empty days in which Valli's words hammered through his head as they had done since they last spoke.

Normally Charles would have filled his weekend with scholarly activities, but now he didn't even have the strength for that, nor did he feel close to his students. It was as if, suddenly, he was no longer one of *them* – families who came from the castles of Scotland or peaceful mansions surrounded by pleasant countryside. Instead, he now came from a poor, small town, and on top of that he had spent the first few weeks of his life hidden in the mountains with a group of guerrillas who were virtually communists. He had always pictured his mother sewing by a gothic window in some little English village, but now he knew for certain that his blood was not as pure as he had supposed. If he was not one of them, as he had always thought he was, then who was he?

Charles eventually uncovered his face and relaxed his shoulders, which had been tense all day. He was tired. He had bags under his eyes and a three-day growth of beard, which was quite unusual and rather frowned upon at Eton, where students and masters were always supposed to appear immaculate. He had also stopped wearing the master's smart uniform at all times, something that he had always done without realising it. But now his life included a new and unpleasant variation that always made him feel dirty next to his colleagues and students. That night after dinner Charles had taken out from the back of his wardrobe an old jumper and an old pair of corduroy trousers that he was now wearing. He had hung up his uniform carefully and with a certain sadness, feeling that the man who had filled that suit for years had now disappeared.

Or maybe he had changed forever. Charles swallowed hard and looked at the side-table that was next to his armchair and served himself a glass of sherry, finishing off the bottle. A bottle used to last him nearly a month, but now he had finished two since returning from Morella three weeks earlier.

He took a first sip and closed his eyes, losing himself in the solitude of his room, where the only sound was the ticking of his old clock and, from time to time, the creaking of the old wood. Sometimes he heard noises coming from the floor below, but not so much on Fridays, since most of the students went down to the local pub. Charles could have called Robin or visited him in his house in the Cotswolds, but he didn't feel like it. All he wanted to do was to hide and hibernate until the following year.

He looked at the clock once more. Minutes seemed like hours. Reluctantly he took hold of the old photo of Morella that he had found in his father's house near Cambridge. He pursed his lips as he remembered that at the time he discovered it he had thought that it was just a great coincidence. Now, against all his predictions, Charles had confirmed that there was nothing accidental about the presence of his father in Morella and that photo, and that what Valli had said was true. As soon as he got back to England, he had called Vicent to check that the story from the detective that he had hired was true. Following that confirmation Charles had hired a detective in London to corroborate all the facts, documents and evidence, and these definitely bore out Valli's and Vicent's stories. He had also gone to the central offices of MI5 to read for himself the report of the English agent who brought him from the Pyrenees to Cambridge in 1955. To his great surprise he discovered that it was Airey Neave, who knew the route well after escaping from a prisoner of war camp in occupied

France during the Second World War. In time Neave would become a member of the British Government and later Margaret Thatcher's right-hand man before he was killed by an IRA bomb outside the House of Commons in 1979.

Incredible stories followed one another in Charles' life, as he now found himself bewildered by a chain of facts and coincidences that linked his past together in a way that he could not make sense of.

After two long draughts of sherry he closed his eyes once more and squeezed them tight, forgetting about the photo that was still in his hand. It fell to the floor and the delicate old glass that was covering it broke. A long silence flooded the room, which was totally still as Charles had remained motionless in his armchair. For the first time since his return a tear rolled down his cheek, followed by another and another. He couldn't remember the last time he had cried, and bent forward, burying his head in his strong hands.

He stayed like that for quite a while, until the sound of the entry phone made him jump. It was nearly ten o'clock at night; it was probably some student who had drunk too much and had pressed the wrong buzzer. For a minute he felt sympathetic towards the putative student, remembering that he, too, was drinking on a Friday night, because life was a bitch. In fact the best thing you could do was immerse yourself in your books during working hours, and in your free time drink and forget. That's how he remembered his father and that's how he lived, too. And clearly that's how the drunken student was living, buzzing the entry phone once more. Charles was not intending to get up, convinced that the best lesson was to leave the little darling in the street, even though there was an icy wind blowing that night, so he would learn more quickly not to forget his keys.

Charles eventually got up to get another bottle of sherry from the cupboard and tried to avoid the broken bits of glass that the cleaning lady would pick up the following day, he thought. But as he looked at them closely in order to avoid them, he noticed the tip of what looked like an envelope appearing out from one edge of the frame, which was partly broken. Charles looked at it with suspicion, but he couldn't stop himself from taking hold of it and lifting it up. He took some bits of glass out of the frame that were still stuck to it and then slowly removed a small envelope that had his father's name written on the front without any address. He closed his eyes for a moment, unsure what to do. Deep down all he wanted to do was to throw it in the waste bin and forget about Morella, his past, everything, forever. But he changed his mind when the entry phone buzzed again for at least the fifth time. He thought about his students and how he reminded them every day that the bravery and courage their ancestors had learned on the playing fields of Eton had been one of the foundations of the British Empire; it was former students of that college who had crossed oceans, explored continents and established colonies on the other side of the world for their riches and the greater glory of the country. Puffing out his chest, Charles cast a quick glance at the entry phone, thinking that the drunken student couldn't be that drunk, because he wasn't constantly pressing the buzzer, but was doing so only at more or less regular intervals and not very forcefully. He was about to answer, but he thought that, drunk or not, it was better to teach him a lesson and for him to spend a bit longer in the cold so that this didn't happen again. One of the principal things that students learned at Eton was to take responsibility for themselves.

With a glass of sherry in his hand Charles sat down in his armchair and felt the old envelope, which was made of old brown wrapping paper. Nothing could be worse than what he already knew, so he slowly opened the letter and took out three small sheets of paper which were carefully written by hand and signed, of course, by Valli.

After another long swig of sherry, Charles read:

Maestrazgo, a day in 1955
Dear Tristan,

I hope that the contact has explained the circumstances that have obliged me to write this letter. I take responsibility for the great surprise that you must be feeling at this time; you probably don't comprehend or you hate me. I would completely understand. I have asked the contact to wait until you make a decision, because such a matter can't be resolved in an instant. Of course, Tristan, you are under no obligation to look after this child, whom I have called Carlos after my father. He is seven weeks old and was born on the ninth of December 1954, just nine months after my visit to London. You are the father.

As you can imagine I have thought of nothing else since he announced his arrival, but believe me this is the best solution. This child is healthy and strong, and I cannot give him a future he deserves, but only a wretched childhood, full of persecution, survival and hunger in a mean, unjust, poor and blind country such as this. If he stayed with me, and in spite of his innocence, he would always bear the stigma of being the son of a Red wanted by the Civil Guard, a liability that would pursue him as long as this country doesn't change, and the possibility of that seems increasingly remote as the years pass. What would happen to him if they catch me, kill me or put me in prison? I have no parents, no siblings; who would look after him?

The last time I saw you, you suggested that I settle in England. It breaks my heart to tell you that it would make us both unhappy, for there is nothing more sad than a love unrequited. This thought fills me with bitterness and I am only consoled by the thought that one day you will meet someone who will love you as you deserve and you will forget all about me. That is what I most wish for in all the world: that you and little Carlos should be happy. I no longer care what happens to me; my life was ruined a long time ago. The only thing that keeps me going is the desire to avenge the death of my parents so that I can at least die in peace. But, believe me, I cannot bring anything good either to you or to our son. I stopped living a long time ago; now I just survive.

My hands are trembling as I write this letter, but I feel I have an obligation to be honest. I have told the contact to wait for two days, in case you don't want to take on the responsibility, which I would perfectly understand. In that case the contact would return to the border with the child and would advise me of the situation via a radio code. I would travel back to Prats de Molló and reconsider the situation when I got there. As you see, you are under no obligation.

But if you are willing to look after him, all I ask is that you love him as I love you, with all the admiration, affection and friendship in the world, and that you teach him, if you can, some words of Spanish or share your love for this country with him – if you still have any after reading this letter. You probably don't want to remember me, or the smell of lavender that you liked so much, or Spain or anything that you knew or learnt in this country, which is now the ruin of millions of lives. It is a real misfortune to have been born in this place.

You, on the other hand, have the privilege of belonging to a free and democratic country, or at least more democratic than mine. It would be wonderful if our son could enjoy the same fine opportunities that I thought I would enjoy one day, until the future disappeared. Until they stole it from me.

That's why I'm telling you, in all honesty and sincerity, that this is the best I can do in the circumstances, even though it breaks my heart to do so.

Until forever,

Valli

Charles closed his eyes tight and dropped the letter on to his lap. Once more he raised his hands to his face, as if he were trying to hide. In case he still had any doubts, here was the definitive proof of a reality that was crushing him.

He looked around him at his peaceful sitting room with its soft old wood, its shelves full of leather-bound books, many of them with his father's initials engraved on the spine. His father had left him some valuable first editions of works by Orwell or Waugh, with personal inscriptions. Charles closed his eyes and furrowed his brow, for he now felt very detached from this calm and rational life. The peace he had felt during the years in the refined atmosphere of Eton, Oxford and Cambridge had now turned into a constant feeling of impatience. His natural habitat was no longer among the black jackets of Eton but in the thorny, arid scrubland of the Maestrazgo or in the fields of lavender. Now he understood everything: it must have been his father and not Orwell who gave the name to the Spanish Club at the college. Charles knew that when he was small Tristan and George Orwell were often involved in the Lavender Club at Eton, giving talks and lectures.

Charles buried his head in his hands once more, unable to concentrate on anything; he repeated over and over again that his mother had been a guerrilla, a lesbian and above all a murderer. Although it would have been in self-defence or by the hands of others, the reality was that she or her comrades had killed Vicent's father, Isabel's grandfather. Charles shook his head several times; he just couldn't believe it.

The entry phone buzzed again, this time twice in succession and more forcefully. Charles stamped lightly on the floor in irritation. He thought that the student was not only drunk or careless, but also stupid, because at his age Charles would have found a way either to jump the fence or to contact some friend or other to get in through a window. What idiot would spend over half an hour, calling at regular intervals, putting up with the freezing November cold? Just to satisfy his curiosity and also because he didn't want to be disturbed any more, Charles suddenly got up and abruptly picked up the entry phone.

'Who is this at this hour of the night?' he said, clearly annoyed.

After a brief silence, a voice replied:

'Isabel.'

Charles felt his heart skip a beat and tightened his grip on the handset as he was about to drop it. It was the last reply that he expected.

'Who?' he asked, despite the fact that he had perfectly well recognised the voice.

'Isabel,' she replied with her usual gentle tone.

Charles felt as if a warm gust of air had suddenly come into his frozen surroundings. He closed his eyes uncomprehendingly. Why had she come to see him? Why was everything so difficult?

'Can you open the door, please?' said Isabel, still in a calm voice.

Charles quickly reacted and opened the door, warning her that she had to come up to the top floor. He opened his eyes and listening carefully he heard the main door to the building open and close and waited for Isabel to climb the stairs, listening to the sound of her shoes on the wood. He looked around, relieved to find the room not as untidy as he had assumed, and quickly went over to the mirror on one of the walls. It had been several days since he had taken care of his appearance and he scarcely recognised himself: he had the beginnings of a scruffy beard, sunken eyes, a tired face, stooped shoulders and a woollen jumper that must have been almost as old as he was. He was about to go off and get changed, but realised he hadn't got time and also wondered: what for?

Charles had written a letter to Isabel a week earlier, in which he said that he had had a wonderful adventure but that his place was in Eton and their lives had different destinies. He knew that what he felt for her he had never felt for anyone, but he was also aware that his life had fallen into a vacuum and the best thing was to forget about Valli and Morella, and regrettably that also included Isabel. He hoped to return to his quiet life as a teacher, which made him happy in its own way, between students, travelling and books.

Before he could think or do anything else, two gentle taps at the door told him that Isabel had arrived. Charles closed his eyes, sighed and slowly headed for the door. Without saying anything he opened it and there was Isabel, slimmer than ever, well wrapped up in an elegant raincoat, scarf and woollen hat. Her green eyes now appeared lacklustre. Her smile was still there but he thought it seemed forced. She looked sad, although she made an effort to hide it.

'Hello,' was all she said.

Charles looked her in the eye and didn't know how to reply. He thought he'd said everything in the letter, but good manners obliged him now to listen to what she had come to say.

'Come in.'

Isabel slowly entered, without taking her hands out of her pockets. She had not brought a suitcase but only a large bag. She stopped when she accidentally trod on the glass that was still on the floor, finally causing Charles to react as he went over to her and took her arm.

'I'm sorry, something fell,' he said, taking her to the middle of the room.

Isabel discreetly looked round the room, her gaze settling on the Poets' Garden painting that she had given him and that Charles had hung in pride of place above the fireplace. Isabel looked at him knowingly, which made Charles relax a little, probably for the first time in weeks.

'Please, sit down,' he said, gesturing to the armchair next to his. 'Sorry about the house, I wasn't expecting visitors.'

Isabel didn't respond. She looked Charles up and down and at the half-consumed bottle of sherry on the table. Her lips were pressed together as once more she looked at the broken glass on the floor and some of the pages of Valli's letter that had also fallen on to the carpet. Nervously she took off her hat and gloves, and finally turned to him and looked him in the eye.

'My mother has told me everything,' she said. 'Valli spoke with her and between the two of them they have sorted everything out without there being a great public commotion. They have saved the school and my father's honour, otherwise the alternative would affect all of us and create even more problems.'

Charles suddenly sat up, because he wasn't expecting such an outcome. The subject of the school frankly now seemed a long way away, but Charles was once again annoyed about Vicent: after how he had treated those two women all his life, the scumbag was now receiving their help. Charles wanted to comment on such an injustice, but he didn't feel it was appropriate, for after all Isabel was his daughter and none of it was her fault. Charles leant back and took a deep breath:

'What have they told you and why?' Charles no longer knew who knew what.

Isabel lowered her head, but immediately looked at him again without saying anything and played nervously with her hands. Unsure as to what to do with them, she finally put them in the pockets of her raincoat, which she still hadn't taken off. Charles hadn't offered to hang it up for her, either, since he didn't know whether her visit was going to last a few minutes or a whole lifetime. His circumstances had changed so much that he no longer felt in control of anything.

Isabel eventually said in reply what he most feared:

'My mother also explained to me how my father discovered the connection between Valli and your father, and how you came to England.'

Charles closed his eyes. He found that reality too painful to share, even with Isabel.

'Why did she tell you?' he asked, angered by the possibility that his secret would get round the whole town.

Isabel noticed his tone of voice and went over to him to place her hand gently on his.

'I suppose my mother wants the best for me,' she said, stroking his hand.

Her touch gave Charles goose bumps, and he recalled the feelings of happiness that night they shared at the hotel less than a month earlier. Neither of them spoke, while Isabel continued to stroke his hand, gently and slowly. Charles didn't dare look at her, feeling ashamed and regretful about the letter he had sent to her. But in spite of that, that strong, brave woman – much stronger and braver than he was – had come to see him. As if he were waking from a nightmare, Charles raised his head and looked at her. There she was, waiting for him. He felt as if his whole body was loosening up: his shoulders, his face muscles, his hands, everything was slowly relaxing, as if he were finally coming to his senses after a long time.

'You must be frozen, you poor thing,' he said, easing the tenseness of the moment. 'I kept you waiting downstairs for over half an hour.'

'Do you always take so long to answer the door? It's not as though there's a heatwave…' said Isabel, who was also anxious to lighten the situation.

Charles smiled.

'I thought that it was a drunken student and I wanted to teach him a lesson.'

His comment made Isabel laugh.

'You and your students, what are you like?' she said, looking once more at the broken glass on the floor and the half-empty bottle. 'They should give you less Latin and more mops. What a lot you are!'

Charles smiled as he thought of his students cleaning the hotel with the brooms and mops that Isabel had given them. That woman really was extraordinary.

'I'm sorry, I'm going to pick it up right now,' said Charles looking at the glass and starting to get up.

Isabel stopped him.

'Don't worry, I'll do it later,' she said. 'I imagine you've got other more important things to worry about.'

He raised an eyebrow and gently nodded once.

'I'll take care of it,' said Isabel sympathetically. 'I only came because after what my mother explained to me and when I received your letter I wanted to make sure that you were all right.'

Charles moved his head from side to side.

'It could be better,' he said, ironically.

Isabel looked at him with her intelligent eyes, without being taken in by his false humour, of course. She knew him well, like the good observer that she was of everything around her, which she captured in her marvellous paintings.

'I've come to offer you my support, if you need it,' she said.

Charles looked at her, this time without concealing how lost he looked or how confused was his spirit.

'No-one can do anything. It's a misfortune that I have to accept and that's it,' he replied with a sigh.

'I don't think it's a misfortune at all,' Isabel stated straight away. 'Valli is a great woman; I have only seen her love and help many, many people. You could give her a chance.'

'Her present isn't as glorious as her past,' Charles responded defensively.

'No-one in this life is free from blame. And she lived through some very difficult circumstances.'

'She killed your grandfather, Isabel,' said Charles, who couldn't comprehend so much compassion for Valli.

'My grandfather was not a good man, not with anyone, and especially not with my father. Let's be clear: he used to beat him from when he was very small.'

Charles held his breath for a few moments. He had always hated violence and he found it impossible to imagine how a father could hit his child. He remembered his own father, always so civilised and rational. No-one had ever laid a finger on him.

'Give her a chance,' Isabel said again.

'Have you come as a messenger?' he spat out, but regretted doing so at once, because the last thing he intended was to offend the only person with whom he wanted to – or could – share these difficult moments.

Isabel looked him in the eye.

'I have a parent who's done awful things, too,' she said. 'But that doesn't mean I should shut myself up in a room and give up on my plans.'

Charles looked at her in silence.

'It's not easy.'

Once more Isabel moved close to him and took his hand.

'I know,' she said. 'But don't shut yourself away like you did in Oxford.'

Charles looked at her intently and pursed his lips. That woman, the only one with whom he had risked sharing the story about the pints that he drank alone, was right and he knew it. If only he had half her courage... he thought.

'At least now I turn to a good sherry; it's not cheap pub beer any more,' he replied.

'Congratulations on your progress,' Isabel answered, raising an eyebrow.

Charles finally gave the hint of a smile for the first time in weeks. It occurred to him that Isabel was the only non-English person of the many he had met on his travels who had learned the English code. She didn't take irony as an ill-timed joke or an attempt to divert attention, but as the best answer for someone who couldn't or didn't know how to communicate in a better way, and who at least had the humility to recognise it, even if in such a subtle manner.

Isabel gave him a very knowing smile.

'I'm delighted to see you haven't lost your sense of humour,' she said.

'Humour, my dear, is the last thing that an Englishman loses in life,' Charles remarked.

They both gave a gentle laugh and Charles got up, with a gesture to Isabel that he would help her take off her coat.

'I'm so sorry, I haven't even offered you a cup of tea,' he said apologetically. 'Let me hang up your coat and I'll move the armchair closer to the fire; you must be frozen.'

Isabel got up, although she didn't seem to be planning to remove her raincoat.

'Well, I'm not sure how long I'm staying,' she said, her eyes lowered. 'I only came to check that you were all right and to see if you needed anything.'

Isabel stopped for a few seconds, raising her enormous eyes that were brighter and more lively than ever. Charles couldn't take his eyes off them, as he felt once more the peace and sense of security that they gave him.

'After I received your letter,' she went on, 'I also wanted to know if it was really true that you didn't want anything more to do with Morella... or with me.'

Charles put his hand to his mouth, as if such an idea terrified him more than he could ever say. How could he stop seeing the only person who really filled him with hope, the only person he really wanted to see in such difficult times? He felt his heart go out more than ever to that woman who was, without doubt, the best thing that had happened to him in his life. Just from having met her, the rest of his past – all those stories of guerrillas, mountains, murders, spies and boarders – now made sense.

Without taking his eyes off her, Charles eventually responded:

'I've got two beers in the fridge. Would you like one?'

25

The smell of Christmas was everywhere in the town, with shops full of trees and horrible wreaths, chimneys giving off wood smoke and people being nicer to each other than usual, apparently full of that spirit that Vicent hated so much.

The former Mayor had never liked this time of year. An only child, a stranger in a strange town and until recently socially inaccessible, his memories of Christmas were confined to a simple meal in a cold apartment with just his mother, while his father was either on duty or with one of his mistresses. His mother, at least, only left him on his own for one Christmas Eve, when she had to go back to Tramacastilla, in the Aragonese Pyrenees, when her father fell ill and died soon after. Vicent spent that night with a cat that he had rescued from the street that same day, but which his father made him give up as soon as he came home. It broke Vicent's heart, because animals had always been his best friends.

The former Mayor felt the coldness of the Morella dawn as he rode just below the Alameda on the back of *Lo Petit*. His most faithful friend for twenty years went slowly around the outskirts of the town at his favourite hour, about six o'clock in the morning when everything was quiet. Since his resignation Vicent had hardly shown himself in the streets of Morella, because he wanted to avoid the inevitable stares and questions. But fortunately his stepping down had remained fairly discreet, thanks to the holidays and because they had already called new council elections which had distracted people's attention. Valli and Eva had also both kept their word and nothing about the investment in the airport had been made public. Instead, following Valli's orders, Vicent had called a halt to the sale of the school and had also withdrawn the promise to give another two million to the airport. He had been able to rescue those two million because it was only a verbal agreement with President Roig, with nothing written down anywhere. It was not his problem, Vicent thought, how the President would explain to the investors in London that in fact the two million didn't exist. Besides, the former Mayor could always argue that thanks to his management, Morella would receive the five million to refurbish the old school that Roig had promised in exchange for the investment in the airport, because those five million had been approved in the Valencian Parliament, so there was no going back on that. What had been paid – but no-one knew about – was the personal commission to Roig that Vicent had promised in exchange for the refurbishment.

With regard to the one million that Morella had paid towards the airport, Amparo, who had been such a blessing to him, had taken that amount out of her personal savings in order to repay the Town Council. Until then Vicent didn't know that his wife had that amount of money, having apparently inherited a large sum from her parents many years earlier. Amparo had told him that there was no reason why the people of Morella should finance such a risky project, and that if that was what it cost to protect his honour, she would pay it because dignity had no price. Vicent had done the council budget again, taking off the three million for the airport and removing the income from the sale of the school – items that he had made Eva include, before he told Valli everything. Vicent had left the Town Hall in debt after the work on the Alameda, the new school and the public swimming pool, but at least such debts related to improvements to local amenities, so that he could always defend his actions.

Cefe had made him put the house up for sale in order to reduce his personal debts and because, of course, without his mayor's salary he could no longer afford such a large mortgage. In addition he had to return the two hundred and fifty thousand euros of public funds that he had received to convert the hotel into a country cottage. Valli had made a claim for them so that they could be returned to the regional government, because she didn't want anything fraudulent connected with the hotel, which was now in her hands. At least she had agreed to keep Manolo on as an employee, for which deep down Vicent was grateful. Everything had been carried out with total discretion in order not to stir up any rumours in the town.

With the minimum of fuss Cefe had already put the house up for sale, hoping to find some English or American banker in search of some peace and quiet. Once again Amparo had saved the situation by proposing a move to a smaller but cosy farmhouse that her family had held on to near the town. In principle the farmhouse belonged to her brother, but he had moved into a council nursing home some time earlier and he hadn't hesitated to help her by handing it over to her. Amparo had also assured him that they didn't need a large house and that in fact she preferred to live closer to the town so that she could walk every day to the square to do her shopping and talk to her friends more often.

With no family or savings of his own, all Vicent could do was to agree to his wife's plan, although in truth he didn't really mind the change. In fact he had always wanted the simple life of the farm labourer in the open air, like his school friends when they were little. The country farm they were now leaving was of course fantastic, but it didn't have the warm simplicity that he had always longed for. Perhaps that large house had been just too big and he could now see that actually he hadn't been happy there, either. By contrast Amparo's farmhouse was smaller, more cosy and more welcoming, and it had a small plot at the back where he could see himself working the land, growing vegetables or keeping some farmyard animals. In other words, keeping everything simple, without the logistical complications or great expense involved in the country farm that basically had weighed him down with obligations.

Buoyed up by these plans Vicent took *Lo Petit* from the Alameda to the Xiva path, where he got him to take a small track to the right. Feeling the need to stretch his legs after two hours in the saddle, Vicent dismounted and walked for half a mile with *Lo Petit* until they got to the ruined farmhouse where the *maquis* had killed his father.

He had not been there since Easter, just after he had inaugurated the new Alameda alongside President Roig. Vicent recalled how that day he arrived there mounted on *Lo Petit*, with his head high, wearing his immaculate Barbour jacket, which had cost him over five hundred euros, and his Wembley riding helmet, imported straight from one of London's leading stores. Today, by contrast, he was wearing a woollen jumper that Amparo had knitted for him at least twenty years earlier, in which frankly he felt more comfortable than when he wore more close-fitting Ascot-style outfits. He stopped eventually a few yards from the building, or what remained of it. That was where, over fifty years earlier, Valli and La Pastora's group killed his father by blowing up the old farmhouse while he was waiting inside on his own to ambush them. According to what they had told him when he was only fifteen, it was such a big explosion that the police found it difficult to find the Civil Guard's remains. Since then Vicent had always gone to this remote spot once a year to pay his respects to his father.

These visits, however, were more by way of tradition or a sense of duty than out of respect or real affection. In fact Vicent didn't really have any good memories of his father, but only beatings, obligations and long absences. What had he learnt from his father apart from living like a dog, grovelling, working his fingers to the bone in the Civil Guard or the hotel, with nothing to show for it?

Just like himself, he thought.

It was only during his nearly two years as Mayor that Vicent had tasted success and the acceptance of the people of Morella. Despite the fact that that dream had now come to an end, Vicent refused to believe that he had to go back to his wretched old way of living. At sixty-seven years of age he still had a good ten years of good health and energy ahead of him and he didn't intend to waste it, nor to live with his head bowed like his father, he said to himself.

Vicent let *Lo Petit* do as he pleased, although after a little walk the horse came back to him, resting his soft, warm back against Vicent's old coat. Animals are always the first to notice things, he said to himself, as he gently stroked his horse.

Vicent moved forward a few yards towards the old farmhouse, bending down to tuck his trousers into his boots and avoid the mud and puddles everywhere. The ground was still wet from the recent downpours, and gave off the smell of damp fields that he liked so much. Moving slowly Vicent came to the ruins, where the lavender and rosemary grew amongst the stones, filling the air with their scent.

He breathed in deeply and looked around him. Basically all he wanted was right there: clean air, fields, freedom and, above all, affection.

Amparo had told him that now, free from the ties of the mayor's office and the hotel, with no interests to defend or fight for, the time had come to rest, to relax and see how the people of Morella would automatically warm to him bit by bit. Vicent hadn't won them all over yet, although it was true that the few old folk he had encountered on his early morning rides through the Alameda had been very friendly towards him. Having worked so hard to get the new Alameda built, he had only used it a couple of times as Mayor, including the day it was inaugurated. Since he resigned, however, he had enjoyed using it almost every morning, for he liked watching the sunrise from there. To his surprise he had discovered that he was not the only regular observer of that spectacle; there were another three or four people who also turned up every morning in silence to bathe themselves in the peace and hope that always accompanied the dawn. His wife was right as usual.

Vicent once more stroked *Lo Petit* standing faithfully by his side, as he distractedly looked at the farmhouse ruins. He pictured his father dying there alone, his shotgun in his hand. He didn't want to end up the same way. He thought about his children, Manolo and Isabel; how would they remember him? His heart shrank as he thought that they might remember him in the same way that he remembered his own father: with empty, cold, dry, even indifferent thoughts. His father, who always treated him harshly, never really loved him and never even taught him anything practical or useful to help him through life. Vicent felt his hands tensing up and growing cold at the thought of the dark, worn skin of that Civil Guard who died alone. Now fifty years later, there was only one person who remembered him – Vicent himself – and that was without any warmth at all. He felt a sudden shudder and, above all, fear. Would he end up the same way?

Suddenly Vicent's legs grew weak and slowly he had to crouch down, holding on to a rock so as not to lose his balance. He knew he hadn't been a good father to his children, despite having worked all his life to help them get on. But that wasn't enough and he knew it. That was his duty, because if he couldn't support them, why have them? He knew full well that the only affection for Manolo and Isabel in the household came from their mother. By contrast, he never had patience with Manolo and even took him straight out of university; maybe he should have gone to Valencia in person and helped him to sort out what it was that took him away from his studies, no matter what the cause, rather than taking him right away from his course and making him return to Morella. Vicent also knew that with Isabel, who had dared to challenge him despite being a woman, he hadn't been fair, either. As with Manolo he had frequently given her a few slaps, although less than his father had given him. But basically Vicent knew that it was unforgivable and that inevitably it would lead to him being forgotten and rejected, the same as he felt for his father. Vicent had never crystallised such thoughts because in his day you were obliged to love your parents. But in today's more democratic and advanced society, parents had to win over their children and he knew only too well that he had never done anything towards it. It was logical that once his children became aware of how life worked they would give him in return the same affection that they had received: none.

Vicent took a deep breath and sensed that tears were welling in his eyes, although the warmth of *Lo Petit*'s firm body at his side gave him the strength to get up and hold back his tears. He looked towards the mountains that surrounded him and promised himself to leave a better legacy behind him than his father had. He had made so many mistakes in his life, towards his wife, his children, the lies in the Town Hall... but at least, he told himself, he wasn't a thief. His time as Mayor had not made him personally rich, as was the case with many others, starting with Roig himself. He was nothing more than a fool who had let power go to his head; he had got into debt up to his neck and now he had to give everything back, including the million for the airport which, for the sake of respectability, his wife had already paid back to the council coffers. He would also give back the funds for the conversion of the hotel into a country cottage so that his conscience would be clear. He didn't want to be looked on as a thief, or have his children feel ashamed of him.

That very night he had asked them all to come to the house, perhaps the last time that the family would meet up in the farmhouse. He was consumed by a mixture of sadness and hope. Sadness at seeing the magnificent house slip out of his life, but hope that it could be a last chance with Manolo and Isabel. At least the two children deserved an explanation about what had happened and about the changes in the hotel, since he hadn't yet said anything to them. He looked towards the ruins of the farmhouse once more. Would he give his father another chance?

Uncertain about what to think, Vicent mounted *Lo Petit* once more and with a light tap on his thigh, the two set off for home.

Vicent had not seen Isabel for five months. Father and daughter did not see or talk to each other more than was strictly necessary since that unfortunate night in July, when she subjected him to the most outrageous insolence he had ever experienced in his life, in the presence of Charles and thereby torpedoing the sale of the school.

Now, barely two weeks before Christmas, Isabel was sitting on the sofa in front of the fireplace next to Charles. They were holding hands, Vicent noticed as he came downstairs and entered the sitting room. Manolo was in the kitchen with his mother.

Vicent made an effort to smile but found he couldn't. With a slight wobble in his legs, he moved towards the fireplace, where the fire was burning and crackling nicely, the only sound in the otherwise silent room. Charles was the first to notice Vicent's presence and immediately got up and proffered his hand like a gentleman, but without a hint of a smile on his face. From the kitchen which was open to the sitting room, Amparo and Manolo watched expectantly.

'Pleased to see you, Vicent,' said Charles.

'How's things?' Vicent replied, barely looking at him and addressing him more as a son-in-law than as a potential buyer. However, Vicent was not paying much attention to Charles, but could only notice the presence of his children, who gave no sign of making a move to greet him. Vicent realised that he would have to swallow all his pride and show humility for once. He recalled the old people from the Alameda and the words of his wife: more humility and less of your own agenda, do as you would be done by and you'll get better results.

He loosened the collar of the nicely ironed shirt that he had put on for the occasion and headed for Manolo, thinking that it would be easier to break the ice with him than with Isabel. Slowly and with a heavy heart Vicent went to the kitchen, where he kissed his wife on the forehead and greeted his son.

'I'm so pleased that you could come,' he said. 'Is everything under control at the hotel?'

'Yes, Father,' Manolo replied with a certain amount of nervousness. 'We don't have any guests at the moment, so everything's okay.'

Vicent was on the point of making some comment about that, but he stopped himself because that evening he had more important matters to deal with. He remembered the thoughts he had that same morning at the old farmhouse and reminded himself that this get-together was to get closer to his children and not to deal with business.

While his wife began to serve glasses of sherry to everyone, Vicent finally turned to Isabel, who surprised him by how attractive she was looking. She was without glasses, looking noticeably slimmer and wearing a fairly close-fitting, elegant dark blue dress, all of which meant that Vicent barely recognised his daughter. Where was that large woman with her head bowed, hidden behind an apron and those thick glasses? It occurred to Vicent that she had begun to blossom just after she had cut the ties that bound her to him. For a second he thought that maybe life would have been better for him if he had detached himself from the legacy of his father much sooner. Although he had been dead for many years, it seemed as though Vicent had only broken away from his hold over him that very morning.

With his head down and almost without daring to look at her enormous green eyes with their long lashes, Vicent eventually spoke to his daughter:

'I'm delighted that you've both been able to come,' was all he could say.

Isabel nodded but said nothing.

He was about to speak, as he nervously took one of the hand-engraved crystal glasses in which Amparo had served the sherry. He looked at the fireplace and then around the house, especially at the stone walls that he had thought impenetrable. Nothing lasts, he thought. Neither the good nor the bad.

'Dear everyone,' he began in a serious tone with sad, downcast eyes.

'Let's start with a toast, shall we?' his wife interrupted in a brighter voice, for which Vicent was grateful, because what he had planned as a reconciliation seemed more like a funeral.

'Of course, you do it,' Vicent agreed, catching sight of the look of surprise on his children's faces. Perhaps they were not used to seeing their mother take the lead, or their father giving way. Although it saddened him, suddenly he felt more comfortable, as he felt that he was going along the right lines.

'To us, as it's been a long time since we were all together, and especially,' she added, looking at Charles, 'a warm welcome to Charles and to say that we hope he feels comfortable and happy among us, and we'll do everything possible from here.'

Charles gave a genuine smile at that point, revealing the dimples on his face that Vicent had never previously noticed, despite having known him for months. Out of the corner of his eye Vicent also saw how Isabel affectionately squeezed Charles' hand, a gesture that he returned.

'To us and to Charles!' Vicent seconded, raising his glass, in a tone of forced jollity.

Amparo was aware of the hard time her husband was having, so she went over to him after a couple of sips of her sherry. As she stood next to him, she took his hand and gave it a squeeze.

Vicent gulped several times. This domestic warmth was a new sensation for him, or perhaps he just couldn't remember it. He turned slightly and smiled at his wife, who nodded and encouraged him to start talking. Vicent started to feel comfortable in a situation that beforehand had promised to be a real torture.

'My dear children,' he began, looking at his audience, who were now all sitting while he remained standing next to the fireplace. 'I just wanted to bring you here for the last time, since your mother and I will be moving soon to the farmhouse of your Uncle Juan, who as you know now lives in a nursing home.'

'Why?' Manolo interrupted, but his mother immediately gestured to him to be patient.

'Because we've, or rather,' Vicent corrected himself, 'because I've been living beyond my means, in both the Town Hall and at home.' He paused briefly to take a sip of sherry. 'You know I've resigned and soon I imagine it will come out that the

Town Hall has more debts than we would like. It's something that I really regret, but I can swear to you that I've always thought about the good of the town, even though sometimes I've made mistakes. I haven't personally benefitted, and everything I've spent without a public project behind it', he said, looking down, 'I've given back. Absolutely everything.'

Charles immediately raised an eyebrow, but his look of surprise disappeared as Vicent continued with his short speech, without giving any more details.

'That's why I resigned, but you can always hold your heads high, since your father has given back every last penny relating to actions that were outside the responsibilities of his office.' Vicent paused once more. 'As far as the house is concerned, without my monthly income as Mayor, the mortgage has become too much for us, so the bank has put it on the market.'

'After all the effort you've both put in here…' said Isabel looking at her mother, as if she didn't understand the situation.

'We're very happy, dear,' Amparo interjected. '|This house has always been too big for us, and it's also so isolated.'

'I've always said that,' Isabel remarked.

Vicent nodded as he looked at his daughter, agreeing with her for the first time in a long time.

'The fact is that I'm also happy with the change,' he explained. 'I've always wanted my small farmhouse where I can grow things, and this is more of a palace than a farmhouse.'

Vicent noticed Manolo give Isabel a look of surprise, which she returned. His children seemed incredulous.

'Don't be surprised,' he said. 'These two years as Mayor have been hectic, but since I was a boy all I wanted was to look after rabbits and chickens and now finally I can,' he said seriously.

Although he meant it, his remark made Manolo and Isabel laugh out loud, because they still didn't know whether to believe what they were hearing or not.

'The thing is,' he went on, 'I've also transferred the hotel to Valli Querol, who you already know.'

'About time,' Isabel remarked straight away.

Vicent looked at her in surprise.

'And what do you know about it?

'I know what Charles has told me,' Isabel made clear, looking at her mother out of the corner of her eye. 'Manolo also knows, because I told him; I thought he had a right to know.'

Vicent briefly remained silent.

'But I think it's a fair and appropriate solution,' Isabel said eventually.

Vicent relaxed his shoulders and lifted his head. At last a sign of approval.

'So do I,' Manolo remarked.

Vicent looked at his son.

'I've also agreed with Valli that she'll keep you on at the hotel reception. She thinks highly of you.'

'The feeling's mutual,' he replied.

Vicent looked at the fire before addressing Isabel.

'As far as you're concerned, Isabel, as it seems that you're now a couple,' he said, looking also at Charles, 'I've been thinking that if you were prepared to take on the debt of this house, you could have it as yours; I'm sure Cefe would help you.'

Isabel looked him in the eye and then at Charles. They didn't seem to need to say anything to each other.

'No thanks, Father,' his daughter replied straight away. 'It's too big for us. I've got a job in Castellón and we're still thinking about what we're going to do. But obviously we don't need anything this big. And if there's still some more debt to be paid off, I think that the last penny from the sale of this house and its contents should be used to deal with those commitments.'

Vicent looked at his daughter, who spoke with resolve, her back straight, her eyes steady, her voice firm. That woman had changed radically, or else she had always been like that and he just hadn't noticed.

'As you wish,' he said. 'I was just trying to help.'

'We can look after ourselves, thank you,' Isabel replied, politely but with a distant coldness that left Vicent feeling hurt. Such a remark made him feel almost redundant, a useless father, unable to offer anything that his children really needed. Or perhaps the only thing they were really looking for was comfort and support, just what he had planned to give them from then on.

'Well, your mother and I will be in the new house in a couple of weeks, by Christmas, but I don't think they're going to put this house on the market until the New Year, so you're welcome to come and have a few days' break here if you wish.'

'I'm fine in the hotel, and there'll be work to do,' responded Manolo.

'We're going to Cuba for a couple of weeks from the twentieth,' said Isabel.

Vicent looked at his wife, who once again got him out of a hole.

'Just think how peaceful the two of us will be in our little house, without any big celebrations; it'll be one of our best Christmases.'

Vicent nodded.

After a tense silence, he looked at his children and opened his hands with his arms out, indicating that he had nothing more to say or to offer.

Isabel understood the message and got up, along with Charles who held on to her hand all the while.

'Well, if that's all, we're going to make a move,' she said, 'as we've got a lot to do to get everything ready for Cuba.'

'As you wish,' said Amparo, as pleasant as ever.

Vicent turned to the fireplace, feeling rather humiliated by the new authority that his daughter seemed to have acquired, and especially by his apparent loss of power. He felt as if he were at everyone's mercy.

As if she could read his thoughts, Amparo went over to him and whispered in his ear:

'You've been fantastic; that's the way, bit by bit and with patience.'

Vicent said nothing and seeing that Charles and Isabel were already by the door holding their coats, he went to say goodbye to them.

He hesitated for a few moments before saying to his daughter in a soft, trembling voice:

'I hope this is the start of a better relationship.'

As he nervously clasped his hands behind his back, Vicent felt as though he were betraying his father: giving in and bowing his head were the opposite of what he would have taught him.

Isabel turned and looked at him without concealing her surprise.

'I have always behaved correctly with you and I shall continue to do so, but don't ask me to do anything more,' she replied.

Vicent looked her in the eye and nodded. He knew he couldn't do any more for now.

As he shut the door, he realised that he would have to spend the last years of his life dedicated to his family and to the countryside, in order to avoid leaving a legacy that was as sad and empty as that of his father. That thought, although it caused him anguish, at least filled him with hope and gave him a reason to go on living.

26

Valli had heard in the baker's shop that Isabel and Charles were in Morella… together. There were odd rumours in the town about Vicent's resignation, Isabel's absence and the impact of her unofficial engagement to Charles on the question of the school. Despite the impressive popular imagination, none of the gossip had got close to the real reasons for Charles' absence from Morella since October.

Since that last occasion Valli had barely kept going and her body, which had generally been healthy and in good shape, appeared to be failing. Her neighbour Carmen made her eat the little she could digest each day, which was only vegetable soup or a little broth, but also a good glass of brandy every morning to keep her circulation going.

Valli had wanted to call Charles or write to him during those two long, cold months, but she had always stopped herself, feeling that what her son needed was time. She also knew, because Amparo had told her, that Isabel had gone to London to see him and that she had spent a week there.

She had been pleased to hear such news and at least it had encouraged her to look after herself, but little more. She hardly used the phone or opened the few letters she received, mostly from the bank or the electricity company. Gradually she had given up her social life, to the despair of her neighbour Carmen, who didn't know what to do to revive her spirits.

The dynamics changed after the gossip in the baker's, since the presence of Charles in the town just before Christmas gave her a window of hope. If he didn't want to see her he surely wouldn't have come to Morella, since he could always stay in Castellón with Isabel, where she lived, or even in London. In any event Valli knew that she had to wait for him to come to her, as she had already put her cards on the table. She knew only too well that relationships – all relationships – simply don't work unless they are two-way.

She was turning over these thoughts when her doorbell suddenly rang, urgently, several times. Initially Valli took no notice of it, which is what she usually did. She carried on calmly running her finger gently around the edge of her small cup of green tea that she enjoyed mid-morning. It was Saturday and she had done her shopping. Now she was resting, safe in her own home and protecting herself from the cold with a heavy woollen shawl, a thick dress and her huge woollen slippers.

The doorbell was so persistent, however, that instead of going out on to the balcony rather than open the windows, she hurried over to the front door to pick up the entry phone.

'Who is it?' she asked, almost shouting.

'Hola, hola!' came the shouts from downstairs to Valli's great surprise, and she had to move the earpiece away from her ear after the fright that the voices gave her.

'Who's there?' she asked again, although her heart began to beat faster as she guessed who it was. That would certainly cheer her up.

'Valli! It's us, Sam and Soledad. Are you okay? Can we come up?'

'Oh, my dear! What a surprise!' said Valli, all excited. 'Come up, come up!'

Valli heard Sam running up the stairs, followed by the Director of the International Institute, coming up behind her as fast as she could but without managing to keep up with her. In the blink of an eye Sam Crane appeared on the landing outside Valli's apartment and immediately hugged Valli who was waiting for them, door in hand, her arms wide open.

'How lovely to see you!' they said. 'We were worried because you weren't answering the phone or our letters or anything, so we decided to come.'

Valli, still amazed, took a small step back. She eyed the two women up and down. They looked good, smiling and confident, straight from the metropolis with their designer jeans and their stylish coats. Their complexion and their teeth were well cared for, like girls from a fee-paying school, and their eyes were shining and full of a youthful enthusiasm that had not yet experienced the more bitter aspects of life. Valli smiled at them. These women, despite the privileged background they came from, were strong-minded and good-hearted. Who would have thought that one day they would come from Madrid to this town where nothing ever happened, just to see her?

With all the warmth and friendliness she could muster, Valli led them into her small sitting room and served them hot coffee and local filled pastries, which despite their perfect figures they ate hungrily and with gusto. They were really lovely ladies, Valli said to herself.

After saying several times that they were amazed at how beautiful Morella was, Sam soon told Valli about the message that they had brought.

'There's some good news, my dear Valli,' said Sam, her red hair in a pony tail that made her face look even younger and more freckled. Her blue eyes shone brighter than ever, suggesting that she had been leading a better and fuller life since the night they drank sherry in La Venencia in Madrid just after Easter. That woman had grown, Valli said to herself.

'As I explained, after a few weeks doing battle with Yale University I finally took ownership of Lorca's pamphlet dedicated to my grandmother and Victoria Kent. Thanks to some of my mother's contacts in London, we auctioned it at Sotheby's and… you're not going to believe this,' she said looking at Valli wide-eyed and with her hands gripping the table, 'we got four hundred thousand euros!'

'Oh, my dear!' Valli exclaimed, leaning back and raising her hands to her head. 'That's amazing! What a lot of money! But who would pay so much for it?'

'Well, the British Library,' replied Soledad, who was calmer than Sam, but brimming with just as much pleasure. 'As you know Lorca is much more respected in England and the United States, or even in Germany, than he is in Spain, and besides, they are rich countries. The dedication is so powerful that the British Library will use it as a symbol of its support for minorities, as proof that it represents a plural and diverse society and not just the British elite. A great coup to keep any critics quiet.'

Valli rolled her eyes in a sign of incredulity. Such demonstrations of good intentions, especially on the basis of a cheque book, didn't mean much to her, but at least on this occasion she benefitted from them. She wasn't going to object.

'Remind me, if you would, what the dedication said,' she asked, still incredulous.

'"For Louise Crane and Victoria Kent, whose love is more true than the laws that shackle it",' Sam quoted straight away.

Valli sighed and leant against the back of her chair. If they had allowed the kind of society to prosper that was championed in the two Residences, how different her life and that of the entire country would have been. Valli took in a deep breath and looked at her new friends, whose sophisticated poise and elegant clothes contrasted with her small and modest home with its few possessions. Sam, at least, came from a free society, whose strength inspired her pure and hopeful outlook. The same as she had when she was young, only to be wiped out by a wretched war, perhaps until this precise moment.

'It's incredible, Valli,' Sam continued. 'We've done it! I told you that my mother had given me permission to sell the Picasso that I was due to inherit, and that we auctioned in New York for one million dollars.'

Sam had to pause, because her enthusiasm was overflowing and she was starting to get her words tangled up. Soledad offered her a glass of water that Valli had left on the table and Sam drank it down almost in one go.

'Well, it so happens,' said Sam as soon as she could, 'that my mother eventually came to Madrid to see me, and after a few days visiting museums and the old Residence, she got so caught up in the project that she decided to join in.' She stopped again before continuing in a more sombre tone. 'I told you that she had always preferred Italy to Spain, which she didn't know much about. I think that having two mothers caused her problems at school and that gave rise to a certain amount of resentment towards Victoria and towards Spain in general. But when she saw, read and above all heard about my projects, she finally understood me and agreed to sell the other Picasso, the one that was sitting doing nothing in a safe in New York. The thing is that we've sold that one as well, and for two million dollars!'

Valli opened her eyes as wide as she could. With her domestic economy based on looking after each and every euro, she couldn't get her head around such amounts of money and she didn't feel that she could possibly have any connection with such plans.

Sam went on like a whirlwind.

'It's all been done with the help of my mother's lawyer, who we needed to protect the family's assets,' she said, pausing briefly to catch her breath.

Valli noticed in the young woman's eyes the same brightness that she saw in those rural children, who had never seen a library or a movie until she and Casona came along with them, carrying them on the back of a donkey at the height of the Republic. To inspire that brightness really did fill her with a sense of satisfaction. Finally her life was beginning to make sense again.

'We've set up a foundation,' Sam went on more calmly. 'I will chair it, with my mother as honorary president. We will allocate the three million plus that we've put together to buy the school in Morella and establish here the extension of the María de Maeztu Young Ladies' Residence, as we would call it.'

Valli's eyes began to mist over, but there were still a lot of loose ends to be tied up.

'Are you sure you're happy with locating it in Morella and not in Madrid?'

Sam got up and suddenly opened a window wide, as if she didn't mind the winter cold of Morella.

'This is a perfect, idyllic place,' she said, as she drew back as many curtains as she could. 'As I said, we already have an agreement with Vassar and Smith College for twenty American women students a year to come and study Spanish. It'll be more peaceful and they'll be more focussed than in Madrid, which is full of English and Americans and it's easier for them to get distracted. This town is marvellous, and they'll be able to integrate themselves better. Besides, today everything can be done by internet, so it scarcely matters where you live, especially for scholars and researchers.'

Soledad and Valli nodded at the same time.

'But who will teach them?' Valli asked.

'We can make arrangements with the local college,' Sam quickly replied. The American girls can teach them English and the teachers at the local school can teach them Spanish language and literature. Then we'll organise cultural and literary courses and festivals to make good use of the facilities, bring in funds and hire teachers.'

'Of course, we'll also bring in resources from the International Institute and hopefully a scholarship or two,' commented Soledad. 'As well as providing accommodation for when the residents in Morella want to come to Madrid.'

Sam looked Valli in the eyes and firmly took hold of both her hands.

'What do you think?' Sam asked her, with tears welling in her eyes.

Valli's body trembled all over; she didn't know what to say. If that wasn't the dream of a lifetime, then what was it? Her beloved and much missed Young Ladies' Residence here in Morella, active and functioning, creative and efficient, the changing of the guard of an institution that was apparently lost forever when the Republic fell, but which now, seven decades later and almost miraculously, was about to come to life again and in her own town.

The old Republican teacher put her face in her hands, unable to contain her emotion. Memories came flooding in of travelling in the cart with Casona, the faces of hunger and illiteracy in Las Hurdes, Victoria Kent's look of determination, talks given by Lorca at Number Eight Miguel Ángel Street, the long, freezing nights with the *maquis*, the bodies of her parents as they slumped down, the cigarettes shared with La Pastora, the letter to Tristan, Charles, exile, Natalie, who must now be weeping with emotion in heaven or wherever she was.

Valli wanted to speak but she couldn't. She stood up with trembling legs and gave a long, strong hug to Sam Crane, the grand-daughter of that young American she met in Madrid in the nineteen thirties.

'Your grandmother,' she said eventually, 'would be very, very proud of you, Sam.'

Valli studied her freckled face and her intelligent blue eyes. That young woman had inherited the same enterprising spirit with which her grandmother filled the Residence. Valli was unable to contain a flood of memories from those years, images of Louise Crane secretly smoking, her open flirtation with Victoria, the drinks shared with Margarita Nelken in La Venencia or the clandestine get-togethers in her room until the small hours of the morning.

Feeling overwhelmed, Valli sat down again still shaking her head, as if she didn't believe what was happening. She looked at Sam and Soledad over and over again to convince herself that they were real and this wasn't all a dream. Soledad seemed to notice this and took her hand, squeezing it firmly.

Sam eventually broke the silence.

'As far as my role is concerned,' she said, 'I have agreed with Soledad that I shall have a small office in the Institute, in Number Eight Miguel Ángel, and I shall co-ordinate the foundation from there. I shall, of course, come to Morella from time to time, but we need to look for a good Director for the Centre who will be based here.'

That sparked Valli's imagination, and immediately she responded:

'I think I may have the right person, but let me speak with him first.'

'A man?' asked Soledad in surprise.

'One day I'll explain, but trust me.'

The two guests agreed, and then Valli went off to fetch a bottle of brandy and three glasses. The toasts were such fun and so numerous that the three women had to go outside after a couple of hours to get some fresh air and walk around the wonderful little streets in the town.

Valli woke up the next day more rested than ever, as if suddenly twenty years had been taken off her. But her optimism vanished a few moments later when, on her way towards the dining room, she thought that the visit had been nothing but a dream. Panic-stricken she ran towards the sitting room, where she saw a very fine woollen scarf that Soledad must have left behind before returning to Madrid the night before. Valli sighed with relief.

She opened the window energetically and breathed in some fresh air, thinking that through some cosmic system of compensation life was now returning the fruits of her labours. She had sacrificed her life to give back to Spain that Republican spirit that she had learnt in the Residence, but had only achieved years of fear, denigration and defeat. Now at last, and unbelievably, her luck had changed.

As she looked over the beautiful views of the Morella countryside Valli felt stronger than she had in many years. She had a great desire to put her shoulder to the wheel and get to work on the project. She wanted to involve the whole town, work with Sam and Soledad, with the hotel and even with the new mayor. That venture would fill the town with young people and those attending courses, study visits and lectures; it could provide the economic stimulus that was so much needed, and so much better than the wretched casino that Vicent was planning, thought Valli with a certain peevishness.

Feeling confident about her plan, Valli washed, dressed and smartened herself up as much as she could. Although she hadn't made any appointments, she was determined that this Saturday she would make two extremely important visits: one to the Deputy Mayor to update him on what was happening, and the other, more important one, to the hotel.

The success of the first, in which the politician received the news enthusiastically, made Valli feel more confident about the second, which was really the only one that mattered. There would be no point in those extraordinary plans without Charles' support. Nothing was worth it if she couldn't rescue her own life, she thought.

Without hurrying, yet full of excitement, Valli arrived at the hotel, where she found Manolo sorting out papers and focussed for once.

'Good morning, Manolo,' she said to her former student affectionately. 'Things are very quiet today, aren't they?'

'It's the crisis,' Manolo replied in a pleasant tone. 'It's good to see you; what brings you here, if I may ask?'

'You can ask what you like, my boy,' she said. 'You don't need to be afraid of anything, much less asking questions. But tell me, is Charles here?'

Manolo seemed surprised by the question, but no doubt because he was aware that he was talking to his new boss, and he replied in a professional manner.

'Well, yes, he's been in Morella recently,' he answered, 'although a little while ago he went out for a walk in the country, with Isabel,' he added.

Valli seemed rather disappointed, but persistent as she was, she said she would wait until they returned. Manolo raised no objections, helped her to settle herself in the little armchair that was in the small room next to the entrance and brought her some magazines to pass the time.

That's how the two of them spent the rest of the morning, listening to the ticking of the clock and the sound of the pages turning, or the files that Manolo opened and closed. Apart from the odd phone call, or conversation about the weather and Valli's occasional snoozes, little else happened until the clock on the wall struck two and Charles and Isabel finally came up the hotel steps.

Charles immediately noticed Valli's presence and after an initial hesitation he headed towards her. Isabel took Manolo off to the kitchen to give them a bit of privacy.

Charles sat on the sofa next to Valli's armchair.

'Hello,' he said, hardly looking at her and taking off his peaked cap that protected him from the cold. However, he kept on his smart navy blue Burberry jacket, as if to indicate that their conversation would be brief.

'Hello, Charles,' said Valli, leaning forwards, aware that a hug or shaking hands were still a long way off. She thought that for what she was going to propose, a walk would be more appropriate than a cold encounter, face-to-face, like this one.

'I know you've only just come in, but do you feel like sitting on a bench in the Placet, or somewhere else, rather than here?' she said hopefully.

'I'd rather stay here,' replied Charles quickly, 'if you don't mind.'

Valli felt a slight stab in the heart because of the detachment of her son, who was being pleasant but cold. She crossed her legs and took a deep breath. Like all relationships, she said to herself, this one would have to be treated with a good deal of care, as if it were an orchid.

'It's lovely to see you around Morella once again,' Valli went on smoothly, trying to set the situation right.

'Yes,' Charles answered in a neutral tone. 'I've come to see Isabel and to finalise the details of our trip to Cuba; we're going for Christmas.'

Valli was delighted to confirm that their relationship was going well, because this could make it easier for her to maintain contact with her son, even if just through geographical proximity.

'Cuba is a wonderful country,' she said with a smile. 'I went there once, when in the mid-sixties Fidel invited a group of Spanish exiles over to offer us assistance and show us their model.' Valli paused briefly. 'Those were the days.'

'I can imagine,' Charles responded, 'but I'm afraid we don't have that kind of visit in mind.'

Valli smiled. She had always loved such subtle English irony.

'Charles,' she began, 'I know this is very difficult for you…'

'I've accepted it,' he interrupted.

'What do you mean?'

'As I said, I did some research and discovered that everything you told me was true,' Charles remarked with a dullness in his eyes and the same serious expression that he had always worn.

'I would never lie to you.'

At first Charles said nothing, but after a few moments he added:

'I also found by chance an old postcard of Morella and the letter you wrote to my father when they took me to London for the first time. I don't know if you remember it…'

'Of course I remember it,' Valli responded quickly. 'They were the most difficult lines I've ever had to write in my life.'

Charles bowed his head, his eyes fixed firmly on the floor. After a few seconds he looked up and carefully turned to his mother:

'Tell me what I can do for you.'

Valli looked at him with a mixture of sadness and hope. She was pleased that at least they had been able to establish a dialogue, but her heart froze at the thought that it could become a superficial and pragmatic relationship, like those he no doubt had in the boarding schools where he grew up.

'As for me, there's no need to worry, I'm fine,' she said, 'but I've come to offer you an opportunity that might interest you.'

Valli felt her pulse rate rising as Charles gave her a look full of surprise but also of a certain smugness, as if she were not really capable of proposing anything that was really interesting.

'I'm listening,' was all he said, leaning back on the sofa and crossing his arms and legs, which Valli took as a sign of imminent rejection.

Despite that Valli felt she had nothing to lose and that this was her great opportunity. She had to try.

'I don't know if you remember, but I told you a few things about the Young Ladies' Residence and the one for Students, where I met your father.'

Charles nodded.

'Since the old school in Morella was put up for sale, I tried on my own account to obtain funding to set up a cultural centre, something rather different from what the Mayor wanted, but not so different from the academic centre that you proposed.' Valli paused briefly. 'Although my idea was more open, or at least, accessible on merit and not due to class or economic circumstances.'

Charles raised an eyebrow, a gesture that Valli interpreted as a warning. She went on more cautiously:

'In Madrid I met some people connected to the Residence, including the multi-millionaire family that owns the Crane empire that makes paper, envelopes and general writing materials.

Charles frowned slightly before conceding:

'Yes, I know the company.'

'Well, I was at the Residence in the mid-nineteen thirties at the same time as the heiress to that empire, who had gone to Madrid to learn Spanish. Her grand-daughter, who is a great admirer of the institution, has now set up a foundation to re-establish the female Residence in our school in Morella once it has been refurbished. She has obtained three million euros to start the project as soon as possible and she already has some exchange agreements signed with prestigious American universities like Vassar College.'

'That's not bad,' said Charles, looking at Valli with some interest. 'I know Vassar; Oxford had an exchange programme with them.'

Valli took a deep breath before she continued. His remark had given her a slight feeling of hope and calm.

'We need a Director, a strong person at the head of the institution in Morella,' she said, looking him in the eye and without fear. 'Someone capable of leading an educational programme, supervising dissertations and organising courses and summer schools that we would set up in order to make full use of the facilities and broaden the range of cultural offerings. In principle the Residence would occupy about half of the old school, with some thirty rooms around an inner courtyard.'

'I think it's a great idea,' said Charles, as if the subject was nothing to do with him. 'But tell me, what can I do to help, exactly?'

Valli looked him in the eye.

'I think you would be the best person to manage the project, should you wish to come to Morella and if Isabel would like to run the hotel. You know it's mine, but I've got everything I need.' Valli paused briefly as she sat down on the edge of the armchair, her hands on her knees, her eyes fixed on Charles. 'I'm thinking of leaving you the ownership of the hotel – who else would I leave it to? Isabel and Manolo could run it, while you manage the Residence.'

'Me?' asked Charles, his eyebrows fully raised. 'That's impossible.'

Valli felt as if her heart shrank. With her back more bent over, she leant back in the armchair to rest her head. It was too soon to give in, she said to herself.

'Why do you say that?' she asked.

'Because I have my life in Eton, a very respectable life and job, and frankly, I've never had a woman in one of my classes, I've only ever taught boys, never women,' he replied, making things quite clear.

Valli would have reproached him for the macho comment, but decided this was not the right time.

'Well,' she said, 'you don't have to answer now. If you like, you can think it over or talk about it with Isabel. I could see you being very happy in Morella, and for a moment I thought you both might like to settle here,' said Valli, looking sad. 'I only wanted to offer you the project because I thought that it would interest an academic like you, apart from all the collaborative cultural links between Spain and England that you could set up through your contacts in London and mine in Madrid. It would be a very nice project that we could share...' Valli didn't have the guts to finish the sentence. She wanted to say "as a family", but she couldn't.

Charles looked away uncomfortably.

'As I say, you don't have to give me an answer now,' Valli insisted.

'I'd rather be honest: I don't think I have much more to think about,' Charles replied coldly.

Valli pursed her lips and noticed that her hands were shaking. Feeling that her heart had shrivelled, she looked at Charles, who remained serious and impassive. Valli realised that the time had come for her to leave.

She got up slowly and without a word she headed for the door. Before she left, she turned round to look at him for one last time.

'Have a good time in Cuba,' she mumbled in a quiet voice.

'Thanks,' was all Charles said in reply.

27

Valli didn't hear the elegant clock in the loft of Durnford House striking half-past two. Nor did she see Charles adjusting his immaculate white bow tie and solemnly coming down the stairs. She didn't suspect that his heart was beating as fast as hers, nor that his life was about to change as much as hers from that moment onwards.

She remained sitting on the cold stone bench opposite the main door of Eton College one cold morning in January, still with her tea in her hand. She had been there for over an hour.

Valli never discovered that Charles had to count to ten before opening the wooden door to find her there, sitting patiently, with the same composure and determination with which she had fought life's struggles. Without knowing why, she turned round at once and saw him there. In fact her son was heading towards her, dressed like a real gentleman with his face looking more serious than she had expected.

She felt the cup of tea slipping between her woollen gloves but reacted in time before it fell. Slowly she got up and opened her dark eyes as wide as she could. After he had rejected the Directorship of the Young Ladies' Residence in Morella, Charles had invited Valli to Eton so that she could get to know the college and its students. She had spent a miserable Christmas on her own thinking she had lost her son forever, and so she had jumped for joy when she received the letter inviting her, dated and posted in Havana. Valli assumed that during their holiday in Cuba Isabel must have encouraged him at least to keep in touch. Deep down Valli had always thought well of Vicent's children, who were kind and gentle and, of course, could not be held responsible for the misdeeds of their father and grandfather. She, in fact, had always tried to offer them some kindness because she had noticed when they were in school how sad and frightened they looked; a sure sign of an almost tyrannical situation at home.

Valli had given Vicent's children the affection that she could never give to Charles, who was now walking towards her with a firm, confident, almost military gait. She didn't care about his ways, she thought; that was her son and she had turned up only forty-eight hours after receiving his invitation. She didn't know what she would say to him, nor if it was a door that was opening or closing. But at her age she had no time to waste. All she had now was hope.

Behind her there was a life of struggle against a class-ridden world, and her own son was now emerging from that world's most symbolic doors. Valli was struck by the image but, old as she was, she knew that she had to embrace it just as it came. It mattered little to her whether those boys in their morning coats were privileged or not. All she wanted was to be at peace with her son and get to see her Young Ladies' Residence in Morella. If, in order to achieve those things, she had to smile at the Eton boys, that's what she would do. Diplomacy wins more battles than many wars; she wished she had learnt that lesson many years earlier.

The immaculately dressed head of the department of languages finally appeared before her. The contrast between the two was striking. Charles' stature and dress made Valli's bent form look tiny, but despite such differences she received her son with her head held high. She was well aware that this was her last battle.

'Welcome to Eton,' Charles said without making any physical contact with her. Not a hug, not a kiss, not even a shaking of hands. His face remained more serious than usual.

Valli said nothing, for such formalities upset her.

'I'm pleased you've accepted my invitation,' Charles went on, filling the silence.

'The least I could do,' Valli replied, adding a touch of naturalness to the encounter.

'I'd like you to meet my boys; don't prejudge them; essentially they're just working hard to carve out a future for themselves, like everyone else.'

Valli chose not to comment on "like everyone else". It seemed to her that those boys didn't have much in common with the world outside, since in other schools they didn't wear morning coats and they didn't pay thirty-five thousand pounds to go to class. But that wasn't the right time to discuss it.

'I thought,' Charles went on, now with his posture a little less aloof at last, 'that they might like to spend time at the Young Ladies' Residence, if it will accept them as male residents for a few weeks in the year.'

Valli's eyes lit up. She no longer felt the cold and started to shake her head, closing her eyes in sheer delight.

'I'm sure that won't be a problem,' she said eventually, looking at him with her big, dark eyes and glowing with happiness. She was greatly tempted to throw herself at her son but, old as she was, she knew that for now the best thing to do was to play the same game as Charles. Raising an eyebrow as high as it would go, Valli added: 'In any case the decision about accepting boys or not will depend on the Director.'

Charles smiled and took a step towards his mother.

'I think the Director will be delighted to welcome them.'

Valli could no longer contain herself and moved towards Charles to give him a long, firm hug, full of tears and emotions that she had not been able to express – nor Charles receive – for a whole lifetime.

A long silence and the tension of the moment eventually separated them some seconds later.

'I'm delighted about your decision,' Valli replied, adopting a very British sardonic tone. She, too, knew how to resolve situations with humour.

'Noblesse oblige,' her son replied, still playing the game and making a gesture of exaggerated reverence.

Valli responded immediately:

'And so does republicanism.'

Acknowledgements

This novel is the result of countless hours of fascinating reading and talking with all kinds of people in several countries.

Starting with Morella, I should like to thank the residents and staff of the Retirement Home that gave me such a warm welcome and where I shared conversations and walks with people who actually lived through the period, such as Manolo Querol. My mother's friends, like Ernesto Mestre and Sara Boix, also provided me with wonderful details about their lives in the farmhouses in the time of the *maquis*. The Elías family, whom I have known since they dressed me up as an Indian when I was very little, welcomed me once more with open arms, and I have been thinking especially of Maita Antolí, who unfortunately is no longer with us. Also Carlos Sangüesa, the well-known local historian and a constant source of help. In the library in Morella I also found whatever I needed thanks to the very kind and efficient assistance of Ángel Viñals.

With regard to people from Morella who are living away, I should like to thank my friend Conxa Rodríguez in London for the books she lent me, and Pedro Sancho in Salamanca, who sent me his amazing account of the Civil War in Morella.

In Mas de las Matas, Javier and Susana showed me their enormous archive and monitoring of everything to do with the Civil War, which can be accessed through the website www.nopasaran36.org. I also had a very interesting conversation in this small town in the Province of Teruel with Avelino, whose father was shot in the mid-1940s for a crime he did not commit.

In the same area of Lower Aragón I have a special affection for the very active bookshop Serret de Valderrobres and its irrepressible owner Octavi, for the number of books I received on loan and for his unceasing encouragement and interest. He is a model of dependability.

In London my friend Jimmy Burns passed me the manuscript of the memoirs of Carmen de Zulueta, the daughter of a Minister and Ambassador during the Republic. The story of her early life in the Instituto Escuela in Madrid, which followed the principles of the Institución Libre de Enseñanza, was of immense value.

Also in London, my friend Gonzalo Coello from Portugal very kindly put me in touch with the Colegio Estudio, the successor to the Instituto Escuela and the Institución Libre de Enseñanza.

It is not an easy task to enter the world of Eton College, especially for a woman, and so I am grateful to my friend Roger Suárez for introducing me to former and present teachers, like Josep Lluís González and Marçal Bruna. I should like to express my most grateful thanks to them and to all the staff at the College. I should also like to put on record the excellent conversations I had with the former student Nick de Bunsen and with my dear friend Stuart Valentine, who told me in great detail about his experience in a boarding school and with students from Eton whom he met when he and they were at Oxford.

As always, living in the English capital has allowed me the privilege of taking part in talks, dinners and lectures with Paul Preston, the well-known historian, and Geoff Cowling, former British Consul in Barcelona, whose research and work on the Civil War and Francoism have increasingly helped me to understand the present.

In Madrid Sabela Mendoza was the first person to open the doors for me to the remarkable world of the Students' Residence. I spent an unforgettable week there, lost among the books and documents of the library and amazed by the atmosphere in general. Almudena de la Cueva, Marta Fernández and Jesús Ruiz helped me to feel closer to an institution that I only knew and admired from books.

On the other side of the Castellana, Pilar Piñón, Director of the International Institute, let me spend time in rooms and with documents and stories of the time when that magnificent building in Miguel Ángel Street housed the Young Ladies' Residence. To share her passion for such a special period only served to make me more excited about everything that took place there.

In the nearby Fundación Ortega, Asen Uña made available to me the archive of the Young Ladies' Residence, where I read letters from María de Maeztu written in her own hand, which helped me to understand the efficient, creative, intellectual and modest character of that place. As I looked through the documents, I was much saddened when I thought about the great legacy that we all lost. How different the country would be if the knowledge and the spirit of that generation of women had not been interrupted, with everything having to begin all over again in the 1980s with barely any models to follow. There is an urgent need to recover that legacy.

It was also thanks to Asen that I was able to visit Josefina Guerra, a former resident. It was her open spirit more than her comments that helped me to gain a better understanding of the values that the Residence instilled in its students.

I am also much indebted to Miguel Ángel Villena of *El País*, for his biography of Victoria Kent and for recommending to me the books of Shirley Mangini about the intellectuals of the period, who she calls "las modernas de Madrid".

I owe my mother Carmen, my sisters Sofía and Susana and my friend Santos Palacios my fondest thanks for reading the first draft of this novel with a great deal of care and common sense. And to my friends, Laura and Shirry Liram in London, warm thanks for their help with the printing of different versions of it.

Of course, the book would not exist without the support of the literary agency Sandra Bruna in Barcelona, and my publishers Santillana, who for the second time have allowed me to make my dreams become reality.

Finally and above all, my thanks to my partner, María, for her encouragement, patience and unconditional support. This book is for her.